CW00968865

The Second Lady

ONEWORLD CLASSICS

The Second Lady Chatterley's Lover

D.H. Lawrence

ONEWORLD
CLASSICS

ONEWORLD CLASSICS LTD
London House
243-253 Lower Mortlake Road
Richmond
Surrey TW9 2LL
United Kingdom
www.oneworldclassics.com

The Second Lady Chatterley's Lover first published in 1999 by Cambridge
University Press
© 1999 by The Estate of Frieda Lawrence Ravagli
This edition first published by Oneworld Classics Limited in 2007
Notes and background material © Oneworld Classics Ltd, 2007

Printed in Great Britain by TJ International Ltd, Padstow, Cornwall

ISBN-13: 978-1-84749-019-3
ISBN-10: 1-84749-019-0

The Forest Stewardship Council (FSC) is an international, non-governmental
organization dedicated to promoting responsible management of the world's
forests. FSC operates a system of forest certification and product labelling
that allows consumers to identify wood and wood-based products from well-
managed forests. For more information about the FSC, please visit the website

Contents

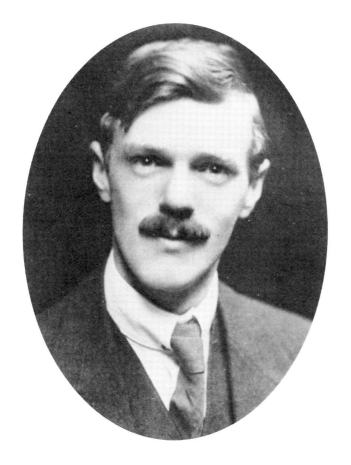

D.H. Lawrence (1885–1930)

Lydia Lawrence,
D.H. Lawrence's mother

Ernest Lawrence,
D.H. Lawrence's brother

Jessie Chambers

Frieda Lawrence

Nottingham Road, Eastwood, *c*.1900. D.H. Lawrence was
born in Victoria Street, off this main road, on the right

D.H. Lawrence's birthplace
in Victoria Street, Eastwood

Manuscript page of *The Second
Lady Chatterley's Lover*

Film stills from Pascale Ferran's *Lady Chatterley*,
starring Marina Hands and Jean-Louis Coulloc'h

The Second Lady
Chatterley's Lover

1

OURS IS ESSENTIALLY A TRAGIC AGE, so we refuse to take it tragically. The cataclysm has fallen, we've got used to the ruins, and we start to build up new little habitats, new little hopes. If we can't make a road through the obstacles, we go round, or climb over the top. We've got to live, no matter how many skies have fallen. Having tragically wrung our hands, we now proceed to peel the potatoes, or to put on the wireless.

This was Constance Chatterley's position. The war landed her in a very tight situation. But she made up her mind to live and learn.

She married Clifford Chatterley in 1917, when he was home for a month on leave. They had a month's honeymoon. Then he went back to Flanders. To be shipped over to England again, six months later, more or less in bits. Constance, his wife, was then twenty-three years old, and he was twenty-nine.

His hold on life was marvellous. He didn't die, and the bits seemed to grow together again. For two years, he remained in the doctors' hands. Then he was pronounced a cure, and could return to life again, with the lower half of his body, from the hips down, paralysed for ever.

This was 1920. They returned, Clifford and Constance, to his home, the home of his family, Wragby Hall. His father had died, Clifford was now a baronet, Sir Clifford, and Constance was Lady Chatterley. They came to start housekeeping and a married life in the rather delapidated home of the Chatterleys. Clifford had no near relatives. His mother had died when he was a boy. His brother, older than himself, was dead in the war. Crippled for ever, knowing he could never have any family, Clifford came home with his young wife, to keep the Chatterley name alive as long as he could, on a rather inadequate income.

He was not downcast. He could wheel himself about in a wheeled chair, and he had a bath chair with a small motor attached, so that he could drive himself slowly round the garden and out into the fine, melancholy park of which he was so proud, and about which he was so ironical.

Having suffered so much, the capacity for suffering had to some extent left him. He remained strange and bright and cheerful: almost, one might say, chirpy, with his ruddy, healthy-looking, handsome face, and his bright, challenging blue eyes. His shoulders were broad and strong, his hands were very strong. He was expensively tailored, and wore very handsome neckties from Bond Street. Yet even in his face one saw the watchful look, the intangible vacancy also, of a cripple.

He had so very nearly lost his life, that what remained to him seemed to him inordinately precious. One saw it in the brightness of his eyes, how proud he was of himself, for being alive. And he had been so much hurt, that something inside him had gone insentient, and could feel no more.

Constance, his wife, was a ruddy, country-looking girl with soft brown hair and sturdy body and slow movements full of unused energy. She had big, wondering blue eyes and a slow, soft voice, and seemed just to have come from her native village.—

It was not so at all. Her father was the once well-known Scotch R.A., old Sir Malcolm Reid, and her mother had been an active Fabian, in the palmy days. Between artists and highbrow reformers, Constance and her sister Hilda had had what might be called a cultured-unconventional upbringing. They had been taken to Paris and Florence and Rome, artistically, and they had been taken in the other direction, to The Hague, and to Berlin, to great socialist conventions, when speakers spoke in every language, and no one was daunted. The two girls were not in the least abashed, neither by art nor by harangues. It was part of their world. They were at once cosmopolitan and provincial, with the high-brow provincialism and the high-brow cosmopolitanism.

Clifford too had had a year at a German university, at Bonn, studying chemistry and metallurgy, and things connected with coal and coal-mines. Because the Chatterley money all came out of coal royalties, and out of their interest in the Tevershall Colliery Company. Clifford wanted to be up-to-date. The mines were rather poor, unprofitable. He was second son. It behoved him to give the family fortunes a shove.

In the war, he forgot all that. His father, Sir Geoffrey, spent recklessly for his country. Clifford was reckless too. Take no thought for the morrow, for the morrow will take thought for itself.

Well, this is the morrow of that day!

But Clifford, first lieutenant in a smart regiment—or what had been so—knew most of the people in Head Quarters, and he was full of beans. He liked Constance at once: first, because of her modest-maiden, ruddy appearance, then for the daring that underlay her softness and her stillness. He managed to get the modern German books, and he read them aloud to her. It was so thrilling to know how "they" felt, to have a feeler into the other camp. He had relatives "in the know," and he himself therefore was in quite a lot of this same "know." It didn't amount to a great deal, but it was something to feel mocking and superior about, for young people who, like Clifford and Constance, were above narrow patriotism. And they were well above it.

But by the time the *Untergang des Abendlands* appeared, Clifford was a smashed man, and by the time Constance became mistress of Wragby, cold ash had begun to blanket the glow of the war fervour. It was the day after, the grey morrow for which no thought had been taken.

Wragby was a low, long old house in brown stone, rather dismal, standing on an elevation and overlooking a fine park: beyond which, however, one could see the tall chimney and the spinning wheels of the colliery at Tevershall. But Constance did not mind this. She did not mind even the queer rattling of the sifting screens, and the whistle of the locomotives, heard across the silence. Only sometimes, when the wind blew from the west, which it often did, Wragby Hall was full of the sulphureous smell of a burning pit-bank, very disagreeable. And when the nights were dark, and the clouds hung low and level, the great red burning places on the sky, reflected from the furnaces at Clay Cross, gave her a strange, deep sense of dread, of mysterious fear.

She had never been used to an industrial district, only to the Sussex downs, and Scotch hills, and Kensington, and other sufficiently aesthetic surroundings. Here at Wragby, she was within the curious sphere of influence of Sheffield. The skies were often very dark, there seemed to be no daylight, there was a sense of underworld. Even the flowers were often a bit smutty, growing in the dark air. And there was always a faint, or strong, smell of something uncanny, something of the underearth, coal or sulphur or iron, whatever it was, on the breath one breathed in.

But she was stoical. She had her life-work in front of her. She had Clifford, who would need her while he lived. She had Wragby, poor neglected old Wragby, which had been without a mistress for many years. And she had certain duties to the parish. She sat a few times in Teated Tevershall old church, that stood blackened and mute, among a few trees, at the top of the hill up which the ugly mining village straggled for a long mile. But she was no church-goer: neither was Clifford. They gave the rector tea twice a year, and subscribed to charities: and let it go at that. Constance tried to get into touch a little with the miners' wives. She wanted to know what that world was like. But the village was so grim and ugly, and the miners' wives so evidently didn't want her, she gave it up, and stayed mostly within the park gates.

Clifford would never go outside the park, in his chair. He could not bear to have the miners stare at him as an object of curiosity, though with commiseration. He minded both the curiosity and the commiseration. He could stand the Wragby servants. Them he paid. But outsiders he could not bear. He became irritable and queer.

So, alas, they had very few visitors. The neighbours, the County, all called, most kindly and dutifully, when they knew the Chatterleys were back. Poor Clifford! That was it! Poor Sir Clifford Chatterley! in the war! so terrible! The Duchess of Oaklands came, *with* the Duke. And she was almost motherly. "If *ever* I can help you in anything, my dear, I shall be more than delighted. Poor Sir Clifford, we all owe him every kindness, every help we can give. And you too, dear!"—But then the Duchess looked upon herself as a very noble charity institution. "I live to do good among my neighbours."

"Thank God they've gone!" gasped Sir Clifford. "I told them we could never go to Dale Abbey."

"But they were rather nice!—a bit pathetic, trying to do the right benevolent thing!" said Constance softly.

"By Jove, Connie, your neck must be more rubbery than mine, if you can stand it."

Constance couldn't stand it. But then she knew she wouldn't have to. The Duke and Duchess would hardly come again. The same with the rest of the neighbours: Clifford was not popular, he was only pitied. He had always been too highbrow, too flippant, thought himself too clever and behaved in too democratic a fashion, to please the County. They knew he made a mock of them all. He had even pretended to be a sort of socialist, besides having written those pacifist poems and newspaper articles. There was no *real* danger in him, of course. The marrow of him was just as conservative as the Duke's own. But he pranced about in that Labour-Party sort of way, and therefore you had to leave him to his prancing. The County knew perfectly well how to do it.

So that, after the ordeal of the first few weeks, Wragby soon became lonely again. Clifford would sometimes have his relatives on a short visit. He had some extremely "titled" relations, on his mother's side, and though he was so democratic, and put "bloody" in his poems, he still liked the fact that his aunt was a Marchioness, and his cousin an Earl, and his uncle—well, whatever his uncle was.—He liked them to come to Wragby once a year, at least. There were Chatterleys, too, occupying permanent-official jobs in the government: good wires to pull, but not very exciting guests to have. And sometimes Tommy Dukes came. He was a Brigadier General now, but the same Tommy really; or an old Cambridge light, or another poet whose brief flower was blown, but who was still good company. Usually, when it was not some relation, it was just some lone man who smoked a pipe and wore strong brogue shoes, and was unconventional but frightfully cultured, and extremely nice to a woman but didn't care for women, and was most happy when cornered alone with Clifford in a bachelor privacy. Constance was used to this sort of young man—no longer so very young. She knew all his sensitivenesses and his peculiar high-toned voice. She knew when she was *de trop*. She knew when "the men" wanted to feel peculiarly manly and masculine and womanless, as if they were still in chambers in Kings or in Trinity. And she had her own sitting-room, up two flights of stairs. Clifford's friends, though they were exceedingly kind and gentle, wincing almost, with her, were not really interested in her. She felt she jarred on them a little. So she withdrew.

But she and Clifford were a great deal alone. The months went by, even years passed. Clifford, with his eyes very wide open, bright, and hard, adjusted himself to the life he had to lead. He read a good deal, though he was not profoundly interested in anything. He never wrote any more. But sometimes he would take a small canvas and go out into the park to sketch. He had once loved trying to paint. Constance too made quaint drawings and illustrations for old books. Sometimes her illustrations were published; she had a little name for her work. Clifford was quite proud of it, and always sent "her" books to his very titled relatives, though he knew they wouldn't *really* admire her for showing such school-mistressy skill. Still, she was the daughter of an R.A., whom the nation had knighted. It was parvenu, but at least it was art in the authorised sense.

The great thrill in being alive began to wear off, with Clifford. At first, it had excited him terribly, to be able to puff his chair slowly to the wood, and see the leaves fall, see a squirrel gathering nuts, or a weasel bound across the path, or hear a wood-pecker tapping. A strange hard exultance would fill him. "I am alive! I am alive! I am in the midst of life!" And when he saw a dead rabbit, which a stoat had caught and been forced to abandon, he thought: "Ha! So you are one more, are you, while I am alive!" And when a little dog from the hall bounded in front of him, dancing with life, he would think: "Ah! you may skip! You are full of life and pep, but at the best you've only got a dozen years in front of you. A dozen years! I shall then be forty-six, in the prime of life. And your little life will be run out."—But at the back of his mind he would be thinking: "Shall I? Shall I live to forty-six? Shall I perhaps live to sixty? Twenty-six more years! If I have that, I can't grumble."—And if he heard a rabbit scream, caught by a weasel or caught in a trap, his heart would stand still for a second, then he would think: "There's another one gone to death! Another one! And I'm not gone!" And he exulted curiously.

He never betrayed his pre-occupation with death to Constance, but she divined it, and avoided the subject. But still she did not guess his strange, weird excitement when he took a gun, in the autumn, to have a shot at his pheasants: the strange, awful thrill he felt when he saw a bird ruffle in the air, and make a curving dive. Afterwards, he was grey and queer. And she tried to dissuade him from shooting. "It's not good for your nerves, Clifford." And for a long time he would not touch his gun. Then, some evening, he would have to go out in his chair and sit waiting for a rabbit, or a bird. It was sport. But at the same time, when he saw a thing fall dead, a sudden puff of exultation and triumph exploded in his heart. And he was proud of his aim. And he thought a great deal of the preservation of his game.

After two or three years at Wragby, when he had settled down at last to the thought of being alive, and was used to himself as a cripple, the excitement which had kept him going began to die down in him. He became irritable and strained. He would sit for a long time doing nothing. Constance tried to get him interested in the old house, which needed repair, and in the small Wragby estate. But he would not bother. The Tevershall collieries were doing worse than ever, the Chatterleys' inadequate income was dwindling.

"You know a lot about mining, Clifford," she said. "Couldn't *you* do something about the pits? Imagine if they have to close down, what a lot of misery for other people, as well as a strain for us."

"Everything will have to close down in the long run," he said, in his hard, abstract way.

"We shall have to leave Wragby."

"Everybody that's ever lived in Wragby, has had to leave it, one day," he said. "So will you and I."

To hear him like this chilled the life in her. He had a terrible passion of self-preservation. He was exacting about food, and ate rather too much than too little, not for the pleasure of eating, but to feed his life. His mind dwelled on the fact that he was feeding his life. He could not sleep, and that tortured him, because he felt he lost strength. It was not the loss of sleep he minded so much, it was the threat to his life. Then he could not bear to be worried about anything: everything must be kept from him, for fear it went to his nerves.

Constance, silent and dogged, plodded on from day to day. She had a silent, but very powerful will, which she had needed to exert. She set her will, when she came to Wragby with Clifford, to seeing the thing through. Her marriage should still be a success. She willed it so, and she would never give in. Clifford could never be a husband to her. She lived with him a married nun, become virgin again by disuse. The memory of their one month of married life became unreal to her, barren. She would live virgin by disuse. To this also she set her mind and her will. And she almost exulted in it. Almost in cruelty against herself, with smooth rigour she repressed herself and exulted in her barrenness.

For the first few years. And then something began to bend under the strain. She became abnormally silent, and would start violently if addressed suddenly. With the ponderous, slow heaviness of her will, she shut sex out of her life and out of her mind. It was denied her, so she despised it, and didn't want it. But something was bending in her, some support was slowly caving in. She could feel it. And if she went, Clifford would go down with her, on top of her. She knew it.

Sometimes it seemed to her as if the whole world were a madhouse, Wragby was the centre of a vast and raving lunacy. She dreaded everything, herself most of all. But still she never gave in. She wept no single tear, she never pitied herself. With a steady, plodding rhythm she went on through the days, with a monotony that in itself was a madness. In the morning, she felt: now I'm getting up, now I'm washing myself, now I'm putting a dress on, the same green knitted dress! now I'm going downstairs: the same stairs! now I'm opening Clifford's door, and I'm going to say Good-morning! to him: the same Good-morning! the same Clifford behind the same door, the same me looking at him to see how he is!—The tick-tack of mechanistic monotony became an insanity to her.

2

IT WAS HER FATHER, old Sir Malcolm, who warned her. He was big and burly and beefy-seeming, and he enjoyed life carefully. But his nose was fine and subtle, if selfish, and he had a certain Scottish eerie aware-ness of people.

"Connie, I hope you're not putting too great a strain on yourself," he said, following her up to her room. He could not stand his son-in-law, but he had a certain selfish affection, or clannish feeling, for his motherless daughters. Now he came after her with his queer Scotch persistency.

"What strain, Father?" She looked at him with big eyes. He too had rather big blue eyes: a handsome man: but he knew perfectly well how selfish he was, for himself, and how selfish other people were, for themselves, without knowing it. Connie could not bluff him.

"You're not yourself! You're running for a fall, the pair of you."

Her heart sank as her father said it. From him, she knew it was true. She looked at him, at bay.

"In what way?" she said.

"I'll sit down if I may," he said, looking round. "You have a charming room. I always liked your way of arranging an interior. You have a gift for it."

Constance didn't like phrases such as "arranging an interior." She felt she never did arrange one. She only made a home round herself, in every room, as far as she could. But she loved her own private sitting-room: she never called it a boudoir. It was up two flights of stairs, at the south-east corner of the house, looking over the gardens behind the hall, and across a corner of the park at the woods.

Her room had delicate pinky-grey walls, and on the floor Italian rush matting, that smelled sweet of rushes, with a few plum-coloured and blue Persian rugs, thin and silky and rather worn, near the sofa and by the fire and by the slender rose-wood writing-table, a very delicate old blue one by the spinet. Her chairs and sofa-lounge were covered with chintz with tulips, and behind the sofa was a piece of *toile de Jouy*.* She had a few modern pictures, and a very fine German print of a Renoir nude.

Old Sir Malcolm stood in front of this last, in silence. He was a landscape painter, sometimes did a portrait, but never nudes. A queer, sad wistfulness came over him as he gazed at the tender, pink, marvellously fleshy back of Renoir's nude woman. He knew he could never have come within miles of such a lovely, living thing.

Constance was sitting in a low chair near the hearth, where a small fire of logs was burning in the yellowed marble fireplace. She loved a finely, delicately-proportioned marble fireplace. This one she had brought from France, and had had it put into her own room.

But now she had almost lost the sensuous pleasure, the glow of warmth, which her own lovely and familiar possessions gave her. She had not many things: a few rugs and pictures, a few pieces of china and ivory. But she had had a great deal of real delight out of them. Now, her nerves were going dead. She knew it. Her room was dead to her.

She envied her father as he stood so fresh and burly and canny, in front of the Renoir nude. His eyelids had a funny wistful tilt, a little plaintive and childish, very celtic. He was feeling mentally the voluptuous desirableness of that Renoir woman. His plaintive childishness came from his own sensuous desire. At the same time, as an artist he was examining the work of art, and was almost depressed by its sensitive fulness. Constance knew him fairly well. She knew the various expressions of his eye-lids, and the subtle changes in his fine, perhaps rather feminine nose. He was not a man of strong character. But he was canny, he poised himself carefully, and he lived scrupulously for himself alone. Nevertheless, if he was to live successfully for himself, he must take others sufficiently into account. He was by no means a blind egoist: rather a far-sighted and very wary one.

He came at last to the chair opposite Constance, and sat down slowly, but gracefully. He made no comment on the picture that had engrossed him, but spread his white, well-shapen hands with the old signet-ring, to the fire, and gazed rather dimly at the glow. Constance said nothing.

"I find your house depressing, though, in spite of your taste in arranging it. I'm afraid I count the hours till I can get out of it again," he said, with amiable poise.

"Yes! I know you do!" she replied simply. He seemed to her so often like a spoilt child, under his worldly grand manner and masculinity. It was his generation. He hated having to bother about her. Yet he was going through with it.

"It would be absurd, Connie, to ask you if you are happy," he said, looking at her warily from under his white eyebrows.

"Why?" she said.

He smiled faintly, dismally, but with a feint of gallantry.

"Well now, are you?" he said. "You don't give anyone that impression. Would you say yourself you are happy?"

"I think I am doing what I ought to do," she said.

"Perhaps! Perhaps! But also, perhaps you aren't taking enough things into count, you know."

"What things?"

"Yourself! You've put the screw down on yourself. You're screwed up—or screwed down!—Your mother did that to herself: and it was that and nothing else killed her.—But even so, she lived till she was over forty.—You know I don't believe in screwing oneself up, not for anything.—What is the point? You screw yourself up beyond a natural pitch, in order to do your duty. As a result, you collapse, and your duty collapses with you. You've neither been kind to yourself nor to anybody else." He spoke in a measured, slightly pompous way. But that was just manner with him.

"Do you think I shall collapse?" she asked.

"Why decidedly I do! I am sure you will! You give me the same feeling of alarm your mother gave me so often."—He looked at her from an anxious, half-wise face. But she knew it was true what he said. And his curious, clannish concern for her, somehow supported her.

"What am I to do, then?" she asked, looking with her big blue eyes at him. Their eyes met. His gave her one glance, then turned aside. His eyes were dark blue like hers. But his were always turning aside, hers gazed full and slow. She continued to gaze at him, though she had met his glance, and knew what it meant. He hated Clifford, he loathed Clifford's special Englishy style, which was ahead of his own style. And he wanted her to find some other man. But of course, he would never say so.

"That is the difficulty," he said. "It is so difficult to advise you.—But you need more life.—You need more society, more enjoyment.—You need young people, of your own age. You need to dance—yes, and you need to flirt a little.—Not with the sort of fellows Clifford has here. They're no good to any woman.—Come away with me to the South of France for a month or two! Come on, now, do, Connie! It will be best for you in the long run—even best for Clifford. I'll stand the racket."

Sir Malcolm had a second wife, a woman much younger than himself, and with a much larger income. But he and she went their own ways a good deal, quite amicably. He had a vast range of friends. He could easily look after Connie for a month or two.

She sighed, and said:

"I can't leave Clifford in the winter."

"Why not? Let him come along then. Other men do, in his condition. Everybody knows it's the war."

"Oh no!" she said.

And he had lived for fourteen years with her mother's obstinacy, he knew quite well when to give up. When you can do nothing with people, you leave them to do things to themselves.

"Well, Connie!" he said. "You are doing yourself an injustice, and you're doing yourself damage, and there'll be a heavy bill to pay for it. Your feelings are going paralysed—not only your legs!—If you want it, have it!—You're going paralysed. Instead of living the life of a young healthy woman, you're going paralysed.—But if you want it, it's useless for anyone to talk." He rose abruptly to leave the room: exactly as he used to do with Connie's mother. At the door, he said: "I want to speak with Clifford this evening. Give me an opportunity, will you? I must leave tomorrow."

She looked up at him as he stood, very portly and very lordly, at the door.

"All right, Father!" she said softly.

It was the quiet way his first wife used to speak to him. But Connie was somehow softer, warmer, she troubled him more.

The meals were always rather a trial. Clifford was wheeled in his chair to the table. An elderly maid waited and carried the dishes. Clifford watched the food in that intense way, that seemed so out of place merely for food. He ate a good deal, and said little. Sir Malcolm, who was very nervously sensitive to his company, hated eating at Clifford's table. The wine was a white claret, and he hated that. He asked for a whiskey-and-soda, and he felt the elderly maid begrudged it him. There was a devastating sense of economy, especially in the drinks. The food was good and sufficient. But when Sir Malcolm wanted another whiskey-and-soda, a certain frosty tension was felt in the air. He, of course, was fully aware of it. If Constance had not been so deadened, she would have minded bitterly. But now she merely thought: "Oh well!"—and drearily took no further notice.

The servants were all old servants of the family, and Clifford was one of those very refined people who *must* put their will over others. The servants were *his* servants, and had to follow *his* feelings. And he, poor fellow, couldn't help begrudging the whiskey. It was one of his economical points. Simpson, the parlour-maid, elderly and grey and neutral, must, however, also begrudge the whiskey, and administer it coldly and contemptuously, with the mean power of asserting her feelings, which trained servants have.

Because her father was so much on edge, Constance decided to leave the two men together after dinner. Let them then have it out. They all took coffee in the parlour next to Clifford's bedroom, the parlour with his books and gramophone and all the gramophone records, and with the small studio easel he sometimes worked at. When coffee was over, Constance slipped upstairs.

Sir Malcolm was smoking one of his own cigars. Since his catastrophe, Clifford didn't smoke, and he didn't like the smell of tobacco. But of course he didn't say so to Sir Malcolm. He begged his father-in-law to smoke, and offered him cigars. But Sir Malcolm preferred his own: and he knew quite well that the smoke got on Clifford's nerves. But it soothed his own, so there you are!

He stood big and handsome and immaculate in his dinner-suit, feet apart, back to the fire, smoking his corona.* Clifford sat in his wheeled chair, in tense silence.

"I don't think, you know," said Sir Malcolm, taking his cigar from his mouth, "that Connie is getting altogether a fair show, do you?" And he put his cigar back.

Clifford went white with anger. For some time he did not answer. It was a devilish silence, that would have blasted any tender heart. But Sir Malcolm was a man of the world.

"I don't quite understand vague phrases like *a fair show*," said Clifford, very quietly, but with deadly, mild superiority.

"Probably it *is* too vague! What I wish to say, is that living a shut-up life as she lives here, without any of the necessary interests and pleasures of her natural youth, she is bound to suffer, and these years may do her a grave damage—a grave damage."

Sir Malcolm was not going to mince matters with his son-in-law. He knew how sharp Clifford was.

"Is she *shut up* here?" asked Clifford.

"She is shut up! Whether by her own will or not, makes no matter. She is shut up, and shut off from the life that is natural to her age."

"She is unfortunate in being my wife, it is true—"

"I agree, she is unfortunate—not exactly in being your wife, but in having to share the very grievous misfortune which has happened to you: and which no one regrets more profoundly than I do."

Another complete and lengthy silence, which Sir Malcolm was too astute to break. The image of calm *bonhomie*, he shook his cigar-ash in the fire. But the tip of his nose was very white.

"What kind of damage to Connie do you anticipate?" asked Clifford, with perfect *sang froid*.

"Damage! Serious damage! Either her nerves will suffer—seriously! Or else there will be a collapse in her health—one of those illnesses that women get, and which are very often fatal."

Clifford remained completely motionless, staring in front of him. Sir Malcolm, going a little yellow under the eyes with rage, turned the stump of his cigar between his lips.

"Where shall I get a drink?" he asked, into the silence.

"Oh!" Clifford started guiltily, and looked round. "Didn't she bring the tray in?" He reached for the bell-push that hung on a cord on his chair.

There was dead silence until Simpson had taken the order, and had re-appeared with the tray. Then there was a hissing of soda-water, and Sir Malcolm took a large mouthful of drink. It so exasperated Clifford, that he said:

"And your remedy? Have you one to suggest?"

"I should like her to come to the South of France with me, for the winter."

"For the winter!—Well, if she wishes to go, she is perfectly free."

"As you know," retorted Sir Malcolm, "she has a very high sense of duty, and therefore she is not free. Perhaps it is *your* duty to see she gets some kind of relief from the life she leads here."

This again Clifford felt as pure insult. At the same time, he knew her father was, in a measure at least, justified.

"I am to force her to go to the South of France for the winter?" he asked, with his perfect sarcastic *sang froid*.

"If you don't use your influence to bring some change and some relief into her life, you will have her as badly off as yourself. I have known her mother. I lost Connie's mother when Connie was a child of nine—"

"And was Lady Reid also shut off from life?" asked Clifford ironically.

"Who, Lady Reid?"

"Your wife, Connie's mother."

"She was Mrs Reid. She didn't live long enough.—If she was shut off from life, she shut herself off. But it had the same result. I always consider she killed herself."

"Yet she didn't marry a misfortune, apparently!" said Clifford. But as he said it, he knew he had gone too far. Connie's mother had been bitterly jealous of her husband, but also, extremely "superior" to him. The two things made a dead-lock in her.

"I am perfectly willing for Connie to winter in the south of France. I am perfectly willing for her to do anything that she wishes to do. But I can't *force* her to live, can I?"

"You might try," said Sir Malcolm. "She knows well enough it is useless to wish for something that there is no hope of ever getting."

"What could she wish for, that she has no hope of ever getting?" asked Clifford coolly. For a moment, he didn't realise how rash he was.

His father-in-law looked down at him from under curious, expressive eyelids. Sir Malcolm's eyes hardly changed, it was the white eyelids that did the speaking—and there was an infinite malice and mocking on his handsome face.

"If you don't know that, I don't," said Sir Malcolm.

And the iron went right down into Clifford's soul. He really had got into the habit of forgetting that Constance might have any conjugal rights: or any conjugal desires. But now, savagely, Sir Malcolm pushed the reminder right home. Then he drank off his whiskey and went to the door.

"I'll see where she is," he said.

And he went out, leaving the dagger thrust home into Clifford's consciousness.

He departed as early as possible the next morning, without having seen his son-in-law. Constance could tell he was pining to get out of the midlands atmosphere. He had just come south from the moors, he was pining to move on to some new congenial set. He just took this little Wragby unpleasantness *en passant*.

"Well, goodbye Daughter! Don't forget what I've been telling you, and try to get a move on. You've got your brake jammed. Believe me, you'd better get help to get it taken off, or your axle's going to break. You know what I mean. Good-bye! Come to Roque-brûne, don't you be put off."

His car buzzed and swung away from the steps. The old knight was gone, on his gay crusade. And in spite of herself, Constance felt against him some of the anger her mother used to feel: the way he slipped through one's fingers! And in spite of herself, she saw her life suddenly with her father's eyes, as a dreary, dismal, priggish, despicable existence, and as a cowardly acceptance of the principle of Hell-on-earth. Sir Malcolm was no butterfly. He believed firmly that life was *almost always* Hell-on-earth, for almost everybody. He had a great dread of Hell-on-earth, and also, a vague dread of Hell-hereafter. He knew it was a cunning fox which died a natural death. He was determined to die a natural death, at as late a date as possible. Furthermore, he was determined astutely to get his paradise this side the grave, like the French lady, "to make sure of it."* It needed a good deal of skill. But then, he had had long practice. There were various hounds of heaven which could make life Hell-on-earth for a man: the hound of duty, the hound of jealous love, the hound of other-peoples'-burdens always snapping at one's heels. He didn't pretend to outstrip these hounds. He had a select little scrip full of dog-biscuits, and when one of these hellish hounds-of-heaven got too close on his heels, he threw it a dog-biscuit and was off again, fleet as any Atalanta.*

So Constance saw him now, disappearing in the direction of the coloured flags of his goal. And he seemed to her at least half in the right. He was a burden to nobody, and he looked so handsome. He was wise for himself!

She wondered a little grimly what kind of medicinal dog-biscuit the old knight had thrown to Clifford. Clifford evidently had swallowed it, he was looking so green. Perhaps it would act as a purge! How extraordinary if it did! She vaguely wondered, and indifferently waited.

3

IN THE LATE AUTUMN, however, came a few very beautiful sunny days. Constance, in spite of herself, kept thinking of the Cap Martin, the brilliant sea, the hills behind Mentone. What would she not give, to be on the dry hills in the sun above the Mediterranean, smelling the thymey herbage as she climbed on the pale rock high into the wilderness! There, the lid was off. In England, the lid was down on one for ever. One was in one's coffin already.

Clifford roused himself to go out in his motor-chair, and Constance walked at his side. The soft, warm wooliness of the uncanny November day seemed utterly unreal to her, in its thick, soft-gold sunlight and thick gossamer atmosphere. The park, with its oak-trees and sere grass, sheep feeding in silence on the slope, and the near distance bluey, an opalescent haze showing through it the last yellow and brown of oak-leaves, seemed unreal, a vision from the past. It was a ghost-day, returned from the late eighteenth century, a day such as lingers in the old English aquatints. The English landscape had revealed itself then, in its real soft beauty. And sometimes the revelation stealthily disclosed itself again, like a ghost, a *revenant*.

Clifford's chair puffed slowly along the path that wound towards the gate in the wood, between the tussocky grass of the park. It was a path of very fine gravel, of a bright pink colour. The gravel came out of a burnt pit-hill. It was the burnt rock and shale from the mine, the refuse, burnt pink and sifted fine. Constance liked the colour so much, the path had been newly gravelled, and Clifford's chair could puff comfortably along it, without danger of slipping or sticking in the clayey places.

Constance opened the wood gate, and the chair puffed slowly through into the wide riding between the hazel thicket. All the leaves were fallen from the hazels, the ground was brown, and strange bright mushrooms had sprung up in the uncanny late warmth. The chair slowly lurched on up the incline, over the pale leaves of the chestnut trees, to the more open oak-wood, part of the old forest. The oaks still clung to their brown leaves. Everything was motionless, in motionless, syruppy afternoon sunlight, that soon would die. It was a purely ghostly day.

Clifford stopped his chair at the top of the slope. To the left, the wood was thick with hazels and trees. But to the right, up to the knoll, it was bare save for a few stalky, ricketty-looking oak saplings. All the timber had been cut by Sir Geoffrey, for the war. Naked and forlorn the big hill looked, with debris of cut timber, and an odd tree here and there, and tree-stumps still showing bare. The hill had been forest, probably, since England was England. Probably, when the weedy oak-saplings that leaned and straggled here and there in so ricketty a fashion had had time to grow up again, it would be forest again, when other, different Englishmen would walk under the leaves.

Clifford gazed round him with melancholy intentness. This devastation in the wood always affected him. He could not help gazing fixedly up to the knoll of the hill-top, that he remembered tree-covered and secret, which was now bald and exposed. Still one could see blackened places where the wood-men of the war had burned up the twiggy heaps, in places where the brown rock came through.

Constance, however, was looking down-hill, down the broad sweep of the grassy riding. At the bottom of the slope it swept to the right, between a dense larch-wood. But on the opposite hill-side a narrower riding went up between the oaks, a riding overgrown with deep grass and burdock.

The sun fell on the chair, and on Clifford's expressionless face. The stillness was a stillness of innumerable ghosts.

"Shall we stay a moment?" he said to her. "Would you like to sit down a bit? See, sit on this stump."

A tree had been cut from the bank on the upper side of the riding. Clifford had stopped his chair just by its roots. Constance sat down, smelling the dying odour of leaves and sun and woodland.

"Who'll come here after us, Connie?" said Clifford. "When you think of the men in green with their bows and arrows, that used to go down this riding—and the Chatterley dames and damsels that have gone on palfreys—then my father and that gang of wood-men in the war, war-working— —and now you and me: one wonders what will come after. I suppose it will be the British bolshevists, and the colliers of Tevershall will turn the place into a sort of Hampstead Heath, with nothing quiet even for a bird to nest in." He spoke with dry, abstract hardness.

Constance looked round vaguely. The wood seemed as yet to hold some of the old inviolate mystery of Britain, even Druid Britain.

"Perhaps it won't be so," she said. "It is never the obvious which happens, is it? Perhaps something quite different will come." She felt she didn't care about what he said, nor about his vision of the future.

"While I live, of course," he said, "I'll have *nobody* in the wood, except whom I may invite. But with a population increasing in millions every year, how is one to prevent the final devastation? They'll burst through every barrier, by mere weight of numbers, and it will be a swamp of common people, profane vulgarity. Thank God, I don't think I shall live to see the worst of it. I wish we had enough strong men to form a small aristocracy, and put the rest back into slavery, where they belong."

But she didn't want to listen. All this dry, material vision of the future irritated her. Somehow, in the wood she felt another influence, something mysteriously alive. And with his talk, he wouldn't let her feel it.

"I suppose the world will come to an end in its own way," she said. "It's no good our wishing anything."

"I suppose not! Give me your hand, will you?"

It seemed as if he were determined to make her aware of him, to pull her into his dry, jarring mood.

He reached over the side of the chair and took her warm, soft hand in his nervous grasp. But as he gripped her hand, she felt the life die out of her, ebb away, away from him, back to her heart, to die there. Her blood seemed to recoil in slow, cold heavy waves.

But the soft, live warmth of her hand started a new train of thought in him.

"You're lonely, Connie, aren't you?" he said. "Wouldn't you like to see more people?"

This was a new line of attack: or so she felt it: a new dodge to make her aware of him.

"Not here! Not in Wragby, no!" she said slowly.—He had not succeeded in dragging her out of her remoteness, not yet. But she was becoming irritated.

"Would you like to go away for a while?" he asked. "Perhaps you ought to."

She was silent for a time. If she could go right away, forever, and forget Wragby utterly and forever, have done with it beyond recall—yes! But as it was, it was a doom that had closed on her. She would have to get to the end of it. A heavy insistence on getting to the end of her doom burdened her heart. Before she could go away, something would have to change in her.

"I'm not keen on going away—not this winter," she said.

"But hadn't you better?" he insisted: always insisting!

"Why?"

"For your health—for your nerves—for your spirits. I'm afraid you may get too depressed."

She frowned under the repeated little strokes of his insistence. He was forcing her attention.

"I don't get depressed," she said, knowing now that he would never leave her alone, and answering crudely. "What would be the good of going away? I should always think of *you*. My thoughts wouldn't really go away. You know you would always keep your mind on me, I should *have* to think of you all the time. You would keep me with your will, no matter how far I went. It wouldn't really be going away."—She spoke with impatience and almost with bitterness. But this seemed to stimulate him. He roused in his chair, quite cheerfully.

"I should *think* of you—of course," he said. "But I should hope you were having a good time, so that perhaps you'd want to come back. Is that what you mean, by my keeping you with my will?"

She was silent. Her hand lay dead in his, her heart lay dead inside her. She didn't *want* to answer him. She didn't *want* to listen to his fair-spokenness, just now.

"You don't think I'd try to *prevent* you from living and having a good time?—no matter how superficial the enjoyment might be, nor how you were deceiving yourself, thinking you enjoyed it. You don't think I'd try to prevent you, if you wanted it, do you?" he persisted. So many words! Oh God, so many glib words! And she had been sensing another mystery, in the wood.

"I think you would," she said dully, attending with the outer half of her consciousness.

"How? Why?" he asked, in bright interest.

She spoke again in a sort of dull brutality, like a prisoner.

"You'd never let me go out of your will. You'd keep me with your will. So what would be the good of going?"

He listened, alert. And he said:

"I don't understand this keeping you with my will. How do I do it?"— It seemed to please him, all the same.

She was very unwilling to answer. But she said at length:

"You *do* do it. You've got your will wrapped round me, like a hundred arms. And no matter where I went, they'd still be round me. I should never get away, actually, not even for an hour." It came out with all the dull apathy of despair.

"It sounds very mysterious: as if my will were a sort of octopus. But do you *want* to get away from me?" he asked, bright and keen.

"I don't want anything."

"No, but think, and tell me! Would you like me to let you go away, and forget you?—It's quite true, I never *do* altogether forget you, sleeping nor waking. I *can't*! If that is having my will wrapped round you, like a hundred arms—well, I suppose it is wrapped round you like *one* arm, at least. But would you like it altered? Would you like me to take that arm from around you. Would you *like* to be free of me? Tell me!—Of course it would leave me with my arms waving in space, like a lunatic. But say what you'd rather. Would you rather be free of me, and the arm of my will *not* round you?"

She pondered heavily, in silence. To her, it was mostly words. He would never do it, whatever he said. He would never let her go, out of his will. That fatal, or beautiful—she still didn't know which—arm of his will, he would keep round her always, like an octopus tentacle—or like a god.

"And don't you have an arm round me, too?" he said. "Do you ever let *me* go out of *your* consciousness and your will? Aren't you always aware of *me*? Wouldn't you be aware of me, and keep the arm of your will round me even if I died, and were the other side the grave?"

She looked at him, frightened. He had light-blue eyes, very keen and terrible. They still had a strange power over her, in their pale, uncanny concentration. She knew they had power over her. And she knew she enjoyed it, or got a strange, unearthly thrill out of it.—She forgot now the other, silent feeling within the wood, that had been drawing her away from him.

"I don't know these things so plainly as you seem to," she said, equivocating.

"Yes—when you choose!" he said. Then he went on, in a voice like a conspirator: "But listen, Connie. You know your father accused me

22

of not letting you live? And in a way—in a way, it's true. In a way, I do prevent you from living the external, superficial life of your body. I realise it. I had thought the inner, *essential* life between us was everything. Now I realise that, though man does not live by bread alone, neither does he live entirely without bread. Especially woman doesn't! Perhaps you need the more superficial life of your body. Probably you do—"

Even as he said it, she felt it was an insult to her. And so many words, so many words! Oh God! for a communication that was silent, unspoken!

"Perhaps you *need* to *enjoy yourself*, like the women at the night clubs. Perhaps you *need* to jazz and flirt and have men make love to you: or *some* man. I can't do it. To me it isn't a necessity anyhow. But if it is a necessity to you—you are your father's daughter—then do it."

Constance listened in silence, attentive to every word. How strange and insulting it all seemed! What voice was this, from a bath chair? What creature was this?

"Do what?" she said. "Dance and flirt and have men make love to me?"

"If you need it," he said. He seemed quite triumphant.

"And you wouldn't mind?" she asked, ironically.

"Of course! But it's come to this. Your father accuses me of starving you of life, of not letting you live the natural life of a young woman. He prophesies all sorts of mysterious penalties, nervous derangements and internal maladies, if you *don't* 'live your life', as they call it. There may be something in it. Man doth not live by bread alone, but without bread, and without cake even, no woman seems able to exist. *I* can't give you the cake: that's my misfortune. But if anybody else can, then take it, by all means."

She had come at last to the bottom of his thought. So! This was what he wanted to say! And so utterly without a spark of tenderness or sorrow for her and him! Only this hard triviality.

"You mean you don't mind if I let a man fall in love with me?" she said.

"I mean it's no use my minding. If you're going to go to pieces, or have a mysterious internal malady through not having some man fall in love with you, then I pray to God some man may fall in love with you quickly, and you may make the best of the opportunity."

So! He had said it! He had said it, and she had heard it! In one sense, at least, it set her free of him; it was a charter of liberty!

"You wouldn't mind even if there were a child?" she asked, after a ruminating pause.

23

"Mind? Why do you always talk about my minding? I accept the consequences of the laws of life—am I not an object-lesson, as I sit in this chair? May the Gods preserve me from going against the laws of life, if I can help it!—or from causing anyone else to go against them!— any more than I have already done. Whoever made the universe, made it stronger than I am. Whoever made woman, made her beyond my jurisdiction. Whoever made me myself, has taught me forever not to play with the laws of life and death. If you need to live to a certain extent according to your father's prescription, then for God's sake, do so. Anything rather than bring down these divine vengeances of ruined nerves or internal complaints and the rest of it."

She listened, and heard it all in her own way. It filled her with a great sadness: it was the end of their marriage, in the inner sense. And that marriage had still been a rock of safety to her.

"But if I had a child, what would you do?" she said, her mind running on cunningly, to get the charter of liberty as full as possible, if the inner marriage *were* dissolved.

He sat motionless, gazing at her in irony. Had she already rushed so far, in imagination? My God, the pace of the woman!

"I shouldn't have to do anything, should I? It would be your affair."

He was a little at a loss, to follow her line of thought.

"Yes! But unless you divorced me, it would be legally your child," she said, showing him where she was.

And again he sat in amazement at the speed at which she went ahead.

"I suppose it would," he said. And still the thing wasn't at all *real* to him.

"Wouldn't you mind that?"

He paused. If she had a child, and the child, in the eyes of law, were his! Still he only vaguely visualised it.

"Mind! Why of course I mind *everything*. But also, I'm willing to put up with everything, in order to make the best of things."

He had not grasped the situation with full imagination. It was still mostly words to him.

"You mean you don't want me to leave you?" she said, now hunting him down to a conclusion, as he had at first hunted her into listening to him.

"I do mean that, among other things," he said. "I suppose that's what it comes to. I don't want you to go away from me. But I don't want to bring more calamities on my head by keeping you. Your father warned me. Well, I'll take his warning. I'd far rather have you have love affairs with other men, and give yourself and me a family of children, if you like—" these words, however, made him pull up short. But it was only words, so he rushed on again: "yes! if you like!—rather than, than have anything else going wrong, more fatal accidents that I can't cope with. I suppose I could cope with the other thing: the lovers and children. But I'm afraid of nervous derangements and diseases.—And—yes!—I suppose I'm afraid of losing you."

Curiously, he was aware of one half of what he was saying: fear of the mysterious stroke of malady, and admission of the probable necessity for her to have "love affairs". But that the "love affairs" would mean other, real men, individuals: and that children, if any were born, would be individuals again, who would grow up to manhood or womanhood: this his imagination failed to grasp. It was still all in the abstract to him, and he wouldn't have it otherwise.

"You don't think you might lose me, to one of the men who were in love with me?" she asked, a little maliciously, trying to force him to realise.

He frowned tensely, and answered with a certain impatience:

"I suppose it's one of the risks I must run. No! You wouldn't necessarily want to go off with a lover—if I know lovers!" He spoke with contempt of the breed. And he looked into her eyes with his irritated tense look, full of a certain cold fire and arrogance and power. When he was driven back into himself, he was so hard and clear, like a diamond. And he always made her feel he was stronger than she, with a strange cold arrogance and power that thrilled her in her remote soul.—And yet, she felt so plainly, now, that he was not quite real. He was too much in the abstract. He was entangling himself in his own net.

"I'd try not to," she said softly.—Yes, he was entangling himself in his own net!

"Not to what?"

"Not to want to go off with one of my lovers."

He gave a quick, cracked laugh.

"That's rich!" he said, "rich! You're already resisting his pleading, and telling him you must be true to your charge! Oh, but women are priceless!" He spoke with profound sarcasm.

"No!" she said, flushing under his ridicule. "I mean I wouldn't *really* want to leave you—if you didn't want me to."

He recovered with a quick little frown.

"Maybe not!" he said. "There are things much more powerful than sex, and that go much deeper. Sex is only an incident; just as dinner is only an incident, even if you can't live without it. And because there is something much stronger between you and me, than sex, probably you wouldn't want to leave me for a sexual lover."

She heard it very distinctly, and kept herself secret. She did not betray anything.

"You'd keep the arm of your will round me all the time?" she said, with quiet acceptance that might contain a sting of irony.

"The arm of my will, if you like to call it such," he said.

They were silent, both very much moved: and moved worlds apart from one another.

Out of a cross riding just below where they sat, a brown spaniel came nosing excitedly towards them, as if it had smelled their emotion from afar, and were tracking it down. It ran towards them, uttering a soft, suppressed little bark.

"Come then!" said Constance, releasing her hand from Clifford's, and holding it out to the dog. But the spaniel stood back, softly waving its tail.

Out of the side riding came the game-keeper, dressed in greenish velveteen corduroy. He looked at the two intruders, and touched his old brown hat in a salute, then was going on, evasive, down the hill, making a soft noise to call his dog. He was striding away.

"Oh I say, Parkin!" said Sir Clifford.

The man stopped and swung round suddenly, showing his red face and enquiring eyes, as if he expected some attack.

"Sir?"

"Turn my chair round for me, and get me started, will you? It makes it easier for me."

Parkin came striding up the slope, with a quick, small movement slinging his gun over his shoulder. He was a man of medium build, his face almost vermilion-ruddy with the weather, wearing a rather sticking-out brown moustache. His bearing had a military erectness and resistance, that was natural to him, and at the same time he was silent, his movements were soft, silent, almost secretive or evasive.

Constance moved from the side of the chair. The man touched his hat to her with a swift, unwilling movement, in silence, and gave her a quick look with his reddish-brown eyes, as he came to the back of the chair to take the push-bar. Constance, absorbed in a confusion of thoughts and emotions, met his glance almost without knowing it. She was hardly aware of him, being so much disturbed in herself by what Clifford had said. But the man's watchful, hard eyes caught the unresolved trouble in the wide blue eyes of the young woman, and the unconscious spark of appeal. He felt the queer spark of appeal touch him somewhere, but he stiffened, and hardened his spine in resistance and in unconsciousness. He did not choose to be aware.

He turned the chair easily, and set it in the tracks, where it would quietly run down the gentle slope.

"Shall yer manage for yerself, or should I wheel yer?" he asked, in a harsh, neutral voice, with the local accent.

"Perhaps you'd better come along, and give her a bit of a push up the park incline," said Clifford, in the voice of an officer speaking to a soldier.

The gamekeeper did not answer, but took the chair by the bar, and started it quietly down the slope. They went in silence, not speaking nor even looking at one another. Clifford and Constance were too much absorbed in what had just passed between them, and the gamekeeper was absorbed shutting the two gentry out of his consciousness, and keeping himself intact from them.

At the gate, Constance hurried forward a few steps and opened. Both the men looked at her: Clifford in remonstrance, the game-keeper aloof. She held the gate open, and waited. She had always done things for herself: it was an instinct with her. She was aware of the eyes of the two men on her, of Clifford's casual reproach, and the other man's distant scrutiny. Clifford started his little engine, the keeper kept one hand on the chair-bar, as the chair ran through the gate. Then the man turned to close the gate, and Constance let him. She bent and patted the dog, which wagged its tail for a second, before it ran away from her. Parkin strode after the chair, and caught it up. She came on a little in the rear, aware of Clifford's face glancing round to see where she was.

Abstractedly, she watched the keeper as he slowly pushed the chair, helping it up the rather steep incline of the park. Its small engine puffed laboriously, even though it was not doing much work. And the keeper went with a slow, deliberate step, taking his foot lingeringly from the ground. Constance liked the colour of his greenish velveteen corduroys, with the fawn cloth leggings. It was the old colour for gamekeepers, but one rarely saw it nowadays. What a strong back the man had!

It occurred to her that he lived a very lonely life: seeing him from behind, one realised it, how alone he was, and how he resisted everything. She knew his wife had left him, gone off with a collier from Stack's Gate, a mining settlement just beyond the south gate of the park. That must be more than two years ago. Constance had seen the woman: a florid, big, common creature, not a native of the district, because she spoke with a queer twang that Constance did not like. As soon as she had got used to the Derbyshire-Yorkshire dialect of the people round Wragby, she found other dialects distasteful, and much more noticeable than they had been before she was accustomed to any dialect at all.

Since his wife left him, Parkin had lived quite alone in the pretty but dark cottage across the wood, at the end of Mickleover Lane. Clifford liked him, because he was a good keeper, and did not drink, and had no pals. During the war, the colliers had roamed everywhere, and had poached at will. Parkin had only been gamekeeper for a year, before he was called up. Till that time he had been a blacksmith at the colliery. But he had had a violent quarrel with the Overhead manager, and there had been a fuss. So Sir Geoffrey had offered him the game-keeper's job, and as he had turned out a success, Clifford was glad to get him back when the war was over.

Now he was a man nearing forty. It was during the war his wife had gone loose. She would entertain men down in the cottage across the wood, to the great disgust of Sir Geoffrey. Constance had heard all the scandal, when she first came to Wragby, She had thought the delinquent wife must be rather a sporting character, till she had seen her, when she disliked her. She was insolent and suggestive, as if she jeered behind one's back. Then she had gone off to Stacks Gate, and there was an end of her.

Parkin was apparently a rather cruel man. He was hated in the village, for frightening children and getting lads locked up, if he found them in the wood with a dog. Constance herself did not care for his harsh, rather tenor voice, that had a peculiar clang in it, in a countryside that spoke broad and rather heavy. Neither did she like the hard, objective way he stared at one, as if to say: What's amiss with *you*!—when one had to give him an order. Nor the too-evident relief with which he backed out of one's presence. Nor the soft furtiveness of his movements, as if he were hiding himself.

But now, as she watched the slow, sensitive way he lifted his feet and put them on the earth again, she realised something—that he was alone, it was his instinct, his necessity, to be alone: that he wanted to avoid his fellow-men, rather than pounce on them when he caught them trespassing. He was alone like some animal that has escaped, and he seemed to feel his fellow-men as the enemy and the danger.

Constance appreciated his solitary quality. She felt that need in herself—to keep herself solitary from mankind. It was no good Clifford talking to her about lovers. She could no more have a score of lovers than a tiger-cat can. And it was useless for her father to want her to "enjoy herself". Even he had to do it on principle. And for her, it was too late. She didn't want people—especially lots of people. She wanted to draw away from them—more and more away. She didn't want contact with them—on the contrary. "Living her life" meant avoiding people, not rushing into their arms. And yet—and yet—some contact she did want—as even a tiger-cat wants a mate, though the mate will probably devour his own offspring.

Clifford waited for her at the top of the slope. The day was already drawing to a close, the damp mist was beginning to close up. An infinite saddened melancholy seemed to settle over the park, in the damp, worn-out air that smelled of sulphur. Clifford's little motor puffed with a forlorn, waiting puff.

"You're not feeling tired, are you?" he asked.

"Oh no!" she replied, and said no more.

She was aware of the keeper looking at her, and she glanced at him, and met his unconscious, searching stare. His eyes were light brown, the hard, reddish colour of nuts, with tiny black pupils. You would never know what he was thinking. She glanced away, and let him search.

As a matter of fact she had vaguely flickered in his consciousness all the time, since he had first looked at her that afternoon, and had met her wide, blue eyes that were full of indescribable trouble, so full of their own trouble, that she had not been aware of him at all. He had realised for the first time that even she, her ladyship, didn't have things all her own way. He always crudely took it for granted that the gentry had things all their own way: even poor Clifford. Even now, it didn't occur to him that

29

Clifford really suffered from his disaster, as a poor man would. No, he was a gentleman, therefore he was above it, the anguish of real suffering.

Now, suddenly Parkin realised that the woman suffered: that she was, so to speak, drowning. That was the effect it had on him.—Yet what cause had she to suffer? she was My-Lady, she was well-off. When you were well-off, you didn't suffer. He resisted having to feel for her, or having to be aware of her at all.

Why should she suffer? she had everything she wanted, except for Sir Clifford's being paralysed. And what was that? She had money and everything to make up for it. It wasn't as if she was a poor man's wife, and would have to go out to work for them both. They had servants, and all they wanted.

None the less, when she came up, he looked at her again, to see if it was true, that she was really in trouble, if she really gave him that feeling, of a young woman who was alone and out of her depth, drowning. A woman, perhaps, who wants something from a man, without knowing it. That was what his hard stare meant, the stare of an animal that lives by the hunt, and watches every danger, every stir among the leaves.

And again he met the strange, dark turmoil of her eyes, the look of one who is drowning, with the spark of appeal unconsciously flying. He drew back, but he thought: "She's got it stiff, she has! Summat ails her!" And again his hostile mind went over the circumstances, and refused to allow she had any justification for taking things hard. She was well-off, she had everything she wanted, servants and all; everything, except her husband was paralysed. Well, other women had to live with their men when they were paralysed. Plenty of women had lost their husbands altogether—sons as well. Let her be thankful for what she had got! He had no use for dissatisfied women.

Nevertheless, something kept stirring. He had kept himself without feeling for a long time now. Feeling was finished in him, with the war, and with his wife. Why should anybody care about other people? Let everybody keep their feelings to themselves, as he would keep his. Especially about women! The war had been bad. But women were worse. Nothing was so bad, to him, as women. They made his heart shut like the jaws of a steel trap. If there'd been no women in the world, no disaster that ever happened would ever have been half as bad as it was. Women made things so much worse. He was determined to keep himself clear now, for ever, and into eternity: his heart shut clean and clear.

Yet still, though his heart had not been touched, a spark had fallen on his sanguine imagination. Yes, he would admit, it was hard on a young creature. She seemed as decent as she could be, being a deceitful woman. Probably it was her trouble made her nice. If she had all she wanted, she'd be as brazen as the rest. So let her bear her trouble. Pity all men's wives didn't have a trouble that kept them down a bit! Anyhow, *he* had nothing to do with her! He closed again into insentience.

After all, she'd drawn rather a blank in the marriage lottery. Parkin couldn't understand any woman wanting to marry Sir Clifford, anyhow. Sir Clifford was all right, as a gentleman: a very good gentleman, you might say. But not the sort that he, Parkin, would have imagined women wanting to marry. Not enough balls to him. But that was apparently what women liked best—that slippy-mouthed sort. So let 'em abide by what they got. Sir Clifford Chatterley was all right for a gentleman. What else did his wife want? Paralysed or not, didn't seem to make much matter.

They came to the house, and at the door in the garden at the back, where there were no steps, Clifford was helped into his indoor chair by Marshall, who was gardener and husband of the housekeeper, an old servant.

"Thanks for the help, Parkin!" said Clifford. "Good-night!"

"Yer welcome, Sir Clifford!" came the harsh, hard voice.

"Oh Good-night!" said Constance's voice, soft and startled.

"Good-night to your ladyship!" came distant and colourless.

That was how it was! Sir Clifford was always so polite, so thoughtful. The very distance between him and his retainers made him so. But she, she was always forgetting the retainers altogether. She had gone indoors now, completely forgetting that Parkin had ever existed. But when Clifford's courtesy recalled her to the fact, then she forgot the distance, and, startled, called Good-night to him as if she were just a woman speaking to him. His *Good-night to your ladyship!* was almost stately. He turned away into the twilight, to get away from them.

4

THE LAST DAYS OF AUTUMN fell into the gloom of winter. Constance took as little heed as possible. She had trained herself to be unconscious even of the English weather: she hated it so deeply. In the old days, they had always gone abroad for the worst months, and even at home, it is not quite so bad near the downs and the sea. But at Wragby, black day followed black day, and black smuts fell in the winter fog, like the end of the world.

She kept herself disciplined, had a thousand small duties to attend to. Clifford gave all the important orders. But the more intimate household affairs, Constance attended to. And she followed the woman's old rule, of keeping herself in order by maintaining a strict rhythm in the house. She had her days for the linen, for the furniture, for the silver, she superintended the making of preserves, she kept a watch on the vegetable garden, and on the fruit, and she worked herself a good deal among the flowers. Then she sewed, making dresses for herself, and for her sister Hilda's little girls. Then she drove into Uthwaite to do the shopping, such as was not done in Tevershall.

As a rule, the greater part of the morning was taken up by the house and the household necessities. In the afternoon she walked or went shopping or paid some duty call. In the evening, she sewed and listened to Clifford, who often read aloud to her. So that really she had very little time for herself, no time at all, in fact, for the piano, and hardly any for her drawing. If it hadn't been for Hilda or her father, who got her commissions for illustrating some children's book or some quaint little volume of verse, she would have let her drawing and painting lapse like the rest, though she really had a certain gift.

So that she was always occupied. Yet she had no real joy in anything. What she did, she did out of discipline: in the routine of life, and as a house-wife, she disciplined herself without relenting. So that everything went well. And yet, she knew it herself, it was dead. Instead of lying dead, she was walking about and doing things, dead.

She wouldn't have minded even that, if her nature had let her remain dead. In a sense, situated as she was, to walk about dead and to do things day after day, dead, was as near the ideal as she could get. It is an ideal to many people, and many people, men and women, achieve their ideal. Corpses that are active, they go on in activity from year to year.

But even if you are a corpse, you are subject to the mysterious processes and explosive reactions of decomposition. And if you are not a corpse, if the passion of life still stirs in you, it will cause violent disturbances and bitter revolts from the corpse discipline, from time to time.

This was Constance's condition. She said to herself: I know I am a corpse, and since there is no chance of life, I ought to be a corpse, I want to be a corpse!—Nevertheless, some second, deeper voice in her rebelled fiercely. And sometimes she would cry to herself: I want my heart to open! Oh, I want my heart to open! I don't want it shut up like this, like a coffin! Oh, if only God, or Satan, or a man or a woman or a child, or *anybody*, would help me to open my heart, because I can't do it myself! I love Clifford, but it doesn't open my heart. He doesn't want it. He's afraid of my heart, if it opened. And I *can't* be religious and charitable: people like the Duchess of Oaklands have used it all up. And I'm not really an artist, I'm only a dilettante. So I can't open my heart, I've nothing to open it to! Oh, if only there was a god I could open my heart to! But I can't open it to Jesus! he's too dead! he's too much of death! he's too like Clifford! He's all suffering!—Oh, if I could open my heart to something! If I can't, I shall die or go mad.—

But there was nothing she could open her heart to, so following the blind yearning came a deep, deafened anger and hate. Sometimes it stormed in, through her sleep, and she would wake feeling strange and livid, semiconscious, burdened with an anger like a sailing ship lurching and flying madly in a hurricane. Save that the hurricane was inside her, not outside. But just the same, she was possessed. And as she looked round her room, she longed to destroy it all, smash the whole thing to smithereens: smash up Wragby, burn it down, anything, anything to erase it and wipe it out of existence. She hated it with a mad and at the same time exquisite hatred. The exquisite relief it would be, if she saw it in flames, and then in ashes; and then even the blackened stones torn apart; and at last, nothing but nettles, just nettles in the place where it had been. The Romans sowed salt on the place that was accursed, but she, with deeper hate, would sow nettles. And the park!—if one could set fire to all the trees, so that it was a bare desert, save for a few black stumps! And burn down the colliery works, and destroy Tevershall, and wipe out all the people! Ah a grand, grand destruction! How her soul gloated on the thought! If something would happen that would *really* destroy the world, and make it into a desert, with a few charred remains and the salty bitterness of ashes blowing on its surface! If *that* could happen, then, then at last one would feel relieved. Even if one were dead oneself in the holocaust, it would still be a relief. It would be good to be dead, if one knew the world was destroyed. But what would be the good of dying, as all the men had died in the war, and leaving the world still wagging, as foul and even fouler than before! Growing fouler every minute! Bah! Fools, to be dead, and not even able to hate it!

On days like this, when she came down and saw Clifford so patient and just a tiny bit smug, sitting up in his bed or in his chair, she would think: *You! You!* what are *you* doing there, hugging your half-a-life and thinking it matters? Can't you see you're half dead, and you'd be much better wholly dead? You miserable thing! You may well gloat over being alive! That's all the half-dead are fit for, gloating on the fact that they're still hanging on, when so many have gone down in the ship-wreck. Hanging on to the raft in a dead weight, making it clogged and unable to move! Oh, how miserable and despicable you are!—

At the same time, though the mood was on her like an insanity, and had possession of her so that she could not shake it off, she had a vague suspicion that her deepest hatred was of herself. She loathed herself, her life, her body and being. She was just another carcase, horrible.

And though she felt so terribly, felt even that the leaves ought to wilt and blacken if she came near them, she behaved just as quietly and mildly as ever. In this mood, she would not kill a wasp that got stuck in the jam, even the daddy-long-legs which she disliked so much in the windows, and usually killed with the flip of a cloth, these days she dare not kill them. She left them alone. And with Clifford, instead of being a little impatient with him, as she often was on her good days, in her evil days she was heavily, almost slavishly patient and attentive, going round him ponderously, and waiting on him like a servant, though in her soul she would be wondering that he did not fall dead under the waves of destruction she was sending out against him. He didn't fall dead, however. On the contrary, during her evil days, when her own existence was torture to her like the rack, he seemed often rather bucked. But at last he flagged. In the end he seemed to collapse like a heap of ashes. And when he began to collapse, she began to recover. So it was!

But her evil days were like some ghastly nightmare. It seemed to her she breathed evil out of the air. It seemed to her that something ghastly and deathly blew in on the air, from the North Pole. The park and the wood seemed just the same, to be going grey and lifeless in the strangle-hold of the death-breathing air. She saw it in the servants too, even in the very sheep of the park, though them she always disliked. Gone, for Wragby, were the days of deer. But sheep were a humiliation even then. And on the awful corpse-days, they huddled and hopped like the greyest of corpse-lumps. The sight of them revolted her innermost marrow. Of all animals, she loathed sheep most. Pigs were poetic in comparison.

Then when the bad days and the intensity of her wild yet cold rage passed, she forgot it all. She thought of herself as always patient and always having a good will to everything. She forgot—as everybody forgets—particularly women. The woman of the evil moods was not herself to her. It was some other, unreal, abstract personage. She herself always had a good will. So she had fixed it in her mind.

But nevertheless, the terrible cold rage that blasted all life for her, never really thawed. She was like the earth in Labrador. The surface thawed and had brief blossoms. But a little way down, only a little way, it remained eternally frozen. So it was with her heart and her deeper self, they were bound in a dead, iron frost that never yielded.

On one of her bad days, she hurried out to walk alone in the wood, ponderously, semi-conscious. In the distance she heard the report of a gun, and that angered her. Why must some fool man be letting off a gun at that hour!—But she walked on, oblivious of everything.

She did not know how far she had gone, nor how long she had been going, when suddenly she heard the sound of voices. She stood to listen, on the re-bound. It was a child crying, sobbing! Instantly the dull rage that was thundering away down in her rose with a rush to her heart. Someone was ill-treating a child! This thought was enough to bring all her evil rage into her suffocated heart. Some-one was ill-treating a child. She heard the snarl of a man's voice. She strode down the wet drive, over the dead and sodden leaves, her face hot, her eyes burning, her body surging as if from a catapult.

Down the narrow path she saw two figures, a little girl in a purple coat and mole-skin cap, crying, and Parkin, in his velveteens, bending over her. What had the brute been doing to the child? She could hear his snarling, irritable voice:

"Shut it up, now, shut it up! Enough on it! If ah dunna kill 'im, 'e kills th' bods (birds) an' th' rabbits, so what's thee got to scraight (cry) at? Are ter goin' ter stop it, eh?"

The voice was becoming a menace, now, the child blubbered louder, in anticipation of the clout that would soon come. Constance strode nearer, with blazing face and eyes. The man heard her, for he drew himself erect and alert on the sudden, as if expecting some attack. He looked into her face, and his eyes too were bright with anger.

"What's the matter? Why is she crying?" demanded Constance peremptorily.

The man's eyes narrowed, and for some moments he did not deign to answer, but looked into Constance's blazing eyes with a narrow, glittering little look of derision.

"Yo' mun ask 'er!" he said, curt and derisive.

Constance started as if he had smacked her in the face, his lack of respect was so complete. For some moments she could find nothing to say. Then she exclaimed, rather breathless:

"I asked *you*!"

Her voice was still peremptory. And still the man looked back at her with that narrowed, glittering look of insolence.

"Ay! Ah know yo' did! But 'er's none towd *me* why 'er's scraightin', so 'appen yo'd better ax 'er."

Constance gave him one glare of contempt, because of his boorish insolence. How she hated the dialect in his mouth. That alone was a mark of disrespect, as if the fellow threw it in one's face.—She turned her back on him, and crouched before the child, which blubbered on mechanically.

"What is it, my dear? What is it? Tell me, dear, tell me!" she said in false sweetness. "What have they done to you?"

But the child only sobbed more chokingly. Constance took out her handkerchief, to wipe the blubbered face.

"Don't cry, then! Don't you cry! Nobody will hurt you!—Tell me what they did to you, dear! What have they done to you, to make you cry like this?"

Her voice was hot with indignation, though really, she was play-acting. Or if she was not play-acting, if she did really feel a motherly distress at the weeping of the child, at least she was trying to find some occasion to turn and rend the man.

"There! Tell me what it is! There! Look, here are some pennies! Tell me what hurt you!"—She had found a sixpence in her coat pocket, and she held it up before the child.

The little girl took her fists from her eyes to look if the pennies were in actual evidence. Seeing the whiteness of the sixpence, her black eyes quickly dried, though she hid her face in her coat-sleeve again, and her body went on with mechanical but subsiding sobs, Constance waited.

"It's the pussy!" came in shaking tones.

"The pussy!" said Constance.

36

The child kept her face covered for some moments, then, rather awkwardly, she gave it another wipe with her sleeve, and lowered her arm.

"What pussy, dear?" said Constance.

The child darted a wary look in the direction of her father, and almost began to speak.

"Tell me! Don't be afraid."

The little girl now lowered her eye-lids self-consciously.

"'E shot it!" she said, in a false sort of plaintiveness.

"Shot a pussy? Did he shoot your pussy?"

The child gave a bold black glance into Constance's face, then a shy side-peep at the forgotten sixpence. Then she brisked up suddenly; and turning, pointed into the brambles.

"'E shot it there!" she said.

"Did he! What did he shoot it for?"

A last convulsive little quiver went over the child.

"I don't know," she said, with affected plaintive pitifulness.

"Yi tha does!" came the derisive, contemptuous voice of the man. "Tha'rt a little liar, when tha says tha doesn't know."

His voice cut like a whip. The child bridled and drew herself up with an air of injured virtue, cool and defiant even at her young age, and ready with the "superior" trick.

Constance rose to her feet, and faced the man.

"I don't think you need use such language to a child," she said, in cold rebuff.

"Is people going to gi'e 'er sixpence for tellin' 'em lies?" he asked, with the same glitter of derision and rage.

"If she was sorry for the cat—!" said Constance haughtily.

"There's the cat! There! If anybody wants to be sorry for him! He's fat wi' Sir Clifford's young rabbits and bods, if that's summat to be sorry about!"

Constance involuntary looked round. There stretched out under the brambles lay a large rusty-black cat with a big head, and amazing flat flanks. Dead, the creature looked like a piece of offal, as alive he must have looked a rather fine, if mongrel poacher. Anyhow Constance didn't like the look of him. She turned to the child.

"There, dear, take your sixpence!" She held out the coin, and a little hand came out readily for it. "Tell me what your name is, won't you?"

The child bridled and twisted and dropped her head, making a display of shyness.

"Connie Parkin!" she murmured.

"Connie Parkin! Well it's a nice name! And were you going for a walk in the wood? Do you like going for a walk in the wood?"

"No! My dad made me go!"

"Did he! And why didn't you want to?"

"I wanted to stop with my gran."

"Did you, dear! Where is your granny?"

"She's at cottage, cleanin' up."

"And would you like to go back to her?"

There was an awkward pause, and more twisting.

"Would you like to go to your granny now, dear?"

"Yes!" came very faintly.

"Come along then! Give me your hand!"

The child had to change her sixpence to the other fist, to give Constance her hand. Then the two set off down the narrow path, leaving the man with his dog and gun and dead cat. With female wisdom, neither the child nor her ladyship looked back to see the anger and malice and derision on the man's face. They walked slowly away, feeling they had scored.

But as soon as they had turned into the long riding, out of sight of Parkin, Constance was bored by the continuance of the excursion. She no longer wanted to hold the hand of Connie Parkin. Connie Parkin was a sly, false, impudent little thing, already full to the brim with tricks. There was a whole mile to go, to the cottage! Constance disengaged her hand from Connie Parkin's and tried to think of something to say to the little creature. But she could think of nothing, and she needn't have bothered. Connie Parkin was much more thrilled by the companionship of the sixpence inside her own fist, than of her ladyship.

At the cottage, the door was open—it was Saturday, cleaning day— and a little energetic-seeming woman was making a great rattle, black-leading the fire-place. The child ran in to her:

"Gran! Gran! Look what I've had given me!"

The little old woman, with smuts on her nose, from the black-lead, turned round to the child, saying with the shrewish, exaggerated fondness of a grandmother:

"Why! 'ave you come back by yourself, love!"

"Look what I've got, Gran!"

The old woman, looking up and seeing Constance in the door-way, rose hastily from her knees in front of the empty fire-place, exclaiming, as she wiped her face hastily with her soiled white apron:

"Why whatever!"

"Good-morning, Mrs Parkin! Don't bother to get up. I just brought your little girl home, as she was crying."

The old woman looked round quickly at her grand-child.

"What has he bin doin' to yer, love?" she asked, in shrewish, grand-maternal tenderness.

Connie Parkin hid in her grandmother's skirts, whence came her chirping repetition:

"'E shot a pussy!"

"Only a poaching cat!" said Constance. "I suppose it upset her, so I brought her along."

"It's very kind of you, I'm sure!"

"Look! Gran!" The child held out the sixpence.

"An' sixpence an' all! Why, you've been doin' well, you 'ave, this morning! An' what did you say?"

"Thank you!" faintly murmured the child.

"Thank you, your ladyship! You know what your daddy said, don't you!"

"Thank you, your ladyship," the child re-echoed very faintly. It was difficult to make the colliery people utter the title as a form of address, but apparently the old woman thought the sixpence was worth it, this time.

Old Mrs Parkin was abstracted. She *felt* she'd got black-lead smuts on her face. She furtively passed her apron over her countenance again, but completely missed the dab on her nose. She felt Constance looking at it, though. So she braved it out, and looked her ladyship in the face.

"I thought as 'ow there'd be a rattle o' some sort, when 'e would 'ave 'er go wi' 'im!" she said, lapsing again into the vernacular. "They never could hit it, them two, though 'e's her dad, an' ought to 'ave more patience. But men never 'as no patience with children, 'ave they?— They're best apart—"

"Oh yes!" said Constance.

"'E's 'asty, an' ever too ready with 'is 'and! An' she's a touchy little mortal, as never forgives! So you may fancy how *them* two gets on together."

"Not at all, I suppose!" said Constance, laughing and drawing away.

"You're right! You've said it! An' me as is 'is mother could never get on with 'im any too bright, I can assure you. Ay! Well! Good-mornin'! an' thank yer for bringin' th' childt 'ome, I'm sure."

As soon as Constance turned into the wood, the old woman rushed to the handbreadth of mirror that hung by the brush-and-comb box near the door, and seeing the smudges on her nose, her already flushed face flushed bright red with anger. She muttered angrily to herself, as she licked her apron and rubbed at the smudges.

Constance walked back to the hall, feeling once more her dislike of the common people. They were not really straight-forward. They resented one, just because one was a little different from themselves and they always hid their feelings up their sleeves. And the man had been insolent, insolent! Yet she could forgive him most easily. He might be a bit of a brute, but he was no cringer, and she didn't mind his temper. How he disliked that brat of his! She could sympathise with him there! It was an unattractive piece of femininity, that one! She could tell his skin simply crawled, at the child's false airs and ways. Crying over a "pussy", and as hard-hearted a little piece of goods as ever emerged!

Constance was glad to get back to her own milieu, and to Clifford. At least it was not so undignified as that squabbling intimacy of the people. Why should the man *want* to take such a brat with him into the woods?— But then, she was his own child, and perhaps he wanted *somebody* in his life. He'd had his finger bitten again that time, though.

It was very soothing to sit in Clifford's room, and hear him read aloud. His voice was cultured, he read well. And one avoided so much vulgar indignity.

The following Saturday, as it happened, Clifford wanted to send a message to the game-keeper. It had been raining steadily all morning, and though the rain held off after lunch, the world was much too sodden for Clifford's chair to venture out.

Yet Constance felt she needed to walk. She wanted to go out, away from the house. Though it had rained so much, still it was not a bad day. The air was soft and still, as if all the world were going to sleep. And once out in the park, in the silence and the suspended softness of the Saturday afternoon, it seemed as if the world had gone unpeopled. It was a soft, grey, deep afternoon, as it may have been before mankind became too many for the natural earth.

In the wood was a great stillness. Heavy drops fell from the bare boughs, with a strange loud noise. Nothing else moved. Life had withdrawn itself, and a deep remoteness had come over the familiar places. Among the trees was depth within depth of untouched silence, as in an old, yet virgin forest.

Constance walked dreamily on. She felt melancholy, but it was the soft, living melancholy of rest, of passivity. She thought she might meet the game-keeper, to give him Clifford's message. At the same time, she knew with deep, dim feeling that there was no-one in the wood.

When she came to the cottage, it too seemed to have withdrawn into a dim remoteness. There was no-one there. Constance knocked, but no-one came. She knocked again. She peeped through the window, and saw a red fire. But no-one would ever come. In all the world, there were no people. This afternoon, there were no people on the natural earth.

Still she did not want to go back without leaving her message. So she went round the cottage, to the little closed-in yard at the back, under the steep bank of the silent orchard. She was so sure that there was nobody, that she came suddenly into the little open gateway of the yard, and there stopped as if she had been shot.

In the perfect soft, grey loneliness of the winter afternoon, there was Parkin washing himself to go out on his Saturday evening. He had stripped to the waist, as the colliers do. His velveteen breeches sagged low on his hips. And he was ducking his head repeatedly into the warm, steamy, soapy water, rubbing his hands over his brown hair and over the reddened back of his neck, while the water ran from his face and over his close-shut eyes. He was so near, Constance could have touched him.

She withdrew in haste and in silence, back to the wood. There, she hastened through the wet trees, to be safely out of sight of the cottage. Then suddenly, a weakness came over her, and she sat down on a low bank, oblivious of the wet, oblivious of the dripping gloom of the forest.

The white torso of the man had seemed so beautiful to her, opening on the gloom. The white, firm, divine body, with its silky ripple, the white arch of life, as it bent forward over the water, seemed, she could not help it, of the world of gods. There still was a world that gleamed pure and with power, where the silky firm skin of the man's body glistened broad upon the dull afternoon. Never mind who he was! never mind what he was! She had seen beauty, and beauty alive. That body was of the world of the gods, cleaving through the gloom like a revelation. And she felt again there was God on earth; or gods.

A great soothing came over her heart, along with the feeling of worship. The sudden sense of pure beauty, beauty that was active and alive, had put worship in her heart again. Not that she worshipped the man, nor his body. But worship had come into her, because she had seen a pure loveliness, that was alive, and that had touched the quick in her. It was as if she had touched God, and been restored to life. The broad, gleaming whiteness!

It was the vision she cherished, because it had touched her soul. She knew it was only the game-keeper, a common man. That did not matter. He did not own his own body. His body was among the beautiful gods. She thought of it, as it arched over in an arch of aliveness and power, rippling then with movements of life, from the fallen sheath of those dead breeches, and her whole life paused and changed. How beautiful! How beautiful! And with what power of pure white, rippling, rapid life!

She quivered in all her fibres as she sat. Were all men like that? Had Clifford been like that?

Again her life stumbled and halted. Clifford? No! Clifford had been handsome and well-made, but there had been something clayey or artificial in his body, at his best. No, not that silky *quick* shimmer and power, the real god-beauty, that has no clay, no dross! Clifford had never had that. There had always been some deadness in his flesh.

Ah well! She rose to her feet. It was no doubt all illusion: just the effect of the grey day, and the complete unexpectedness.

And still she felt an ache in herself, as if she were moving a cramped limb. There was an ache, and a vague, heavy yearning, like a stream, started to flow in her. She was afraid of this yearning, so she suppressed it quickly from her consciousness. She would be matter-of-fact.

She hurried now towards the cottage, to get there before he should have gone out. And she wondered if he would think it queer, her coming to speak to him, in the absolute loneliness of the afternoon.—At once she caught herself up. Such a thought had never even vaguely occurred to her, before. Now she was angry with herself, and confused. The game-keeper!

She stood on the threshold of the cottage, flushing and quivering inwardly. She was very angry with herself! A mere game-keeper! Didn't he always have a body! If it had *really* been anything wonderful, of course she would have sensed it through his clothes. Which she hadn't done, she had never given him a thought. So that obviously it was all the effect of her disordered imagination.

But it seemed to her wrong, that, being a commonplace individual, he should have that pure body, that arch of white, living power.

She knocked. And then she heard him coming downstairs. Almost she fled away. Yet when he opened the door, she was there on the threshold. She looked up into his face, and stammered:

"Oh! Sir Clifford wanted to send a message—"

He held open the door.

"Shall yer come in?—Have yer bin afore?"

"No!" she said, making big round eyes.

"I sort of wondered if I'd 'eered somebody knock."

He stood there in a clean shirt, and navy-blue Sunday trousers and pink braces. His damp hair was carefully parted on one side, his ruddy face shone with soap and with shaving. He was getting ready to go out. He had on his Sunday neck-tie, of shot silk. And his hard, rather hostile eyes examined her keenly as she stammered her message. She stammered uncontrollably, to her rage and despair. And he just listened and watched her.

She did not like him. He seemed hard and impudent. She did not like his ruddy, vermilion face. She did not like his pink braces, nor his shot-silk neck-tie. And she did not like his shirt of grey and pinkish-striped flannelette. All very well, having a pure body under that striped flannelette shirt! And with that red, common face!

"All right, my lady! I'll see to it, as Sir Clifford wants."

"Oh, thank you! Good-afternoon!"

"Good-afternoon to your ladyship."

She was always flattered when he said that. But how curiously he looked at her, as if he wanted to say something else! She hurried away. And as she went, she knew he stood in the doorway looking after her, and she felt her dark-blue mackintosh was ugly.

No matter! No uglier than his cheap navy-blue trousers and his cheap shot-silk tie! No uglier than his damp, carefully-parted hair! And his red, impudent face. She realised that she was weary of people's faces. They were always so full of small conceit, and of the monotonous, impertinent things they always thought. Did he really have that white, curving, lonely body she had seen? Ah no, it was an effect of her imagination. He was what his face was; and his grating voice.

She wondered if he were still watching her. But she did not turn round. She felt him looking after her, as she went forward to the gloom. He would be thinking something stupid and mean. Ah well, let him think! People were all like that. The hidden loveliness of his body, even if it were there under the flannelette shirt, was not his. He knew nothing of it. He was too common and stupid. She was bitterly bored by common, stupid people.

Yet once she was among the trees, she looked back. The door was shut. And she was disappointed. She even resented the fact that he was going to the village for the evening—leaving the estate. The red fire in the cottage had seemed so cheerful. And he was alone. And ahead, towards Wragby, seemed such gloom, such encircling gloom. Lead kindly light,* amid the encircling gloom!—She saw the red twinkle of fire in the cottage. And the beautiful body of the man. Those were her kindly lights, for the moment. But she was going away from them.

When she was home again, she seemed to be haunted by another self inside herself. It was a self which had seen powerful beauty, seen it alive, and in motion, and seen it as the greatest vision of her life. She was well accustomed to beauty in the world of art, and from this she had derived, truly, the deepest satisfactions of her life: from beauty and from knowledge. Human contact, love, sex, marriage had all meant little to her, strictly, compared to the curious rapture and fulfilment she had got from certain Beethoven symphonies, or from a book like Les Liaisons Dangereuses,* from some poetry, from some pictures, from the sight of Florence in the sunshine: or even from a course of philosophy lectures. Life! they talked about life! But what was life, except experiencing the beautiful experience of works of art or works of nature, or acquiring the never-ending gleaming bits of knowledge that came to one? What was life, besides that? What point was there in being Mistress of Wragby, unless Wragby was beautiful to her? What did she care about being her-ladyship, unless it stood for something fine in life, above the ignoble? What was her marriage with Clifford, save the sharing of the evanescent raptures of some poetry, some picture, some landscape, the joy of making some critical analysis of life or of some work of art, the thrill of acquiring through him, or along with him, some new idea, some glimpse of new reality, what one might call a discovery of truth? What was life, beyond this? Nothing! And she was sure it would go on being nothing.

Love, that mysterious fetish-idea, what did it amount to? In her own case, nothing. The word was a portmanteau-word, and inside the portmanteau was little or nothing. Her feeling of clannish attachment to her father and sister!—her thoughtful and aesthetic companionship with Clifford!—what were these? If Clifford had not been able to read to her, talk to her, keep her critical and appreciative faculties sharp and alert, what would Clifford have been to her? Nothing.

As for sex, what she had known of it—and she had had brief experience of other men, before Clifford—what had it meant to her? Not much! Sex in itself didn't mean a great deal. Even her father knew that. But perhaps it was a function necessary to the health of the young. Leave it at that. Clifford was right in what he said.

Even if she had had children, she did not imagine they would *really* have mattered deeply to her: not to her own, individual life. She knew it was so with her sister Hilda. Hilda wove a lot of importance round her little girls, round herself as a mother. She took her duties terribly seriously. But it was, really, in the same way as Constance took her household duties to Wragby Hall. It was a sort of self-discipline and a sort of self-importance. It was part of the mechanistic activity of life: if that was life. There was nothing at all profound in it. There was even no real experience in it: neither in Hilda's motherhood nor in her own housewifery. It did not amount to a great deal more than another set of physical and emotional exercises, a sort of drill.

And that was life! And that was all there was to it. Constance accepted it with a certain stoicism, which nevertheless left her exposed to devastating storms from within.

But now! But now! A new flicker of experience had just licked her heart, and had left a burn, an inflamed place which she could not smear with forgetful ointment. What was it? It was nothing, surely, that the portmanteau-word "love" could contain. It was much more like beauty, but beauty come alive and dangerous, something dangerous to touch, like perfect white fire, arched over.

The man's body! It seemed to live in itself, perfect, powerful, hidden, a life of its own, godly, apart from the man, who was vulgar. The man's mind, and his spirit, were crude, uninformed, vulgar. His body alone was a lovely plunging thing, divinely living on, ignored. It was beauty that rippled and made quick movements, and was dangerously alive, curving in the white arch of life.

Did she wish to touch it? Did she wish it would touch her, and fold the white, clean, warm arms round her? Ah!—and a new misgiving came into her. If she too had a body that was alive with beauty—then yes, yes! But had she? Had she a body of beauty like that, alive like a quick soft flame? Had she? Had she?

She listened to Clifford reading. He had found an old copy of the second part of *Hajji Baba*,* and was reading that aloud. He now preferred, usually, to read aloud an amusing book: and they both found Hajji in England very amusing. In it, yes, Constance could feel some of the old Persian delight in the original bodily life, as distinct from the mental and spiritual life. Yes, with all their ridiculousness and cruelty, those Persians had live bodies that glistened, she knew, with aliveness, even when they had grown fat and ungainly. But then, poor Persians, they were so at the mercy of the logic and the mechanism of the west. It made them so helpless and silly. Surely one could live the life of the body, without being so foolishly naïf!

Clifford was very much amused when Hajji exclaimed with such loud woe over the nakedness of Englishwomen's faces. Ah! if only these houris had covered their faces, what fire of passion would have flamed in the Persian's portly body! But the bald naked indecency of the exposed countenance quenched all Hajji's fervour, and left him repelled. Oh, if only a little handkerchief had been put over the faces in London, what lovely houris these women would be! But no man, no, could survive the bald sight of the faces of endless women. Every spark of desire left him.

Constance had been silently embroidering. The lamp-light fell on the knot of soft brown hair in her neck. She was so still! But oh! the thoughts that teemed endlessly, endlessly in the small, rounded, womanly skull! Clifford never suspected them.

She lifted her face to him and looked at him with her wide blue eyes. He seemed so arch and amused. Yes, even Clifford, how tiresome his face was, really, nakedly grimacing and showing all his mind-born feelings.

"Don't you think Hajji is right?" she said. "Don't you think people's faces *are* the worst part of them?—"

He thought a moment: Then he said:

"No, I don't exactly see it."

"They're like clocks, to tell the time of their personal feelings by. I rather hate people's faces. There are so many of them, and they all tell more or less the same time, like clocks."

"They express more or less what their owners feel," said Clifford. "What else can you expect?"

"I know! That's just the trouble! Their owners all feel such monotonous, and usually mean things, and usually they're pretending something else, like clocks that tell the wrong time. I'm tired of people's faces. I wish there was a law making them all cover them up, like Mohammedan women. If they did that, I wouldn't mind if they went with all the rest naked—so long as one didn't see their faces."

"You'd find their bodies infinitely uglier than their faces," said Sir Clifford. "You'd soon wish there was the law against nakedness again."

"I don't think so. I believe most people might be ugly. But anyhow they'd have to be ashamed of it: which they aren't now. Truly, Clifford, I'd rather see any portion of people's anatomy, than their faces."

"Even their posteriors!" he teased.

"Oh much!—their innocent posteriors! They wouldn't be like clocks, showing all the mean, stupid personal ideas and thoughts on the dial."

"No, I don't suppose they'd be expressive of much. But still—" He burst into a loud, jarring laugh.

When Constance went to bed, she did what she had not done for some years. She took off all her things, and looked at herself naked in the huge mirror of the huge mahogany cupboard. She did it almost without thinking, and without knowing what she was looking for. Yet she moved the lamp so that it would shine full on her.

She knew she was supposed to have a good figure. But after all, what does that mean? She was not very tall, a bit stocky, but she had a certain fluid proportion. Her skin was not white, a little tawny, and her limbs were rather full, soft and slow. She should have had a certain voluptuous fulness of body, and a soft, downward-sinking flow.

But somehow, she felt, it had not come off. Instead of ripening into a warm, voluptuous, curving fulness, her body was like a fruit still greenish at the end of summer. There had not been enough sun to swell it to its delicate, ripened curves. Her breasts already were sinking a little flat, her belly had lost the young, expectant beauty, and was becoming a little slack, meaningless, her thighs too, that used to glimpse so quick in their odd, female roundness, that looks almost like a subtle, fleet spiral, now were becoming heavy and inert. Inert! Inert! That was what was happening to her body, it was sagging a little and going expressionless. It was not yet deadish, like poor Clifford's. But neither was it *quite* alive. Not *quite* alive!

She twisted to look at her back, her waist, her hips and buttocks. She was not fat. Perhaps she had grown a very little fatter in the years she had been at Wragby. But her body had somehow lost distinction. The crumple of her waist at the back was not so alive, so gay-looking as it used to be, and the long, rich slope of her haunches and her buttocks was not quite, not quite so sensitive in outline.

But this was the part of her that seemed most alive, the beautiful, long-sloping hips and the buttocks. Like long yellow grapes! Like hillocks of sand, as the Arabs say, long and soft and heavy, and downward slipping! The long, full, heavy contour, so rich and full of female life! What did Clifford know about women!

But the front of her body made her miserable. Was it already beginning to slacken, to move towards age before even it had approached maturity? Was the bloom gone, and the delicate glad contour, while still it was a green fruit? All she would know in her life, would it be just girlhood and old-woman-hood? Was the body of an old woman already beginning to steal upon her, invidiously?

She slipped on her nightdress and went to bed, feeling infinitely sad. And in a sort of despair she wept the first tears she had cried for many a long day. Long and bitterly she wept.

But afterwards, she felt that even tears made her younger.

5

CHRISTMAS WAS NEAR, and they were having visitors. Though she did not like the "festal season," and always wished she could disappear to some utterly heathen country for the Christmas fortnight,—or else go to sleep—still she busied herself making preparations, and allowed herself to think of nothing. The approach of Christmas always inspired her with indefinable dread, as if something bad were going to happen. But perhaps that was because Clifford had been wounded on Christmas day. Anyhow, she had to prepare for mild festivities.

In the wood she had seen a holly tree with many red berries. It was very bright, and very gay, with the jolliness of the pre-Christian Christmas, the heathen mid-winter excitement. She sent word for the keeper to bring a few branches to the house, along with a few brace of pheasants. Simpson came to her one morning, to say that Parkin had come with the holly and the birds, and was it as much as her ladyship wanted.

Constance went down to the big kitchen which was also the servants' hall, since there was no butler or footman. On the huge table was the dark sparkle of a huge, black-and-scarlet bunch of holly, and the long, brown-gold lines of the pheasants' tails spread along the board. It gave her a sense of richness and wildness. The game-keeper, in his dark velveteens and red face, seemed part of the wild out-doors, as he stood and watched.

"That's splendid!" said Constance. "Splendid! That's beautiful!"

"If your ladyship'd like any more—"

"No, no! That's enough! It seems a pity to cut it."

"Or a bit of spruce fir, wi' cones on?"

She turned and glanced at him. His red-brown eyes with the tiny black pupils, disarmed for the moment of their watchful hostility, seemed as near to being kindly as they ever could be. But also they showed a peculiar fear, fear of all that she stood for, and that Clifford stood for, and that all the house-servants stood for.

"No!" she said. "No! Let the trees keep their own branches. It is a pity to bring them indoors, to get dusty!"

He gave her a sharp glance of intelligence.

"Then I'll go, if there's nothing else," he said.

"Nothing else!" she replied.

He gave a quick salute, and seemed to melt from the kitchen.

Constance put up the sprigs and tufts of red-berried holly where they pleased her: just a hint, here and there. She did it all against her instinct, really. Since the war, Christmas nauseated her.

There were only five guests: Clifford's aunt, Lady Eva, his cousin Olive Strangeways and her husband Jack, then Tommy Dukes and Harry Winterslow. Olive and Jack came for Clifford's sake: Olive had always had a *tendre** for Clifford. Lady Eva, who belonged to one of the very titled families, but was slightly in disrepute because of her gambling and her brandy, came because other people were scared of her play. Once she started, she was a demon, and she infected others. Money gushed from pocket to pocket in a way that was the ruin of any house-party, the day after. So nobody wanted her for Christmas. There would be no cards at Wragby. Resigned and angelic, Lady Eva descended on her nephew Clifford. She was his mother's sister, after all.

Tommy Dukes, the Brigadier General, was tall and thin and erect, with a reddish bony face and a reddish, plucked neck and ginger hair going grey, though he was not yet forty. He was fond of Clifford, and he was very good company, witty, amusing, dry, original, and an authority on Arabic and Arab literature. But he could talk to anybody on any subject, he got on famously with Lady Eva, one would have thought he had a tenderness for her.

Perhaps he had, of a sort. Lady Eva was sixty, tall and thin and with a small, shapely red nose (brandy) and vague, light-blue eyes that only really woke up at cards. She was as simple in her manner as a girl, and withal had the remains of a real grande dame about her, of the Queen Alexandra period. She was intelligent, too, but like a child, detached. Everything was vague and far-away, to her. Probably it was this childishness, combined with the remains of the grande dame, that appealed to the General.

Harry Winterslow was the General's friend. He was a moody young man with a pale face and dark hair and a rather petulant manner, who wrote poetry that Constance could not understand, and who seemed to labour under some cloud of doom: though it was probably only a cloud of self-importance and self-consciousness. He very often did not answer when spoken to, was always retiring to his room, or disappearing somewhere, and altogether was one of the young men that Constance had learned to leave to themselves. Lady Eva and Olive Strangeways did the same. So that sometimes, the young gentleman, who was of good family and "knew everybody", *had* to put himself out and start charming one of the ladies. And when he started, he was quite good at it.—But it happened to be Olive whom he spasmodically tackled. He seemed afraid of Constance.

This left Jack Strangeways more or less alone. So Jack made up to Connie. He had been for a long time what is called "a good-looking boy". Lady Eva still said it of him: "Poor Jack is such a good-looking boy." But Jack was thirty-five, and it was time he left off being a boy. Moreover, he was getting really fat. And if anything exasperated his wife, it was to hear people calling him: "Poor Jack!" They did it so unconsciously.

"I don't mind people getting fat," said Olive, "if they didn't lay it on in the wrong place."

CHAPTER 5

Olive was always saying deadly things about her husband, "the good-looking boy". And it was true, he did have too large a posterior, and there was something almost female in his big thighs. But men, as a rule, didn't like him. He was too fond of the sound of his own voice, and he loved to get some sympathetic woman into a corner and tell her all about the war, and himself in the war. He terribly wanted to make women *feel* for him: but he rather overdid it. His big, rather childish blue eyes would get wider and wider, his low, secret voice hotter and hotter, as he talked on about himself, or expounded some idea of his own about Spanish architecture, which was his pet subject. And he seemed so convinced that the woman must, simply must feel tremendously *him*, his appeal, and what he was saying, that most women laughed at him a little spitefully.

So it was with Constance. She did not even think him a good-looking boy. He was flat-faced and a little insipid. And his posterior *was* too large. Nevertheless he followed her about as if she must, simply *must* want to be listening to him, must want to be taking him up: like a persistent little boy dogging his mother. He was not little at all. He was big, and good-looking in the romantic style, like a young Siegfried already a bit too fat and vapid. Yet he, too, had his own peculiar intelligence, a certain insight into things, though it was the insight of a rather timid child who wished things could be made "safe". He was, like many young people after the war, a neo-conservative and a neo-aristocrat and everything that was anti-democratic.

This bored Constance. Even in Clifford, when he kept saying that democracy was a dead dog, most people should be put back into slavery, there should be a small and ruthless, armed aristocracy, and so on, she felt it was mere stupidity, really, ineffectuality. In Jack it was still worse. When he said to her, so hotly: "My God, if ever we get a revolution here in England, how I should *love* to charge the rabble with machine-guns," she felt like kicking him. "What rabble?" she asked. "These damned bolshevist-socialist lot."—"But how do you know they are rabble? How do you know they are any more rabble than you are? Perhaps it's we who are rabble, really—people like you and me, who stand for nothing, really!"

"Oh come! Look here! Look at Russia!—" and off he went again.

"Very well!" she said. "But when the time comes, take care that it isn't the rabble who are charging *you* with machine guns, not you them. Don't you think so easily of mowing them down. The mowing-machine may be in their hands."

"That's just what we don't intend it to be!" he cried.

But she walked away, her face flushed and angry. There was nothing infuriated her more than this puppyish talk about "mowing down the rabble". The rabble, coming down to brass tacks, were to her the Tevershall colliers. And though she didn't love them, exactly: still, they were at least as manly as Jack Strangeways, and she hadn't yet heard them talk of "mowing him down".

Olive looked up from her deep conversation with Clifford.

"Oh, don't you get cross with him, Connie!" she said. "Lascialo sfogarsi—let him blow off his steam!"

Which was just what Constance didn't intend to let him do: not upon her, at least. He could go into the garden to blow it off.

The general conversation happened to turn on the future. Suppose this civilisation *did* blow up, what might we expect after. A woman had written a book* about such a future: with "immunised" women who had definite activities, and other women who were "breeders"; and a strictly-regulated society, like a superlative ant-heap that had at the same time marvellous flying-machines and all that: just an extension of the scientific-materialistic Wellsian ideas.

"It's so perfectly repulsive," said Lady Eva, resignedly sitting the whole evening with no brandy to sip, "that it probably will happen."

"Probably if the men had their way, it would happen," said Olive.

"Not if I'm one of the men," said Tommy Dukes.

"I think I might apply for a job as breeder," said Jack.

"Where's your testimonials?" cried Olive contemptuously: she had no children.

"Testi-monials!" said Tommy Dukes.

"It will never happen," said Winterslow. "Because by the time we have reduced ourselves to the ant-heap psychology, society will have gone quite mad, and we shall have murdered one another. I consider society the most dangerous madman alive. The mass is much more insane than the individual, though he's bad enough—But if we go on as we are doing—"

There was a pause.

"Of course!" said Constance. "The whole thing is based on hatred—a hatred of life. It becomes a system of hate."

"Now that had never occurred to me before! I believe you are right, child, it is just hatred!" said Lady Eva. "One must love *something*."

They looked at her, as she sat in her black dress, with her slender, still-girlish arms. Her face was reddened with brandy. She was a pathetic instance of not being able to love anything. She couldn't do it: so she drank brandy and gambled.

"I don't know," said Clifford. "It seems to me that sufficient civilisation eliminates the love-necessity. The need to love is only half civilised. And if the fully-civilised have no need to love, we may easily come to the bee-hive community."

"Even that requires a queen bee," said Dukes quietly.

"*Cherchez la femme*!"* added Olive's satirical voice.

"And what woman could lay three-thousand eggs?" said Jack.

They all laughed.

"Oh!" said Tommy Dukes. "Let them talk! Let them talk about immunised women and sterilised men, and flying to Mars. It won't alter things! Men only talk like that, because they're sterile already: and the women because they're immune—even if they've not been immunised. They're immune enough!—It's not from that sort of talk and that sort of talker any change will come. So let them buzz. They're the flying ants of the present ant-heap. Who cares!"

"Exactly!" said Olive. "Who cares?"

"Well, I do!" said Lady Eva. "I should hate to think that anything of that sort was going to happen. It's bad enough, what has happened. Imagine if I had to be an immunised woman, or the other sort, in that kind of London University society! I should hate it."

They all laughed, and it was only by a miracle that the impudent Jack saved himself from saying: "Well, what are you now?—if not immunised, you're immune." He was always a bit second hand.

"No, don't trouble!" said Tommy Dukes softly. "If I know anything about human nature, the ant-heap is here and now, and soon a big ant-eater will come along and lick it up with a curly tongue!"

"How nice!" said Olive. "And what then?"

"Ask the ant-eater," said Jack.

"Something really nice might come after, don't you think?" said Constance. "Don't you think it's time things took a rather lovely turn, instead of always a more horrid one?"

"Quite time, my child, quite!" said Lady Eva, pursing her lips.

The men laughed.

"I can imagine a world where nobody cared terribly about money, or owning things, or bossing other people. Personally, I wouldn't care a bit if the land and the mines and all those things belonged to everybody. I only want to live. And I don't seem to make a very startling success of it!" Constance persisted.

"But you want to own Wragby," said Jack. He certainly did.

"Not necessarily. I can imagine lots of nicer things than Wragby," she said.

"Scotch castles and Italian villas!" he smirked.

"No! Where one needn't be desperate about owning anything. Where a bit of life flowed."

"You're quite right, Connie!" said Dukes, looking at her with his shrewd eyes. "A flow of life, and contact! We've never had proper human contact— we've never been civilised enough. We're not civilised enough even now, to be able to touch one another. We start away, like suspicious hairy animals. The next civilisation will be based on the inspiration of touch: believe me.—But we shall never live to see it, so why talk about it."

Everybody sat silent, not understanding him.

"But *you* never want to touch anybody," said Constance.

He laughed short.

"Don't I?" he said.—"No, I don't want to *paw* anybody—and I don't want anybody pawing me. But *touch*?—" he considered a moment— "well, perhaps it's too late for me now. Too late for me, or I might even want—ah well!" He looked at her oddly, and her heart gave a queer lurch. This man might have been in love with her—if he'd had enough hope, if the weight of disillusion hadn't been too heavy. But the old thing, the dead civilisation, was clamped down on him too hard. That was why he never married, never would marry—he had no bodily hope for himself. "Apart from me, personally, though," he added, "there *will* be a new civilisation, the very antithesis of tabloids and aeroplanes: believe me! There will be a civilisation based on the mystery of touch, and all that that means; a field of consciousness which hasn't yet opened into existence. *We're* too much afraid of it—oh, stiff as wood, with fear! We paw things—but probably we've never truly touched anybody in all our lives, nor any living thing.—Oh, there'll be a democracy—the democracy of touch. For the few who survive the fear of it. We shall be swept away, and all the tabloiders and white ants and brown and black ants, and soldier ants and artisans. We're only an experiment in mechanisation, that will be properly *used* in the next phase."

A sense of fear fell over the room. This soldier seemed to see all his own world so definitely swept away, to replace something else.

"I belong to the mechanistic experiment," he said. "But I wish I could have crossed over, to the democracy of touch."

"Well, I never heard of the democracy of touch before!" said Lady Eva. "We used to think there was only one democracy, when my husband was radical member for Darlington. But I suppose we were wrong, as usual."

"Quite wrong, Aunt Eva! There are as many democracies as there are people—every man his own demos," laughed Clifford.

"It seems so."

"I don't get your democracy of touch, you know," said Olive, in her casual, brutal way. "Touch what?"

"Ah, there you ask me! We've had two thousand years of *Noli me tangere*. Just imagine *voli me tangere*,* for a change."

"Sounds to me like pawing."

"Ah, well it isn't!—any more than *noli me tangere* is not-pawing. A great deal of pawing goes with *noli me tangere*."

"I'm afraid you're getting mystical."

"To you, I'm sure I am."

"Touch is the one thing that is entirely mystical, to a materialist," said Harry Winterslow, turning with a saturnine gleam on his pale countenance, to Olive. "Especially the idealistic materialist."

"You mean the materialist has only got paws, anyhow," said Olive. She knew that Winterslow scorned to make love to her; and by instinct, she knew he didn't find her quite, not quite touchable; he thought her hands insensitive paws, her body a clumsy animal arrangement that just pushed against things.

"Clever of you!" he retorted to her.

"And of course, all women are materialists!" she said sarcastically.

"Clever again."

"I'm sure you're wrong there!" said Lady Eva. "I've known women who were anything but materialists."

"I agree with you, Lady Eva!" said Dukes. "Yet perhaps women *are* more out of touch, than some men. Most men, of course, we don't speak of at all. Delenda est Cartago!* But a few men might know what touch meant—and I doubt if any living woman would."

"You'd be jolly well determined not to let her!" said Olive. "Men like you! You talk about touch-me-not! It's touch-*her*-not, with men like you."

"I tell you," laughed Dukes, "she's not yet ascended into touchableness."

"Poor darling!" said Olive. "Who's going to give her a heave up, do you think?" She looked at him with malicious sarcasm.

"I tell you, I'm too old," he said.

"And far, far too modest!" she mocked.

"Perhaps it is rather modesty than age that ails me," he laughed.

"Of course, I think it's hate," said Connie, in a faint voice.

"You would, Connie darling!" laughed Jack. "Everybody that sees you says how adorable you are, so it must be hate."

"Connie certainly is a wonderful girl," said Lady Eva.

"We're to be pawed—but never really touched. That's how men treat us," she said. "We're untouchables! But they'd like to paw us about."

"Not necessarily even that," said Dukes. "And men? are men touchable, to women? Is any man really touchable, to you?"

He looked at her shrewdly, sarcastically.

"I think we've talked about touchables enough now," said Lady Eva. "It used to be one of the problems of India, as far as I remember. But we've got it on the domestic hearth now, apparently. I think you ought to stop, General. You're much too clever for us, so why rub it in?"

"I'm sorry, Lady Eva! I'm wrong."

"Yes, you are wrong."

"Set me right, then," he said good-humouredly.

"Will you dance with me? I should just love a fox-trot."

"I should like it more than I can say," he replied.

"There, then! Now you're being human. You don't really mind holding my hand in a dance, you see! I simply don't follow you in all that untouchable talk."

"We'll manage better with music, Lady Eva, if I'm not presumptuous," he said.

"Much better! Much better with music!"

And Connie had to dance with the fat Jack.

She didn't know what to make of the "untouchable" talk, either. She only felt that Dukes was trying, in his own way, to get somewhere eventually. There was something a bit heroic about him. And as a human being he was generous, even to a woman. But why did he have that funny thread of hate for women altogether? He liked them, as creatures. Yet, because they were women, they were, to him, untouchable, in some subtle way. And he had no control of this feeling in himself. It was something more than physical. He didn't mind having Lady Eva's hand in his, nor his arm lightly round her, as they danced. Because, of course, there was no real contact. It was hardly more physical than talking to her, and not really so near.

No, it was not just physical, in the scientific sense of the word. Connie knew this when he was dancing with her himself. He held her hand lightly, but kindly, and his arm against her shoulder had a certain protectiveness in its guidance. But essentially, he was a thousand miles away from her, he held himself most perfectly out of contact with her, at the same time sharing the rhythm of the dance with her.

"Why do you talk about a democracy of touch, when you can't really touch any woman, not to save your life?" she asked him.

"I tell you, I'm on the wrong side of the fence," he said. "I don't belong to the democracy of touch myself: I only prognosticate it."

"If you did belong to it, you'd have to be in touch with a woman, wouldn't you?" she asked.

"Yes! Yes, I'm sure I should. But something would have had to change in me, and in women, before it took place. And it hasn't changed in either of us, and won't. I tell you, I'm a long way on the wrong side of the fence."

"You mean you're not touchable, either."

"I suppose that's what I do mean. Don't touch me! for I am not yet ascended unto the father! Perhaps that's about where we stand."

"And I too?" she asked.

"I don't want to judge about you. You must decide for yourself."

The dance came to an end, and he left her. But vaguely in her consciousness the words of Jesus were moving: *Noli me tangere!* Touch me not! for I am not yet ascended unto the Father!—What did they mean?

It meant they had died, these men. In the war, finally, they had died. And though they were still walking about in the flesh, and were still struggling for the life that should be theirs, after the resurrection, they had not yet got the body of the new life.* Their bodies were the old, tormented bodies which had died, but which had not yet come to life again. The spirit was struggling into new life, a resurrection. But the body was not yet filled with new blood and new fire, which was the Father, the resurrection into full life.

How terrible the story of Jesus! It was the epitome of the story of all men. They had all been crucified, these men: all except Jack, who had balked it. But Clifford and Tommy Dukes and even Winterslow, they had all been killed, in some subtle way. And it was the strange, dim, grey era of the resurrection, with them, before the ascension into new life.

And perhaps they would never ascend really into life. They would remain the shadowy, almost incorporal beings of the era between the rolling open of the tomb, and the ascending into the firmament of a new body. They lived and walked and spoke, but theirs was still the old, tortured body that could not be touched.

There was no hope, in them, of a new body, that did not wince with the unspeakable memory of death. And between the old bodies, there was no possibility of contact. Those that had never died, who had, in a way, dodged, like Olive and Jack and so many second-rate people, were utterly out of touch with those who had died and were walking now in the dim, grey days before ascending unto the Father. There was no touch with that which lay behind. The new body could not touch the old. The old must be connected with the old, the new with the new.

Clifford, at least, could never rise to a new body: no, nor even hope for it. Lately, since the excitement at the rolling back of the gates of the tomb had died down in him, he had known. That was why he had told her to have lovers. He thought she could be connected with the old body of life, like Jack—men who had got the old body, which had dodged the descent into hell.*

But she knew, the old body of life, these second-rate men, were to her untouchables. She could have loved Tommy Dukes, but for the dark, cold death that was still at the centre of his heart. But men like Jack she could not even touch: nor any of the ordinary men, who had dodged the real descent into hell. Brave men had made the descent: but they were still wincing and saying *noli me tangere*—It was malicious, really, of Clifford, to suggest she should find lovers among the second-rate men who had never suffered the awful adventure.

But Clifford was becoming a little malicious. He was gradually coming to the old position, of those who did not believe in the resurrection of the body. He talked a great deal about immortality. The subject obsessed him. But it was the immortality of the spirit he insisted on.

The resurrection of the body—the bodies of living men, even if not one's own private body—this did not interest him. It was the private and egoistic resurrection of his own spirit, into the ideal eternity, that obsessed him.

Constance could see that he and Tommy Dukes were no longer in accord.

"I believe in the resurrection of Man, and of the Son of Man, and that is a great comfort to me," she heard Dukes saying to Clifford. "Somehow, I shall always be part of mankind. That's what I feel. So that if men can rise up again, with new flesh on their spirits, and new feelings in their flesh, and a new fire to erect their phallus—that is immortality to me."

"But that is merely temporal," said Clifford. "Even granted it happens, give it, say, another two thousand years, and it will be where we are once more—descended into hell!"

"What does that matter? Even eternity is in rhythms. What can rise up to life again is eternal, in the fact that it rises from the dead. If once there is a rising from the dead, then death is part of the life rhythm: and that is immortality. And if we have died, and only got as far as pushing back the stones of the tomb, without ever ascending unto the Father, we've performed one of the great acts of the life-cycle. If we never ascend, and never know the joy of new life: well, those that come after us will know it! We've died: that's patent. But if we've even pushed open the doors of the tomb a chink, we've kept up the immortality. What does it matter if we go through the rest of our lives with sore, untouchable bodies, and the incessant *noli me tangere!* in our mouths? We have done the worst bit. And those that come after, even if they aren't my children, will be able to make the ascent on to a new earth. By which I mean have new bodies, with new good blood in them, born for a new epoch of mankind. Surely that's heaven on earth! It would be to me! though I shall never experience it. But I believe I've made a bit of a way for it, and I'll go on trying. If I can't have a new body, and new blood in my veins and a new song in my mouth, I can at least go on shoving the stone from the mouth of the tomb, so the others will come a little quicker to the ascension and to the next day, the human tomorrow, that'll be theirs all right, though we only shiver in the darkest hour before the dawn."

There was an obstinate pause on Clifford's part.

"But I still believe the individual spirit is immortal!" he insisted. "I still believe that my spirit, after having striven sincerely after truth, or knowledge, or self-awareness, will enter into the realm of perfect knowledge, perfect universal self-awareness, the great light, or the godhead, or the nirvana! I still feel that as the greatest truth."

"Then for you it *is* the greatest truth, and therefore it is true," said Dukes. "I suppose men only surge out towards one door of truth at a time. The survival of my individual spirit, and its incorporation into the great light, or the perfect knowledge—I've no doubt it's quite true for me too—but I feel it isn't a poignant truth. The poignant truth, for me, is the resurrection of the body. That's what I yearn for. But if there is one perfect knowledge, and one eternal light, so, ultimately, to me there is one body: the body of men and the animals and the earth! And if this body is capable of newness, then that is my resurrection. But only that is born again which rises from the dead. And so, knowing I have died, I want to make at least the first grey movements of the resurrection: the pushing back of the rock from the tomb.—We are not divided, all one body we—The hymn says it:* and I feel it is acutely true, of all those who rise from the dead."

"But women?" said Winterslow.

"They die too, the best of them. And they're as bad as we are, just as much wincing from being touched. But they've got to roll back the stone from their own tomb. We can't do it for them: nor they for us."

"I can't see, honestly I can't, that the body matters, in the face of death. Admitting the obvious fact of dust to dust—can the body *really* matter?" Clifford insisted.

"If matter is indestructible, there is only one body, and that is eternal," said Dukes.

"And why not leave it at that?" said Clifford.

"Because my soul yearns for a new body of man."

"I'm afraid I don't feel that way," said Clifford.

"Why should you then, if you don't?" said Dukes. "Every man his own immortality!"

"Myself!" said Winterslow. "I don't so much yearn for a new body, as set my teeth absolutely against the fact of being nothing but spirit. I *am* a body. I am even somebody. And that I'm going to be, forever."

Connie had been eavesdropping. The men were talking in Clifford's bedroom, where he lay in bed. And she sat by the folding doors, listening to every word. If they'd known she was there, they wouldn't have talked. But she wanted to hear.

So! the immortality of the body! It set her yearning for children. If only she could have children, by a man with a risen body! Even by Dukes!—if only he hadn't got that fatal little memory of death occupying his heart! No! Not Tommy Dukes! He was still too overshadowed.

And perhaps she herself had not sufficiently risen from the dead. But then, she did not feel she had died, with all the absoluteness these men seemed to feel. Died! yes! she had died many deaths. But none so awful, such a cold time in the tomb, as these men seemed to think they had known. Though probably they exaggerated, as men, in women's eyes, nearly always do, in order to make themselves more important to themselves.

Anyhow, the talk, though it moved her, did not settle her own problems. What she wanted, for herself, was that her body should not go dead. She was by no means anxious to have it dead, so that it could gruesomely resurrect and push at the cold stone of the tomb, and murmur continually, with cold lips: *noli me tangere!* No no! her great problem was to keep her body alive. And between second-rate men who had never died the death, and first-rate men who, overshadowed and benumbed by death, could only murmur: *noli me tangere!* where was she to go? Perhaps even her father's way of knowing so much about the mouth of the tomb that he trained a Dorothy Perkins rambler rose* over it, and a profuse pink geranium, perhaps that, after all, was best. Yet one can never repeat the excellencies of one's parents! alas!

She felt repelled by the men, and very much more drawn towards Lady Eva and Olive. Olive tried to live by Sir Malcolm's principles. She tried gathering roses while she might.* She picked up a lover where she could. But invariably she found him terribly unsatisfactory, and invariably she returned to her tension with Jack. That seemed to her the only real thing in her life: the tight string that tied her to Jack, and made her spend most of her time strangling his soul, while he, equally canny at the game, had tight strings round all her limbs and pulled them till he paralysed her. A great deal of it was mutual torment! And that was the most real thing she had in her life. She felt herself like an embodied demon. She envied her cousin Connie her placidity and her soft, if ridiculous, abstractedness.

Lady Eva was another matter. Constance liked her, but was always depressed by her. In her simple, very well-made black dresses, the elderly slim woman had the look of a girl, when she sat still: and she sat so often so very still, just murmuring her gossip. But when she came to walk, she creaked with rheumatism. And it was the same with her manner: she was so simple, almost like a child, yet she managed to preserve the curious prestige of the *grande dame*. But when you came nearer to her, you found the joints of her soul as stiff as those of her body. At the centre of her, she was completely insentient. At the middle of her, she had no feelings at all. She didn't even know that, at the centre, anyone *could* have feelings. She thought that the core of everybody was quite hard and quite without feeling, as every crystal is centred upon a grain of cold dust. Only, of course, the way you were elaborated upon this centre of nothingness mattered. It was that which established your quality.

And she didn't think her niece Constance had any very definite quality. That peculiar quality of the diamond, which makes it able to cut all the other stones, Constance had not got; whereas Lady Eva, in her own way, had it, and so, she thought, had Clifford. It was the quality of the ruling class, That the diamonds were mostly flawed, and not very much wanted, didn't matter to the diamonds themselves. Nothing mattered to them, because they had the quality of ultimate imperviousness. Only they *had* begun to realise that they, like diamonds, were nowadays mostly used merely as settings for baser, more coloured stones.

Constance understood Lady Eva fairly well, and expected absolutely nothing from her: not one single deep or warm feeling. The diamond is the most bloodless of all stones. But she liked her: and she felt sorry for her. Poor Lady Eva, the *grande dame* in her was her trump card, when she was dealing with people. And it didn't always work. All sorts of other trumps were continually being called. She had to fall back, at last, in her aristocracy, upon an infinitely cunning impudence. That was what her aristocracy amounted to, in the very last issue.

But still—why jump to ultimates? She *was* a figure! And she *was* interesting, in a quaint way, with her frail grandeur of the queer, unreal days of Queen Alexandra.*

She loved to talk tête-à-tête with women, in a slightly whispering voice. So she came limping slowly but still aristocratically up to Constance's room: and Constance gave her a brandy-and-water.

"My dear, you have by far the pleasantest room in the house. You really are wonderful!"

"Am I? Why?" said Constance, by no means caught.

"Oh, altogether! The way you manage as you do! I was always such a bad house-keeper! And your patience with Clifford! Wonderful!"

"But he is patient with *me*," said Constance.

"He is! He is wonderful too! It *is* dreadful! Of course his brain is as perfect as ever—he can be so witty!—and that's the part that matters most in a man. I think brains so much more important than looks in a man, don't you?"

"Yes, I do! But Clifford is quite good-looking!"

"Quite! Oh quite! Very good looking. But you know what I mean!— only half a man, as you may say. It *is* dreadful."

Lady Eva sipped her brandy, and her moist blue eyes became vaguer. And yet there was a determined point within the vagueness. She was after something or other. Constance remained silent.

"Being a woman, it's your side that appeals to me," Lady Eva went on. "It's so dreadful for you to be deprived of—of one side of a woman's life, as you may say! Almost worse for you, because you're healthy."

"But what am I deprived of?" asked Constance.

Lady Eva looked at her with those vague blue eyes, in which yet was some remote point of determination.

"You're bound to miss not having a real husband, you know," she said. "You're bound to suffer, with that being taken away from you.—Or don't you really mind?"

Lady Eva was probing very close, in a queer, female curiosity and intimacy.

"But I've got a real husband," Constance said. "I mind for his sake that he is paralysed. But why should I pity myself?"

"No! Perhaps you're right! Perhaps you don't care for a man in that way! I believe most women don't, if you ask me. If a man gives a woman an interesting life, that is what she really wants of him. She isn't very keen on the other. I know I wasn't. But I had a wonderful life, in politics, with my husband. It was wonderful at the time. You know ours was a real love-match, mine and my husband's."

She looked at Constance queerly! And it was as if some queer long, elegant insect, a stick-insect, or a mantis, were talking about its love-match.

"Yes, I know!" murmured Constance.

"Isn't it queer, how it's all gone! My husband has been dead only five years! Yet it seems to me as if all the years I lived with him had never been real: all that reform and the politics I thought so much of, and the electioneering down there in our own place!—oh, it *was* wonderful!—yet it doesn't seem any more real to me now than a cigarette one has smoked. A man makes a woman's life for her, but he never enters into *her* life, don't you think?"

"You see I don't know very well," said Constance.

"No, you don't, really!—" Lady Eva rather waveringly lit a cigarette, having reminded herself. "No, I don't think men enter really into a woman's life. They make her life for her—but they never really come in to it. That's how it seems to me. When I look back, and think of my husband, I can see him making my life for me: and of course, I adored him, I'm almost sure I did. Yet he's hardly more real to me now than Lord Palmerston,* whom I just met, or than other men whom I remember. No, he never really came into my life at all. No man has."

"Perhaps men *don't* enter into a woman's inner life," said Constance.

"That's what I mean!" said Lady Eva quickly, pointing her cigarette. "When I think of all the men I've known, not one of them has ever affected my inner life no more than Collingwood, my butler, has. Yes! And he's my butler."

Lady Eva pursed her lips and looked oddly at her cigarette point. Constance knew Collingwood. He was a big, burly Lincolnshire man, about Lady Eva's own age, who had come with her when she married from her father's place. All these years he had been with her, and was the same huge, strong Lincolnshire fisherman's son, with a face redder than Lady Eva's, by far, through drinking whiskey where she drank brandy. But he had a genuine gentle feeling for her. To him, the girlish pathos of her was complete. He knew her very well, and he loved her with the queer passion a man might feel for his slender, girl-like sister, who was just a little younger then himself. He had a wife and grown-up children, but when Lady Eva moved to her house in Dieppe, he moved with her, and kept house for her. He was like a big, burly brother to her: but of course, always the butler. And she could never have got on for a month, without him.

"What I mean, you know," said Lady Eva, becoming more involved in her own vagueness: "men don't mean much to a woman, in her real life. Women mean a lot more to one another. Don't you think so?"—She looked round, with queer searching.

"Yes, perhaps!" said Constance, thinking of her sister Hilda.

"Still some men do give you a warm, safe feeling. I know that," continued the elder woman. "And as you grow older, that's what you value. It's so awful to be alone and always to make your own decisions. My father was a tyrant, but one did feel safe when he was about."

"Yes!"

"And what I mean to say, with you and Clifford—perhaps you ought to fall in love with a nice, strong young fellow who would think the world of you—if only for a time—"

She drifted off vaguely, and Constance waited.

"I think, if I had to live my life over again, I should marry one of those nice, healthy, fresh-faced young policemen, you see, with lots of fun in their eyes. I do seriously!"

Constance only laughed at this Ethel M. Dell touch* suddenly coming out in her well-born aunt.

"A woman nearly always chooses the wrong thing for herself," Lady Eva rambled on. "I chose Edward because he was so refined-looking, and interested in politics, and so clever; and of course, because I was wildly in love with him.—But I was wrong, you know, in a way!—It's awful to be growing into an old woman, and feel no safety anywhere round you. And feel you've never had the right man's arms round you, you know, to make you feel safe, really safe! I wish I'd let a young, fresh-faced policeman fall in love with me!"

"Then why didn't you?" laughed Connie: thinking that Lady Eva had let the good-natured Collingwood fall in love with her, in his own way, without taking much notice of him.

"Oh, I could never *give* myself to a man of that class! never! Women having their chauffeurs for lovers! it seems to me so humiliating!—But still! if one only had some warm and comforting thought somewhere!—It's so awful to grow old!"

She turned her vague blue eyes on Constance like some spectre, and Constance shuddered.

"But you're not old, Aunt Eva!" she said.

"Oh! I'm an old woman! I'm sixty-one! And believe me or not, it's pretty awful. It's pretty awful, going on making your own decisions, without any idea, or any feeling at the back of you, to keep you up.—But you're strong-minded, and I never was that!"

"No, I'm not strong-minded!" said Constance, in a murmur.

"You are more than I was.—But if I were you, I'd be awfully careful

65

what I did with my youth. It seems to me, if I'd ever had the arms of a real nice man—you know! I say a nice policeman with a jolly face! you know what I mean!—well, if I'd had the arms of a man like that round me when I was young, perhaps I shouldn't feel so stiff and stark now I'm getting old."

"But Sir Edward was in love with you," said Constance.

"Oh yes! Oh, deeply, deeply! But you know what I mean, there's ways and ways of being in love! My husband was a higher type of man altogether. So it was very different."

"And wasn't it enough?" said Constance.

"You mean isn't that enough for me to remember?—That's what's so awful! It seems like nothing at all. My sides feel so cold and stark, if you know what I mean."

"And don't you think policemen's wives feel their sides are cold and stark, when they grow old?" asked Constance, laughing.

"No!" said Lady Eva, with a queer snap. "No! No, I don't believe they do."

"But you've never known any!"

"I haven't! But I don't believe they do! And if I were you, I wouldn't drift into a stark old age if I could help it: I wouldn't really, Clifford or no Clifford. He won't thank you, in the end. Believe me, you must look out for yourself, and look out in time.—You're a faithful girl, as I was. I was always faithful to my husband, I couldn't help it, if you know what I mean. And that's how you are! Not like Olive! She's quite another plate of soup, is Olive—"

There was silence for some minutes, then Constance said suddenly.

"But your children! Don't they make you feel less lonely?"

She had suddenly remembered her cousin Elsa, who was at the moment exploring Darkest Africa, or whatever place was to be considered as darkest; and her cousin, Sir Egbert, who had married a New York Jewish millionaire daughter, kept up a great country establishment with very expensive stables and gentlemen forever in "pink"* and ladies in whatever they thought was most surprising, and who was a little impatient of his mother, "poor dear Lady Eva!"

"Yes!" said Lady Eva, suddenly reminded of them. "Yes! I love to hear that they are happy. I love it when I hear they are doing well—"

6

CHRISTMAS WAS OVER, the guests were gone, Constance was alone with Clifford once more. Clifford seemed irritable and exhausted, now the excitement of the strangers had passed. He had a good deal of pain, and lay a good deal in bed. And Constance felt she could not do much for him. He would remain for hours in the ashy silence of a sort of burnt-out resentment. Of her existence he was strictly unaware. And it seemed to cut her off even from her mere existence.

If ever she could have made him better, she would not have minded. If she could have hoped. But there was little or nothing to hope for. And there was no faith. Sometimes she sincerely wished they could both have been good christians. But they couldn't, so it was no good wishing.

As it was, they were nothing, and they had nothing to draw upon but the resources of their own, stoical will. The will itself did not fail. But the power of life which kept the will alive, that did collapse. It collapsed completely in Clifford, and he merely lay in bed and was ash. But it collapsed also in Constance, and that frightened her. She foresaw the day when she too would lie in bed unable to think or to will any further. And that terrified her.

She kept on her plodding round from day to day. But she felt as if she were labouring inside a vacuum. No life came in to her, and what life she had oozed out spent. Her mere vital energy was giving out. And this produced in her a sense of profound terror.

She began to go thinner, and her heart did queer things. There was a pulse in her neck which she could see shaking, when she looked at herself in the mirror. She began to see now that the pride in her own will was a mere conceit. She could not do as she wished, even with herself. There was that mysterious flow of life-energy, which she had never known existed, until it began to fail her. She had thought her life was her own, till she came to the point where she needed it most bitterly, it failed her. Her own life failed her. No energy flowed into her, from the sources. It seemed all used up, the fountains run dry.

In six weeks she was a changed creature. She kept her golden-ruddy colour, but it had gone earthy. And she was thin as a rail. She had never been thin in her life before, so it was strange to rub her thin arms and thin thighs. It filled her with a dim wonder. She felt like a grey, unreal changeling.

At last she wrote to Hilda. "I haven't been well lately, and seem to have gone very thin, but I don't know what's the matter."

Hilda at once prepared to descend on Wragby. She came in March, alone, driving herself in her small car. When she saw Connie, really a mere ghost of the old Connie, pathetic and dumb like one who is dying, tears of rage and pity sprang to her eyes.

"But Connie! What's the matter?"

"I don't know."

"But you're really ill! What do you imagine it is?"

"I don't know. I haven't much energy, that's all."

Hilda went to interview Clifford, and found him remote, irresponsive, also dead.

"What's the matter with Connie, Clifford? She's gone so dreadfully thin."

"She is thinner! But I don't think there is anything wrong with her, is there?"

"Well! I think we'd better find out."

Fear roused him a little from his dismal apathy, and he made arrangements for Connie to see a doctor. But Hilda insisted she should be taken up to London, to Hilda's own doctor. So the two sisters prepared to drive off.

"We shall only be away one night, Clifford! You won't mind?" said Constance to him.

"I do hate being left to Marshall!" he said, with an irritable, resentful sort of pathos.

"You must have a nurse," said Hilda to him.

"I don't want a nurse. I've had enough of nurses," he replied.

"When you've worn Connie out, so that she can do nothing for you, what will you do then? Then you'll have to have a nurse each. You're not a cheerful man to wait on, Clifford. I should think you know that."

"Am I expected to be cheerful?"

"Not if you don't want to be. But you mustn't pour all your depression over Connie. You can see what it does to her. You'll have to have a nurse."

"Are you the person to tell me so?"

"It looks like it, doesn't it."

They went down to London, the two sisters, to have Constance examined. The doctor made a careful examination: then he asked about

Connie's life. And he said: "There's nothing organically wrong, that I can find. But the vitality is terribly low. Lady Chatterley will have to make a change in her life. She is living too much off her reserves—and now she's got no reserve left. She *must* get away, and take her mind off the things that trouble her. She must. If she doesn't, I wouldn't answer for the consequences, within another six months."

"What sort of consequences, for example?" Hilda insisted.

"Well! Her mother died of cancer, didn't she? Those things start out of some depression, or repression which lowers the vitality—"

Hilda was determined now to take her sister away from Clifford. But she had reckoned without Constance.

"I can't leave him for long, Hilda! I can't!"

"But if you're going to bring something awful on yourself?"

Constance pondered for a long time, then she said:

"Perhaps we'd better get a nurse for Clifford. And when he's used to her I might leave them for a time: in the summer."

The two sisters struggled together. Hilda wanted to take Connie straight away to Italy.

"I can't, Hilda! I can't! I can't!"

And Hilda had to give way. But about the nurse she was firm, and Connie did not resist her. Only she pondered: she knew how Clifford disliked efficient and trained nurses.

"Perhaps we could get Mrs Bolton," she said at last.

Mrs Bolton was a widow of forty-five or forty-six, who had been parish nurse for Tevershall for ten years and more. Constance had met her once or twice, in connection with charities. She was a Tevershall woman, her husband had been killed in the pit, years ago. Constance rather liked her, she seemed so sensible and so human. She was good-looking, too, in a quiet way, with strong features and grey eyes. Her manner was just a little bossy, with having handled the colliers and their families for so many years. But there was a certain dignity about her, of a woman who really is able to put herself aside to attend to others, but who, at the same time, insists on being properly respected. Oh yes! she was used to obedience and a certain amount of deference from the colliers and their wives, she took it as her due, almost as one of the ruling classes.

Clifford probably would not object to her. He had known her by sight, and known about her all his life.

Constance therefore at once suggested Mrs Bolton to Clifford, when she got back to Wragby. He agreed very unwillingly: he hated giving himself into strange hands: and Connie knew how cruel it was for him. But Hilda was there, so there was no getting away from it.

The two sisters called to see Mrs Bolton, in her house in Tevershall. She was in her nurse's uniform, very clean, rather handsome, and with an odd, girlish impulsiveness in her manner that was rather attractive, contrasting with her professional benevolent severity. It was evident she had a very good opinion of herself. She received so much respect from the collier people, and had so much authority with them, she considered herself one of the bosses, as it were. And as such, she was not in the least daunted by the visit of the two ladies.

"Why yes! Lady Chatterley's not looking at *all* well. She's usually so bonny. But she's been failing all winter. Oh, it's very hard on a woman, nobody knows—"

As it happened, Mrs Bolton was glad of Lady Chatterley's offer. She was getting tired of the heavy work of parish nursing, and felt herself due to rise a little in her profession. But of course, she would have to serve a month's notice—unless Dr Shardlow would agree to get a substitute.

Off went Hilda to Dr Shardlow, who, of course, was willing to do anything to oblige Sir Clifford, but he'd have to get the consent of the Board. Obstacles, however, only roused Hilda to greater speed. Round she went! She got the consent of everybody necessary, and she speeded up Dr Shardlow. So that Mrs Bolton would be able to come to Wragby Hall on Monday.

Hilda went to have a talk with her.

"I'm so glad you can come!" she said. "Sir Clifford does so hate the thought of a nurse. But he knows you, so that makes it much easier."

"Oh yes! I've known Sir Clifford since he was a tiny toddler, and a lively one he was—"

Hilda drew Ivy Bolton's story from her. Queer, how young the woman seemed, how the passion would flush in her cheek and the light in her eye! She was forty-seven years old, and seemed hardly forty.

Ted Bolton, her husband, had been killed in the pit twenty-two years ago: twenty-two years last Christmas. He had left her with two little children, one a baby in arms. The baby was married now, and had a baby of her own. The other was a schoolmistress in Sheffield. Yes, they'd both done well.

It seemed to Hilda, Ivy Bolton had loved her husband: he had been so steady, and so good to his wife! He was only twenty-eight when he was killed in an explosion. The butty ahead had called to the other men to lie down, feeling it coming, and they'd all lain down in time except Ted, and he was round the corner and didn't hear. So the explosion caught him, and never hurt the other men.

At the enquiry, they said, on the master's side, that Bolton had been frightened and tried to run away, and that was how he came to get killed. They found him lying on his side as if he'd been running away from the explosion. That was what they said. If he'd lain down, he would have been safe like the others. But his own cowardice was the cause of his death. Yes! That was what they said.

So the compensation was only three hundred pounds, and it was more of a charity gift to the widow, under the circumstances, than legal compensation. Yes, that was what the Company said! And even then she, Ivy Bolton, wasn't allowed to have the money down. They said she might drink it, or do something wasteful with it. She wanted to start a little shop, with the money. But they wouldn't give it her. They doled it out to her, thirty shillings a week. Yes, she had to go every Monday morning, with her baby in her arms, down to the offices, and stand waiting with a lot of others who wanted their accident pay, or whatever it was: sometimes she'd have to stand for a couple of hours before she got her thirty shillings, and a baby in her arms!

Well, three hundred pounds at thirty shillings a week didn't last long: not four years! And what could she do, with two little children on her hands? But his mother had been very good to her, oh, very good! Nobody could have been better than Ted's mother. She'd look after the children any time, when Ivy was learning to become a nurse. So Ivy worked hard, and attended courses in Sheffield, and had special ambulance courses. She was determined to be independent, and to bring up her children in independence. So she had got a place as assistant nurse at Uthwaite hospital for a time, and then they'd made her district visiting nurse for Tevershall. She would say that for the Company, they'd always treated her well, as nurse. But what rankled in her was what they'd said about Ted: as steady and fearless a fellow as ever went down a pit, and then to give it out as it was his own cowardice that killed him!

Hilda wondered at the fire in the woman still. She spoke of Ted as if he were just as much alive as ever, as if he would be coming home from work soon. And she spoke so curiously of the Company. All her queer suave ladylike way fell off her when she mentioned the Company, and it was very obvious she had never forgiven them the insult to the dead Ted, nor to herself, doling her out the thirty-shillings. Somewhere very deep in her was a resentment against all bosses and all owners. Her sympathy was with the colliers: but of course she liked to play my-lady-benevolent to them.

And it was obvious she did not like Sir Clifford. She did not like the Chatterleys. In a subtle, undefined way, they were to her the enemy. Yet she envied them their power. She wanted to find out about that, and to get the secret of it: the power of the gentry. She did not believe them to have any heart, and ordinary human feeling at all. That you found among the colliers, and that was what made you lower class: your ordinary feelings. The upper classes didn't have them. What then did they have? What was the secret of their supposed superiority? She was keen to find out.

Hilda could see this: but she did not mind. Only she wanted to get the woman's sympathy for Constance.

"And I do wish you'd do what you can for my sister—for Lady Chatterley. I'm afraid Sir Clifford is just using up her life, and killing her. Not that he means to do it, of course! But he can't really help it. He *will* have her there all the time. We've had such a fight to make him agree to have a nurse. But the doctor in London said plainly that my sister wouldn't live, unless she got some relief. And naturally we don't want to see her killed off.—I do hope you'll persuade her to go out, away from that house, as much as she can."

"I will indeed! I will! It always was a doomed house, to my thinking: a depressing place."

"And of course one *can't* blame poor Sir Clifford. Paralysed like that, he can't help being selfish, and thinking of himself first.—Yet it's a dreadful thing for a young woman—a husband who can never really be a husband—and no hope of a cure, nothing to look forward to—"

"Oh, yes! It's terrible! I only had *my* husband for three years and a bit. But my word! While I'd got him I did have a good husband, if ever a woman did—"

So Ivy Bolton appeared at Wragby, and for the first two or three days was very nervous, feeling her way about. Her rather bossy, open, talkative, coaxing manner, that she had with the colliers, would never do at the Hall. She was extremely circumspect and subdued. However, Clifford let her do things for him, though his resentment amounted almost to hatred of her. She felt this, through all his extreme politeness, and it was, curiously enough, not surprising to her: so different to the colliers. They were shy with her, when she had to bandage their legs or wash their bodies, but they always trusted her with a childish sort of trust. And that made her proud and pleased.

But Sir Clifford only coldly resented her, and disliked having to submit to her. She knew it at once, and kept very quiet, never trying to coax him, or command him for his own good, as she did the colliers. She kept herself quiet and a bit mysterious, with her long, handsome face, and her grey eyes rather downcast.

"Shall I do this, Sir Clifford, or would you rather I didn't bother you?"

"Do you mind if we leave it for half an hour?"

"Oh, not at all! It is just as *you* prefer."

"Very well then! Half an hour!"

"All right, Sir Clifford!"

And she would retire again. But in her heart she was saying: "Very well, Sir Bossy! if you *must* show that you're master!"

Hilda went, and the house took on a new rhythm. The old tense intimacy between Clifford and Constance was gone. Mrs Bolton was always there, a curious link between the world of the servants and Clifford's rooms. Before, the servants had lived and acted far-off, off the stage. Now, they all seemed to come nearer.

Mrs Bolton helped Clifford to bed at night, and slept across the passage, so that she came in the night if he rang for her. She also helped him in the morning, and even shaved him when he was not feeling well. All the heavy, intimate jobs that had fallen to Constance now fell to her. And she was very good.

Clifford, however, resented it deeply, and never felt quite the same again to Connie. It made a cleavage through his feeling for her, that she had relinquished his wrecked body into the hands of a stranger. He never any more felt the close oneness between himself and his wife.

Constance knew, but did not really mind. It was a relief to her. That other oneness had almost destroyed her. Sometimes, upstairs, she would sing to herself the song: "Touch not the nettle!" It has a refrain: "for the bonds of love are ill to loose."* She had never quite understood that, till lately, when she was trying to extricate herself from the intense personal love that was between her and Clifford.

She found that it was as if thousands of little roots and threads of consciousness between her and him were entangled and utterly grown together in a mass, and all these roots went unnourished, they devitalised the plant itself. Now she was quietly and subtly trying to break these threads and roots of consciousness, with patience and impatience. The coming of the nurse had torn quite a lot free. But there were others. And the bonds of love are ill to loose: like any other bonds.

He would still read to her in the evenings: Mrs Bolton was free after dinner, till ten o'clock. Mrs Bolton took her meals with Mrs Marshall and the others in the kitchen.

"Oh, I'm not proud! I should look well, shouldn't I, thinking myself too proud to have my meals with Mrs Marshall, my word! No thank you, my lady, I'll eat with them in the kitchen, if I may. It's no good putting on any pretences, is it?"

So that, after dinner, Constance and Clifford were still alone. He was still harping, with an insistency that Constance felt was purely destructive, on the problem of immortality, and on the reality of mystical experiences. He had had mystical experiences—sort of exaltations and experience of identification with the One. Constance mistrusted these experiences terribly. They always seemed to her conceited, egoistic, anti-life. But he insisted on them: and insisted that the necessity for everyone was to have this mystical experience of identification with the One— which seemed to him like pure Light—and to bring this experience with them down into life again. So that a bit of his mystical experience of the great Oneness had to enter into his dealings with Connie—even with Mrs Bolton.

But to Connie, this was both boring and irritating. When he insisted on his unification with the One, it seemed as if he insisted that he *was* the One, the great I Am:* and to Mrs Bolton, though she knew nothing of it openly, as yet, it came as a new sort of subtle, sublimated arrogance, superiority, and bossiness: a queer sort of bossiness and arrogance she wasn't used to.

Clifford, however, insisted on it. Connie once said to him: "Surely, Clifford, if the mystical experience were real, you needn't bother other people about it. You sound as if you had to convince yourself." But that only offended him deeply. So she just held her tongue and let him insist on his immortality, and let him inflict his immortality on her. For that was what it amounted to. This Mystic One was like a great pompom on the top of his cap, to show his personal superiority and importance.

He read her again Plato's *Phaedrus*. She never minded listening to Plato, because, though she felt that he too was on the exalted ecstatic track—a line she hated, personally—still, he started from such a strange old world, where so many deep things were still alive and potent, which in our world have been falsified to death, that there was always a thrill in him. Even the ecstasy had a touch of the Bacchic in it, for her.

And the Phaedrus myth had a certain fascination for her: the glimpse of another world. She didn't care about the progress of the soul, nor for pure Truth nor pure Knowledge, nor the Philosophers' heaven. But the imagery still fascinated her. At the end, however, when it came to criticising the meaning of the thing, she could only say:

"I do think Socrates seems awfully stupid and overbearing with his black horse. I do dislike men who treat a horse like that."

"But my dear child, the black horse is merely a symbol!"

"Oh, I know!—is the black horse Passion and the white one Desire? or vice versa? Anyhow it's the only team the philosopher's got, so he might learn how to handle it. If he's such a bad driver, he should try walking up to heaven on foot: he'd still have his precious charioteer Νοῦς to keep him company."

Clifford looked at her in wonder. She was really in revolt.

"And when the grasshopper has become a burden, and desire has failed,* I don't think even a philosopher will get far," she added.

"You don't agree that desire and passion must be curbed?" he said.

"Oh, curbed! Philosophers and their curbings! What will curb desire except desire, and how can you handle passion except with another passion? Oh Clifford, I am sick to death of your philosophy and your immortality! It deadens everything out of existence. Look at you, how dead you are! Your black horse and your white one are dead. And now you can chuff up to heaven in your bath-chair—with not even a gamekeeper to give you a push!"

Clifford watched her with eyes that glowed with cold hate! The strangest of strange things, was how a speech like this, which seemed to her only rather natural, made him full of cold rage. However, at length he controlled himself to smile a rather sickly smile of frustrated superiority.

"Ah yes!" he said. "We know what a woman is after."

"She doesn't want a philosopher's heaven, nor his immortality either. And if I had a black horse to drive, I'd learn to drive him, no matter how bloodshot his eyes were.—Are they both supposed to be stallions?" she added suddenly.

"Plato wasn't a woman, so he doesn't specify."

"And philosophers don't notice such things," she said laughing.

But she felt wave after wave of revulsion going over him, revulsion away from her. She felt great masses of the roots that bound them together tearing asunder. And she was glad. A queer joy came over her.

"It is all conceit," she said. "Plato isn't even a good black horse, he's a conceited mule, sterile. That's what they all are, full of the conceit of their own Νοῦς and their own immortality. Loathsome conceit! And they all use petrol: all the white and black horses are dead. The intelligent kippers have killed them all.—I wish I could find one."

"Don't flatter yourself that you'll find any black horse willing to let you ride him," he said.

At which she looked at the mystic Clifford in astonishment. Was it *all* sham?

She went up to her room, even before Mrs Bolton came. Why drag out the evening with him? At last she was in rebellion. Against Clifford and all his sort she was in rebellion. But she was not yet free of him. Who could tell, how many of her roots, perhaps even mortal ones, were entangled with roots of his, roots of men of his kind? The bonds of love are ill to loose. And when they are the bonds of a whole civilisation, they are very very ill. One can only make a good start.

Mrs Bolton, however, was an ally, always urging Constance to go out, to take the air, to drive to Uthwaite, to do anything that would get her away from Sir Clifford. While she had been so ill, Constance had hardly walked in the wood at all. But on a blowy day late in March, Mrs Bolton said to her:

"Now why don't you take a walk through the wood, my lady, and look at the daffs behind the keepers cottage? They're the prettiest sight you'd see in a day's march. I'm sure you'd like some in your room."

Constance did not mind the woman's semi-professional coaxing. She took it in good part.

Daffodils! and were there daffodils? Behind the keeper's cottage? Her heart gave a queer little burn. For a long time she had never even thought of the keeper. Even now, she did not think of him. It was the vision of the cottage, the dark cottage on a dark, lonely winter afternoon, that gave her the queer burn on the heart.

But she went! She felt stronger, she could walk better, though still she was weak. But the world was alive! The body of men, and the animals, and the earth!—it could all come alive again. Tommy Dukes had said it. And it was true. If only that hateful pale Spirit which men had in them didn't prevent it. "Thou hast conquered, O pale Galilean!"*—But there was to be a resurrection, the earth, the animals, and men.

She didn't want any more dead things and pale triumphs. No more engines, no more machines, no more riches and luxury. She wanted live things, only live things: grass and trees on the earth, and flowers that looked after themselves; and birds and animals, stoats and rabbits, hawks and linnets, deer and wolves, lambs and foxes. There *must* be life again on earth, and fewer people. There *must* be fewer people!

There must be the resurrection of the body, not forever this tomb-stricken spirit creeping about. It must end. Pallid miners, creeping like caterpillars by the thousand, from under the earth! What for, what for? And gentry in bath-chairs and motor-cars. What for? It was all bodiless and ghoulish. The resurrection of the body. Even the true Christian creed insisted on it.

But these dead larval creatures called people had such invulnerable wills. That was what they wanted immortality and eternity for: to go on exerting their pale cold will forever. They were like a huge cold death-worm encircling the earth, and letting nothing live. It was Will, the will of dead things to make everything dead. Nothing, nothing must remain free and wild and alive. Men would prevent it. Men and women, millions of carrion-bodied personalities who imagined themselves to be the ideal and the non-such, these would kill off all life, with their relentless wills and their good motives and their determination to be "kind". These, and the other ghastly people with relentless wills and spiteful motives, who were satisfying themselves by knowing better. But they all had a cold, relentless will, and a determination to get the better of life. One thing, and only one, seemed evil in all the world. And that was the unyielding, insistent human Will, cold, anti-life, and insane.

But how to get free? How to get out of the clutches!

She went slowly across the park. It was a blowy day, and she felt weak. But the sunshine blew in sometimes, and the world was bright.

It seemed strangely bright. She was glad to flee into the wood, like a stricken thing.

Pale the wood seemed, even, with pallor of wind-flowers sprinkling the shaken floor. Cold draughts of wind came, and overhead there was a rushing of entangled wind among the twigs. It seemed to try to tear itself free, too, the invisible wind! How cold the little anemones looked, on their crinoline green skirts! A few primroses, too, by the path, seemed bleached with cold, and hardly could bear to unfurl their little fists.

Yes, there was a rushing and a roaring, as if the black horse were let loose among the cold stagnancy, and the flowers had come out to see him. She was strangely excited, in the wood, in the sound of the wind. She gathered a few violets, and held them in the palm of her hand. Then the scent came out like summer, between her fingers.

She went slowly, slowly, drifting feebly yet gladly, across the mile of woodland towards the cottage. She came to the clearing, and looked at it shyly. It was just the same, silent. But there was a bit of yellow jasmine by the door, in flower, and a few last crocuses.

It was quiet: no sound of a dog. Softly she went round to the back. All was still. Nobody! But on the orchard slope, behind, the little wild daffodils were rustling and fluttering and shivering so bright and alive, but with nowhere to turn their faces to, as the wind pounced on them with its invisible paws!

Perhaps they liked it! Perhaps it excited them too, when they had to shiver and flutter and try in vain to turn away their faces from the blow. They shook their bright, sunny little rags in such distress! But perhaps they liked it, really.

Constance sat down with her back to a young pine-tree, that swayed against her like an animate creature, so subtly rubbing itself against her, the great, alive thing with its top in the wind! And she watched the daffodils sparkle in a burst of sun, that was warm on her face; and she caught the faint tarry scent of the flowers; and gradually everything went still in her, so still, so still and disentangled!

The shade and the cold roused her again. The daffodils were dipping now in shadow. And so they would dip all through the night! How strong, in their frailty! From the grey slate roof of the chimney a faint waver of smoke whirled. Perhaps someone was at home. She hoped not.

She rose, rather stiff and cold, and took a few daffodils as she went down: although it was always with a pang that she broke off the flowers.

They belonged to their own outdoor world. It seemed so unfitting to take them inside the walls of Wragby. Walls! Walls! How weary she was of walls! Yet how she needed their shelter. Even at this minute she would have liked to go into the cottage and sit quite still in the wooden arm-chair by the fire, safe within the four small walls. She wished she were strong enough to live without walls.

The afternoon was fading. It must be already past four o'clock. She ought to be home for tea with Clifford.

She took the broad riding that swerved round and down to the larch wood, past the pure little spring of water that was called Robin Hood's Well. It was cold down this hill-side, and there was not a flower on the sombre riding. The well, however, bubbled brilliantly clear, from its bed of red pebbles. The keeper kept it clean. And there was a faint, faint tinkle of water, as the thread of a streamlet ran down-hill past the larches. She could hear the sound even above the hissing boom of the larch wood, that seemed so bristling a twilight spreading away in its own wolfish darkness.

Slowly at last she climbed the up-slope, towards where the timber had been cut away, and the sky was bare. She was tired. As she came near the brow, she heard a faint tapping away on the right, and she wondered if it were a wood-pecker, or the keeper. It came from the direction of the little clearing where the hut was. Instinctively, she turned down the narrow side-track, to see.

The hut and the clearing were in a hidden place among the oak-trees and the remnants of last year's bracken. It was here the pheasants were raised, when the time came. It seemed one of the old secret places of the forest, very still and remote. But it was from here that the hammering came.

The brown dog, Flossie, came running towards her, but did not bark. She saw the keeper, in his shirt-sleeves, bent over one of the chicken-coops that he was repairing, ready for the nesting time. He lifted his face suddenly, having heard some sound, and saw her. By the startled look in his eyes, she knew his instinct was to reach for his gun, as if he were being attacked. For a second he was absolutely still, watching her. Then he rose slowly to his feet, and saluted her, still watching her from his red face, as if she might be an enemy.

She approached slowly, her limbs melting as she did so, so that she wanted to sit down, to relax.

"I wondered what the hammering was!" she said. "I'll rest a minute before I go on."

She felt so weak and breathless. He looked at her, and seeing her so thin and so lost-seeming, something stirred in his bowels.

"Shall yer sit i' th' hut a while?" he asked.

"I think I will."

He went before her, and got the rustic stool he had made, brushed aside the lumber, and set the stool facing the door.

"Should yer like door shut?" he said.

"Oh no!"

He looked at her sideways, as if he didn't want to look at her really. But he was kindly. He felt for her the sympathy one fugitive feels with another. He went back to the coop he was repairing.

She sat with her back to the timber wall of the hut, and leaned back her head, closing her eyes. She was so tired, so tired! Fugitives from the social world: that's what it was. The man had fled too, and now guarded the wood like a wild-cat, against the encroaching of the mongrel population outside. This was at least a little sanctuary. Here she could rest. She closed her eyes, and all her life went still within her, in a true quietness. She heard the soft tapping of the keeper, but that only made her more peaceful. He gave her stillness, and rest.

He worked quietly, troubled. His instinct told him she had come to be near him, nearer and nearer she would want to come. And he wanted nobody to come near him, never any more while he lived. He had never, all his life, felt at ease and free with other people. The war had made it worse. He recoiled from contact more than ever. And his wife had been worst of all for him. He had, somehow, been mistaken, and had made a fool of himself with her. Now he was humiliated, and the one real gratification he had in life was in being alone, always alone.

Especially he did not want to be mixed up with a woman again. His nature was passionate and inflammable. But he had had the lesson of his life with his wife. The feeling of shame was deep and permanent.

Like all really passionate people, he was born solitary, and born incapable of vulgar, promiscuous contacts. There were so few women he could touch. The mass seemed to him repellant, when not repulsive. Yet the true sex desire was strong in him, and very deep. It had been balked and humiliated in his wife. Now he hoped to be alone for ever, apart from women altogether.

The common sexuality of most men, and of his wife among women, was now repulsive. When he was young, and incapable himself of that cheap and nasty sexuality most people seem capable of, he had almost envied other men their squalid sexual facility. But in his wife he had met the vulgar sexuality—which is so utterly different from the true, silent stream of sex—and he knew its worth for ever. It was humiliating and repulsive. He wanted to be left alone, only that.

And as sure as he had reached this point: not to think any more about women, nor to lust steadily after them, nor even to dream of them at night, came this woman seeking him. There she sat in the hut, with her eyes shut, thin, and with shadows under her eyes, at last a fugitive too from the nasty world of people; and the unconscious stream of her sex flowed towards him. Already he could feel the stirring of his bowels, and the hot fusing of his knees.

Did she know? Did she know what she meant? Did she know? If she knew, then—! The sudden irrepressible flames of desire ran up his body. She remained so still, and for such a long time. He had finished the one coop, and took another. But he glanced at her. Poor thing! There was a touch of death in her face! But she was breathing softly with peace and with life. Was she waiting? Was she waiting for him?

The strange, soothing flood of peace, the sense that all is well, which goes with the true sex, flooded him now. But the damaged human being in him dreaded more than ever exposing itself to the false thing, the false sexuality, which is of a rasping egoism, and the false social virtue, which is utter humiliation. The man in him, the natural male man inherent in life, wanted her to open her eyes and look at him in the softness of desire, so that they could enter that soothing flame of peace which is true sex. But the maimed human being which had only suffered from human contacts, wanted her to go away, to go away and leave him uninsulted.

She was a woman: and he doubted if women had any left of the genuine, deep sex of womanhood. They all had the modern self-sexuality which rasps a man raw. He loathed them, the self-sexuality women: and most of the young collier lasses were that way. But this one was a lady. Who knows what she wanted! Anyhow it would be just her own hard, female pleasure, at the best. No, and he was not going to fall for that! Was she coming after him out of brutal feminine curiosity? Ah well! he would not fall for it! No no! How much better to be alone, than to entangle oneself in endless humiliation, just for the sake of a moment's bad gratification!

Let her go to her own class! Let her find a lover among the gentlemen. What was she after? Let her go home! There had been enough young men in Wragby at Christmas, and enough fooling about! He hated them, the gentry, with their callous pleasures and their inward selfish brutality. Let her go home. Let her leave his wood, like any other trespasser.

No, he could not turn her out. She was my lady, and the wood belonged to her and to Sir Clifford. Himself, he was only a servant, they could turn him off, run him out like a stray dog, if he displeased them for a moment. The wood was not his own. He knew in his bones he would have to leave it. He would be jockeyed out into the world again before long. And they, the gentry, they would go on and on, there in Wragby, selfish, empty, pleasant-spoken and cruel in their will. They cared about nothing, and yet they kept all the best places on the earth. They did nothing, yet they gave all the orders, and took all the fruits. They ate the pheasants Parkin reared. And why? Why? Were they good people, good, fine people who *should* have the best?

They were not. They were fools, who did nothing and cared for nothing except their own importance and their own luxury. Parkin hated them. He hated the well-spoken fools who came to shoot in the autumn. Some of them were mere Ha-has!—"Here, I say, come here!"—they would call to him, as if he were a dog. The others were perhaps affable, and pretended to be man to man with him. Man to man! He knew what a bluff it was, and he smiled with contempt, to himself. They'd be man to man with him, would they? Ah well, he wasn't having any! They could keep their man-to-manliness for one another. He noticed they did very little of that. They were cat-wary with one another. Bah! Call them men!

He hated them, and hated the gentry altogether. He found himself gazing fixedly, with hate, at Constance, as she sat in the hut. She opened her eyes, anxiously, as if she had lost something. And the strained look came on her face again.

She rose, looking at Parkin. But he was bending over his work. She went across to him. He glanced up at her quickly. Her face was stiff and tired again.

"It's nice here," she said. "So restful!"

He did not answer, not seeing anything to reply to.

"I should like to come to the hut sometimes, to sit awhile."

He still did not answer, only looked at her, and she found it rather difficult to finish what she had to say.

"You lock the door when you're not here, don't you?"

"Ay!" The monosyllable was abrupt and hard.

"Are there two keys?"

"No! There's no other but the one I've got."

"Could you get me another one?"

Her voice was soft, but underneath was the well-known ring of a determined woman speaking to a man who would have to obey.

"Another key for th' hut?" he said, looking at her with the remembered sparkle of derision in his eyes.

This made her angry.

"Yes! Don't you understand what I say?"

"I understand, my lady, what you say. But where am I to find another key, if Sir Clifford hasn't got one?"

"Has Sir Clifford another?"

"He might have."

The man still looked at her with the sparkle of derision.

"Very well!" she said. "I'll ask him. And if he hasn't got one, you will have another made, from the one you've got."

He looked away into the wood, with anger.

"I suppose it would only take a day or two to have one made?" she insisted.

"I couldn't tell yer, my lady. I know nobody as makes keys, round here."

"Then I'll take yours to Uthwaite, and get one like it."

Their eyes met, in silent hostility. How small and piggish his eyes could look, when he was acting up.

"If you'll let me know when you want it!" he said, with the last sparkle of derision upon his rising anger.

"I'll let you know," she said. "Good-afternoon!"

"'Afternoon, my lady!" he said, saluting and turning away.

Constance walked home again, feeling unhappy and angry. She could not bear to be thwarted.

He resumed his work in silent, cold anger. It had begun. He would be driven away. The day was not far off, when he would have to leave the wood. He saw it. She knew he was quiet by himself, so she could not rest till she had disturbed him and ousted him. He knew it. It was so like his own wife. To show her power! Her power! An impotent rage took hold of his soul again. He was impotent, under the power even of that woman. With anger and the sense of impotence, came the idea of death. To die, and to be free at last!—Or else to fight! If a man could but fight, and tear them out of Wragby, the Chatterleys, and make an end of the gentry! Either that, or die, and be rid of it all!

Constance was late for tea. She found Mrs Bolton out under the great beech tree on the knoll in front of the house, looking for her.

"I just wanted to see if you were coming, my lady. Sir Clifford was asking for his tea."

There was the subtlest smile of indulgence and mockery of Clifford's petulance, in the woman's face. He did so hate to be kept waiting. And how his nurse knew him already!

"Am I late?" said Constance. "I was sitting in the wood, and it seemed so quiet. Why didn't you make the tea, Mrs Bolton?"

"It's not my place, my lady. I don't think Sir Clifford would like it at all."

"Why not?" said Constance.

She went in to him with her few wild-flowers in her hand.

"I'm sorry I'm late, Clifford. Why didn't you tell Mrs Bolton to make the tea?"

"I never thought of it," he said ironically. "Wouldn't you have been surprised if you'd come in and found Mrs Bolton sitting behind the tea-pot?"

"No! Not really! Why should I? There's nothing sacrosanct about a silver tea-pot, is there?"

He glanced at her curiously.

"What did *you* do?" he asked.

"Look! I walked right across the wood! Aren't the daffodils fresh and lovely! Isn't it wonderful, what comes out of the earth!"

"Just as much out of the sky and air," he said.

"But modelled in the earth. Anyhow it doesn't matter. Oh Clifford, is there another key to the wood-hut?"

She had laid her gloves and flowers on the small round tea-table—they always took tea in Clifford's study—and was pouring the boiling water from the silver kettle into the old silver tea-pot. Clifford watched her, wondering if he could bear to let Mrs Bolton do it. But Constance was so unconcerned. Her gloves and the few flowers lying there were much more on her mind than the sacred process of making tea. In fact, as soon as she had popped the silvery-grey tea-cosy over the tea-pot, for the tea to mash, she rose and found a little glass bowl for her flowers, arranging them lightly, the few daffodils and primroses, the odd violets and drooping wind-flowers, the two bits of pussy-willow. She touched the rather wilted flowers lightly.

"They'll come up again," she said.

And she put them down on the tea-table.

Clifford watched her narrowly. She irritated him. He was not there for her at all.

"What did you want a key to the hut for?" he asked her.

"It's so nice there. I sat still and listened to the wind. Parkin was mending coops for the hens and the young pheasants. I thought I might rest there sometimes. I asked Parkin about a key, but he said he hadn't another, and perhaps you had one."

"I doubt it. But we can look."

She brought him his tea, and the bread and butter.

"I thought Parkin wasn't very keen for me to have a key. Do you think he'd mind?" she said.

"Possibly! I think he likes to feel that that is his private reserve."

"But there's no reason why it should be, is there? He only does carpentering and little jobs there. Why shouldn't I have somewhere where I can rest, and still be in shelter, in the wood?"

"Quite! *He* feels that the hut is his private lair, where he sleeps sometimes and keeps watch."

"But do you think I oughtn't to go there, then?"

"Ought! There's no ought about it. You do as you wish. You may as well be prepared for Parkin to be offended, though. He's easily offended."

"And shouldn't I offend him?"

"I tell you, that is as you wish."

"But surely, he shouldn't be offended!"

"Quite! You have a perfect right to go into the hut. It isn't his private house. But I think he's none too pleased even if we go into the wood."

"But really—!"

"Oh, I know! But that's how the lower orders are. You put them in charge, and they think they're in possession. I suppose he'll find some way or other of getting even with me, if you take to sitting in the hut."

"Why what could he do?"

"He knows, better than I do. Raise about half the number of pheasants he might raise—or never hunt up the nests—or feed them in some place apart, so we could never find out how many there are—and maybe sell them *sub rosa* to his Tevershall friends."

Constance held her breath.

"He wouldn't be so treacherous!"

Clifford laughed.

"He wouldn't call it treachery. He'd say he had a right to the birds he'd raised himself."

She still held her breath.

"Do you hate him?" she asked at length.

He laughed.

"Hate him? I'm not personal about him at all. He's an excellent gamekeeper. But he's also a malcontent, and none too civil, as you'll no doubt find out, if you insist on using his hut."

"But is it *his* hut?"

He smiled at her with fine malice.

"Why not ask him?" he said.

Clifford had touched a sore spot in her. Nothing made her more angry than when servants or poor people treated her merely as a member of the possessive class. She wanted to be herself, not a member of any class. Any demagogic display, or any show of the vulgar class grudge and class spite, on either side, made all her nerves run the wrong way.

So that was how Parkin would treat her! It made her very angry.

The next afternoon was sunny with white clouds. She asked Clifford to go to the wood with her. And she walked at the side of the chair, feeling very wifely and true to her own sphere.

The ground was fairly dry, the chair went easily. It was behaving itself. The wind was still rather cold, but light and without buffets, and the sunshine was a wonder. In the hazel copse, the lambs-tails were hanging like a curtain, coming soft in the filtered sunshine. The wind-flowers in the sun-filled places were wide open, wide white little things, exclaiming with the joy of a little life. And they had a faint scent like apple-blossom. Constance gathered a few, and brought them to Clifford. So wide-open with new delight, they were.

He took them and looked at them.

"'Thou still unravished bride of quietness,'" he quoted. "Spring flowers always seem like that to me, much more than Greek vases."*

86

Constance's heart sank. But she had to come back at him.

"Ravished is such a horrid word!" she said. "And they don't look like foster-children of silence and slow Time, do they?"

"I think they do," he said.

"But they look so light and alive and quick, and nobody's foster-child!" she persisted, depressed.

"'Thou foster-child of silence and slow Time'" he quoted. "But look! Look at these anemones, and tell me if anything could be more fitting!"

She looked, but only felt immeasurably depressed. And she went away, looking for wide yellow celandines, with their varnished points. And as she gathered them she thought: "Nobody ravishes the flowers, bees don't and beetles don't—unless we do when we pick them and say things about them."

She said she was tired. Today the keeper did not come. But the chair performed its duties, and slowly rolled its own way home, Constance walking beside it in silence, feeling tired, and her spirits low, in spite of the sunshine. And the evening with Clifford seemed interminable. She went up to bed at nine o'clock.

The next day was rainy, but in showers. In a sense, Constance felt relieved. When the sun shone, she felt she ought to be alive, to live. The sunshine was a reproach to her half-deadness. But when it rained, it didn't matter. One might just as well be half-dead.

Nevertheless, in the afternoon she felt stifled. The house weighed on her insufferably, with its heap of old masonry. She must get out. The wood drew her as by some silent magnetic force. In an interval when there was no rain, she put on her old blue waterproof and escaped. That was always how she felt when she got into the park: escape.

She walked slowly, dimly, heeding nothing. The sky was grey, but not cold. One could be still. She determined not to go to the hut. Yet when she was in the wood, there came such a sharp shower of rain, and walking was so clayey and heavy, she turned in the isolation of the rain down the narrow track to the hut clearing.

No-one was there. The hut was closed and locked. But there was a little pent-roof over the door, and the rain blew from behind. She sat on the wooden door-step, gathering her mackintosh round her skirts. Yes, and the place was a sacred place, silent and healing. Unravished! Yes, it was one of the unravished places of old stillness.

She sat blindly watching the rain, listening to the subtle manifold noise of it, that sounded apart from the sudden queer soughings of the wind in the forest. Old oak-trees stood around, and the ground was fairly free of undergrowth, the rushy remains of bracken on the floor, purplish ropes of bramble tangled up, and an odd weak elder-bush. Then the space of grey old oaks, making the everlasting silence of Britain. This was all in front. Only behind the hut was the dense hazel-copse, through which the path came.

She sat a long time, and was still. It was all she wanted, to be still. But she was growing cold. And the rain was abating. She would go. Yes, the rain was still dripping in trickles off the hut, but it was hardly making ghosts among the oak-trees any more. She would go. She felt it was time to slip away.

Yet she sat on, and did not rise to her feet till the brown, wet dog ran towards her, waving the wet feather of its tail. The keeper followed, in a short oilskin coat, like a chauffeur. She had risen to her feet, and stood vaguely under the hand-breadth of porch roof.

The keeper saluted very hastily, his face red and hot with rain, but he did not speak. Constance moved away from in front of the door.

"I'm just going," she said.

She looked cold, and a little wan. He glanced at her with silent resentment, and met the wide, vague, rather miserable look of her blue eyes. Instantly a pang went through his bowels.

"Had yer bin waitin' ter get in?" he asked, his accent broader than usual when speaking to her. And he made a small gesture towards the door of the hut.

She thought she detected the touch of derision again in his voice.

"No, I didn't want to go in," she said quietly.

He waited. He would not open the door of his hut.

"Didn't Sir Clifford have no key, like?" he asked. "Did yer ask him?"

She wondered why he spoke with more of the vernacular than usual.

"No," she said, "he hasn't got one. But it doesn't matter. I don't care about it. If I want to be out of the rain I can sit perfectly well on the door-step. Good-afternoon!"

He did not reply for a moment. Then, as she was going, he said rather loudly:

"I'm 'ere a good bit my-sen, this time o't' year."

Almost she walked away without attending to him. Then something made her turn round and look at him. He had the most peculiar unsmiling sort of smile on his ruddy, rain-washed face.

"What do you mean?" she said.

He pressed back his head with a little jerk, as a cobra does.

"I mean now t' bods (birds) 'll start layin'."

She wondered what he meant.

"Of course!" she said vaguely.

"What you want is to be here by yersen," he said. "Yo' wunna want to be here, like, wi' *me* potterin' 'round a' t'time."

She looked at him vaguely, still not following.

"You don't make any difference," she said.

He watched her with queer, narrow eyes.

"I don't want to be in your ladyship's road, if you follow me," he said.

"You won't be in my way," she said.

"'Cos yer see it's like this! Winter-time I might give th' key up to you, an' stop away fra th' hut. This time o' th' year, I canna. There's eggs to sit—"

She felt only dazed. Why this lapse into a half-dialect?

"But I don't want you to stay away," she said. "I should *like* to be able to come when you're here, and help you with the little pheasants when they hatch out—"

She looked at him with her wide, wondering, curiously innocent gaze. In his red-brown eyes little lights flickered, as he seemed to be trying to search her out.

"It's as your ladyship likes, as far as that goes. If it was any other time o' th' year, I could give th' hut up, like—"

"But I don't want you to give it up. You don't *mind*, do you, if I come sometimes in the afternoon when you're here, to see the hens sitting on the eggs?"

"Me!" he said. "It's as your ladyship likes, that is! It's your own place! On'y I thought as 'appen—"

"Happen what?" she said, trapped herself into the vernacular.

He gave a quick, odd smile with his eyes. Then he dropped his voice.

"'Appen you wouldn't want to be here wi' on'y me about, like," he said, in a low, soft, cold voice.

She suddenly, vividly flushed, and felt the pulse beat in her neck.

"Only you about!" she said, indignant. Then she stopped. After all, it was perhaps what she secretly wanted. She changed her feeling, bewildered. Then she looked at him with that wide, blue, vague look of innocence which she could assume. "There's no reason for me to be afraid, is there, of being here alone with you?"

He was baffled. He put back his shoulders with a little jerk.

"Afraid! No!" he said almost angrily. "I on'y thou't as 'ow yer'd 'appen not like it." And he looked away into the wood.

"Yes!" she said softly, with that vague, straying innocence still. "I like to be here when you're here. Then I'm not lonely at all."

He was completely bewildered. Did she mean she wanted to be with him? What was she after? Did she want to make him feel small? To make a fool of him? Or did she just want the protection of another presence? It must be that.

"It's as your ladyship likes," he repeated, quietly.

"But I don't want you to feel I'm in the way," she said.

"It's Sir Clifford's hut," he said. "An' your ladyship pleases 'erself."

"Very well! Thank you! I may come sometimes, then. Good-afternoon!"—then she added to the dog: "Good-bye, Flossie! You know me, don't you?"

Flossie waved the plume of her tail slightly, and the man watched.

7

CONSTANCE DID NOT GO NEAR THE HUT again for some time, and did not see the keeper. She felt confused, and a little humiliated. Was it the half-suggestion of illicit sex?—surely he had half-suggested the possibility of it. Then he had been thinking about it!

She disliked so intensely any sort of conscious sexuality. It was so ugly and egoistic. Had he been thinking perhaps he could snatch a moment of ugly gratification front her? She shuddered a little. Never that! Better to avoid all sex, than start messing about in ugly self-seeking. A nasty, mechanical sort of self-seeking was the normal sex desire. Not spontaneous at all, but automatic in its cunning will to get the better of the other one, and to extend its own ego.

Was that what he wanted? She knew it was what most men wanted: just to get the better of a woman, in the sexual intercourse; the self-seeking, automatic civilised man trying to extend his ego over a woman, and have a sense of self-aggrandisement by possessing her.

And women? Women, she knew, were worse at that game than men. Take Olive for example. She picked up a man for the sole and simple purpose of putting herself over him, just putting her will over him, and thereby getting a sense of power and enlargement in herself. It was not true sex that she wanted at all. The thing that people call free sex, and living your own life, and all that, is just egoism gone rampant.

This had become very plain to Constance, from her knowledge of women. The true, sensitive flow of sex, women sometimes had with one another. But with men, almost invariably, the whole thing was reversed. The woman's acquisitive ego rose rampant, and the strange, tender flow of sex was utterly stopped. The acquisitive ego rose rampant, and she saw woman after woman half-insane to "get" a man, in the same sense that they were half insane to get a new gown or set of furs: to parade herself in the skins of dead animals, or to parade a live animal called a man, it was the same thing, sheer acquisitive greed and self-seeking. The men revolted. But poor things, the next female that wanted to pick them up could always catch them with a little flattery.

It was horrible. It was most horrible in rather elderly women, women between forty and sixty. These were the hyaenas. Unscrupulous, and with a callousness that put the hyaena to shame, their only lust was to acquire a new grip over some man. The men seemed to fight in vain: except men like Tommy Dukes, who fought off all women, as wounded animals still fight off the vultures. All that the woman wanted was to impose her own will and her own ego over the man. It was the same sort of insanity as the money-getting insanity. The heroes of wealth and the heroines of "love" were very much the same: semi-insane horrors of unscrupulous acquisitiveness: mine! mine! me! me! got it! got it! got him! got him! It was the horror of our insane civilisation.

Our civilisation has one horrible cancer, one fatal disease: the disease of acquisitiveness. It is the same disease in the mass as in the individual. The people who count as normal are perhaps even more diseased than those who are neurotic. The neurotic at least show that something is wrong. But the normal consider the very disease part of their normality. They carry on the hideous insanity of acquisitiveness in masses, or in solitary enterprise, with a firm conviction that it is the right thing to do.

And what is this acquisitiveness, looking deeper? It is the lust of self-importance. The individual, the company, the nation, they are alike all possessed with one insanity, the insanity of conceit, the mania of the swollen ego. The individual, in his normal insanity, wants to swell up his ego bigger and bigger, at any cost. He must be bigger than he is. So he fights and fights and fights to get rich, or to get on. Not many men fight for women any more, to swell up their own egoism that way.

But women, leaving the men to fight for the money, fight for the men. This is called love. "She is terribly in love with him," that cant phrase, means really: "She is mad to get him under her will." It is all it amounts to. Gentlemen prefer blondes, but they like bonds, especially those that pay well, better still. And blondes prefer gentlemen. They want, more than the money even, the strange sense of power and self-aggrandisement that comes when they've "got" a man. Got him!

The whole process is one of helpless insanity. All the complexes that were ever located are swallowed up in the grand complex of helpless acquisitiveness, the complex of the swollen ego. It possesses almost every individual in every class of society in every nation on earth. It is a vast disease, and seems to be the special disease of our civilisation or our epoch. If you haven't got the disease, you are abnormal. You have to have the malady in some form or other: either the fearsome clawing tyranny of "love" and "goodness", which is the horrible clawing attempt to get some victim into the clutches of your own egoistic love, your own egoistic virtue, your own egoistic way of salvation; or you have the less high-minded, more ignoble but perhaps not so deadly clutch-clutch-clutch after money and success. The disease grows as a cancer grows, ever extending its clutch. And now it grows very rapidly.

It is useless to talk of the future of our society. Our society is insane. Its most normal activities, money-getting and love, are a special form of mania. And for the maniac there is no future. None, either, for a maniacal society. Insanity can only be cured by death. The devil is the arch-alienist.

A good deal of this is vaguely felt, by the young: or by some of them. They are paralysed by fear of a maniacal society, into which they have to grow up. The rest are possessed by the mania, and are maniacs of love and success, pure and simple: success being money, and love being something very close akin.

Constance felt the fear paralysing her own soul. The keeper had seemed so alone: his white, lonely body, no more acquisitive than a star! But even he had flickered a queer smile of self-seeking self-gratification at her: even though, perhaps, he didn't want to.

But at home she had a more subtle example. This was Mrs Bolton getting Clifford under. Mrs Bolton was fascinated by Clifford: his cool detachment, and the way he almost invariably, quite calmly frustrated the will of his nurse.

"It's a lovely day! I should go out in my chair a bit if I were you," she would say.

"Would you? Perhaps I may—and perhaps I may not. Do you mind placing that jar of narcissus where the light falls on them?—on the bureau! There!—no, a little more forward!—to the right a little! So! Now I can see them at their best. They're very beautiful, don't you think?"

"Oh, they're lovely!" she would chime in, baffled and frustrated. "And their scent!"

"Their scent I don't care for, it's a little funereal."

"Perhaps it is," she would add.

He was always getting the better of her. Yet by always giving in, she was getting the best of him.

"Shall I shave you this morning, or will you shave yourself?"

"I don't know. There was something I wanted to think about. Do you mind coming again when I ring."

"Very good, Sir Clifford!" she said, so soft, so submissive. But she stored it up. It was all converted into energy for subduing him.

When he rang, after a little while, she would appear in silence. And then he would say:

"I think I'd rather you shaved me."

Her heart gave a little thrill, and she said with extra softness:

"Very good, Sir Clifford!"

She was very deft, with a soft, caressive touch. At first he had resented this infinitely soft touch of her fingers on his face. But now he wanted it every day. He let her shave him every morning. Till she knew in her finger-tips his cheeks and lips, his jaw and under his chin, and the front of his throat, perfectly. They both took a voluptuous pleasure in his morning toilet. His face and throat were handsome, and he was a gentleman. She too was handsome, pale and her face absolutely still, revealing nothing, her eyes bright but expressionless.

She now did everything for him, and he felt less ashamed than with Connie. Mrs Bolton *liked* handling him and putting him into shape. She liked having him, having his body at least, quite in her power. She had a peculiar pleasure and triumph in it, that Connie had never had. And he gave way, and enjoyed her handling him. He really got a voluptuous pleasure from her soft, lingering touch. But he still bullied her. It was almost a sort of marriage.

Connie watched it at once with relief and with repulsion. It relieved her of Clifford. He wanted less and less of her. When she had pleaded a head-ache in the evening, he had said:

"Never mind! Mrs Bolton will play chess with me!" Connie thanked her stars she herself needn't, for she got intolerably wearied at chess. Nevertheless she found it curiously objectionable to see Mrs Bolton, flushed and tremulous like a young girl, touching her knight or her pawn with uncertain fingers, then drawing away again. And Clifford, faintly smiling with superiority, telling her:

"You must say *j'adoube*!"*

And she glanced up at him with bright eyes, and murmured very shyly, but obediently:

"J'adoube!"

Yes, he was educating her, and he enjoyed it. And she was thrilled. She was learning bit by bit all the things the gentry knew. And she was making herself absolutely indispensable to him.

Constance saw it all, saw them both rising in their own conceit. Ivy Bolton was flattered when he took trouble with her, and he was flattered by her submissiveness to him, and her girlish thrill. They played into each other's hands marvellously. And to Connie, he seemed to get more commonplace, more foolish and complacent every day. But perhaps his wife was not a fair judge of another woman's influence on him. And to Lady Chatterley the tricks of Ivy Bolton seemed crudely transparent. But she had to admit one thing, Ivy Bolton *was actually* thrilled by her intimate contact with a gentleman, and by the sort of education he was giving her. True, she already had him like a fish on a string. But Connie didn't want to unhook him. What was the good? At least he was cheerful now, and seemed to enjoy his life more, even if he were getting sillier. But in his case, anything, let him love anything that could keep him cheerful.

Connie couldn't even really dislike Mrs Bolton. Something about her she loathed: her false submissiveness and her almost unconscious scheming. But if any woman at this late hour could get a tremendous thrill out of being taught chess by Clifford—of course he invariably won, but it didn't seem to weary him—then let her! She must have something naïve and aspiring in her.

And Connie heard long conversations going on between the two, Clifford would ask Mrs Bolton for all the local news, and she, a born talker, fascinated all her life by the psychology of other people, having lived the lives of the colliers and colliers' wives vicariously for many years, would tell him all the news. The figures he had known as a boy, when the world still seemed safe, and which he had almost forgotten, she created for him again. There was Henry Paxton, the burly self-made grocer who had been so loud upon the parish council and the urban district council: he was over eighty now, and paralysed, but still a tyrant. His daughter Cassandra, still an old maid, now fifty years old—how Clifford remembered the tall, wild, raw-boned, rather simple young woman—waited on him hand and foot. No, she would never marry now, and she had been born for marriage. But her father, bully as he was, had kept her for his own purposes, and at the age of eighty-four was still making a slave of her. There was old James Allsop, the boot-and-shoe Allsop, also over eighty, but nimble as a boy. You would see him walking up Tevershall hill from the station and he never sat down on the seats Lewie Rollings had made the Council put on the hill. Yes, Lewie Rollings was still alive: and married again. Yes, he still talked socialism and wrote for the "Tevershall and Stacks Gate News." But he hadn't much influence any more. His kind of socialism was all words and being funny about people like Henry Paxton: the colliers laughed and took no notice. Oh, things were changed! There was more rushing about, and more discontent. Why, the boys thought nothing of going in to Sheffield four or five times a week, with these buses. And then the pictures—and the Miners' Welfare—oh, things weren't as they used to be. The young fellows drank too much at the Miners' Welfare, and they had no respect. The women, though, had changed most. They had got so much cheekier, and commoner. The things they did, and the things they said, you'd never believe. Swear! they'd as leave swear at you as look at you, many of them. Oh, it wasn't like that before the war. And spend! they'd give as much as nine guineas for a winter coat, and two guineas for a little girl's Sunday hat. Oh, with the women it nearly all went in clothes. They didn't believe in saving. Since the war! Since the war they believed in nothing, good nor bad, and they had no respect for anything. They'd go and give contributions for a wedding present for the Princess Mary,* and then, when they saw in the papers all the grand things that had been given, they'd say: "And what right has she to it all! She's no better than I am.

It's a shame, she marries one of the richest men i' th' country, and then the big shops go and give her ever so many sets of furs, at thousands of pounds. And I should like a fur coat myself, this winter, but I know I'm not going to get it, pits doin' so bad. It's time there was a revolution, my word, when some women slaves their insides out and gets nothing, and others has things poured over them by the million, just because they've got Princess before their name. There's plenty of Marys in Tevershall every bit as good as she is, and every bit as good-looking. But where's the tradesman as'll give them a pair of gloves, let alone a thousand-pound set of furs. It's not right—"—oh, the women, it was they who were the mischief nowadays, among the colliers. There was no satisfying them, and the young ones just did as they liked. It had been as much as Mrs Bolton could do, to put up with their ways and their impudence. There was no pleasure in going among the miners any more, the women were that off-hand and nasty with you: far worse than the men.

Clifford began to get a new vision of his own village. He tended to think of it as unchanged and unchangeable. But he knew in his bones it was not so. There was a new ferment working, a new danger. The malcontent ferment, that peculiar germ, was working actively, especially in the women. It brought with it a certain excitement, like raw whiskey. And an infinite danger. He could feel, even through Mrs Bolton's skilful paraphrase, the hostility to himself, to Wragby, to the Chatterley name, to all colliery owners, all managers, even all minor bosses. There it was, not loud-voiced yet, but potent as a ferment.

And it stimulated him. The sense of hostility against himself and his class stimulated him into action. He suddenly wanted to go out again, to go down to the mines. The colliers were hostile, were they? Then he would face them. He had thought they looked on him only in commiseration, with pity. But not so. They also hated him. Very well! Then he would show them what he was good for.

The pits were doing badly. The colliers looked forward with grim satisfaction to the time when they would have to close down, and they, the miners, would have to go on the dole! But then the master's pay would stop too. So at least it cut both ways. Wragby was delapidated already. But soon it would have to tumble down, for lack of money to hold it up. If the pits stopped. For money held everything up.

Clifford ordered a motor-car. So far, Wragby had managed with just a dog-cart. But Clifford wanted to go down to the mines. So he ordered a car. And he discussed with Mrs Bolton a man to drive it and to help him, Clifford, in and out. It was Mrs Bolton who thought of Field.

Quite a new look had come into Clifford's face. While he had thought he had only to sympathise with his miners, he had been inert and apathetic. But now, Mrs Bolton had subtly injected into his veins the stimulus of a fight. The colliers were waiting to see Wragby wiped out, were they? They were anxious to see the Chatterley name obliterated in Tevershall? Good! Let them wait!

A queer, subtle hatred of the lower classes had taken hold of Sir Clifford. He was still a sort of Conservative-anarchist in his expressed views. But in his veins was a new excitement, a new stimulus, a new virus. And it was the virus of hate. Nothing loud-mouthed and fascist. But a keen, tingling, subtle hate of those who were really nearest to him, his own colliers. His father, Sir Geoffrey, had always said "our colliers." Clifford had been brought up to that: "our colliers". And now, with a sudden flare of elation, he found he hated them. He kept the fact secret, even from himself. He even pretended he wanted to save the situation for them. But the stimulus, over and above the desire to restore his diminished fortunes, which roused him to a new, keen interest in the mines, was his vivid, secret hatred for the colliers, the lower classes, who wanted to drag him down to their level. Yes, they wanted to drag him down. Mrs Bolton had very subtly and unconsciously made that clear to him. They wanted to wipe their feet on him at last. Good! Then he would see.

The moment he hated them, he could face them.

Connie felt relieved, seeing him rouse to new activity. He was moving, with meteor-like rapidity, away from all contact with her. In a few months they had become, he and she, almost startling strangers to one another. She was interested and excited in his new activities, his new struggle with the mines. Clifford was clever, and keen. He could do something still. He would do something, too. But it would be something to which she was almost uncannily alien.

In spite of the new excitement, she felt again a gathering sense of doom. And again came over her her hatred of those doomed, dreadful Midlands, with all their clang of iron and their smoke of coal. But the doom was taking on a new, bristling sort of terror. In the peculiar stagnancy of the depressed conditions a strange poisonous gas seemed to be distilling. Dimly she could feel some new sort of disaster accumulating: accumulating slowly, with awful, serpentine slowness, but with peculiar cold dread. It was something she dreaded coldly and fatally, the working-out of this new, unconscious, cold, reptilian sort of hate that was rising between the colliers of the under-earth, the iron-workers of the great furnaces, and the educated, owning class to which she belonged, by the accident of destiny. She did not want to see it. She did not want to live through the results of English class hatred, that is so deep and still unacknowledged. If society was insane, as Winterslow had said, surely this class hate was the most dangerous manifestation of the insanity! It was a hate that would go so deep, so deep. It would go to the very bottom of the human soul. And it would be so awful!

Yet for herself, she felt she did not belong to it. She did not feel any class hate. She would have liked to be at one with the colliers. She did not want to live under their conditions, but she felt she would even have done that, rather than have this awful hatred upon her. She would even rather be a collier's wife and live in a collier's dwelling, rather than be swept like a straw on the livid, destructive wave of hate. Touch! Ah yes, Tommy Dukes was right. It was touch that one needed: some sort of touch between her class and the under class.

It was so frightening, men divided off into two spectral halves, each spectral to the other. In the old days, the gentry were the heroes on the stage, and the people were the audience. It was so. The gentry played to the audience, as all heroes must, and the audience, the people, identified themselves with the heroes, as all audiences do.

But now! Now the lights were out. The gentry were still masquerading on the stage, but all the illumination was spent, and in the grey, monotonous daylight of reality the actors were no longer heroic, they were futile. The glamour was gone, the artificial illumination had collapsed, and the actors were revealed as paltry human beings, looking more paltry even than the audience, because raised to greater conspicuousness. Yet still they held the stage. And the audience was beginning to howl at the deception.

How horrible! How ghastly, now, is this division into upper and lower classes! How resolve them back into a oneness?

Constance shuddered. She felt she belonged neither to the actors nor to the audience. She wanted to come off the stage and be in touch with the people. But once the audience had started to howl, there was no being in touch with it. And the stage, the place of the upper classes, was becoming a place of pure humiliation. What was to be done? Merely wait for the fracas?

She felt she would surely die, in the interim. Her soul would have to have some relief, some hope, some touch. It was that she wanted. Not any revelation nor any new idea. A new touch. Just a touch.

She went to the wood at last, one evening immediately after tea. Spring was here. In the green light of an April evening, blackbirds were whistling with the old triumph of life. There was a fresh, cold wind, and the wind-flowers, passing over-wide and raggedy now, were shaking with spring life. Many primroses now showed their cold faces, which yet had a bright, wide-open fulness of life. The dark-green spears of the blue-bells were opening and spreading like velvet under the oaks, strong and unhesitating, so filled with dark-green life. Birds whistled, whistled, whistled, and called aloud in the voice of life. The wood was like a sanctuary of life itself. Life itself! Life itself! That was all that one could have, all that one could yearn for. And yet the human will cuts off the human being from living. Alone of all created things, the human being cannot live.

Life is so soft and quiet, and cannot be seized. It will not be raped. Try to rape it, and it disappears. Try to seize it, and you have dust. Try to master it, and you see your own image grinning at you with the grin of an idiot.

Whoever wants life must go softly towards life, softly as one would go towards a deer and a fawn that are nestling under a tree. One gesture of violence, one violent assertion of self-will, and life is gone. You must seek again. And softly, gently, with infinitely sensitive hands and feet, and a heart that is full and free from self-will, you must approach life again, and come at last into touch. Snatch even at a flower, and you have lost it for ever out of your life. Come with greed and the will-to-self towards another human being, and you clutch a thorny demon that will leave poisonous stings.

But with quietness, with an abandon of self-assertion and a fulness of the deep, true self one can approach another human being, and know the delicate best of life, the touch. The touch of the feet on the earth, the touch of the fingers on a tree, on a creature, the touch of hands and breasts, the touch of the whole body to body, and the interpenetration of passionate love: it is life itself, and in the touch, we are all alive.

THE SECOND LADY CHATTERLEY'S LOVER

It is no good trying to fight life. You can only lose. The will is a mysterious thing, but the golden apples it wins are apples of Sodom* and bitter, insane dust. One can fight *for* life, fight against the grey unliving armies, the armies of greedy ones and bossy ones, and the myriad hosts of the clutching and the self-important. Fight one does and must, against the enemies of life. But when you come to life itself, you must come as the flower does, naked and defenceless and infinitely in touch.

Connie went on down the broad riding, and up the little way to the well. It bubbled the same, always the same, so bright and so shinily cold, above its ruddy pebbles. She sat a moment looking down into it, as it came up gaily out of nowhere. And she watched the unfurling of a bright-green frond of fern, harts-tongue that grew there so bright and without restlessness, by the well. It was unfurling even as she watched, though she could not see it.

A cock pheasant called, and she looked away into the bristling gloom of the larch-wood. But there was no movement. The silvery calling of blackbirds and thrushes seemed farther away here. It was chill and sad, at the well. So many ghosts, so much memory! So many men must have drunk the cold water, in the days of the free forest, when the broad riding was a green road that travelled across country. That was why the riding swerved down the hill, to touch the well.

But now, no one passed, and the bright water bubbled, but no one camped on the bank above, in the nook of the trees. Connie felt eerie. She rose to go home. And she went in the thrilling wonder of the first twilight of spring, while the birds still called wildly, and the yellow light of evening mingled among the tree-buds that were just for opening. What lovely, ghostly presences of life the wood was full of! Each tree had a presence of its own. And each hidden bird. Each squirrel, each stoat, each mole just under earth.

She turned at last down the path to the hut. She wanted to come merely into the presence of the keeper.

He was there, building a sort of little straw house, or roof on four posts, among the oak-trees, for the birds. Against the north was a screen of boughs and straw, and the roof was of real thatch. And he was pegging down the thatch. The dog gave a little wuff! and he turned, to see her approaching. He seemed at once startled and not surprised. He stopped his work and touched his forehead in the slight, hasty salute, watching her without speaking.

"How nice, a little house for the birds!" she said.

"A bit of shelter, like!"

"It's so pretty!"

They both stood silent. She was aware of his deep, quiet breathing.

"It is spring!" she said. "Have the birds made their nests?"

"Ay! There's a jinny-wren's just theer!"

"Where? Oh show me!"

He took her across to a tree, where a wren had inserted his nest in a cunning fork of the boughs. It was a little round ball of moss and grey hair and down, with a little round hole of a door.

"I wish I were a bird!" she said, with infinite wistfulness.

"Do yer! Such a little un as that?"

He was laughing at her quietly. He went back to his work.

"You won't see much longer," she said.

"I shan't, shall I!" and he straightened the long wheat straw. She stood vague and motionless, watching him.

"I got yer that key, if you want it," he said suddenly, in a lowered, altered voice.

"Did you? How kind!" she said, a little startled.

"I'll get it."—And he strode across to the hut, where he had left his coat. He was in his shirt-sleeves.—After a moment, he came back with the key.

"Thank you so much! You're sure you won't mind if I come?" she said.

He looked away into the wood.

"If your ladyship doesn't mind me, I—you're very welcome to—I mean, you do as you please, it's your own place."

She was silent for a moment.

"Yes," she said quietly. "But I didn't want to interfere with you—or to seem to."

"You won't be interferin' wi' me, my lady—"

"Very well then," she said softly.

He stood for some moments motionless, staring away into the wood. Then automatically he reached for some straw from the heap, and began straightening it with his hands. The sun had set, and real shadow was coming among the tree-trunks, though there was still yellow light beyond the boughs.

"It's the end of the day," she said, unthinking.

"Ay! Another!" he replied.

And that Another! rang strangely in her soul.

"Good-night, then!" she said.

"Good-night to your ladyship."

And as she went home she saw a new moon, bright as a splinter of crystal in the western sky.

After this, she went almost every day to the hut. She had her key, and when he wasn't there, she entered and sat in the doorway. He had made one corner tidy. Across, there was a carpenter's bench, and some tools hung on the wall. There were also traps hung up, and an old coat: and there was a truss of straw, and a couple of bags of corn for the pheasants, and on a shelf, a couple of old blankets, a lantern, an enamel mug and plate: a queer accumulation of things.

He had set only four hens. Constance would offer them a bit of corn in her hand, but the fierce mothers would rarely eat it. They would peck almost savagely at her hand, instead. But soon they got to know her, and pecked less savagely.

She felt curiously at home in the place, as if it were her *real* home. It did not matter whether Parkin were there or not. Like the hens, and like his dog Flossie, he had got used to her. He would go about at whatever he had to do, quietly and unconcernedly, without troubling her. Sometimes she talked to him for a little while, though never of anything that she could record. Mostly they were just silent.

Yet it was that she lived for: her hours in the wood. Some days she could not go at all. Sometimes she could only go after tea. But whenever she went, she found him there, or he was sure to come. And she could tell, by the quick, eager way he looked round when he emerged from the path, that he was looking for her.

They seemed to be drawing together. Though they never touched, they seemed to be coming strangely, closely into touch, a powerful touch that held them both. When she saw him coming, a queer fire would melt her limbs, and she would wait, wait. But always he would look at her with those inscrutable eyes of his, and salute, and move aside.

He always looked for her to be there, and wanted her to be there, and dreaded it. He wanted the contact with her, and dreaded it almost as much as he wanted it. His queer, round eyes watched her at moments with infinite desire, but he stayed at a distance: With his whole soul, he wanted *not* to start an intrigue with her, not to involve the two of them in the inevitable horrible later complications. With all his soul, he hated the humiliating complications of the human world.

Yet from his bowels, from his knees, from the middle of his breast he felt himself streaming towards her, and the flow gradually growing stronger, even while he was unaware of it. Gradually he was losing the sense of time and of consequence.

But still, the iron bar of reserve that held him back from her, something unconscious and absolute, never relented. He could not, and would not take the first step. He did not want to start the thing. Even now, he would be glad if he could escape this kind of doom, of taking her.

And therefore he would not think about her. He would not let his mind entertain her. The desire he had was in his body, and his mind tried not to acquiesce. Yet gradually a sort of sleep or hypnosis was coming over him, he was losing the sense of time and of consequence, it was melting away in an unknown, but infinitely desirable flood of wholeness. What could a man do!

The young pheasants began to hatch out. The first little trio she saw pattering about on tiny feet, little alert drab things, under the straw shelter, she gave a queer, startled cry of delight. It was true, they were born. And when they were under the hen, and poked their tiny cheeky heads through the yellow feathers of the old bird, suddenly poking out a beady little head from the midst of her, Constance wept with excitement. She was thankful the keeper wasn't there to see her. And for the first time in her life she loved an old hen, the bright, fierce warm creature, with the chicks under her feathers so softly!

For two days Constance could not go to the wood. One of Clifford's Aunts descended on them, with her husband, and it was a busy house. Even on the third day they did not leave till after tea. But then she slipped away, breathless and bewildered, to see how many more little pheasants had hatched out.

It was a lovely warm evening, but the sun had set by the time she entered the wood. The chicks would be gone to sleep, under their mothers. She hurried on towards the hut, and arrived in the clearing flushed and breathless. He was there, in his shirt-sleeves, just going to close up the coops and make them safe from any depredation. She went straight towards him.

"How many more are hatched?" she said.

"Oh, they're nearly all out," he replied.

She quivered, he stood so near to her. Then she crouched down before the coop he had not shut up.

"Look!" she said in a low voice. "Look! They are peeping out at me! Oh, I *must* touch them."

Tiny heads were poking out inquisitively between the yellow foliage of the old hen's feathers. Constance looked up at him to see if she might touch the little birds. He stood above her, his face queer and bright and expressionless. And he looked into her wide, bright eyes as if he did not understand.

She put her hand gingerly through the bars of the coop to touch one of the chicks. But the hen pecked at her savagely, and Constance drew back, startled and frightened.

"How she pecks!" she said in a wondering voice. "She won't let me."

He crouched down at her side, knees apart, and put his hand softly, slowly into the coop. The old hen pecked at him, but not so viciously as at Constance. She knew him. Slowly, softly he drew forth his closed hand, with one of the faintly-piping chicks. He put it into Connie's hands.

"Isn't it adorable!" she cried, her voice trembling as the chicken stood chirping and quivering its light little life between her hands, "Oh, isn't it adorable! so little and so cheeky!"

In spite of herself, tears came into her eyes, and she bit her lip.

"It's one o' th' lively ones!" he said, his voice so close to her.

But she had bent her head, to hide the dropping of the tears. At first he was unaware. Then he knew, and he said queerly:

"There's nothing amiss, is there?"

She shook the tears from her eyes and looked up at him with a wet face, trying to laugh through her tears.

"It's—" she said, with a broken laugh—"it's that they're so unafraid—" and following the laugh came a sob.

He laid his hand softly on her back as she crouched there, and slowly, softly his hand slid down her back, to her loins, in a blind caress.

"Yo' shouldna cry!" he said, softly.

But then came another sob. She held the chick to him, between her two hands.

"Put it back!" she wept.

He quickly put his hands to hers, and taking the little, piping bird, ushered it gently back under the mother hen.

But at once his hand had returned, unconscious, to touch her, to the delicate caress of her flank. She had found her scrap of a handkerchief, and was trying to dry her face. His hand slid slowly round her body, touching the breasts that hung inside her dress.

"Shall yer come?" he asked, in a quiet, colourless voice.

But his fingers did not cease delicately touching her breasts.

Her tears had suddenly left her. His hand touching her breast was like flames. She grasped it in her own hand, and rose to her feet. He was afraid she was rebuking him; but no, she tremblingly clung to his warm, relaxed, uncertain hand.

He had risen, with his arm round her, for she clung to his hand at her breasts. He drew her to him, and she hid her face against him, which was what she wanted to do. He held her quite still for a few moments and with her face buried against his shoulder, she seemed to go to sleep.

"Come to th' hut," he said, in a low voice.

She turned submissively. He stooped and shut the coop, and followed her. In the hut, she sat down weakly on the stool. He followed her, and closed the door, so that it was almost dark. Then he turned to her, feeling for her body, feeling with blind, overwhelming instinct for the slope of her loins. And she submitted, in a kind of sleep. The groping, soft, helplessly desirous caress of his hand on her body made her pass into a second consciousness, like sleep.

He held her with one hand, and with the other threw down an old blanket from the shelf.

"You can lie your head on the blanket," he said.

And with queer obedience, she lay with her head on the old blanket. She felt him slowly, softly, gently but with queer blind clumsiness fumbling at her clothes, then the quiver of rapture, like a flame, as he touched the soft, naked in-slope of her thighs. But she was not aware of the infinite peace of the entry of his body into hers. That was for the man: the infinite peace of the entry into the woman of his desire.

She lay still, in a kind of sleep. The activity, and the orgasm, was his. And afterwards, the stillness, the great stillness when he lay with his arms fast round her, his nakedness touching her, and did not leave her. She remembered what a woman had said to her: "You'll know if a man loves you, if he doesn't want to get up, away from you, when he's had you."

No, he lay with his arms round her, holding her fast, in the mysterious stillness that she dared not break. Till the desire came on him again, and that exquisite and immortal moment of a man's entry into the woman of his desire.

It was quite dark when he roused, and tried to help her modestly to adjust her clothing. And when he opened the door of the hut, they saw through the oak trees the thin moon shining with extraordinary brilliance.

"Ah well!" he said to himself. "It had to come!"

He seemed almost rueful, in a peaceful way. She gave a little laugh.

"I suppose it had!" she said.

And he turned sharply, looking at her in surprise. Then he touched her face with his fingers, softly, as a man touches the woman of his desire. That made her proud.

"I shall have to hurry home," she said softly, looking up at him and wanting him to kiss her. "You won't come with me.—I shall come again soon.—You aren't sorry, are you?"

But he only looked down at her, and softly stroked her cheek again, and her throat.

"Say something to me," she said plaintively.

"What should I say to thee?" he said, displeased, putting his arms round her and holding her close, kissing her. That was really what she wanted. Yet she said again:

"You aren't sorry, are you?"

"Me! No! Are you?"

There was a queer fluctuation in him. She was the woman of his desire. Then he remembered she was a stranger, not belonging to him.

"I'm glad," she said.

But even her very saying of it seemed to put her apart from him.

She walked home quietly, and glad. But he only was conscious that she was gone, and gone where he could not follow; and the complication already had started in his own heart. He was not sure of her. What did she *really* want? What was it that his own heart wanted of her, and was not sure of?

He tried to shake off the spell of her, and the yearning, and the subtle sense of anxiety. When she was gone, and it was night, he went his round of the wood. All was still. The moon had set. He waited in the darkness under a tree on the knoll, whence he could see the lights of Stacks Gate, and some lights of Tevershall. It was a still, lovely spring night, full of life. Yet also, full of dread: that queer, ever-shifting dread of the Midlands.

CHAPTER 7

The lights at Stacks Gate and at TeHershall seemed wickedly sparkling, and the blush of the furnaces, faint and rosy since the night was cloudless, seemed somehow aware. A curious dread possessed him, a sense of defencelessness. Out there, beyond, there were all those white lights and the indefinable quick malevolence that lay in them.

He turned home, to the darkness of the wood. But he knew that the wood was frail, in its darkness and loneliness, as a hollow nut. Like a hollow nut the spiteful spirits of those white lights could crack the solitude of his remnant of old forest, and let in the malevolence. He was not safe. And by taking the woman, and going forth naked to her, he had exposed himself to he knew not what fear, and doom.

It was not fear of the woman, nor fear of love. It was a dread, amounting almost to horror, but of something indefinite. It was not that he regretted what he had done. He had wanted the woman intensely, and still wanted her. Slowly, carefully, with a hermit's scrupulousness, he got his supper of bread, cheese, onions and beer, and prepared the porridge in the double cooker, for morning. He kept his kitchen very bare, rather homeless-seeming, but clean, tidy, and curiously silent. It was a room in which one felt an accumulated silence, a silence which almost had a will.

Having finished his few chores, he went out again for half an hour with his dog. The fear that was on him was not a fear of poachers: not a fear of anything definite. Neither was it a sense of having done wrong. In this respect, he had no conscience. He often felt he had been a fool, but he never felt he had been wrong. The word "sin" had no meaning for him. He went round the wood without any fear of the darkness, yet with a sense of dread almost pulling down his shoulders, and contracting his heart. It was the dread an independent, solitary individual has of society, of the human mass.

Constance, for her part, felt more buoyant than she had felt for years, as if all the troubles of the world had rolled away. She would be in time for dinner, at half-past seven, so no one could question her.

She found the doors of the house all closed, however, and had to ring. This annoyed her. Mrs Bolton opened.

"Oh, your ladyship, I was beginning to wonder what had become of you!" the woman said *sotto voce* and roguishly. "Sir Clifford has never asked for you: he's got Mr Linley in with him, talking over something important. Shall I put dinner back a bit?"

107

"Perhaps you might—ten minutes."

"Very good, your ladyship. That'll give you time to dress—if Mr Linley is staying to dinner."

Mr Linley was the general manager of the collieries: a thin, red-faced, quiet man from the north, with not quite enough punch for Clifford: not up to post-war conditions. Connie liked him, however, but could not stand his wife, a blonde, over-dressed woman out of a country vicarage, very obsequious and toadying. However, she was not there.

Linley stayed to dinner, and Connie was the hostess men liked so much, so modest, yet so aware, with big, wide blue eyes and a soft repose that sufficiently hid her cleverness. She had played this woman so much, it was almost second nature to her. And it was curious, how everything disappeared out of her consciousness while she played it.

Yet with joy she was cherishing her memories in reserve. She had achieved a great triumph: the man loved her with his body. That she knew. She knew he had felt an overwhelming desire for her, and a profound, passionate pleasure in going into her. It surprised her a little. She had felt nothing so extreme. But it pleased her that he had felt it. "With my body I thee worship," says the man to the woman in the marriage service. And she felt it had been so with him: an act of bodily worship. That surprised her and moved her, and made her glad.

But she was still vague, confused. She wanted the experience again. It had not, as it were, gone right home to her.

She went to the wood in the afternoon, the next day. It was a grey, still afternoon, with the dog's mercury coming dark-green near the hazel roots, and the trees making the silent effort to open their buds. In the unconscious one felt it, the heave of the great weight of powerful sap in all the trees, upwards, outwards, to the bud-tips. It was like a tide running out to flood, very full, filling every outreaching twig to surcharge. And overhead, all through the wood, the tree-buds faintly stirred, like bees slowly waking.

Constance, however, was not conscious of anything save her own waiting. She came to the clearing of the hut. He was not there. But the pheasant chicks were running lightly abroad, light as insects, from the coops where the yellow hens clucked anxiously. Constance crouched and watched them, and waited. She only waited. Even the chicks she hardly saw. She only waited.

And he did not come. The time passed with a dream-like slowness, yet when it was gone, how quickly it had gone! He did not come. And it was half-past four. She must go home to tea. She hesitated. Something tenacious and obstinate in her made her want to stay on at the hut, if she had to wait till midnight.

But she reproved herself. It would be far better to go home to tea, and to come again after tea. Perhaps he only expected her after tea. That would be better. Then Clifford would have nothing to be surprised about. And *he* would be there waiting for her when she came. Yes, that was what she would do.

She hurried home. And as she went, a fine drizzle began to fall.

"Is it raining again?" said Clifford, as she shook her hat.

"Just drizzle."

"We might have a game of bezique after tea."

She looked at him in her slow, inscrutable way.

"I think I'd better rest till dinner," she said. "The spring makes one feel queer."

"Unsettled, doesn't it! There's nothing wrong, is there?"

"No no! Perhaps Mrs Bolton will have a game of cards with you."

"She will if I ask her. But probably I shall just listen in."

When Constance heard the loud speaker idiotically, in a velveteen sort of voice, announcing a series of street cries, she slipped out of the side door. The drizzle of rain was like a veil over the world, mysterious, and not cold. She got very warm in her old blue mackintosh, as she hurried across the park.

How still the wood was! how secret and full of the mystery of buds and eggs and unsheathing! how wonderful all of it in the silent rain-mist, the trees glistening naked and dark, as if they had unclothed themselves, and the green things on the earth seeming to glow in greenness.

She arrived in the clearing expecting to see him. He was not there. The hut was locked. The chicks were gone under their mother-hens, but the coops were not shut up. He had not been. Perhaps something was wrong! She hesitated, whether to go to the cottage for him.

But no. She was born to wait, and in waiting lay her strength. She opened the hut with her key. It was all tidy, the corn put in the bin, the straw neat in one corner, the blankets folded on the shelf, the lantern hung on a nail. It looked, for some reason, forlorn, now it was so tidy. No litter on the work-bench, no litter on the floor. It had the look of a man's shut-up workshop.

She sat down on her stool, and watched through the open door, sitting in the doorway. How still everything was! how secret and retired into itself! The fine rain blew softly, filmily, but the wind made no noise. Nothing made a noise. Everything was silent and twilit, and alive. And the time passed. He did not come.

It was half-past six, night falling, when suddenly he came into the clearing, ducking rather in his walk, and looking ghostly. He gave a quick look towards the hut, and saw her sitting there, another ghost. He gave a little, half-finished salute, and swerved aside to the coops, bending over them in silence, shutting them up and seeing they were well protected.

And Constance waited. She sat on in the doorway of the hut, watching the shadowy, unwilling man, and waiting. Till at last he came slowly, unwillingly towards her, glancing at her with a swift, unwilling glance. His face was ruddy, but a bit abstracted, as if he were holding himself absent.

"You are late!" she said softly.

"Ay!" he replied. And nothing further.

She looked up into his face, but did not meet his eye.

"Didn't you want me to wait for you today?" she asked sadly.

He glanced swiftly at her.

"Won't the folks at the hall be thinking something, you coming here every night?" he said, in his harsh voice.

"It isn't every night. They don't know where I am. They won't think anything," she said.

He looked away, not saying anything.

She rose from her stool in the doorway.

"Did you want to come into the hut?" she said.

"Only to lock up."

She paused. Then she flushed deeply as she said:

"Are you sorry—about yesterday?"

He looked at her, and saw the deep blush burning her cheek and throat.

"Me?" he said. "It's you! Aren't you?"

Her lips quivered a little as she said:

"I was so glad."

He dropped his head, and said in a low voice, rather hard:

"Don't you feel as you've lowered yourself, with the likes of me?"

There was something satirical in the question.

"Do I feel I've lowered myself? Why? Do *you* feel I've lowered myself?" she asked, puzzled and hurt.

He had his faint, yet somehow vivid little ironical smile on his face.

"Wi' one o' your husband's servants, like," he said.

"You're not a servant, you're a gamekeeper," she replied, hurt. "But perhaps *you* feel you—you've lost something—"

"It's not that, your lady—" He broke off, and added in the vernacular, with a twisted grimace: "I canna ca' yer *your ladyship* an' then—" He flung back his shoulders and pressed back his head in his own queer gesture.

"I don't want you to call me *your ladyship*," she said. "I don't care about it ever. I don't really like it, ever. And if you like me—"

She paused, and he watched her narrowly.

"Do yo' like *me*?" he said.

She gazed up at him with her wide blue eyes.

"Yes!" she said pathetically.

He continued to gaze down on her.

"Ay!" he said. "'appen tha does, tha 'appen does! But 'ow do we stan', thee an' me?" He spoke rapidly, taking a kind of ironical refuge in the dialect.

"How?" she said naïvely, not following.

He did not answer her, but gazed on her with bright, concentrated eyes.

"Tha'lt be sorry, tha'lt be sorry!" he reiterated.

"Oh no!" she replied, starting. "Why? Why should I? I don't think you need be afraid."

He gazed down on her, with a queer baffled smile in his eyes.

"Well," he said slowly. "If *tha* doesna care—if tha wants it—! On'y when tha'rt sorry for't, dunna tell me."

"If you knew how much it meant to me," she said truthfully.

"What way?"—he said, still ironical.

But she only gazed up at him, unable to say more.

And then she saw a strange thing. Suddenly his eyes changed, seemed to grow large and dark and full of flashing, leaping light, that leaped up and down in the dark, dilated pupil. He came towards her and took her against him.

"Ay," he said, in an abstracted voice, "let's gi'e in, then! What's good sayin' owt! Tha knows what ter't doin'."

Suddenly his resistance left him, and he folded round her, wrapped her with his body. He had ceased to resist or to remember, letting his body live of itself. She wanted him to kiss her and speak to her, but his hand wandered with the blind instinct down to her loins.

"Let's go inside," he murmured.

He closed the door on them, and put the blankets on the floor, folding one for her head. Then he turned to her again, and put his arms round her. He held her close with one hand, and felt for her body. She heard the catch of his intaken breath, as he touched her. Beneath her frail petticoat, she was naked.

"Eh! tha'rt lovely to touch!" he said in a dim murmur, as his fingers caressed the delicate, warm, secret skin of her waist and hips.

He kneeled and rubbed his cheek against her thighs and her belly, and when he took her, he seemed to know her already so much better. And still she wondered a little over the sort of rapture it was to him. It made her feel beautiful, and very glad to be so desirable. And for the first time in her life she had felt the animate beauty of her own thighs and belly and hips. Under his touch, she felt a sort of dawn come into her flesh, the dawn of desirableness. And yet still, still she was waiting.

"I can't stay long," she said gently, when he lay still. "You came so late."

He held her closer, and tried to cover her naked legs with his.

"Are ter cold?" he asked. But he did not let her go.

"I shall have to go, or they'll wonder," she said.

He gave a sudden deep sigh, like a child coming awake. Then he raised himself, and kneeling, kissed her thighs again.

"Ay!" he said. "Time's too short this time. Tha mun ta'e a' thy clothes off one time—shall ter?—on'y it'll ha'e ter be warmer."

He drew down her skirts and stood up, buttoning his own clothing unconsciously.

"I'll go wi' thee as far as t' gate," he said. "There wunna be nob'dy."

He took his gun, and looked for his hat, which had fallen off. Then quickly he locked the hut, calling the dog.

"'Appen as yer'd come ter th' cottage one time," he said. "If yer could slive off for a night. If we've made up us minds to it, we needn't be balked."

She did not answer: it seemed so far away. He seemed near, yet his voice far away. They were walking side by side over the wet grass, but not touching. The night was dark grey, peculiarly obscure. Sometimes she jostled him. And it puzzled her, that queer, persistent wanting of his, when he seemed so far from her. She did not quite know where she herself came in.

"Dost want ter walk wi' me?" he said, still uneasy.

And he put his arm round her waist, and walked half raising her against him, in a peculiar unison, so that his hip moved against her like a pivot. She realised it was the way the colliers walked with their lasses. It was queer. She was not sure whether she liked it.

And when they came to the gate, he suddenly whipped his hand under her skirts again.

"I could die for the touch of a woman like thee," he said to her, adding: "an' if they knowed, they'd just about hang me as it is!—Eh! dost want ter goo?"

"Yes! Don't keep me," she pleaded.

"No!" he said suddenly, in a changed voice, releasing her, and becoming part of the obscurity.

"Kiss me," she said, lifting her face to him, to the shadow of him.

He kissed her cheek and her brow, in the dark, and held her.

"Ay!" he said. "It's a pity you look to me. You should look to one of your own sort. Yo' canna mate wi' me, yo' know. Yer'll on'y be sorry, after!"—and yet he held her warm and tender.

"I shall come tomorrow, if I can," she said, moving away.

"Ay!" he replied. And in the darkness he opened the gate.

"Goodnight!" she said softly as she passed him.

"Goodnight your ladyship," came his voice.

She stopped suddenly, looking back. She could not even see him, against the darkness of the wood.

"Why did you say it?" she asked, into the gulf of darkness.

"Nay!" he spoke. "When you've gone, that's what you are."

Strange, his voice in the dark! It frightened her a little.—But she had no time to stay.

"Goodnight," she repeated, wanting to get away.

"Goodnight then," came his voice, from the blackness beyond the gate.

And she plunged on, in the dark-grey obscurity.

She found the side door open, and slipped into her room unseen. Though she was late, she would take her bath. She felt a little uneasy: a little afraid of the man she had been with. He too was a risky element.

8

T HE NEXT DAY, TRY AS SHE MIGHT, she felt she could not go to the hut, to him. What kept her away, she did not know. It was some kind of reluctance, that overmastered her. She was afraid of the intimacy. She winced when she thought of his voice, speaking to her in dialect: "—Tha mun ta'e a' thy clothes off one time, shall ter—?"—Surely it was not *she* he was speaking to? surely it was some other woman, some woman of his own class, whom he had known! not herself, not Constance Reid, not Lady Chatterley! She felt herself lumped in with all women as just a woman, and she shrank away.—Then his walking with his arm round her waist, and his hip working against her with such male assurance: no, just like a soldier and a nursemaid! Surely it was not herself! He was mistaking her for some-one else, some common woman. And she felt herself very special.

Yet when afternoon came, a quiet grey day of spring, she could not keep still. She made a dozen plans. She would go to Uthwaite in the motor-car. She almost rang for Field. And then no, the thought of going to Uthwaite sickened her.—Or she would call on Mrs Linley: she ought to. Yes! She could walk there.—Then again no. It was loathsome to call on Mrs Linley. Clifford even suggested she should go with him to the colliery, to look at some new arrangement he was making in the overhead works. But no!—peevishly she told him she had a headache. And indeed bright spots glowed in her cheeks. So Field and Marshall helped him into the car, and he went alone.

She was miserable and angry with herself, feeling today more paralysed than Clifford. He had gone off actively, and she was there at home like a dog on a chain, chewing the chain. No! at least she must go out. She rushed and got her hat. But she would not go to the wood. No! She would go to Marehay, through the little iron gate of the park, and round Marehay farm.

When she was out, she felt better, but she walked on stupefied, noticing nothing. She had seen nothing and known nothing, when she came to Marehay farm. And even there she was only roused by the commotion the dog made, bellowing round her.

"Come, Bell, have you forgotten me!" she said. She was afraid of dogs.

But Bell stood back and bellowed.

Mrs Flint appeared. She was a woman of Constance's own age, and had been a school-teacher.

"Why Bell! Bell! barking at Lady Chatterley! Bell! be quiet!" the woman commanded.

"He used to know me," said Constance.

"Why of course he did. But it's so long since he's seen you.—I do hope you are well again."

"Oh yes! I'm all right, thanks."

"Shall you come in and look at baby? He's grown you'd hardly know him."

Constance was glad to accept at once. Mrs Flint was a rather pretty woman, already beginning to fade. The two women went into the living room, where the baby, a child of about ten months, was sitting on the rag hearth-rug. Constance played with it—she had given it a shawl when it was born, and a rattle for Christmas.

Table was laid for tea, though it was only four-o'clock.

"I was just having a cup of tea all by myself. Luke's gone to market, so I can have it as early as I like. Would you care for a cup, Lady Chatterley—?"

She always offered so shyly, Constance would never have been able to refuse, even if she had wanted to. But she didn't want to. The quiet female atmosphere, just Mrs Flint and the baby, and the servant-girl, was infinitely soothing. Mrs Flint insisted on opening bottled strawberries: but they were good, too. And the two women enjoyed themselves, talking about the baby, and everything that came up.

But at last Constance rose to go.

"My husband won't know what's become of me," she said.

"Well, perhaps it's good for him not always to be too certain. Men have to be kept on tenterhooks now and then, don't they?" said the woman, hostile to Sir Clifford.

Constance laughed. Mrs Flint insisted on opening the locked and barred front door. In the little front garden, shut in by a privet hedge, there were two rows of auriculas all in flower.

"Oh, how pretty!" said Constance.

"The recklesses?" said Mrs Flint. "Yes, aren't they a show! I tell Luke, it's my doing. I split them and bedded them. But take a few!"

So Constance set off again with velvety, pale-eyed auriculas, and dusty yellow ones that smelled sweet.

"I think I'll go across the warren," she said.

"You'll have to climb, you know."

"Oh, I don't mind climbing! It's the cows," said Constance.

"Why, they're not in the warren close. They're in gin close—"

Constance walked across the rough pasture to the dense corner of the wood, planted with young fir-trees, that was called the warren. She climbed the wooden fence, and went in the narrow path between the dense, bristling green fir-trees. She didn't like that part of the wood. But once out of the warren, she would slant down to the broad riding just near the gate of the park.

She had forgotten Parkin. She never associated him with this part of the wood. And she was thinking so deeply of Mrs Flint's baby. It was a nice little thing, with hair like red gossamer, and such a delicate skin. She wondered if its legs would be a bit bandy, like its father's.

As she turned a bend in the dark, lonesome path, her heart suddenly stood still. A man had stepped out in front of her. It was Parkin. She gave a cry of fear. He looked at her in surprise, and did not salute:

"Why, how's this?" he said.

"How did you come?" she asked, breathless.

"Nay, how did *you*? Was you coming to the hut?"

"No! No! I was going home—"

He looked down at her in a flare of anger.

"But you said—" he began.

"Yes I know—but—"

She looked at him mutely. He glanced rapidly over his shoulder, then stepped up to her.

"You wasn't sliving past and not meanin' to see me, was you?" he said, putting his arm round her, determined.

"Not now! Not now!" she said, trying to push him away.

"But you *said*—" he replied, rather angrily.

And his arms tightened instinctively, against his will, around her, and his body pressed strangely upon her. Her instinct was, to fight him. He held her so hard.—Yet why fight? Why fight anybody. Her will seemed to leave her, and she was limp. He held her in his arms, glancing round again cautiously. Then he half carried her through the dense trees, to a place where there was a heap of dead boughs. He threw out one or two fir boughs, and folded his coat. She stood by mute and helpless, without volition. Then he took her and laid her down, wasting no time, breaking her underclothing in his urgency. And her will seemed to have left her entirely.

And then, something awoke in her. Strange, thrilling sensation, that she had never known before woke up where he was within her, in wild thrills like wild, wild bells. It was wonderful, wonderful, and she clung to him uttering in complete unconsciousness strange, wild, inarticulate little cries, that he heard within himself with curious satisfaction.

But it was over too soon, too soon! She clung to him in a sort of fear, lest he should draw away from her. She could not bear it if he should draw away from her. It would be too, too soon lost. He however, lay quite still, and she clung to him with unrelaxing power, pressing herself against him.

Till he came into her again, and the thrills woke up once more, wilder and wilder, like bells ringing pealing faster and faster, to a climax, to an ecstasy, an orgasm, when everything within her turned fluid, and her life seemed to sway like liquid in a bowl, swaying to quiescence.

And he was still too, in the same stillness as herself. It was a perfect stillness, in which she lay, and he lay upon her.

When she woke to herself, she knew life had changed for her. Changed with him. And she was afraid. She was afraid of loving him. She was afraid of letting herself go. It seemed so like throwing away the oars and trusting to the stream: which was a sensation that, above all others, she dreaded. Yet she loved him. When she looked at him, she felt a strange flame fill all her veins. Ah, she adored him! And she longed to abandon herself to the luxury of adoring him. At the same time, she mistrusted yielding to her love. It was not safe to yield to such love for a man—a mere man, after all.

So she searched his face, when he roused, seeing the glisten, the god-glisten, and trying to deny it. And he looked at her, into her eyes, with eyes that seemed still to know the stillness they had brought about together.

"We came off together, that time," he said.

She waited a moment before she answered.

"Did we?" she said.

"Ay!" he said.

She rose and adjusted her clothing.

"Am I tidy?" she said.

He dusted the fir-needles from her dress, and took them quietly from her hair, quietly and carefully.

"There," he said. "You'll do!"

She turned and looked up at him.

"I'm awfully grateful to you," she said hesitatingly.

His eyes looked into her, wondering, perplexed, and hurt.

"How do you mean?" he said, resenting such words.

"For *this*—"

He looked at her in deeper resentment, and a sort of pain.

"It's nothing to do with me!" he said, inconclusive.

In spite of herself she resisted the implication.

"But I want to thank you," she said.

He walked with her as far as the big riding, silent, not knowing why he felt trodden on, or humiliated, since she had spoken.

He returned into the trees, whence they had come, and she ran on into the park, running with a kind of frenzy. It was the power that passion had assumed over her. She felt strange, different from herself. Ah yes, it was easy to embark on these adventures, but they carried you away, even beyond yourself, over the edge of your own world and into another world, where you did not recognise even yourself. She was aware of a strange woman wakened up inside herself, a woman at once fierce and tender, at the same time soft and boundless and infinitely submissive, like a dim sea under the moon, and yet full of fierce, remorseless energy. She had been known all her life for her quiet good sense. She had seemed to be the one reasonable woman on earth.

Now, she knew, this was gone. It had never been real, only a kind of sleep. She had awakened, and come out of the chrysalis of her dream another creature, another beast altogether. Why had no one ever warned her of the possibility of metamorphoses, of metempsychoses, the strange terror and power and incalculability of it all? The danger! She was aware of the danger.

She had thought to take this man in the wood, and appreciate him, and he grateful for his service to her, all in the same range of emotion as she had known all her life. She remembered her intense emotion when she had seen him washing himself that Saturday afternoon. And at the thought, a vivid, consuming desire for him flared up in her. She wanted him, with wild and rapacious desire.

She was like a volcano. At moments she surged with desire, with passion, like a stream of white-hot lava. At other moments she was still and marvellous in a wonderful, incandescent quiescence of passion, an infinite, incandescent submissiveness, submissive and fathomlessly tender because of the very fulness of white fire, like the pool of white-hot lava deep in the volcano. And then queer rumblings and surgings of frenzy filled her. She felt herself full of wild, undirected power, that she wanted to let loose.

Had it all happened merely through that man? She did not know. But if so, he was merely the instrument, the key that had unloosed the torrents. This she decided in herself, imperiously, arrogantly. It was curious. At moments she flamed with desire for him, like a volcano, streaming with lava, and he was the only thing that mattered in the world. Then in a few minutes she had changed to an infinite tenderness, like the soft ocean full of acquiescent passivity, under the sky which was the male embrace. He was like the sky over-arching above her, like god that was everywhere. And then, having tasted this mood in all its ecstasy, she shook it off, and became herself, free, and surcharged with power like a bacchanal, like an amazon. And he dwindled in her esteem to a mere object, the male object, the instrument. And again, as she felt his curious power over her, power to release life in her, he became the enemy, the one who was trying to deprive her of her freedom, in the arms of his greedy, obtuse man's love. In some mysterious way, she felt his domination over her, and against this, even against the very love inside herself, she revolted like one of the Bacchae,* madly calling on Iacchos,* the bright phallos that had no independent personality behind it, but was pure ecstatic servant to the woman. The man, the mere man, with his independent soul and personality, let him not dare to intrude. He was but a temple servant, the guardian and keeper of the bright phallos, which was hers, her own.

The vivid dream of passion is many dreams in one, and of a terrific glowing iridescence. One aspect of the dream the woman fixes upon. And the destiny of mankind depends upon which aspect it shall be.

But to the man also passion is a multiple dream. And he alone of the two, perhaps, can dimly apprehend the whole of the dream, and be true to the whole. Then he can resist the woman's fixity upon the part.

The disaster is, however, that mankind can never accept the whole of the dream of passion, which is the dream that underlies and quickens all our life. Always and invariably man insists that one meagre and exclusive aspect of the great dream is all the dream. Thus he casts his own prison within the mould of his own idea, inside his own soul, and tortures himself all his life. Man is a creature of reason, and therefore he gets drunk, says Byron.* But the truth is, man thinks he is a creature of reason, and therefore he alone, of all creatures, must needs get drunk. Why? Because he has made for himself a prison of his own reason, and sometimes, in mad irrational frenzy, he must burst out of it, in one form of drunkenness or another. If man could once be reasonable enough to know that he is *not* a creature of reason, but only a reasoning creature, he might avoid making himself more prisons. Man is a creature, like all other creatures. And all creatures alike are born of complex and intricate passion, which will forever be antecedent to reason.

To this stage, however, Constance had not reached. She was in the wild turmoil of passion, and had not yet fixed upon any one aspect or phase of the passion, with which to identify herself.

She came home flushed and panting, and, although it was still bright day, not much after six o'clock, she immediately began her explanations.

"I walked over by Marehay and went in to see the baby. Mrs Flint made me have tea with her: Flint was gone to market. It's such a bonny baby, such a dear, with hair like red cobwebs: but such a dear!—Did you wonder where I was?"

"Well, we wondered! But we didn't think of sending round to the police-station just yet," said Clifford, eyeing her curiously.

"I saw you go across the park to the iron gate, my lady," said Mrs Bolton. "So *I* thought you'd perhaps gone over and called at the rectory, and had tea there."

"I nearly did," said Constance, looking round at the nurse. "Then I changed my mind and went round by Marehay."

The eyes of the two women met, Mrs Bolton's grey and bright and cool, Constance's bright and burning. And with the infernal instinct of her kind, Mrs Bolton knew that Constance had a lover of some sort. She had suspected it before. Tonight she was sure. And a curious pleasure, a satisfaction almost as if it had been her own lover, leaped up inside her. Only the question began to burn in her mind: who was he?

"Well it's good you did!" she said, in reply to Constance. "I was telling Sir Clifford, we ought only to be too glad if her ladyship *will* go out and find a bit of company among the ladies round about.—You don't get out enough, really you know, your ladyship. If only you *would* go out to tea sometimes, it would be so good for you."

Mrs Bolton was presuming on her rights as nurse. Clifford and Constance were silent for a moment. Then Constance said,

"Yes, I'm glad I went. I like Mrs Flint, she's a dear creature. And the baby is really adorable, Clifford, really adorable. Its hair is just like spider-webs, so fine, and bright orange!—and it has the oddest, queer cheeky blue eyes! Adorable!"

She spoke with a new, hot passion of maternity, strange in her. It made Clifford very uneasy.

"Curious how red-haired people breed their own type!" he said.

"But wouldn't you like to see it?—the baby?—I asked Mrs Flint to bring it one day," she said.

Clifford looked at her curiously.

"You can have a mothers' tea-party yourself that day, up in your room," he said, not unamiably though.

"Why? Don't you want to see it?" she cried in resentment.

"Oh, I'll see it. I'll kiss it too, if you like. I'm sure it's a cute little thing, right enough. But you must let me off a whole tea-time with it."

"Very well," said Constance. "Then when she comes, Mrs Bolton, we'll have tea in my room."

"You're quite right, my lady! Then you can have a nice woman's talk all to yourselves," said Mrs Bolton.

But in her mind she was thinking: Who can he be? Is there any man over Marehay way? It would never be Luke Flint, no! Then who? who?— She could not hit upon any man that would do for Constance's lover. Yet she exulted within herself, and pined for a demonstrable proof. And she exulted with queer malice over Sir Clifford. There, Sir Clifford! Now who is the gentleman, and Sir Bossy Benjamin! Now what about the grand Chatterleys! My lady's got a lover somewhere about. Put that in your pipe and smoke it.

She forgot that Clifford smoked no more.

After dinner, Constance asked Clifford to read to her, so that she needn't listen. And for some reason, he chose Racine. She heard his voice going on and on, in the grand manner of the French. She bent her head over her sewing, and heard mere sounds. She was full of a strange triumph, and a sort of glory of new pleasure. She could still feel the echoes of the thrills of passion in her blood, ebbing away down all her veins like the rich after-humming of deep bells. The whole of her life had a new throb, in which she exulted. And she remembered the soft, moist mouth of the man kissing her in a soft, straying, absent manner, after he had loved her, and she triumphed.

Clifford made some comment to her about Racine. She caught the words even after they had gone.

"Yes! Yes!" she said, looking up with glowing eyes. "It's very splendid, even the sound of it."

He wondered over the deep, blue blaze of her eyes, and was a little afraid. He resumed his reading, and she bent again over her sewing, hearing the throaty sound of the French as if it were the wind in the chimneys. Of the Racine, she heard not one syllable.

She was absorbed in herself, her own new experience. All her body was alive, and softly vibrating, like the woods under the pulsing of the sap. It was as if passion had swept into her like a new breath, and changed her from her dead wintriness. She was like a forest soughing with the soft, glad moan of spring, moving into bud. And she felt sure she would have a child, a baby with soft live limbs, and a little life of its own, ensheathed in her own life. She could feel her body like the dark interlacing of the boughs of the oak-wood, humming inaudibly with myriad-myriad, unfolding buds. Meanwhile the birds of desire had their heads on their shoulders, asleep in delight, in the vast interlaced intricacy of her body.

A baby! The thought thrilled through her like the thrill of coition. What if it had *his* tight reddish-brown eyes, with the passionate potency, the flames shut down in them! She hoped it might have: for the sake of some woman in the future. Passion like that was a gift indeed. And his beautiful silky skin, that was finer than her own! But not his mouth, that was rather angry. And not his figure!—taller, more graceful. He was not graceful. She could imagine him dancing a Highland reel, but not a fox-trot nor a tango. He would never be elegant. And she wanted her son to be elegant too.

She thought of the man in a detached way now. When she closed her eyes and thought only of his kiss, and the touch of him, she seemed to lose herself in him. But when she had her eyes open, she could detach herself from him. She had got the best of him, got it in her veins and her womb and her soul. For the time being, she needed him no more.

Meanwhile Clifford's voice went on, clapping and gurgling with unusual sounds. She glanced at him. And she thought, suddenly, what a queer rapacity there was in his naked face and his alert, cautious eyes. The rapacity of our civilisation, suave but insatiable, cautious and remorseless. He had, in his own soul, got over his accident, and now his will was more than a will-to-live. It was the steely, flexible but insentient modern will to assert himself. He still was going to make his mark on his environment: even if the mark should only be a scar! But he was no longer personal. He no longer cared about persons. It was the mines that occupied his attention, on them his will was fixed. He was going to pull them out of the depression: he was going to make money.

How he had changed, from the once pale, poem-writing, idealist Clifford! Now he was like some bird with a red beak, that flapped its wings and looked with intent, beady eyes for what it should eat. It was a dangerous face, revealing a fixed, insentient will. She would have to be careful of him. She shuddered a little. But then, she thought she could manage him. Her soul was as astute and steely as his.

She tried to retire again into sacred and sensitive forest of herself, herself filled with passion, a communication delicate as the scent of young leaves. But she found the sacred grove for some reason violated, or it had lost its virtue. She thought of the other man. Well, of him she need not think. She need not be afraid of him.

The reading finished. She was startled. She looked up, and was more startled still to see Clifford watching her with a faint, cruel smile in his eyes.

"Thank you so much!" she said, with a ready instinct of self-preservation. "You do read Racine beautifully."

"Not more beautifully than you listen to him," he said ironically, putting the book away.

She knew it was wisest not to answer.

"After all," he said, "you've got all the important feelings there in Racine. The feelings modern novelists and people pretend to feel are only vulgarisations of the classic emotions, just as the curves of the *art nouveau* furniture are vulgarisations from the true line of the curve."

She watched him with wide, vague, veiled eyes.

"Yes!" she said slowly. "I'm sure that's true."

"The modern world has worked emotions up to such a false vulgarity," he said, "the only way is to have as few emotions as possible: none, for preference."

"Yes," she said again, again with that slowness, as if she were carefully deliberating what he said. As a matter of fact, she was most carefully screening her own new emotions. "One does get terribly tired of people's feelings. They seem as if they stencilled them on for effect, don't they."

"Exactly!" he laughed, with queer savageness.

Mrs Bolton brought in the tray with a cup of some nourishing hot drink which she had introduced as the night-cap for the two. It helped Clifford to sleep: he slept so badly. And it had been useful to help Constance get fatter, when she was so thin.

Constance was so glad she need no longer help Clifford to bed. Mrs Bolton had taken over the task. It was Connie's gradual abandonment of all her intimate duties towards him, that had finally hardened Clifford's heart, and cut him off from her, emotionally. Tonight, she lingered queerly, took his cup and put it on the tray, then picked up the tray.

"Good-night Clifford! *Do* sleep well!—The Racine gets into one like a dream.—Good-night!"

As she spoke, she drifted dreamily nearer the door. She was going without kissing him good-night. He watched her with lynx eyes. Even that she could forget! And he was too proud, too offended to remind her. Though the kiss, indeed, was but a formality. Yet so much of life is just formality. It is these formalities that hold the structure together.

She drifted out vaguely with the tray, and closed the door behind her. He gazed angrily at the door-panels, too angry to ring as yet for Mrs Bolton. Ah well! Let the last vestiges of the old love disappear! He could not make love to her! and therefore she was withdrawing every tiny show of love. She forgot, no doubt. But the forgetfulness was part of her whole intention.

Ah well! He was a man, and asked charity from nobody, not even his wife! He was a net-work of nerves, it is true, and suffered terrible nervous torments of fear and gloom, dread of death, dread of the future. But after all, Mrs Bolton was his best tonic. She did not understand the awfulness of his mental condition, as Connie did. And therefore she was the best help.

He was remarkably healthy, considering. And he *looked* so well, in the face. He was proud of that. He knew he was crippled for life. But the will-to-exist was very powerful in him. It gave his bright, light-blue, over-conscious English eyes an odd look, at once secret and assertive: the half-concealed look of the intense will-to-exist and to hold his life and his possessions against all odds. It was the look of the cripple in his eyes, something bright, slightly furtive, almost impudent.

His dread was the nights, when he could not sleep. But now he would ring for Mrs Bolton, and she would come in her dressing-gown, with hair in a plait down her back, strangely girlish and secretive, and talk to him, or play chess or cards with him. She had a queer faculty of playing even chess while she was three parts asleep. And this, and the peculiar intimacy of the silent night, the reading-lamp, the woman with her plait of hair down her back, soothed Clifford and perhaps sent him to sleep again. If not, she would make a cup of bovril or of some milky food, one for herself and one for him, with a dry biscuit.

Tonight, at the back of her mind, she was continually wondering whom her ladyship had found for a lover. There seemed no gentleman possible. And she always went across the park towards the wood. There was even no house in that direction, except Marehay: and surely Marehay was impossible, there was nobody there.—She must inquire if Mrs Flint had a lodger: if it was possible one of the young engineers lodged there. But it was unlikely.

There was Parkin in the wood, of course!—alone too, and living alone!—and a man who could run after a woman, in his common way. Oh, Mrs Bolton knew that! But then her ladyship would never stoop to him!—he was so common, and that wife of his had made him commoner. He might be attractive to a low sort of woman, if anyone could stand his overbearing, nasty way. But for a refined woman, he was just a snarling nasty brute.

Still, you never knew! When women did fall, they sometimes liked to fall as low as they could. Refined ladies would fall in love with niggers, so her ladyship might enjoy demeaning herself with that foul-mouthed fellow, who would bully her the moment he got a chance. But there, she'd had her own way so long, she might be asking to be bullied.

In her half-sleep, thoughts like these drowsed through Mrs Bolton's mind, as she rather drearily played cards with Sir Clifford. They gambled mildly, to keep the game alive. It was one of Clifford's bad nights. He wouldn't go to sleep till dawn. Luckily, dawn was fairly early now.

Constance was in bed, and she slept deeply. Parkin, after Constance had left him in the drive, went to the hut, and as night fell, he closed the coops and locked up. Then he went home to the cottage and made his evening meal. But he was unsettled, in a ferment. As darkness deepened into night, in the clear spring evening, he put on his coat again and took his gun. He could not rest. His dog Flossie looked up at him.

"Come on then," he said. "We're best outside."

It was a starry night, with no moon. His eyes, like a cat's, dilated in the darkness, and he was at home in the wood. He went his round stealthily, cautiously. But his heart was not in it. The real hunter's instinct abandoned him tonight. He more or less knew it would be so. A woman always interferes with the true hunting or war-path instinct in a man, if she gets beneath his skin.

And this woman had disorientated him. He did not care vastly if there should be poachers setting silent snares for his hares or for his pheasants. He didn't really care. He wanted the woman, who had gone away from him.

Nevertheless he made his round cautiously and thoroughly, till the night was getting late, beating the bounds of the wood like one in a dream. He wanted really to come to the woman. For some reason she had trailed away with her the thin end of his desire, and it drew him, drew him after her.

But he refused to be conscious of it. He was weary, he knew he was weary. He went at last to the hut, and sat awhile in the doorway, looking out at the stars and the silent darkness of growing trees. Somehow, the stars looked slippery between the boughs of the trees. And for some reason, they were like the body of a woman.

After gazing a long time motionless into the night, becoming again conscious of a certain weariness that was upon him, he shut the door of the hut, and wrapping himself in a khaki blanket, remainder from the war, he went heavily to sleep.

Yet he woke, uneasily, after a while. It was still dark night. He looked at his phosphorescent watch. It was half-past three. He sighed—and got up. It was cold. He put on his coat and his hat, took his gun, and went out, followed by the dog. It was still night, but night towards morning. The stars shone imperturbable. But he was restless and cold. He walked away into the wood, without knowing in which direction, merely going on in the night.

So, with prowling quietness, in the heavy chill at the end of night, he climbed uphill to the knoll, to listen and look out. There was not a sound: and in the distance, scarcely a light, save the electric arc-lamps at the colliery away beyond the park. The world was utterly still and wan and dead, and he felt an unbearable melancholy weighing on his heart. He wanted to come to the woman, to lose, in contact with her body, the sense of dread and of heart-chill. He felt he needed her, needed her infinitely. He needed the contact with her, needed it terribly, to save the life in his heart. Yet he remained for a long time on the knoll, looking out into the hollow of the invisible world, where was nothing, except a hollow sort of dread.

At last, he slowly descended, and slowly, as if drawn by a magnet, went across the wood to the park gates. And when he got there, already the faint, ghostly pallor of the outer air announced that dawn would come, though not at once. He stood at the gate, gazing into the outer intangible obscurity. The chill that was on his heart, and the pain of uncertainty that was in his bowels, wanted the woman, if only for one moment, for one touch of re-assurance. The terrible chill sense of being cut off, of not being linked up with life, tortured him blindly. If only he could see the woman, and have one warm touch, one gentle word, the world would be all right again.

He opened the gate, and went slowly into the park, slowly, slowly along the colourless path, that would be pink gravel when the dawn came. Dawn, however, had not come, only a deathly sort of greyness, that became more livid. Not even the first flush of colour. And yet, undoubtedly, the sky was paling, and the trees were detaching themselves darkly from the monotone obscurity of the park. It was like a mist. Yet there was no mist. This was the advance of light.

He went slowly, slowly up the incline, towards the house, hoping for the woman. It was a necessity, that he should see her, should come to her, should touch her if only for a moment. If he found his way into the house!—or if he made her know he was there!—or if he waited, waited, waited for naked day.

He came to the top of the knoll, where the great trees were, and the lozenge where the two big beeches grew, encircled by the sweep of the drive in front of the house. There was the house, low and vague. He could see it, so it must be nearly day. Nearly day, though the dawn had not even yet flushed into colour, and all was ashen grey.

There was a light burning downstairs, in Sir Clifford's room. Parkin knew that was his room. But which room was she in, the woman who had carried away with her the frail thread of his life and his desire? He did not know. He stood there on the drive, with his gun in his hand, motionless, as the first flush of day entered the sky. And motionless he remained.

He saw the light go out. But he did not see Mrs Bolton come to the window and draw back the old dark-blue silk curtains, and stand herself looking out, looking for the longed-for dawn, waiting, waiting for Clifford to be assured that it was really daybreak. When he saw the day breaking, he would be able to go to sleep.

So she stood semi-consciously at the window. And as she stood, she became aware of the figure dim but detached upon the drive. At first she was afraid: a man! She woke up, and watched closer, closer.

She could just make out, in the flushing dawn, his rather baggy jacket, and his gun. Yes, and the dog was running round. It would be Parkin, the game-keeper. And gazing motionless at the house. Motionless! The figure detached itself more and more distinctly, as the light of day, beyond the great guardian beeches before the house, grew rosy and alive. Parkin, standing there small and transfixed!

What did he want? Did he want her ladyship? Was he like a male dog sickly waiting outside the house of the bitch? Should she, Mrs Bolton, go out and speak to him.

But he, as the day grew, felt the futility of his yearning. He would not see her. She would not come out. And he could not get in. And if he could, she would not want him. She would not want to be disturbed, to be sprung upon. She would not want him. She would want to be safely apart from him, now.

This knowledge drove deeper and deeper into his bones. Till at last, with a curious sudden snap, the thread of bleeding desire which she had carried away with her, and which held him helpless, snapped, even at the moment when his soul finally, deliberately broke it, because it was no good. There was no coming to the end of the desire, to the infinitely yearned-for contact. She did not want it, not now, absolutely. So at last came the break of the thread of the desire, at last he was able to go. And he turned away, slowly, ponderingly, departing. He had been able to break the spell, this time at least. But his heart was still immeasurably sad, and bleeding in some way. Yet he walked back to the wood with quickening feet. It was broken. A man must not *depend* on a woman.

And Mrs Bolton, who was just making up her mind to go out and speak to him, saw him turn and disappear. Yes, he was gone! And his going made her more certain than ever.

"Well would you ever now!" she said to herself, dazed with sleep. "And not a young man either!"

9

CONSTANCE WAS SORTING OUT A LUMBER ROOM on the top floor, under the roof. The rooms on this floor were all really attics, except the two in the centre, which were over the hall. These were a little higher: and one of them was Constance's sitting-room, at the top of the second, hidden flight of stairs. She rather liked this lonely top floor of the old, low-pitched house. She always felt she might discover treasures, if she looked long enough.

Now, with Mrs Bolton's help, she was sorting out the long store-room, lifting aside the old, usually ugly pieces of furniture, looking through everything. There was a very nice old painted bureau, painted with scenes and inlaid with mother-of-pearl: but it was rather badly disfigured. It would be pleasant to restore it herself, and put back the old landscapes complete. It was a job that appealed to her. Then there was a lacquer screen— but indeed, there were many things, crippled or damaged, which she could have a go at.

And among the rest, carefully wrapped up to preserve it from dry-rot, was a charming cradle of rose-wood, two hundred years old at least. It had such touching proportions, its hood, of soft old rose-wood, somehow looked so like a cosy, subtle bonnet to shield the child under the coverlet, Constance was moved. How many Chatterley babies had lain in it. Perhaps Clifford himself.—Well, and perhaps her own baby!

"Isn't it sweet!" said Mrs Bolton. "But a bit cumbersome, don't you think, my lady?"

"No!" said Constance. "I like it very much. It seems almost alive. I suppose it's been used so much."

"You may be sure it has! I expect Sir Clifford's father and grandfather were rocked in it. And who knows how many before them! Fancy though! In these old houses and old families things linger on, don't they, no matter how the world changes!—It seems a pity there isn't a little baby to put in it now, don't you think, your ladyship!" Mrs Bolton said, in her peculiar suggestive way.

"Yes!" said Connie vaguely. "I suppose it is."—She hesitated, before she added: "But there may be, you know." And as she said it, she looked up into the grey, inquisitive eyes of the nurse, her own eyes wide and veiled and innocent. The eyes of the two women met, and there was a moment of silence more arresting than a scream. Then Mrs Bolton adjusted herself, and said quickly:

"Oh, your ladyship, that *would* be good news! Oh my word, that *would* be good news!—But you're not expecting it, are you?"

"No," said Constance slowly. "Not as a certainty. But it may be—" and she turned away.

"Oh, I do hope so, I do!" Mrs Bolton concluded, a little lamely.

And Constance left the subject.

But the heart of Mrs Bolton exulted wildly and explosively. A pink colour mounted her cheeks, she could hardly contain herself A baby! Her ladyship having a baby! And herself confided in! Yes, she needed no more than a hint. Her ladyship had looked at her, as one woman to another, and they had exchanged the secret!

Strange thrills of exultation went through the woman. The cradle fascinated her now. It seemed like the shell of all the mysterious revolt of womanhood, and the subtle revenge of the ages. Oh yes, her ladyship was a real woman, a real woman, afraid of nothing or nobody. A baby! quite openly and innocently! And nobody knew better than she, Ivy Bolton, that it was none of Sir Clifford's. Poor Sir Clifford! Even while she pitied him, the bowels of the nurse gave a thrill of triumph.

Was it though, *was* it Parkin's child? Oh my dear, just think of it!—in that old cradle! Oh my dear! But no doubt it would be as good a baby as ever a Chatterley produced. She would say that for Oliver Parkin, no man had a fresher, healthier skin, nor a quicker eye. Leave the man's character alone, his body was fresh and healthy enough!—oh poor Sir Clifford! *Poor* Sir Clifford, if he ever knew! My word, there were troubles ahead.

"Look!" Constance was saying. "Shall we send this to the bazaar?"

She was hunting something for a grand bazaar which the charitable Duchess was to open: a bazaar garden-party affair in the grounds of Cotmanhay Hall. And "this" was a largish, black japanned work-box, evidently made some fifty or sixty years ago, out of some man's would-be-ingenious mind. It really *was* ingenious. It had compartments for everything: probably it was intended for a travelling companion. And what a curse it would be, of that unhandy in-between size! Such a big thing to pack in a trunk: and impossible to carry unpacked.

But it contained everything, and in perfect order. On the top was a concentrated toilet set, brushes, bottles, combs, mirrors, even small razors with safety sheaths; then small clothes-brushes, boot-brushes; then an ink-well, pens, small blotter, and diary: then a perfect sewing out-fit, with three different pairs of scissors and everything to fit. It was wonderful. And everything bran-new, the ink-well had never had ink in it, the silks and cottons were untouched, the small brushes were immaculate. And everything was of the Victorian best: wonderful fine scissors, beautiful bristles in the brushes, everything perfectly made! And the whole thing fitting together like the most intricate puzzle.

It really was a surprise-packet. Connie kept on discovering and discovering, and the very unexpectedness made the women laugh. Another invisible compartment! Lo, sealing-wax, wafers, coloured as gay as life: and at least fifty years old! Never been touched!

"It must have been a present," said Connie. "Do you think it will do for the bazaar."

"Oh, my word! Why it's lovely! It perfectly fascinates *me*!" said Ivy Bolton, her eyes shining in a kind of ecstasy over this box of innumerable intricate treasures. "I think it's *too* lovely to give to a bazaar! Why it must have cost pounds and pounds."

"I suppose it must, for it must have been specially made, by a quite clever workman. But whoever would use it?"

"Oh, your ladyship, but *everything* is useful! Look at that *sweet* button-hook! And even three corks, three silver-mounted corks, for if you opened a bottle and wanted a cork. Oh, and a screw-driver, and a perfect little hammer, and pincers!—There's not a thing that doesn't come in!"

"Even travelling razors and shaving-brush, not to mention those clumsy tooth-brushes!—Do you think anybody would ever use it?"

"Why, your ladyship, if it wasn't for fear of spoiling it, I should think *anybody* would just *love* having it to use!"

"You have it then!" said Connie.

"Oh no! I *didn't* mean that, your ladyship."

"I know. But *do* have it. I love people to have a thing if it thrills them. And it rather thrills you, doesn't it?"

"Oh, it *does* thrill me! But—"

The glisten of innocent, or at least childish covetousness gleamed in the nurse's eyes.

"Then take it!" said Connie with finality. "That's yours!—and we'll send these four pictures to the bazaar, shall we?"

The four pictures were by two R.A.'s who were only *just* a little more old-fashioned than Connie's father.

Mrs Bolton was ecstasised for days by her box. She *had* to carry it to the village, to her cottage. And she *had* to ask a few "friends" in to tea. And it took hours, simply, to examine everything. But in between she had time to say:

"And would you believe it, Lady Chatterley still has hopes of a son and heir?"

"Never!" cried the women. "Why it's impossible!"

"You'd have thought so, wouldn't you? And I always thought so myself. But it seems it isn't so. No! Sir Clifford's *legs* are paralysed, but—" and a series of suggestive nods. "And you know he's *so* much better! Wonderful, really! I know she's hoping, poor thing. She mentioned it to me herself. I *do* hope, for her sake, it is."

"Wonders'll never cease!" said Mrs Draycott. "It seems you can all but kill a man, but he'll be able to do something *that* way, with a woman. I would *never* have believed it!"

"Oh, but you should see the strong arms and shoulders and chest he's got: a splendid chest! Only at the hips, you know—" and she began a few more hints and suggestive nods.

The word flew round among the women of the place, and came before long to the doctor who sometimes looked in on Sir Clifford.

"Well," said the local doctor, "I should have said it would take a miracle. But women can perform miracles.—And there's no sign of any baby *yet*!"

The word went on and on. Mrs Linley, the manager's wife, said to Constance one day, in the hushed intimacy of tea tête-à-tête under the "arbour" at the manager's house:

"And I hear there are hopes for a son and heir at Wragby. Oh, *wouldn't* that be wonderful for Sir Clifford and all of us! Oh dear, I do hope it's a certainty!"

"No!" said Constance, flushing. "It's not—not a certainty.—It's only a hope."

It was marvellous, with her stammering hesitancy, how she kept her winsome, innocent attractiveness. Even Mrs Linley felt motherly towards her, at the moment: excited and motherly. She nodded her head up and down, and repeated:

"Time will show! Time will show!"

Constance agreed that it certainly would.

And as Connie went home, she had something to think about. Mrs Bolton had evidently been preparing the way for the "event", if it should ever come off. Constance had herself no signs that it would actually come off. Yet she believed that it inevitably would. She *felt* she would have a child by Parkin.

In that case, perhaps it was just as well for the village to be prepared. Perhaps Ivy Bolton was right, in letting out a hint. But also, perhaps now it made the meetings with Parkin more risky. Wouldn't everybody be on the watch?

But evidently, the hint had gone further than the village. It had spread into the county. Mr Winter, from Shipley Hall, called one afternoon. He too was a coal-owner, and a friend since Eton of Clifford's father, Sir Geoffrey. He was a lean, well-bred man of about sixty-five, wealthy, and twenty years ago had been considered very go-ahead, both in politics and in the mining world. But the world has itself gone ahead, or gone astray, with such startling rapidity since the death of Queen Victoria, that Squire Winter, as the colliers still called him, seemed like a gentleman from some old régime which nobody can remember any more.

"I'm delighted to find you so much improved, Clifford, delighted," said the old man: who did not think himself old, in the least; and who really was not old, in himself; only, in some queer way, out-of-date.

The two had a very keen and interesting talk about coal-mining. Winter was shrewd enough.

"That's right, that's the way, Clifford! We can keep up our heads for a time yet. If coal isn't what it was, it must become something else, that's all. Oh, I think, with the new additions, we shall keep the works going and the men employed for *my* life-time, and for yours too. Men must be employed, and we must employ them. Oh yes! we shall last my life-time, and we shall last yours; and if we had sons, I hope we should last their life-time too.—By the way, Clifford—forgive me if I'm touching too near, but I feel, in a sense, we are all one family, here in our corner of the country—!—There was a rumour that we might have the pleasure of welcoming the birth of an heir to Wragby. No foundation in it, I suppose?"

The old man seemed wistful. It was obvious he honestly hoped for it.

There was a silence. Clifford was startled, frightened, infuriated, bewildered, and a little flattered.

"Well Sir!" he said, fetching a quick look at this lean man with the white moustache, of whom he had always stood just a little in awe. "Of course nothing is certain.—But we can *hope*!—" He gave a wan, indefinite smile, under the keen and imperious eyes of his father's friend. "We can always hope, I think, Sir!" he added.

"Ah! I see! I see! No definite expectation?—But there *is* hope?" said Winter, with an eagle glance at Clifford. "There is ground for hope?"

"Oh, there is every hope, Sir!" said Clifford, with a boy's naïveté. And he was amazed at himself.

"I am glad, Clifford, more glad than I can ever say. For your sake, for Lady Chatterley's, for our sake here in the county. I hope and pray it may be so! A son and heir at Wragby, and the world will still wag on. My world comes to an end with myself—! Ah well! You are wise to have married! I shall leave my people employed, that is all I can say. But Shipley, when I am gone—"

He lapsed into silence, and Clifford could feel the touch of death in the room. This man, who had been a friend of King Edward, was almost willing to die. The world was no longer his world.

Clifford had a new thing to brood over. And he brooded over it for some days before he mentioned it to Connie. But one morning, when she was arranging some yellow tulips in his room, he said to her:

"I say, Connie, have you heard a rumour that you are going to provide Wragby with a son and heir?"

She did not start, she made no movement. Only in perfect unconscious silence she waited for some moments with the tulips in her hands. Then she came to. And she said, with queer quiet:

"Why, have you heard such a rumour?"

And she went on arranging the flowers, though it cost her a great effort to control her breathing.

"Yes," he replied. "You would hardly expect it, but I have."

"From whom?"

He hesitated whether to answer. She always parried his questions by asking others.

"Well, if it interests you, from Winter—he asked me if the rumour had any foundation in it. Has it?"

"And what did you say?" she asked, still one by one placing the silky flowers in their jars.

"Do you mind turning round?" he said.

She took her flowers and the vase and turned facing him, but still went on with her arranging, in silence.

"Do you mind telling me if you know how the rumour started?" he asked. "And whether there *is* any foundation to it, as John Winter said?"

She looked up at him. How queer he was: so apart from her! He seemed to see things, and know things, but never to *be* anything quite real. No breath entered him, from any other living being or creature or thing. He knew *about* life, but he was not life. No breath of life came from him. Only this queer knowing *about* things.

"There is no foundation to it, as far as I know," she said, looking at him with that queer blank candour. "What did you say to Mr Winter?"

He was at once relieved and disappointed. But he answered:

"What *could* I say? I said the same: there was no foundation for it."

"That there *couldn't* be?" she asked simply.

"No! I didn't go so far. I didn't know quite— when it came on me all in a moment—quite where *you* stood.—I thought I'd better leave you a loop-hole, considering what I said to you before."

She pondered for a while.

"And what did you say, then, to Mr Winter?" she asked.

He was a little reluctant to tell her.

"Why—" he said. "It's a little ridiculous, no doubt! But I was so taken aback.—And when he pressed me to know if there was any *hope* of such a thing as a son and heir—" here Clifford tilted his eyebrows with odd irony—"I just said there was every *hope*—"

He looked at her oddly. She was still softly touching the flowers. She looked up at him.

"Do you think it's funny?" she said.

"Rather, don't you?—even if we have to laugh on the wrong side of our face! Rather funny, don't you think?"

"But if I *did* have a child, after all?" she said, annoyed.

"Whose?"

"Oh—" she brushed the question aside like a vexing fly. "It would be my child, wouldn't it?" She looked him in the eyes.

"Quite! But you hardly expect a virgin birth."

"There are men in the world. Does it matter?"

"Is there *a* man in the world, may I ask?"

"Why should you ask, Clifford? There might be," she said, with that queer, unseizable simplicity that made her seem so innocent and remote from certain actualities.

"Quite! There might be! But between might-be and may-be is such a long stride—"

He felt for some reason so very sure of himself and his prerogatives, at the moment.

"But if I said, I *may* be going to have a child: what would you say? What would you feel?"

"Is it true that you *may* be going to have a child?" he asked, with a mocking insistency.

"No-o!" she said, with hesitancy. It was not true. She was not pregnant. "But it *might* be," she said.

"When might changes to may," he said, "then I'll tell you how I feel. Till then, it seems to me I've no need to rack my feelings imaginatively, rumour or no rumour."

"I suppose not," she said slowly.

But inside herself, she was thinking: "You perhaps need only wait till April changes to May." And she wanted to go to Parkin, to give herself into his arms again.

Not that she wanted, really, to be bound to either man: or to any man. It was as if a stone had fallen into her consciousness, a clear round stone of awareness, and had sunk deep, deep, to the bottom of her depths. And there she could see it, far down, still faintly glimmering its awareness. And it said: "I don't want to be committed to any man. I am attached to Clifford, and I am in love with Parkin. But I don't want to be fastened tight close up to either man, or to any man."

She recognised, emotionally, that the idea of eternal love, or life-long love even, and the idea of marriage, had a disastrous effect upon the will. The idea of permanency stimulates the possessive instinct, the possessive instinct rouses the egoistic will to self-assertion, and there is a vicious circle. Let there be permanency if it happens so. But let there be no convention of permanency, especially in emotional or passional relationships.

So, Constance found herself moving more alone. She wanted to go out, but not under anybody's wing. It was May, but cold and wet again. She could not stay indoors. She decided to drive to Uthwaite, if Clifford did not want the car, or the young man Field, who was his man when he went out.

The car was free, and in the afternoon she set off. In spite of the buds on the trees, the country was dismal. It was rainy and rather chilly, with smoke upon the rain. One had continually to live from one's endurance. But that is more natural to the northern peoples.

The car ploughed uphill through the long, sordid straggle of Tevershall village, the blackish-red miners' dwellings, the glistening black slate roofs, the black earth, the wet, dark-grey asphalt pavements, the utter hopeless absence of any beauty, any cheer at all. It was as if the dismalness of the climate had penetrated into every human expression, and all was dismal, dismal, dismal, fatally and fundamentally so. In the shops were stacks of soap and soap-powder packages, or in the green-grocer's, yellow lemons, pink rhubarb, foreign apples, in the drapers, models of garments, quite expensive, and of an innate dreariness to make one sink down. A load of coal had been tipped up in the street, and, wet with rain, was waiting to be got in, when the collier came home from pit. The Wesleyan Chapel stood behind iron railings. It was of blackened red brick, with stone facings, and black notice boards. The Methodist Chapel, higher up, was newer, still rather pinky-red in comparison with the rest of the buildings, and like a large cinema building, with a big slate roof. The cinema itself was built of concrete, and had lurid posters with the original heading "A Woman's Love",* posters which helped, for some reason, to add to the rainy dismalness even by their would-be dramatic luridness. Beyond the chemist's and the shoe-shop was the congregational chapel which, considering itself the aristocrat of nonconformity, was built of sandstone and had a steeple. And just behind it were the new school-buildings, very modern and grand, but giving off the most awful sound of Standard Five's singing lesson. How could they call that noise singing? It had as much relation to song, spontaneous song, as the squeaking on the brake of the coal-cart coming down the hill. And there was the Sun Inn, the only approach to an hotel in Tevershall, where the commercial travellers stayed. And that was Sam Black, the landlord, who had been a school-teacher but made a far better job of the *Sun*. Down to the left stood the old church, among black trees. Then the car began to slip greasily downhill, past the Mechanics' Hall and its much more modern successor, the Miners' Welfare, on towards Stack's Gate.

Tevershall!—the home village for Wragby. How utterly and unspeakably dismal it was! Connie had been accustomed to Scotch hills,

Kensington, or Sussex, and she had always felt a certain connection still with the old England, Shakespeare's, Chaucer's even, Jane Austen's, Dickens'. But transplanted into these Midlands, she seemed to have left England altogether, to have entered some weird and unnatural country where everything came from underground. It was no country. It was another no-man's-land.

Yet, gradually, it came to have a certain hold over her. It was sad country, with a grey, almost gruesome sadness. Yet it was not dead. It was alive, labouring under a queer, savage weight of dismalness and acquiescence. It was not cowed nor broken, either. No, the very ugliness seemed to have preserved a manly relentlessness in the men, a sort of slow, smouldering courage of death and desperation. But no hope. No immediate hope. There was a grim sort of acceptance of hopelessness, something underground and uncanny. And, when the disillusion was complete, a capacity for a ruthless destruction. That she felt. When the disillusion was finally complete. Because it was still a country of men, men with weird, incomprehensible underground natures, like trolls. On the surface, they were usually decent, and deferential to a woman. But that was only in the overhead works, so to speak. Below, down pit, they were womanless, and partook of the elementality of the minerals.

Parkin was one of them—with a difference. He had been sent down pit as a lad. But he could not bear it. And he could not really mix in. Colliers, in truth, are a tribe, they have an elementary tribal instinct. Parkin, who inherited the instinct, had also a recoil from the underground tribal association. He *had* to get clear. He *had* to be alone.

Connie thought of him, as she drove on. Coming out of all this ugliness, he had his share of it. He had a mineral sort of ugliness, imperviousness, too. But he had also another kind of beauty, another kind of manliness. She wanted his children. And she had never very definitely wanted Clifford's children. But there was a certain mystery to Parkin, even if it went with a certain gruesomeness. He was passionate, too, with the underground passion.—No, she did not want to be committed to him. But she wanted to go to him. At the thought of him, a flame went through her bowels. She wanted his children.

But he did not touch her heart. That, as usual, remained free. Nobody touched her heart, except, perhaps, children. Yes, her heart belonged to children. Clifford, she was attached to him personally. The other man held her with passion. Nothing and nobody held her altogether, and she did not want it.

The car began rising again to Stacks Gate. It had ceased raining, and in the air was the queer pellucid gleam of early May, the grey gleam which yet is bright with spring. The country rolled away in long waves, south towards the Peak, east towards Mansfield and Nottingham. She was running south.

On her left, hanging over the rolling country, she could see Warsop Castle, a shadowy, powerful bulk. And below it was the pinkish plastering of newish mining dwellings with dark slate roofs, and plumes of dark smoke, plumes of white steam rose from the great colliery that had put hundreds of thousands of pounds into the Duke's pocket. There it was, away on the low sky-line, the hanging bulk of the castle, with the black plumes and the white waving on the damp air just below.

Stacks Gate, as seen from the high-road, was just a cross-roads with a huge and gorgeous new hotel, the Coningsly Arms, standing red and white and gilt, in barbarous isolation. But if you looked, away on the left, you saw rows and rows of spick-and-span pink dwellings, set down in blocks like a game of dominoes that was going to be played on the surprised earth. And beyond them, the huge pit-bank and all the astonishing and frightening over head erections of a really modern mine, chemical works and long galleries, all the new apparatus for by-products. Downhill, below the hotel's isolation, was the blackish-red old village, and the grey pit-banks of the little old mine. Down there were the brick chapels, the little pubs, the shops. Up at the new colliery were the weird works, the plumes of smoke and vapour, the proud and awful activity of the devil: and also, the spick-and-span model dwellings. Up here, they needed no chapels. Even the grand hotel stood a little aloof. The monstrous new colliery was the Eleusis,* the sacred place of the terrific modern demon. The grand hotel was really nothing but a miner's pub. But it was to scale.

A strange world! Even in Constance's little day these model dwellings had arisen, and the people had flowed in, from nowhere. Loose families had come in quickly, but at random, from all over the place. And now Stacks Gate was on the sign-posts, it was a place of importance, the miners there had money to jingle, not like at poor Tevershall. And it was these new, riff-raff colliers that poached Clifford's game.

The car ran on, along the uplands, seeing the rolling country spread out. The country! One might well have been proud, once, of being a lord of such a country. In front, looming again and hanging on the brow of the sky-line, was the huge and splendid bulk of Cheswick Hall, one of the most famous Elizabethan halls in England. Noble it stood above its great park, yet with a forlorn nobility. It was still kept up, but as a show place. It did not live. Looking at it was like looking into the past.

The future was below. Already the car was turning, between blackish-red old miners' cottages, to descend to Uthwaite. And Uthwaite was sending up its smoke and steam to the gods that care to receive them. Uthwaite down in the valley, with the dark stripe and steel threads of the railway to Sheffield, and the coal-mines and the great steel-works sending up smoke from long tubes, and the pathetic cork-screw spire of the church, that is going to tumble down, still pricking among the fumes, always affected Constance deeply. It was an old town, a centre of the dales, an old market-centre. And the Chatterleys knew it as their home town. There, Wragby was known as Wragby, as if it were a place: not, as it is to outsiders, merely Wragby Hall, near Tevershall.

The miners' cottages, dreary, but dreary with that queer, exciting smallness and crudeness of a hundred years ago, now lined all the way, the road became a street, and you forgot instantly the open, rolling country where the castles and big houses had once dominated like lions. Now you were above the tangle of naked railway-lines, and foundries and other works rose above you, so big that you were only aware of walls. And iron clanked, and lorries shook the earth, and steam whistles screamed.

Yet again, once you got into the twisted and crooked heart of the place, behind the church, you were in the old world, in the crooked streets which would lead out towards the open, wide region where the castles and the stately houses hung couchant.

Yet at the corner the policeman held up his hand as three lorries rolled past, shaking the poor old church. And not till the lorries had passed could he salute her ladyship.

So it was. Upon the old, crooked burgess streets hordes of oldish, black-red miners' dwellings crowded, lining all the roads out. And immediately, these gave way to the pinker, newer, rather larger but still more depressing blocks of more modern dwellings. And beyond again, in the wide, rolling region of the castles, smoke waved against steam, and patch after patch showed the new mining settlements, sometimes in the hollows, sometimes gruesomely ugly along the skyline of the slopes. And in between, bits of the old, Robin Hood England, where now the miners prowl with the dismalness of suppressed sporting instincts.

They talk about England, but this is the heart of England. One meaning blots out another. The great houses, "stately homes of England,"* still loom and make good photographs. But they are dead. The handsome old halls are there, smuts falling on their drab stucco, that is no longer gold. And one by one they are abandoned. Fritchley Hall, a beautiful old Georgian mansion, was even now being pulled down, though it was in perfect repair. It was too big, and in the wrong place, next the mines which had made its wealth. It was derelict from the eighteenth century.

This is England. One meaning blots out another. So the mines were blotting out the halls. It was inevitable. When the great landowners started the mines, and made new fortunes, they started also their own obliteration from the English countryside. One meaning blots out another.

It had taken Constance a long time to accept the inevitable. The old England was doomed to be blotted out, with a terrifying absoluteness, by a new and gruesome England. It was inevitable. Nay, it had *almost* happened. Fritchley was gone, Eastwood was gone. And Squire Winter knew perfectly well that, once he was dead, his beloved place, Shipley, would go too. They would just tear it down.

Shipley was a very pleasant stucco hall, of the middle of the eighteenth century. It had suave round bays with winking Georgian panes, and a beautiful alley of yew trees, much older than the hall. Inside, the rather low, beautiful rooms were panelled and delicately painted, and furnished with excellent old-fashioned taste. Squire Winter loved the place.

But his little park was fringed by three collieries, and had right of way through it, so that the colliers were everywhere, save across the little lake where the house itself stood. The squire had been a generous man, in his ideas. He had almost welcomed the colliers into his park. Had not the mines made him immensely rich! So, when he saw gangs of colliers lounging by his ornamental water, and furtively looking for a chance, maybe, to poach a bird, he would say: "The miners are perhaps not so ornamental as deer, but they are far more profitable."

He had said this to King Edward, when, as Prince of Wales, the latter was staying for a few days at Shipley. And the Prince had replied in his free way, in his rather guttural English:

"You are quite right. If there were coal beneath the lawns at Sandringham, I would open a mine there, and the miners should walk through the park. Of course! And I should think it fine landscape gardening."

But then, the Prince had perhaps an exaggerated idea of the value of money and the wonders of industrialism.

Now, Squire Winter felt almost swamped. There were these new mining villages crowding on him, and so many new colliers, and a whole new world. He used to feel, in a bright, almost grand way, lord of his own domain and of the colliers. Now, by a subtle pervasion of the new spirit, he felt more and more a nobody. Mining had become less and less a personal affair, it was part of scientific industrialism, with the artizan hordes on the one hand, the exploiting capitalist on the other. He no longer liked to walk across his park after dinner, in his dinner jacket and his lacquer shoes. He winced away from the colliers. They did not salute him. They stared at him a moment, and turned away, muttering to one another. And he had to walk by, wincing, pretending not to see them. Yet he saw them well enough, and that little smile of derisive resentment on their faces. They resented him. They resented all the upper classes. It was rather a subtle, derisive resentment than dislike. No no, they didn't *dislike* him. But they *resented* him, resented his "superiority." That was it. When they saw him there in the park in his dinner jacket and silk socks and lacquer slippers, a deep grudge rose up in them, not against him personally, but against the *difference* that there was between them and him.

They would never accept the difference. They couldn't any more. And somewhere in his secret English self, he didn't even want them to. Yet they drove him away. By simple force of mass resentment they made him wince, and withdraw himself, and go away.

He died rather suddenly a little while after his visit to Wragby, and he left Clifford, who was his god-son, some quite valuable shares: in copper, not in coal. But to Shipley, there happened what he had expected. The heirs would not live there, neither would they keep up the place, with its forty bedrooms. It was a white elephant nowadays.

So, with the consent of the joint heirs, it was just broken up, pulled down. Nothing else could be done with it. The timber of the park was cut, even the splendid rows of yews. Beech trees, chestnuts, ash-trees, they were all cut. With startling rapidity the hall was torn down. A strange bald desert the park looked, another weird no-man's-land, when the clearage was made. But then they began almost at once to erect rows of dwellings where the hall had stood. It was so near to Uthwaite, there would be a rush for the houses, and a solid profit. "Shipley Hall Estate", they called the settlement of new dwellings.

And this is the second stage of that landscape gardening which has a coal-mine on the lawn for ornament. And this is the England we have to reckon with.

Connie knew it all, and accepted it far more inevitably than Clifford did. The world of the Cliffords and the Winters was doomed. Another, more awful world was coming. Yet perhaps the more awful world had more life, more weird passion in it; and life, no matter how weird the form, is the only eternal conqueror. The weird passion that was in Parkin, the volcanic something she felt in him, perhaps had the germs of a new life. She didn't know. She didn't want to know. She didn't want to think too far. It was all too weird and too fearsome, it would have to wait for fate.

She spent some time shopping in Uthwaite, and chatting a little. Then she had a cup of tea in the clean, awkward little tea-shop kept by Miss Bentley. Constance felt she was out in the world again, as in the days when she went to the Academy School, in London. After all, though the outer world scared one a little, it also refreshed one. She felt stronger, and more inclined to accept fate, and much less sure of her own ability to direct fate or destiny, after her trip to Uthwaite. The world was so big, so weird, so fearsome. The common people were so many, and, really, so terrible. So she thought as she sat in the car, going home, and saw the colliers trailing along the pavements, going home from pit, in their underworld grey clothes, with underworld grey faces, rolling the whites of their eyes and cringing a little at the neck, as if they had the rock still down upon their heads. Yet they were men! Ah God, men!—that one might bear children to! She quivered with fear and dread. Yet her Parkin was almost one of them. How awful the world was!

And again, she knew it was not true. For her, the colliers were not quite men, men one might bear children to. They were weird, shapeless creatures, no doubt as good as gentlemen, if the word "good" means anything in that connection. But they were not quite men. No-no! Ghoulish and uncanny, they had been born apart from life.—And Parkin was not one of them. He was solitary, fighting for his own solitude. He was a man, though even he was limited by some of the weird, mineral elementality of the colliers.

The future! The far future! Out of the orgy of ugliness and of dismalness and of dreariness, would there, could there ever unfold a flower, a life with beauty in it?—as a pure antithesis to what they had now. Could the descendants of these colliers ever make life a new and rather gorgeous thing? Could they? In the far future? After all this that existed at present was gone, smashed and abandoned, repudiated for ever—could the children of miners make a new world, with mystery and sumptuousness in it? Her own children's children, if she had a child to Parkin? She shuddered a little, at the awful necessity for transition.

As she went home in the car, it began raining again, the cold rain of spring. "A cold wet May is good for corn and hay."* How insignificant corn and hay seemed, in this countryside! And coal is not susceptible to the changes in the weather.

She was thinking of Parkin, whom she had not seen for some time. And she found a tenderness for him springing up in her again. He was uncouth and passionate, yet at the same time, she realised, tender, and fragile, as all really lonely living things are. A certain compassion mingled in with her desire for him. Yet, of course, she still saw him *outside* her own life. For the passionate contact with him, she had to go outside her own sphere. It was an excursion. And the desire for the excursion was coming over her again.

Thinking of him, a certain tenderness came over her, for this disfigured countryside, and the disfigured, strange, almost wraith-like populace. To her, there was something grey and spectral about them: and something so inflexibly ugly. Ugliness incarnate, they seemed. And yet alive! But with an uncanny, underworld sort of life.

What would become of them? They had appeared in their thousands, out of nowhere, when the coal was opened in the bowels of the earth. And when the coal was exhausted, was gone, would they go too, disappear off the face of the earth? Were they merely the strange human fauna of the coal-seams, destined to vanish like other fauna, when their special habitat and means of subsistence was exhausted? Or were they capable of undergoing change, and bringing a new sort of life to light?

She shuddered again at the thought of them: and even her Parkin was one of them. Creatures of another element, they did not really live, they only subserved the coal, as the steel-workers subserved the steel, the workers in the potteries, the clay. Men not men, but merely the animae of coal and steel, iron and clay. Strange fauna of the mineral elements, of carbon and iron and silicon!

If ever they did emerge, it would be with weird luxuriance, something in heavy contrast to what they were now. From ugliness incarnate, they would bring forth, perhaps, a luxuriant, uncanny beauty, some of the beauty that must have been in the great ferns and giant mosses of which the coal was made: some of the beauty of the weight and the resistance of iron, and the blueness of steel, and the iridescence of glass. When at last they had risen from subservience to the mineral elements, and were really animate, when they really *used* the iron, for the flowering of their own bodies and anima, instead of, as now, being used by it. Now the iron and the coal used them, not they the iron and the coal.

She told Clifford she had had tea in Uthwaite.

"Oh really! In Miss Bentley's tea-shop? And how was the assiduous Miss Bentley?"

"Just the same."

Miss Bentley was a sallow old maid, dark-skinned, with a rather large nose, who served teas with careful intensity, as if she were administering an oft-repeated sacrament.

"It must be rather splendid," said Clifford, "to be able to make tea for strangers, and put so much soul into the tea-pot, along with the astringent Ceylon tea. She really should have better tea, if she is the vestal and the virgin ministrant of that tea-temple of hers. Did she ask after me?"

"Oh yes!"—Constance imitated Miss Bentley's hushed murmur: "*May* I ask how Sir Clifford is, my lady?"

Clifford laughed.

"And I suppose you said I was blooming?"

"Yes! I said you were wonderfully well; and if she came to Tevershall she was to come up to Wragby to see you."

"You did! Why good Heavens, what an idea! A pretty fool I should look, with Miss Bentley kissing my hand; as I know she would if she dared.—Did she say she would?"

"She blushed: quite prettily! and lowered her eyes for a moment; and looked quite a pretty young thing. She must have been really good-looking.—And she said she didn't think she would dare to presume."

"Dare to presume!" he laughed. "She is an absurd old thing.—Do you think she has a special feeling about me?"

"I'm sure she has. You are her *roman de la rose*."*

"Her romance of the rose! Come Con, don't be too far-fetched."

"I think you are. It's quite easy for you—"

She laughed, and went upstairs to take her bath, and change. At least this part of her life, the material and comfortable part, ran with a regularity and a smoothness which was like a sleep, and which she loved: so long as there was also an escape, an excursion into the outside. She did not want to *be* outside the comfortable routine of her days. But she wanted sometimes to make a sally, a sortie, and have a strange tussle with different life.

She had managed, in a great measure, to detach from Clifford that part of herself which no longer belonged to him. For the rest, as an occasional companion, and as a presence in her life that was always *there*, but not pressing upon her, she accepted him.

"We are a queer couple, you and I, Connie," he said that evening. "In a sense, we belong to one another, don't you think?"

She was in an acquiescent mood.

"Yes, I think so," she said.

"There is even something eternal between us, don't you think?"

That frightened her a little. She was so mistrustful of these eternities.

"Yes, I think there is," she answered, to get it over.

"There is a certain conjunction, so to speak, between our immortal selves," he went on.

But now she began to lose him.

"You know I rather hate long-drawn-out immortality," she said, as if perplexed.

"I know you *say* you do. But that is chiefly contrariness on your part."

She pondered, or pretended to. But she was really only making sure of her own resistance.

"I think it's absolutely no good talking about immortality," she said. "It is something one has by not thinking about it.—I'm sure a striving after immortality is a sign that you've lost your natural immortality."

He mused over what she said. And then, slowly, reluctantly, he veered to his real point.

"Has your father settled where he is going, in June?" he asked.

"Near Biarritz—to the Villa Natividad."

"And you are going?"

"Yes! Aren't I?"

"I know you've *arranged* to go."

"You don't want me not to?" she said, puzzled.

It had been a long settled thing, that she should spend a month or six weeks abroad, with her father and Hilda, in June and July.

"Oh no! Oh no!" he said. Then he added, rather awkwardly: "I only hope that you won't make any serious—entanglement—while you are away.—I would like to make sure that you feel the same as I do—that whatever is between us—*is* eternal, whatever you may say."

She looked up at him, conscious of a rising resistance in herself.

"I think it is eternal," she said. "But many things are eternal."

He made a gesture of impatience.

"Quite!" he said. "But not mutually-exclusive things."

"What do you mean?" she said.

"I will put it in words, then.—I know you have got this idea into your head about having a child. And if you could bring it off without any further entanglements—well—I don't think I should mind altogether. For your sake, I should be glad if you could have children. And I've no doubt I should be very glad for my own sake, once the child was there. It would be something to plan for into the future, even if it were not my own. It would anyhow be *yours*.—It's the question of the other man— and the entanglement.—For God's sake, be careful what sort of a man you let be the father of your child."

She looked up at him.

"But there *is* no child," she said.

"Quite! But, to use your own words, there *might* be.—Do you think you can promise not to get tangled up with somebody else, over the business?"

"In what way tangled up?"

"Oh, you know what I mean—love affairs taken *an grand sérieux**— the mess of being in love—and wanting to be *free*—bah, *free*!—"

"You mean free of my marriage with you?" she asked.

"Quite!"

She was silent for a time.

"I don't think I want to be free of that," she said slowly.

"That's just what *I* want to feel sure about," he said, with relief.

Again she waited before she replied:

147

"I think you can be sure of it."

There was a note of finality in her voice.

"Then I needn't worry," he said. "There *is* something eternal between us, and if I know you *feel* it, I don't much care whether you admit it or not."

But she herself only felt rather indifferent as to whether there was something eternal between them. Long-drawn-out eternalities bored her, and irritated her.

10

COMING DOWNSTAIRS IN THE MORNING, she found Parkin's dog Flossie running anxiously round in the hall, making faint whimpers.

"Hullo Flossie!" said Constance softly. "What are you doing here?"

The dog ran towards the door of Clifford's room, whimpering. Constance listened. That was the voice of Parkin, speaking to Clifford. Her heart stood still for a moment, with fear. Then she said to the dog:

"You want your master? Come along then!"

In spite of herself, the dog's pain and anxiety to go to the man moved her, and a new flush came into her blood. She opened the door of the room softly. The dog slid in, and she followed.

"I had to let Flossie in," she said in her soft, breathless voice. "She was so distressed."

The dog had lain down at the man's feet, quivering. He was standing near the door. He looked down at the animal, and said harshly:

"Why didn't you stop outside!"

The dog only looked up at him.

"I shut her out," he said apologetically to Clifford, not looking at Constance.

"I suppose she slipped in through the kitchen," said Constance. "I found her in the hall, poor shut-out Flossie!"

He turned to her ladyship with a hasty salute.

"She'll find a road in somehow," he said, glancing at the woman and away again, with perfect reserve.

Once she was physically near him, Constance was only aware of *him*. Clifford was a mere cypher. And something in her rejoiced. But she wanted to know what his business was.

"Did I interrupt you?" she said to Clifford. "I'm sorry! It was the dog, she was frantic."

"No no!" said Clifford. "There's nothing very important—a question of taking up two colliers from Stacks Gate for snaring rabbits down the warren hedge."

She looked at Parkin. He had on his furtive, game-keeper's look, which she did not like. Yet his physical presence fascinated her.

"When did you catch them?" she asked.

"Just at daybreak this morning—me an' my nephew Joe. We was waitin' for 'em, I'd seen 'em settin' the snares night afore," he said rather hurriedly, being game-keeper pure and simple.

She turned to Clifford.

"And will you prosecute them?" she asked.

"I think so! I think so! Eight snares, in the middle of breeding season! It's a bit much! l think there's nothing to do but to have them up."

There was silence for a moment. She was thinking that Parkin would be making more bitter enemies.

"The colliers hate it when you prosecute anybody," she said.

"They do! But it's Stacks Gate, not Tevershall. And after all, snaring at this time of the year—!"

"They'd got three rabbits apiece on 'em," said Parkin, in a burst, like a witness; "an' two of 'em was does as would ha' cast in a day or two."

She felt Clifford stiffen at the coarseness of this, in her presence, and she smiled to herself.

"It *is* awful, those snares!" she said. "And when the rabbits cry!—They *deserve* to be prosecuted, for torturing the rabbits with those snares. *Do* prosecute them, Clifford, and stop them if you can at that. It's so cruel."

"And it's the only way to stop them," said Clifford.

"Brutes!" she said.

Parkin remained motionless, at attention, his face a game-keeper's mask. She was rather piqued that her presence had no visible effect on him at all.

"How are the little pheasants?" she asked him, looking him in the eyes with her wide gaze.

He glanced at her swiftly, but remained stiff.

"Getting on nicely, my lady," he said.

"I shall come and see them soon," she said, looking again full up at him. And again their eyes met.

"You'll find 'em runnin' round nice an' independent," he said.

But his eyes did not change in the least. He might never have known her save as Lady Chatterley, never have touched her in his life.

How clever of him, to play his part so well! It made her a little angry.

"Nothing you'd like me to do for you, Clifford?" she said, turning to her husband.

"Not now, thanks, dear!" he said.

And she left the room.

She went upstairs to her own room, and stood at the window till she saw Parkin going down the drive. The skirts of his big coat flapped as he strode with aggressive importance, his brown dog ran at his heels. He was going once more to take the world by the nose. And he looked ridiculous, his legs prancing out in their stride, his old hat worn with a certain defiance, his baggy coat flapping! Especially those prancing legs annoyed her! And so cool! Not even the judge of judges would ever have suspected that he had more than once made so free with my lady's person, and walked with his arm round her in the dark. So cool, and so completely detached, as if he didn't know her!

Yet she went that very evening to the hut, and found him there, apparently waiting for her.

"You see I've come!" she said.

His eyes smiled in a curious secret amusement, and he did not salute.

"Ay, I see it," he said.

He was in his shirt-sleeves, working at something: a flannelette shirt with bone buttons at the wrists. Yet his wrists looked so full of life!— and under his clothing, did he have that beautiful white body she had seen? One day, she must see it, touch it, know him altogether! The flame of passion went over her.

He was looking at her with that curious look of amusement, and preparing himself to come and take her. Suddenly she said:

"I told Sir Clifford I might have a child."

He stopped as if he had been shot. Dumbfounded!

"You told him *that*?" he said, in complete astonishment and some dismay.

"Yes! You see I might."

He gazed at her with blank eyes. Then he took off his hat, and stroked his hair, bewildered, thinking hard.

CHAPTER 10

"You don't do nothing to stop it, then?" he said, in a secret voice.

"What do you mean?—to prevent me from having a child?—no, how could I?" she said.

"Because *I've* not taken no precautions," he continued, as if he might be to blame.

"I should hate it if you had," she said.

He put on his hat again, and thought it over.

"You was reckonin' on havin' a childt, like?" he said, cunningly.

"Yes! I should be glad," she said.

The rather hostile look of amusement came into his eyes.

"An' Sir Clifford 'ud take it for his own, would he?"

"He says so."

He gazed away at the little pheasants, that were grown all out of shape, but were very brisk. Then he looked very keenly at her.

"But there was no mention of me in it?" he asked, ironically.

"Oh no!" she said.

"Well!" he said. "He'd have to think it was somebody's childt."

She was a little angry with him, so she said coldly:

"I'm going abroad with my father and sister next month, so he could think I had found somebody then."

"Are yer going abroad? For how long?"

"Six weeks or so."

"Next month?"

"Yes—about the middle of June."

"Not long yet."

He gazed at her! So, he was going to lose her for a time! He was thinking fast.

"Sir Clifford'll think you've found somebody higher up, eh, to give you a baby?—What would he say if he knowed it was me?"

She paused again, in anger at his mocking tone.

"He'd hate it," she said, off-hand. Then she looked up at him. "But you'd never want to tell him, would you? You'd never want to give me away?"

There seemed to him a certain dumb pain in her face.

"Me! No! You may bet I should never want to tell him. He'd never be no wiser if he waited for my tellin'."

"Nor anybody? You wouldn't tell anybody?"

"Me! You can back your life, I s'll tell nobody. I've had enough o' what

151

one woman's said about me, wi'out ever startin' any more talk.—No, if God knows, he'll have to. But I'd not let even him know, if I could help it."

They were both silent, and awkward.

At last he turned to her, with a quick, awkward movement.

"That was what you wanted me for, was it? A baby?" he said.

She was silent, so confused, she did not know.

"I don't know!" she said, looking up at him with lost eyes. "I—I wanted—I don't know what I wanted. I wanted—I wanted *you*, yes, I did. I do!—And, perhaps, a baby," she concluded, in slow, dumb syllables.

"You didn't think much of *me*, like?" he said slowly and ironically.

She looked up at him dumbly.

"I liked your body!" she said.

"My body?" he repeated, incredulous and amused.

She looked up at him without speaking.

"An' do you like it now?" he asked.

"Yes," she murmured.

"Then we're quits! I like yours!" he said. "I imagined it was no pleasure for you, to touch me, as it is for me to touch you.—My wife, she had her bouts of liking the touch of me. But you're different."

"I—I don't think I am," she stammered. "I want to touch you."

He looked at her a little mockingly.

"Nay-nay!" he said. He knew she wanted to keep really free of him.

"It's because I'm—afraid," she said.

"An' do you like it, when I feel of you?" he said.

"Yes, I love it," she admitted.

"Eh well then—what's amiss!—Have you left your underthings off for me?" he asked rather brutally.

"Yes!"

His eyes were now flashing, but his face had a hard look.

"Let's go inside, then, and be private."

He closed the door of the hut, and sitting down, pulled off his boots and leggings and trousers, and stood in his shirt.

"Now you can feel of me if you've a mind to—" he said, coming to her and lifting back her skirts, and coming to her naked body with the queer, constrained smile of passion. But she knew his heart was heavy. And she put her arms round him, under his shirt. But she was afraid,

afraid of his smooth naked body, with its violent muscles. She shrank afraid, away.

And when he said, in the queer heart-sad croon of the voice of his passion:

"Tha'rt nice! tha'rt nice!"—her body loved it, and was glad. But something in her spirit, and in her will, stiffened with resistance, from the intimacy, and from the peculiar haste of his possession. And if the sharp ecstasy of her own passion did not overcome her, if her spirit managed to keep aloof, then the butting of his hips would seem ridiculous to her, and the sort of anxiety of his penis to come to its conclusion would seem almost farcical. And then it would occur to her, that *this* was love, this ridiculous butting of haunches, and wilting of a poor little penis. And she would say to herself, as so many men, poets and all, have said, that surely the God that created man, created him a reasoning being, and yet forced to procreate himself in this humiliating ridiculous posture, created him surely out of savage irony and contempt for his own creation.

It was difficult for her mind and her critical spirit to submit to the throes of love. They wanted to dominate. They wanted to throw the man aside, escape his grip and his butting over-riding haunches. They found his body a foolish and pretentious, imperfect, perhaps disgusting thing.

But then again, caught unawares, passion overcame her, and the body of the man seemed silken and powerful and pure god-stuff, and the thrusting of the haunches the splendid, flamboyant, urgent god-rhythm, the same that made the stars swing round and the sea heave over, and all the leaves turn and the light stream out from heaven. And then inside her the thrill was wonderful and the short, sharp cries that broke from her was in the wild language of the demi-gods. And then, the strange shrinking of the penis was something so tender, so beautiful, the sensitive frailty of what was so fierce a force, she could feel her heart cry out.

She was at the mercy of her two selves. But the self that mostly ruled, was the self of her own, critical spirit, that was fiercely independent, and resented his clutches, and his blindness, and even the soft, lapping intimacy of his voice, the *thee* and the *thou* of his dialect. When he was warm with passion, he was so unaware of the ridiculousness of things, and of himself: the ridiculousness of buttoning down those corduroy breeches, there in front of her. He was so pleased and so satisfied, and it irritated her so. Out of sheer perverseness, she *made* herself be irritated, she *refused* to let herself be carried away by the soft, vague, uncritical pleasure of passion.

"Whether tha gets thee a childt, or whether tha doesna, we'n 'ad summat for us-selves," he said, with that darkening glow of afterwards. But there was a tension on his brow. And she felt his heart accused her.

And in spite of herself, in spite of her critical standing apart from him and jeering at him, she could not retort on him. He, or his mood, had a strange power over her. And the moment he came really near to her, it was as if something radiated out from the front of his body, that put her in a spell, *made* her submit to him and his desires, whether she wanted to or not.

"An' if Sir Clifford gets th' childt, we've 'ad *this*!" he said, as he sat down fastening up his leggings. It sounded so fatal, as if they were parting for ever.

Nor could she retort on him. Nor could she even prevent him, in his complication of mixed emotions, from using the dialect to her, the dialect that made her feel so curiously *caught*, netted. The very sounds of it cast a spell on her, spoken in the warm, physical, yet fatal voice he used when he was roused, and the physical man in him became defiant, in conflict with the other, personal man. Then she was merely woman, merely female to his male. And partly she loved it. The body of her loved it. But her spirit wanted to get away, to run, to get out of his presence.

"Tha mun com' ter th' cottage for a naight, sholl ter?" he said to her, his speech getting broader. "Tha mun com an' slaip wi' me, afore tha goos wi' thy feyther. Shall ter? When sholl ter?"

Her mind flickered like a wavering candle, under the sound of the curiously-varied dialect, which sometimes said *maun* for *must*, and sometimes *mun*; then *sholl* or *shall* apparently indiscriminately. "We'n 'ad summat fr' us-selves!" he said, and all her skin turned, it was so unspeakably intimate and stuck together. And *we* he pronounced like a sharp *wai*, with Italian vowels: really unwritable.

He seemed to slide through centuries, thousands of years of human culture, in his hour with her. When she came, he was an ordinary man, not very different from Tommy Dukes or Clifford. But when his eyes began to dilate and flash, he began to slide back through the centuries. His curious hiss of passion, sudden indrawn, when he touched her naked body, was far back almost as the snake itself.* And that crooning voice: Tha'rt nice, tha'rt nice!—was something pre-human. And then he used the dialect as a sort of armour and a weapon, forcing her to physical compliance.

Now, in another breath, he had moved forwards again another thousand years.

"Shall yer come one night ter th' cottage?" he repeated, quite changed and distant, in an almost ordinary voice. And now, instead of *naight*, sharp, it was *ni-ight*, with a long heavy *i*.—And now, also, he did not urge further. He left her to it. And even now, she had to say yes to him, for fear he should not ask her again. She wanted to go to the cottage: but he made her admit it.

"Yes! Shall I? Do you think I dare?" she said.

And back he went the thousand years again, but warmer, more assured.

"Yi, yi!—tha durst! What's goin' ter stop thee? Tha oppens one o' t' doo-ers, an' tha coms."

She stood and wavered. He glimmered with a faint smile at her in the darkness. He was taunting her, daring her.

"When sholl ter com?" came the near, caressive, lapping voice.

"Sunday?" she said faintly.

"Ay! Com o' Sunday!"

He quickly opened the door of the hut.

"Should I dust thee?" he said, taking her gently by the arm.

And he gently dusted down her dress, his hand passing softly over the curves of her body, firmly, without any seeking any more, but with memory.

"Tha'rt good cunt, aren't ta?" he said softly, using one of the indefinable sexual words of the dialect.

"What is that?" she said.

"It's what a man gets when 'e's inside thee!—Yo' wouldn't know what *cunt* is, though," he added, a little mocking, taking a great stride suddenly, and landing in the twentieth century.

He was cold again, returned back to the man of her own day, but not of her own class: silent, with a restraint on him. Only when he was leaving her, he said:

"Sunday then! What time?"

"Why—some time after ten."

155

"All right! An' I s'll wait for yer here, at this gate.—If anything stops you though—?"

"If I don't come," she said, "you walk towards the house, and see if there's a light in my bedroom. If there's a light in my bedroom, after ten o'clock, it means I can't come.—But I shall see you before then."

"All right! I know which is your bedroom."

She left him, but in a kind of dreaminess. The world seemed like a dream. The trees seemed to be bulging and surging, at anchor on a tide, and the heave of the slope of the park was alive. She herself was a different creature, sensitive and alert, quietly slipping among the live presences of trees and hills and a far-off star.

It was new and wonderful, but she was still uneasy. She knew she had got it from him. She had really touched him at last, like the woman who touched Jesus,* and who found the world changed. Stars were coming out. Time was a full soft urge, with no minutes to it. And the universe ceased to be the vast clock-work of circling planets and pivotal suns, which she had known. The stars opened like eyes, with a consciousness in them, and the sky was filled with a soft, yearning stress of consolation. It was not mere atmosphere. It had its own feeling, its own anima. Everything had its own anima.

The quick of the universe is in our own bodies, deep in us. And as we see the universe, so it is. But also, it is much more than we ever see or can see. And as the soul changes in us, turns over with a new creative move, the whole aspect of all things changes. And again we see the universe as it is. But it is not as we saw it before. It is an utterly new reality. We are clothed with a new awareness, in a new world. The universe is all things that man knows or has known or ever will know. It is all there. We only need become aware.

Connie felt this change happening in herself. The man had caused her soul to turn, to become aware in a different way. She felt frightened and shrinking. She had got a new nakedness, an old, hard sheath was gone. And she was frightened, exposed, yet invisible, in her new nakedness.

And now, she felt, with a dim inward knowledge, he had impregnated her body as well as her soul. Now she believed she would have a child.

He, walking in the wood when the night deepened to a magnificent night of May, felt a peculiar surging joy. In some way, he had won a great victory, broken through into a world where he could live. The struggle was long, and like a tense dream. But with his loins he had won a victory. His life had been a long, tense dream of resistance and of pressure against some constraint. And now, for the moment, he had broken down the resistance and emerged loose and free in the night. The intense hour with the woman was only the culmination, and, for once, the triumph, of the life-long passion of his soul and loins, a passion for a new space in life. His whole life was a resistance and a fight. But this was one of his moments of emergence and of a new splendour.

Connie remained under the spell of him, her mind feeling dim and inert, but in her limbs, in her body, in her loins and her womb, a new, strong awareness and aliveness. For some reason, she felt drawn to Mrs Bolton, as if she had something in common with her.

The two women were working together in the garden, pegging down carnations and putting in small plants of flowers for the summer. It was a lovely warm morning, and a work they both loved. Connie especially felt a delight in softly putting in the roots into the soft black earth of the borders. She felt her womb quiver with pleasure, as if something were taking root there too, in the same way.

"It is many years since you lost your husband," she said softly to Mrs Bolton, as she dug a new little hole with the trowel, and carefully prepared it for the plant.

"Twenty-three," said Mrs Bolton, waiting with the columbine plant ready. "Twenty-three years since they brought him home."

Connie's heart gave a lurch. If they brought home the body of one's man, dead! It must not be.

"Why should he have died, do you think?" she asked, glancing up. "Why shouldn't he have escaped, like the others?"

It was a woman's question to a woman.

"I don't know. He was too obstinate, if you ask me. He hated ducking his head, for anything. He ought never to have been down pit, if it hadn't been for his father, he never would have been. His mother always said: our Ted's not the lad for down pit, he's too much of a wezzle-brain—"

"What is a wezzle-brain?" asked Connie.

"Why, he wasn't that either, exactly. It means careless, and never know where you've put things, forgetful. He wasn't really wezzle-brained, it was that he *wouldn't* care, he wouldn't *take* care: there, that's it! He wouldn't take care. He was like some of those lads in the war, going off gay and lively. And they were always killed first. And that was how our Ted was: that fresh and happy-go-lucky, and *wouldn't* be careful. It wasn't that he couldn't. He could have. I knew that when my first baby was born, an' I had such a bad time. But he stopped with me all through it, an' held my hand, else I b'lieve I *should* 'ave died. An' I never saw him, you know, like you don't when you sufferin'—not till after, not till I was through. An' then I looked at him, an' he was white as a sheet, an' such a look in his eyes, oh!—angry, angry! I said to him: *It's all right, lad!*—An' he said, in such a funny way: *A body 'ad better die than suffer.* An' that made *me* mad, as you can imagine. *Well!* I said. *If you mean I'd have better have died, it's a nice thing to say!*—An' he gave me such a look! But I was too weak to notice any more. Only I always remembered it.—Ay, an' I remembered it when he lay dead. I thought to myself: *Ay, you've died without sufferin', that you have done!*—I believe 'appen it was the pit. He should never have been down pit. It wasn't his nature, like.—Eh, I wished afterwards as I'd made him take a job on top!—But when a man's married, he doesn't like choppin' an' changin'."

Connie had gone on bedding her plant, and watering it with her secret tears. But she managed to compose herself.

"And you never forgot him?" she said softly.

"No! It seemed as if I couldn't. It came as such a shock. An' I'd been so happy with him. I was brought up with a step-mother as was none too good to me, an' it was lovely havin' Ted, as was just the opposite. I'd never had anybody be fond of me; my father was fond of me, but he never dared show it. I never had anybody to make a bit of fuss of me, like, and hold me in their arms. And then Ted was so good to me. Nobody knows! I *did* love him to hold me—an' I've kissed every inch of his body. After my first baby was born, he didn't want me to have any more children, an' I had such work with him, to make him get over it. He was a thousand times more done by what I'd had to go through, than I was. I said to him: *Well, I've forgot it! An' look at me, if I'm any the worse! Why I'm stronger than ever.* But it 'ad made such an impression on him.—But in the end, he got over it, an' we had us good times again. He said to me not long before he died, he said: *I dunna reckon much o' life, Ivy, 'xcept f'r thee!* An' I said to 'im: *I don't know what you have to grumble about life for!*—An' 'e said, so funny an' quiet: *Ah'm non grumblin'! I'm sayin' I dunna reckon much on't. Tha'rt a nicester woman than I am a man.*—I don't know, but I couldn't make him out.—He seemed that jolly an' good tempered, an' a good foot-baller, an' never drank *much* after he was married, though he used to take too much before. Yet when he lay there dead, you'd almost have said he *wanted* to die. An' that was my cry, when he lay there dead: *What did you want to leave me for!*—"

"But he *didn't*, did he?" asked Connie.

"No! Of course not! But that was what I kep' on sayin'.—But it was the pit, really, that killed him. I believe inside himself he couldn't bear it. But he wouldn't own up—not even to himself."

The plants were set, Connie rose from her knees, and looked down the softly steamy garden, full in the sun under the old sandstone wall.

"It was terrible for you, to have your life end there," she said, glancing at the handsome, brooding face of the other woman.

"It's true. One part of my life ended there. One part of me went with him. I could never alter it. It was as if I could only feel his arms round me, an' his body against me, an' his legs against my legs. It's the touch of him that I can never really get over."

"But do you want to?"

"No! Only sometimes I've felt bitter, being left. And sometimes I feel it was other folks, an' the pit, as killed him. It seems silly, doesn't it! But sometimes I feel, if it 'adn't been for the pit, an' them as runs the pit, other folks, he'd never have left me."

"But which other folks?" asked Connie.

"Oh, I don't know, my lady. There's a lot of hard-hearted folks in the world."

It was queer how even Ivy Bolton could change. Connie had seen her with Clifford, soft-footed, pale-faced, sly, mock-submissive, intimate in the wrong way, and rather hateful. Now here she was, a woman indeed, in love after twenty-three years, with a dead man, caring for nobody else, rather hating the world for having killed him.

"But can a touch last so long?" she asked suddenly, quite apart even from her own thoughts. "Can a man's touch on a woman last so long?"

"Eh, my lady, what else is there to last, if it's the right man!" replied the nurse, almost mocking.

Constance looked at her.

"I think you're right!" she said. "It's when he touches you—"

Mrs Bolton's eyes suddenly filled with tears.

"And even *that* they'd kill if they could," she said fiercely. "They'd like to kill his very touch that he left inside you. If they could!"

It was spring, a warm day, with a perfume of earth and auriculas, and yellow flowers down the garden, and many things in bud, and a blue sky.

In the afternoon, she felt she must go and speak to Parkin. The first dandelions were wide-open, giving themselves off in yellow rays. The hazel-thicket was a lace-work of half-open leaves, green, and purplish stems, and the last dusky catkins. Yellow celandines in myriads were flat-open, pressed back in urgency and the yellow glitter of themselves. They were in myriads, in the abundance of May. And primroses were broad and full of a pale abandon, broad, thick-clustered primroses. And the bluebells were a thick, lush dark green, with buds rising like pale corn, while in the riding the forget-me-nots were fluffing up, and the purple ruches of the columbine leaves were getting wider, and showing a bud-knot.

He was not at the hut. She walked on slowly, hoping to find him, on towards the cottage, where he so rarely was. The double daffodils stood in tufts near the door, and the red double daisies were all out. The door was open, and he was sitting at table, in his shirt-sleeves, eating.

"May I come in?" she said, as he rose and came to the door.

"Come in!" he said, wiping his mouth, still chewing.

The sun shone into the room, which still smelled of a mutton chop done on the grid-iron. The black potato-saucepan was on a piece of paper by the white hearth, the fire was red, rather low, the bar dropped, the kettle singing.

And he had his plate with potatoes and the remains of the chop on the table, that was covered with dark chocolate oil-cloth. He had also bread and salt, a mug of beer, and a piece of cheese on a blue plate. The place was tidy, but rather comfortless. All the nick-nacks and little cloths and things that delight a woman, were gone, the yellow-painted little dresser was bare, the sofa had no soft cushions, only the same oil-cloth, dark chocolate, as covered the table.

She sat down in the Windsor arm-chair by the cupboard.

"You are very late!" she said. "Do finish eating."

"Yes! l had to go to Uthwaite," he replied, wiping his mouth again on his red handkerchief, and sitting down at table, but not taking up the black-handled knife and fork.

"Do eat!" she said.

"Shall yer have something?" he said. "Shall yer have a cup o' tea?—th' kettle's on t'boil." He half rose from his chair.

"May I make it myself?" she said, rising.

"If you like!—Tea-pot's in th' cupboard, an' th' tea's on t' mantel over your head."

She got the black tea-pot, and the tea-canister from the mantel-shelf. Putting water to rinse the tea-pot, she went to the door and threw the rinse-water down the path. How lovely it was! So still, the wood seeming so primeval, the oak-trees ochreous gold with spring. She looked at the big, hollow sandstone of the threshold, that was now crossed by so few feet.

He had begun to eat again, rather hurriedly and unwillingly. But he knew perfectly well how to use his knife and fork, and how to behave. As a matter of fact, he knew how to behave in most ways, and even how to speak correctly, at least much more correctly than the way in which he usually spoke. His broadness was wilful. So were his manners.

She made the tea, in silence, and he pushed his plate aside, and cut bread, eating large mouthfuls, chewing steadily, and eating the cheese simply, taking it with his fingers.

"Shall I take your plate away?" she said, leaning over and lifting his plate from the table.

He looked up at her with an amused little laugh.

"If you've a mind," he said.

And she tramped across the uneven brick floor, to the dark scullery at the back.

"You'll see milk i' t' pantry," he called.

She opened another door, and in the white-washed, narrow pantry found a little milk-jug. The place was clean and bare. But there was a barrel of beer.

"How do you get your milk?" she said.

"Flints' leaves me a pint in a bottle, at th' warren gate, an' I fetch it when I can. That's what I was goin' for that time—you know—"

She remembered the time he met her, but she did not speak.

"Ay—" he said, laughing at her. "You thought I shouldn't catch you, didn't you? Yet that was the first time you *come*, wi' me—"

It was not a question, but a reminder that he had heard her short, sharp cries of passion. He was watching her curiously, to see if she resented it.

"Will you have a cup of tea too?" she asked him.

"Don't mind if I do," he said, finishing the beer.

She found two cups in the cupboard, and the sugar, but no spoons.

"Where are spoons?" she said.

He reached and pulled open the table drawer in front of her—he was sitting with his back to the wall, the light of the window falling sideways

161

on him. She took the spoons, and put herself a chair at the table, facing the window and the open door.

"Ay!" he said. "That's where my wife sat. I c'n fancy I'm set up again, can't I? Not so much to your fancy, though, I'll be bound!"

His eyes were laughing at her tauntingly all the time.

"I don't understand," she said, puzzled.

"I'm sayin' it looks like you was my wife, sittin' there!—You'd hardly fancy it, would you?"

"I should like it sometimes," she said, simply.

A quick laugh went over his face.

"Ay—sometimes!" he said. "You're about right! Sometimes!—I say though," he added, more seriously, "if anybody *did* happen to come an' see you—I don't know who it would be, but you never know—" He glanced at the open door.

"It wouldn't matter. They wouldn't think anything," she said.

"They mightn't," he said. "It's but a cup o' tea, when all's said an' done.—An' you like it, you say, to be my wife *sometimes*?"

"Yes!" she said. "Do you?"

"It suits *me* down to the ground—as long as it lasts," he added, less good-humouredly, apprehensively.

"Why do you say, as long as it lasts?" she reproached him.

He looked at her a long time, into her eyes, and she lowered her lids.

"Ay! Why do I?" he said at last, with vague melancholy.

He drank his tea, and sat with his hands in his pockets, in silence, while she gazed out into the sunshine. Suddenly he lifted his head, and pressed back his shoulders, stretching his body in the quiver of desire.

"Shall we go upstairs?" he asked softly.

She looked at him really startled.

"No! Not today! Not that today!" she cried.

He looked searchingly into her eyes, searching for the latent desire in her. Today he didn't find it—there was another sort of wistfulness in her look. His shoulders gradually relaxed, and the tension slowly subsided in the muscles of his body. He sank into silence again.

"Will you have some more tea?" she asked him.

He pushed forward his cup without looking at her. She poured out the rather strong tea, and watched him pour in the milk. Then at last he drank, wetting his sticking-out brown moustache, and wiping it automatically on his fingers.

"Do you like having a moustache?" she asked him.

"Me!"—And he looked at his wetted fingers. "I usually have that other cup," he said.

"It hides your mouth—one can't see what sort of mouth you've got," she said to him.

He looked up at her, smiling ironically.

"Why? Do you think it's a bad one?" he said. And with a queer face, he took his moustache in both hands and lifted it aside, sticking his mouth out a little as he did so. "There!" he said. "That's what it is!"

There was something infinitely sad, in the still, mute, rather pushed-out lips.

"Kiss me!" she whispered. "Kiss me because you like me, not because you want me."

And she looked at him pathetically.

He pushed back his chair and opened his arms, with a little gesture half of command.

"Come then!" he said.

She went over to his arms, and he bent his head over her, kissing her tenderly, and with a sort of grief, and holding her fast to his breast.

"If it's but for a minute," he said, "it's there while it lasts."

"What lasts?" she said, looking up into his thoughtful face. But he did not answer.

"Tha'rt but a lass," he said gently. "How old ar ter?"

"I'm twenty-seven, which isn't so young at all.—How old are you?"

"Are you as much as that? I'm eleven years older."

"Thirty-eight—nearly forty—!"

"Ay!"

"But you love me?" she asked.

He frowned a little.

"It looks like it," he said. "But who knows!"

"And don't you care whether I love you or not?" she said.

His eyes came back to hers, with that swift, searching look.

"Nay!" he said, with a faint smile. "What's the good o' carin'?"

She did not understand him.

"Why not?"

He pulled himself together.

"You an' me!" he said. "It's not as if we could think o' marryin'."

"Couldn't you think of it?" she asked, searching his face.

Back came his eyes to her, always giving her heart a shock.

"Why, could you?" he said.

She thought about it in a wavering fashion.

"I feel married to you in a way," she said.

His eyes began to look amused.

"Ay—*sometimes*!" he said.

"Yes! Why shouldn't I be your wife *sometimes*, as long as we live? Why must it be a regular marriage?"

He pondered her words.

"And you think it *could* be like that?" he said slowly. "Off and on, while we live?"

"Why not?" she said, pushing back his moustache with her fingers, and kissing him on those hidden lips, and quivering at her own temerity.

"Ay, why not, if it could be so!" he said, taking no notice of her.

"Why couldn't it? You wouldn't want me *always* in this cottage, always, always, always, till doomsday, would you?"

"I know you wouldn't want it yourself," he said.

"But you wouldn't *want* me to want it!" she insisted.

"No! I don't want you to want it," he repeated, smiling. "It'd be nice if you could be my wife *sometimes*, while we live: while ever we wanted it! If it could be done!"

"Why not?" she said. "Off and on!"

She was sitting on his knee, and still stroking his moustache, and touching his lips, teasing him.

"We'll see!" he said.

"Yes!" she said, clinging to him suddenly. "Let us see! Let me be your wife off and on. And you be my husband. Will you? Will you be my husband, like now: off and on?"

"Yes!" he said, in good English. "I will! I will while ever we can."

"Why not always!" she said, pressing herself to his breast.

"Sometimes always, always sometimes!" he said, smiling.

"Yes! Why not? Why not?"

"We'll see!"

"And you'll *like* me, won't you?" she said. "You won't always just want me!"

"Ay, I'll like you," he said, with peculiar acquiescence, as she rested against the unconscious rise and fall of his breast.

"And what will you call me?" she said.

"Call you?"

"Will you always call me my-lady?" she teased.

"Back your life I shall!"

"Call me Connie!"

"Connie!"

"What is *your* name?"

"Oliver."

"Shall I call you Oliver?"

"If you like."

"Oliver! How queer that you should be Oliver!"

"Why?"

"I don't know. It just seems queer.—Give me your hand, Oliver, will you?"

He began to laugh.

"Why do you laugh? It does sound queer, doesn't it? Speak to me, call me by my name."

"What am I to say to you, Connie?" he said, in a funny artificial way.

"It does sound not quite right, somehow," she said.

"We'll call one another by no names," he said hastily.

"Perhaps not. But give me your hand. Hold my hand fast!"

He clasped her hand fast in his right hand.

"There!" she said. "Now I feel safe."

He was silent for some time, as she sat on his lap, leaning her head against his chest, and holding his hand clasped. It was a moment of perfect peace.

"Ay!" he said at last. "But th' door is wide open, an' if anybody chanced to come afore we 'eered 'em!"

She rose suddenly and closed the door. Then she said:

"Then sit here in the arm-chair, and hold me still, will you? Will you? Or don't you want to?"

He rose silently, and went over to the arm-chair. She stood troubled, near the table, a little forlorn.

"Come then!" he said, with a queer, sipping movement of the head. "Come then, be a little lass, an' we'll be quiet."

She went straight to his arms, and he held her close, in silence, in the still, warm little room, with all the wild sunshine of spring outside. And clinging close like a child, she went to sleep. And he, his head drooping above her, passed also into doze, infinitely soothing and still. He was vaguely conscious, and conscious of the passage of time, and of the dog at the door. But Flossie lay down to sleep outside the door, and Connie slept heavy and still, in his lap, indoors, and his consciousness flowed vague and still and warm, like the pouring of sunshine.

And the sun moved slowly, slowly across the room, shortening, lingering, gathering itself to depart. And the dog roused outside, and settled down again with a sigh, in the shade from the sun. But the woman curled heavy in the man's lap lay still, and did not move, and his arms softly held her, as she lay against him. And he too was motionless, in a stillness, only faintly, faintly conscious of the outside world, as the soft heavy weight of the woman lay full on his life. Sometimes, at long intervals, she woke and looked up at him, and saw him looking down at her, as he lifted her and moved her a little, upon his thighs. But she quickly nestled down to him again, for fear she should have to leave him. And he leaned his face down again against her hair, and lapsed into semi-consciousness, in the pure forgetfulness which is perhaps the best experience of life.

As the sun left the room, however, she began to stir, to wake. And when it was gone, she lay against his breast with her eyes open. On the wall by the door was a big enlarged photograph of himself and his wife, at the time of their marriage: he young and alert and defiant, the woman with curled black hair, and a black satin blouse with a big brooch, rather common, vulgar.

She opened her lips after what had been an eternity, and said:

"Why do you have *that* there?"

"Eh?" he said, startled, not knowing she was awake and thinking.

"Why do you have that horrid enlarged photograph of yourself and your wife?—Was it when you were married?"

He looked at the framed carbon enlargement.

"Just after!" he said. And he looked again. It was years since he had even seen the thing,

"Why do you have it?" she persisted.

"I don't know! Folks does have 'em!" he said.

"I think they're horrid. They always look like dead people," she said.

"I don't suppose it's got much of either of us now," he said. "It's neither me nor her."

"It's hideous!" she said. "Did you like her when that was taken?"

"I expect I must ha' done, some way or other," he said.

"And do you still?"

"Me? Like her? Christ, no! I never *did* like her," he said, roused.

"But you loved her?"

"She was the only woman I had—an' I never wanted another, after her, I can tell you.—No, don't make me think about her, if you want me to feel—as I could iver like a woman."

He spoke with some violence of feeling.

"Why don't you burn it?" she said.

"Burn the likeness?"

"Yes! It's so ugly."

"I'll burn it, if you've a mind," he said.

"When? Now?"

"Ay! Now! If I'd ever looked at the thing I'd a' done it long enough ago."

She rose from his lap.

"Do burn it now!" she said.

He rose rather stiffly, stood on a chair, and lifted down the heavy, dusty picture.

"Not worth while dusting it now!" he said.

"You can save the frame if you like," she said, "though that's ugly too!"—It was!—a chocolate-coloured moulding with a gilt pattern.

"We'll save th' glass," he said, "an' that's a'!"

He tore off the brown paper from the back of the picture, and put it in the grate, where the fire was nearly out. He was very tidy, putting all the bits in the fire as he went. Then he inserted his fingers in a crack of the back-board, and pulled that out too, with a tearing noise, breaking it small and putting it on the fire, which had begun to blaze up. Then he pulled out the huge crayon portrait, that was mounted on very thick cardboard. He looked at it, with a queer expression on his face:

"A man's a fool!" he said quietly.

And putting the huge square of cardboard over his knee, he broke it across, and broke it again and again. Then he waited for the fire to sink again, so as not to set the chimney on fire. But the first bits he picked up to burn were the pieces showing his own face, and hers. When these were blazing, he fetched the pincers and pulled the sprigs out of the frame, so that he could remove the glass. The glass he carried away. Then he stoked the fire with more bits of the portrait, and went out with the frame. She followed him.

167

He went to the chopping block on the bank at the back of the house, under an old plum-tree. And there, with quick strokes, he smashed the heavy frame to pieces, so that the plaster of the moulding flew abroad.

"It's nowt but grey plaster, at that!" he said.

Then he gathered the bits of the frame, and carried them to the hearth.

"If we leave nothing," he said, "there'll be nothing for my mother to open her mouth about, when she comes a Sat'day."

He carefully swept up all the bits, and put them in the fire, continuing to burn pieces of the heavy cardboard.

"Dirty stuff to burn!" he said. "But I can poke it out tonight.—I might as well wash up while it's finishing."

"Shall I wash up?" she said.

"You? You dirtied no plates, so why should you wash 'em up."

"Then I'll dry, shall I?"

"If you like."

Curious how he had become hard and angry again, at the mere thought of the photograph.

He stood at the sink washing the dishes in boiling water, putting his fingers in the very hot water with quick haste.

"You'll scald your hands," she said.

"I'm used to it!" he replied. "I've done my own Polly-anning* long enough for that."

"Don't you mind doing your own housework?"

"I'd rather do it than have a woman in. Seems to me anybody ought to he able to do for themselves. Mother comes a Sat'days an' cleans up an' black-leads, an' takes my bit o' washin. But if she didn't, I'd do it myself What cleanin' an' sewin' an' cookin' I need I can do for myself, an' bother nobody!"

The cardboard was a red and grey mess in the fireplace. He poked it somewhat clear, and put on the frame, piece by piece. It burnt up quickly, and the plaster cracked and flew. Meanwhile he looked at the bare place on the wall.

"It shows, doesn't it!" he said. "I s'll have to nail up a Church almanach."

"Aren't you glad it's gone?" she said.

He shook his head in a queer sideways jerk of assertion.

"Ay! I'm glad to be shut of it."

He tidied up the house quickly and carefully, till it had its usual bare look of a place half-inhabited, a sort of cabin used just for meals and sleep. Then he put on his coat. It was past five o'clock, when he glanced up at the time. He mended the fire carefully with coal, to keep it going, washed his hands, and put on his hat, taking his gun.

Connie had been sitting in the arm-chair, musing, as he moved quickly and quietly about. Now, she didn't want to go.

"Shall we be going, then?" he said. "You won't be at the Hall for tea, shall you?"

She looked up at the clock.

"No," she said.

"What will they be thinking?" he said.

"I don't know," she said, with indifference, not moving.

He waited a few moments at the open door, looking out at the full ripe sunshine of the evening, and listening to the calls of the birds. Then he looked indoors again, to her who still sat in the arm-chair by the hearth.

"Shall we be going?" he repeated.

"I suppose so!" she said, rising with a gesture of impatience, and moving resentfully towards the door.

"Where's your hat?" he asked.

"I didn't bring one," she replied curtly, passing out of the door and stooping to gather one of the red double daisies, which she threaded in her dress.

"Hat nor nothing?" he asked.

"Nothing at all," she said impatiently.

He shut the door and locked it. Flossie ran round in silent joy, lifting the feather of her tail. Then she started off towards the wood.

"It's a beautiful evening!" he said.

"Lovely!" she cried, impatient at having to go home.

He looked at her closely.

"Has something nettled you?" he asked.

"No!" she said, with assumed indifference.

And again he looked at her.

"Folks'll tell where you've been, by that red daisy," he said.

"Surely they grow in other places besides at your cottage," she said, rather rudely, looking at the flower threaded into her dress.

"Ay, they may! But—" he said no more.

The wood facing the cottage was hazel brake, out of which rose the grey, twiggy oak trees. The hazels had myriad downturned buds, half opened, like a kind of dew in the full evening sunlight. And underneath was a dense, dark-green sward of dogs-mercury, without any colour but the dark green. Over this dense green poured the early-evening sunlight, and the birds already seemed very busy and happy.

Connie resented bitterly going home. Yet he walked beside her so without feeling, accepting the fact of her departure. She almost despised him, for his mechanical acceptance of facts.

He walked through the wood, alert, listening for every noise, watching everything that moved. He did not look at flowers nor trees. These he only noticed when there was something unusual. But he watched all the time, with trained alertness, for sounds and for movements. And suddenly, out of nowhere, he said to her:

"If you come to th' hut and I'm not there, an' you want to find me, what you want to do is to take the hatchet an' chop a bit o' wood. I s'll hear you—an' Flossie will. Chop a bit o' wood on th' block, you know. We s'll hear that."

"All right!" she said. But the idea pleased her.

"An' if I don't see you afore Sunday, I s'll be waiting for you at ten o'clock. An' if you don't come, I s'll walk up to th' house. That's right, isn't it?"

"That's right!" she assented.

"I won't come to th' gate with you, for fear there's somebody in th' park.—You know about that daisy, don't you?"

Again she glanced down at the inoffensive button of a flower threaded in the bosom of her dress.

"Quite! I'll throw it away in the park," she said.

He hesitated at the turn of the path.

"Well!"—he said, looking at her.

She looked up at him.

"Good-bye!" she said.

He gave a hasty salute, turned, and was gone.

She went on blindly towards the gate, and out into the effulgence of light, in the park. There, as if from force of habit, she began to hurry. The sun was sinking, in clarified gold, towards the rookery beyond the hall, and rooks were dropping home in dark specks from the sky.

Clifford had come in his wheel-chair to the top of the drive, outside the screen of the yew-trees at the corner of the curving sweep, and was sitting looking out into the living glow of the evening, that was full of the wild, uncanny disturbance of an English spring, She saw him, and waved her hand quickly, as she came up the incline. Then she stroked back her hair from her flushed face.

"It is so lovely, Clifford!" she said. "I went to sleep."

"To sleep!" he re-echoed, looking at her flushed, sensitive face, that was clear again, and fresh like spring with the warm tenderness of the flesh. Suddenly she struck him as lovely: the fresh, tender flush of her face, of her flesh, the flushed, sensitive flesh! "You went to sleep!" he re-echoed, fatherly. "But how? Where did you go to sleep?"

"In the keeper's hut, sitting in the sunshine. I went fast asleep."

She still looked as if she had only just wakened up.

"And was the keeper there?" asked Clifford.

"Not at the hut," she said. "Why didn't you come and meet me? I kept expecting to hear the chair."

"I didn't know where you'd gone," he said. "And on a day like this—especially an evening like this—" he looked up into the sky—"I was by no means sure you would want me and my chair."

"Why not?" she said quickly. "I was thinking of you, as I came home, and wondering if you were out of doors, as you ought to be."

"If there were any point in my being out of doors!" he said, with a touch of bitterness. "You look so lovely this evening, Connie! You want something different from me to come and meet you."

She stopped, and looked at him.

"Why, Clifford?" she said.

"Why!" he answered ironically. "A bath-chair, in the month of May! There goes the cuckoo, he's at it all day! I can't bear May, I wish it was always winter, and dark and rainy. Then I don't mind."

"Oh Clifford, don't! It's *so* lovely!"

"Am *I* lovely!" he said desperately. "The cuckoo only jeers at me, even the rooks. How *dare* I come and meet you, in a bath chair!—as you come flushing home like a Dryad! Why doesn't somebody shoot me!"

"Oh Clifford, don't! Oh don't! *Don't* spoil it all! It is *so* lovely. Don't say anything against it!"

She laid her hand reluctantly and tremulously on his, that lay on his steering-wheel. He controlled himself with difficulty.

"You missed your tea," he said. "Don't you want to go in and have some?"

She looked at him. She didn't want tea. But if it would please him—! Yet no! She wouldn't drink any more tea.

"It's not long to dinner now," she said, hesitating.

"You look so happy," he said, watching her with a sort of gnawing misery inside him. "*Are* you happy?"

She looked at him, startled, wondering what he saw.

"I didn't think I was so happy," she said. "But I *loved* today.—Was it horrid of me not to be home to tea?"

"My dear child, the only thing that is absolutely horrid is my existence. I ought to be shot, as a horse with broken legs is shot."

He spoke in dry, nervous anger and misery.

"No Clifford!" she said. "Stop! Stop! I won't hear any of that! I won't hear it!"

"Then don't come home looking so damned lovely," he said.

"Must I come home ugly?—Don't make me wish I needn't come home at all," she said, turning to the house. And she left him there in the chair on the drive, at the crest of the park slope.

Mrs Bolton was in the hall.

"Have you seen Sir Clifford?" she asked. "He was fretting a bit about you not being home for tea, though I said to him: *Do* leave her ladyship free, in such a small matter!—I told him you'd just be having tea at Marehay—Thursday, market-day, and no men home.—How *well* you're looking, my lady! you're a different woman!"

"I didn't go to Marehay, I went to sleep in the wood," said Connie.

"Well I never now! Well it's done you good, that's all!—We ought to have a border of those red daisies here at the Hall, don't you think? They're so winsome!"

Constance took the flower quickly from her dress.

"We might get some later on from the keeper's cottage," she said, looking Mrs Bolton in the eyes. "Some plants."

"Yes! Mightn't we!" said Mrs Bolton, flushed and excited. "There goes Sir Clifford! I'll go to the back door to him, don't you bother, my lady! I think he frets a bit when he doesn't know where you are—and *such* a lovely day! If only he'd have gone out for a drive in the motor! But I couldn't persuade him."

"No!" said Connie thoughtfully.—"I mustn't be out unless I let him know."

"That's right, your ladyship! He doesn't mind a bit if you've *told* him you'll he out—"

"But how is one always to know!" said Connie resentfully. "People make life so tight."

"I know! And if you just doze off in the sun!—But don't you bother, my lady, he'll be right in a minute now you're here."

She went to the back door, to help Clifford, and Constance went upstairs.

Dinner was a little constrained. She could not help feeling him a dead weight. And he was feeling uneasy and trammelled. She was in love with the other man, and did not get clear this evening. And she did not want to be interrupted in her flow. She wanted to be left alone. Yet after dinner he started again.

"You mustn't mind, Connie, if I grouse a bit sometimes. The spring makes it gruesome for me, you know."

"But why don't you forget!" she said. She wanted to say, *forget yourself!*—but that would have offended him.

"Quite! But when the larks go up into the air, and you have gone off into the void of spring, and I have nothing to do;—and you come home at evening lovely and expectant like a Dryad, and I sit waiting for you in a bath-chair, then I can't help thinking, why wasn't I finished off, why was I left this mutilated thing, encumbering other people's lives?—and encumbered with my own deadness!"

She frowned slightly.

"But you encumber nobody's life, Clifford," she said.

"Not yours?" he asked, with a queer look.

"No!" she said.

"Do you mean you love me as Heloïse loved Abélard, after he was mutilated?"* he said, in a queer ironic tone.

"I don't know!" she said. "I'm not Heloïse. But Abélard never wished they had *killed* him. He was very much alive and active."

"He had his feet," said Clifford.

"And his mind! and his courage! he was a brave man."

"Which you don't think I am?" he said.

"Not when you repine!" she said. "Imagine if I sat in a corner of the house on a lovely spring day and moped because you were ill! How would you like it?"

"Not at all! I'd far rather you went off into the woods like a Dryad."

"Well then! And after all, you can hear the larks, and feel the sun, and smell the wall-flowers under the window, and see the trees looking so queer and fleecy, in bud. After all, Clifford, *think* what life still offers you!—And you have the mine to be interested in, and all the things you studied in Germany, you can make use of them now!—After all, Clifford, don't be too poor-spirited to accept life, as far as you can."

He was quiet for a while.

"Quite!" he said, rather ironically. "Quite!—I suppose I've no right to cry and howl, when it comes over me, no matter how much I may want to."

"I don't think you have!" she said, rather brutally. "Why should you cry and howl! You are healthy, and have lots of interests. You are alive and well-off! Why should you want to cry and howl? If you are sure you are alive, live in every way you can live. But if you want to die—well really—don't burden other people with it—not even Mrs Bolton! I *hate* Hamletising men!"*

Again he listened in silence.

"Quite!" he said at length. "Quite! Not even Mrs Bolton!—You're quite right, Connie! Lash out at me, when you see me starting to Hamletise.—And another day, I'll come with you to the wood, if I may."

"Come then, do!" she cried. "So long as it will make you happy."

"Quite!" he said.

But when she went upstairs, she felt an irritation in her blood, and she resented it deeply.

She went down again to Mrs Bolton's sitting-room.

"I'm going up early tonight, Mrs Bolton," she said. "So if Sir Clifford rings early, you'll know! Don't get up! No, don't get up!"

"Very good, my lady."

Mrs Bolton was seated at a little table, spectacles on her nose, writing a letter. A small fire was burning in the grate. Some sprigs of pink blossom were in a jar on the window-sill.

"Peach-blossom!" said Constance, touching them.

"I'm afraid I stole it," said Mrs Bolton.

"One may just as well, the peaches are never any good.—How I love Italy when the almond and peach-blossom is all pink clouds under a blue sky!—Sometimes one wants to run away, don't you think?—even from oneself.—I seem to have known such a lovely world, and then lost it. But today was lovely. I looked in at the keeper's cottage. Did you know his wife fairly well?"

Mrs Bolton put down her pen and took off her spectacles.

"I knew her, but I never had anything to do with her. Will you sit down?"

"A minute perhaps," said Constance, sitting by the fire. "What was she like? Who was she?"

"She was a Bertha Coutts, one of those Irish Couttses that live down Beggarlee," said Mrs Bolton. "A common lot."

"Why are there Irish here? are there others?"

"Oh, quite a number of families—that's why there's that Catholic chapel at Bog End. Couttses, and Donellys, and Burns, and Mays, and Roddys, and Hunts, and Fitzpatricks—no end of them. They used to come in the old days, for harvest time. Then they got jobs at the pits, carpenters' jobs or something on the bank, not many of them went down. And so they settled. They're mostly very nice, decent people, a bit mean, being catholics. But the Couttses were a rough lot. And this Bertha was a rough one, the only girl in a houseful of lads. They went down pit, the Coutts lads. But they were low, my word! even the other colliers didn't have much to do with them. But it was a common place to live in, Beggarlee. The Parkins lived down there for a long time, till the children was growing up. Then they moved up the hill."

"Which is Beggarlee?" asked Constance—and she had to be told all about the two rows of very old cottages, miners cottages built down by the brook, in the old days when there were only gin pits. Connie thought Beggarlee rather attractive, by the old stone bridge.

"It may be all right outside, my lady, but it's a rum lot lives there. The same even now. But the Parkins moved when Oliver started to work. I think Mrs Parkin wanted to get away from the Couttses. I know they were trying to shove one another out of Beggarlee for years—till Mrs Parkin had to give in, and go. Oliver would be a lad of fourteen or fifteen then: and that Bertha, she must have been years older than he was, a brazen hussy!—Then she went away, to Sheffield or Nottingham or somewhere: not into service, oh dear no! the Couttses wouldn't let *their* girl go into service, they were above it, they were. I never knew rightly what she did: but I believe she was a bar-maid or something in some hotel. Anyhow I can remember she used to come home dressed up to the nines, and parade about showing herself off. That was what she loved, to parade about the roads in fine clothes. She dressed quite smart, she was no fool. And she'd talk in that Nottingham way, *carstle* for *castle*, all the lardy-da! But she wasn't above sitting in the pub and having half-a-pint with the men, even then.—I suppose she must have been away some years. I know I'd started nursing, when she came home all at once with a broken arm. It must be—oh, fifteen or sixteen years ago, quite. Because I used to bandage her arm for her, and she'd talk to me that superior, my word, fairly made you sick!—And then she got Oliver Parkin. She was getting on, nearer thirty than twenty, so I suppose she thought she'd better nab what she could—"

"Was she good-looking?"

"In a way! In a bold sort of way! A very good colour, and a high-and-mighty way with her, showing off! But you could tell she was a trolly. You'd only to see her go down Tevershall hill, marching in that slow way, with her head up, and looking round with her bold eyes, wanting everybody to stare at her. And clothes! my word, she had some clothes, good ones too! And jewellery!—worth a sight of money!—But where had she got it from?—*men!*—Everybody knew! Though the colliers weren't good enough for her! oh dear no, common colliers! She turned up her nose at them.—But she married Oliver Parkin as soon as her arm was out of splints, and they went to live in a new house in Chat'ley Road—"

"Why did he marry her?" asked Connie.

"You may well ask me. He wasn't one for the girls, either. Never spoke to one.—I suppose she thought she'd better marry somebody, so she got hold of him."

"But why did he let her?"

"There you're asking something. His mother wouldn't speak to him for years. Oh, old Mrs Parkin and Bertha Coutts hate one another like poison.—But I suppose her finery dazzled him. And he was young."

"How old?"

"Why how old would he be?—William Allcock was building those new houses in Chat'ley Road when their Cassie was born. And Cassie Allcock is eighteen. So it must be seventeen or eighteen years ago. And Oliver Parkin—he'll be how old? He was a lad of about—"

But Connie knew how old he was. And she silently calculated that he would be twenty or twenty-one years old when he married.

"Not much over twenty, anyhow," concluded Mrs Bolton.

"And were they happy at first?"

"Oh I don't know, I'm sure. I never heard anything of them. But I

176

know she'd be sailing out dressed up to the eyes, and paint and powder and all in the afternoon when she should have been getting his dinner ready. And he'd come home to a cup of tea and a kipper. He was working in the blacksmith's shop on the pit-bank then, and took his snap like all the others. His mother told me herself. And they used to have rows royal over *that*. She told him he could cook his dinner himself, and he told her he'd see her in hell afore he gave her a penny on Friday night: and there'd be some language, when they both started. For she could rip as hard as he could, and he was a foul-mouthed beggar. I suppose he got it from old Bob Pawney, his father; or his step-father, by rights."

"Whose step-father?"

"Oliver Parkin's. His name is Oliver Leivers, only nobody ever called him by it. His father was Dicky Leivers, a cricketer, who went off all summer professional cricketing. Mrs Leivers was only married to him a year, and Oliver was just born, when he died o' somehow, when he was away somewhere. And Mrs Leivers went and married Bob Parkin, old Bob Pawney, they called him, who was years older than she was, and a widower with two growing girls. And a bad step-mother she was to them, for they ran away to service as soon as they left school. Nobody ever heard of them, not even old Bob. And she led him a dance, too, till he was finished off. She had a demon of a temper. She fairly bullied old Bob's life out of him, and he never said a word, till he was blind drunk. Then he came out with language to make your hair stand on end, and smashed whatever he laid his hands on. They say your heart would stand still, of a Saturday night, when old Bob seized the poker and made for the cupboard, smashing cups, plates, teapot—everything he could lay his hands on—and then after her. And she running like a demon up Bestwood Lane, for the police-station.—And then next day, old Bob as still as a mouse, and she raving and tearing—! Oh my word, it was an awful house!"

"Poor little boy!" said Connie.

"Who, Oliver? Yes, it's hard on the children. But to Bob's two girls she was really cruel: made them bath in the back yard, even in winter, so they shouldn't make a slop. One of those women who wouldn't let a speck of dust settle even on the floor. Old Bob had to take off his pit-boots and trousers in the outside scullery, before she'd let him in the house. And all the children, of a muddy day, had to take their shoes off before they could come through the door. And not allowed to stir in the house: not allowed to stir, for fear they made a foot-mark on the floor. They were always in the street, freezing or snowing, raining or blowing, always in the street, shivering in other people's entries.—And then thrashed if they weren't in at eight o'clock, to go to bed."

"What a devil of a woman!" said Connie, stifling with rage. "Did she have any children by that Bob?"

"Two!—a boy and a girl! Both left home as soon as they left school. Like old Bob's own girls, who ran away when one was twelve and the other thirteen, and never heard of again, as far as I remember. Oh, she was a demon! She favoured Oliver, if she favoured anybody. But she thrashed him just the same, and I believe he hated her. He always stuck up for old Bob. He died—Bob Pawney—when Oliver was a lad of fifteen, I should think. It was before I really started nursing, but I used to go in sometimes, to see the old man. He was about sixty. They'd just moved up the hill. He died of hardening of the liver. Pitiful, he was. He used to whisper to Oliver: *Oliver, lad, could ta fetch me a pint?* And if Oliver had got threepence in the world, he'd try and sneak a pint in for his Dad. Of course it was bad for the poor old man! But what was the use! He'd got to die!—But if she, Tanky Parkin, as they used to call her, caught sight of the beer, oh, there was a scene to bring the roof down. And she'd snatch it from poor old Bob and drink it herself. And he, poor old man, would cry, really cry, when she snatched his beer from him and drank it up herself.—And Oliver would call her such names! Oh, awful! I've heard him myself, and him a lad in his teens. *I'll break your neck for you one of these days, you stinking bitch!*—I was well-brought-up myself, strict Wesleyan, and my blood ran cold.—But Mrs Parkin had a hard time of it, taking in washing to earn a shilling or two, and old Bob lingered—years, it seemed—and two children at school, Oliver just beginning to earn—And Bob had drunk himself to death—"

"Did the children drink?" said Connie.

"Not to speak of! Their father had cured them of that. When the father drinks badly, the sons are usually rather sober.—No, I never heard any harm of Oliver Parkin—except the awful language he would use when he was put out. And of course he'd sit in the pub and take his pint, but not too much, as a rule.—But people didn't care for him. He was never free and easy, and if you asked him anything, it was always: Who asked *you* anything?—so surly and spiteful.—Then when he'd been married a year or two he went as gamekeeper to Sir Geoffrey, and I hardly saw him."

"And had he still quarrelled with his mother?"

"Oh!—old Mrs Parkin!—she got converted, just after old Bob died, at one of these revivalist meetings: not Gipsy Smith, a young fellow as there was so much talk about with Hatty Smithurst. She got converted, and fell at the mercy seat, and confessed her sins, how she'd been a hard woman to her husband and her children, and if the Lord would forgive her—oh, a great show. And she went to the Primitive Chapel and to prayer-meetings, and prayed and carried on—for about six months. Then she dropped off, and now she never goes near a place of worship, and has her pint regular.—But she's much quieter, very different—and as hard as nails. The work she gets through!—And she spoils Oliver's little girl down to the ground. That's how it is, after being cruel to her own and to Old Bob's children. It's the way of the world—"

Connie was silent with dread, thinking of the awful lives people led: there in Clifford's village.

"And after Oliver Parkin came to the gamekeeper's cottage, was he happy?"

"Oh no!—She started her old games, dressing up and going off to Tevershall, and sitting in the pub. Pretending she was fetching the shopping, she'd be gone hours. And he coming home and finding the fire out, and knowing where she was—Then there'd be another row when she came in."

"But couldn't he control her?"

"It seems he couldn't. His mother says he was too soft with her the first year, and let her have her way with him, and now he's paying for it.—But she's older than he is, and a woman who'd had goodness knows what life before he married her—well, what can you expect. Though I can't quite see him being soft with anybody."

"And did she have other men still?"

"Oh, I don't think so. I don't think so. Not before the baby was born. The baby was born the year of the war—and he joined up in 1915, I believe. He said he joined up to get away from her. The cottage was shut up, and she went with the baby to live with her mother in the new buildings. And when he came home on leave he went to stay with *his* mother, not with her. I know, because there was a lot of talk. But when he came home from the war, and went back as gamekeeper to Sir Clifford, Sir Geoffrey having died, she went with the child to live with him in the cottage. But I believe it was a dog's life. Till she went off with that collier

Swain from Stacks Gate, and she said he drove her to it. That's what she always said: that her husband turned her out, and drove her to another man: that she'd been the best wife on God's earth to him for fourteen years, and then he turned her out and told her to find a man as 'ud keep her, for he'd keep her no more. And that's—but you remember when it was, between two and three years ago—three years come December: it was near Christmas time."

"And does she live with the same collier still?"

"I believe so: in that row of houses just after the level crossing at Pye Hill—about a mile out of Tevershall, that's all. But she doesn't often come into the place, she goes more to Stacks Gate and Uthwaite. She would, if she'd any shame in her."

"And is she happy with the collier?"

"They say the pair of them drink and swear together. He's a bad lot, one of the boastful, loud-mouthed, blathering sort, always talking about what *Ah* did and what *Ah* said and what *Ah* s'll do if th' bloody—you know the sort. His wife left him, and took the children. He's a rather fat fellow with sticking-out eyes, a bully, and just a bit off it, if you ask me. I don't know how she lives with him. But she says if Parkin went on his knees and licked the dust on her shoes, she wouldn't go back to him—"

"He's hardly likely to want to," said Connie shuddering.

"I should say not."

There was a dead pause. Each woman was thinking the same thing: what a man to he mixed up with. And yet, after all, it wasn't *his* fault.

"Don't you think he's a nice man at all?" Connie asked at length, a little wistfully.

"Who, my lady?" said Mrs Bolton, looking up with troubled grey eyes. She knew the intimate life of Tevershall so deeply. And somehow, it always moved her very much.

"Oliver Parkin! Oliver Leivers, you say, really!"

"That's right, my lady, Oliver Leivers!—Well—I know no harm of him, as I say, except his bad language. He seems to keep himself to himself. That's perhaps what folks have against him. He's not liked.— And then to marry that woman—"

"Wasn't there anything nice about her?"

"Oh, I don't say that! She was clean, and she never made debts. She was honest, the Couttses were that. And there's no denying she was handsome, and had a way with the men—but a bit too free for a nice man.—Perhaps she might have been all right, but for *clothes*!—and that came of being a bar-maid, or whatever it was, all those years."

"I wonder where all her clothes are?"

"Oh, he sent them after her, by Knighton's fish cart. He sent everything of hers, everything she'd ever bought. And she said an awful thing. She said he'd better cut off his member—only she used another word—you know!—and send her that, for she'd more right to it than he had, because she'd had to get it alive for him."

"Did she say such a thing in public?"

"In a public-house full of men. His mother told me. They say she was wild because he sent her things on Knighton's fish cart. But then Jacob Knighton carts things for lots of people. But that's how she behaves: as if her clothes should be sent after her in a cab with a pair of white horses.—And then takes up with an outside fellow like Swain, a man as has got himself on the brain, and isn't quite right in his head—"

Connie sighed deeply.

"What awful stories! What awful lives people have!—It makes one dread coming into contact with them."

"It does, my lady. Yet I don't know. Life's *always* awful one way or another. Better-class people's lives can be awful too, in another way. You never know. Old Mrs Parkin says that Oliver ruined that Bertha by making too much of her when they were first married. You never know how a man will be. The nastiest can sometimes be nicest. And those that seem so nice turn out the biggest swindle as a rule. My husband wasn't very nice with people. He was off-hand with them, and never wanted them in the house. Yet with *me*—ay! It's no good judging from outside!"

11

CLIFFORD WANTED TO GO WITH CONNIE into the wood. There had been some hot days, the pear-blossom and the plum-blossom had emerged out of nowhere, in creamy and silver-white, upward-breathing snows, little hills and mountains of bloom.

It was indeed cruel for Clifford, that he had to he helped from one wheel-chair to another. His legs were quite useless. But his arms and shoulders were very strong, and he was very clever at swinging himself from one place to another. And Constance hardly felt the shock any more, of lifting those long, heavy, inert legs, and covering them up.

She was sorry for him, as he puffed away all round the house, in his chair. But then, he had always believed in the immortality of the soul, or rather of the spirit, and the comparative worthlessness of the body. Nobody had stolen his soul or his spirit. He could still assert that stone walls do not a prison make, nor iron bars a cage.*

She waited for him at the top of the drive, at the turn of the loop, by the great beech-tree, as he came chuffing along behind the yew trees. His low chair, with its little motor, puffed softly, and moved at a meek, invalid pace. As he came near her, he smiled.

"Me on my foaming steed!" he called.

"Snorting, at least," she replied, laughing.

"A little nearer," he replied, as he glanced round at the long façade of the low, brown-stone house. "Wragby doesn't seem to open its eyes any wider, no matter how I'm mounted," he added. "After all, I ride upon the achievement of the mind of man, and that beats a horse."

"Quite!" she said. "And Plato's soul riding to heaven on a two-horse chariot* is all out of date since petrol."

"Absolutely! No black steed, no prevention of cruelty to animals!— We'll have some repairs done to the old place next year. I hope I may have a few hundreds in hand then."

"That will he good! If only there isn't another strike!"

"What in the name of heaven would be the use of their striking! Just ruin the industry.—It's no good, you know, Con! The human animal doesn't know when it is well off. It's worse than children: it's vicious. It's no good, there has either got to be *compulsion*, or anarchy."

"But I thought you said the other day you were a conservative-anarchist."

"So I am. People can be what they like and feel what they like, privately, so long as we keep the *form* of life intact. It's the form that matters."

"That seems to me silly—like saying the egg can go as addled as it likes, so long as we don't break the shell. But the shell will break of itself."

He was in rather high feather this bright May morning. The larks were singing over the park, the distant pit was chuffing and rattling merrily. It seemed like the old days, before the war. She did not really want to talk about strikes or any of those things. But then, she didn't want to go to the wood with Clifford at all. So, as she walked beside the chair, that edged cautiously down the incline, and the rooks rose in a hover from the hollow, she said:

"You don't think there is any solution in any form of socialism?"

"Oh don't!" he cried. "Nothing is more of an apple of Sodom than an exploded ideal. No! What the mass of the people want is *masters*."

"And who will be the masters?" she asked.

He looked at her quickly, then answered, after a pause:

"We! I! Even I!"

"But will they let you?"

"We shan't ask them. We shall do it while they're not looking.—It's for their own good: to save them from starving. Stop any part of the big industrial machine of this tight little island, and, *for the workers*, it means starvation. Not for me. I could still live without *them*. But what they must realise is that they cannot live without me. And therefore they're not going to dictate terms."

At the curve of the path, on the slope, they looked down the shallow valley at the mine, that sent up its usual white plumes and black plumes. Beyond, climbing the hill, was the glister of dark slate roofs of Tevershall, and topping all, the old square tower of the church, of brown stone like Wragby, among dark trees. The dwellings seemed to crawl up the hill in curious overlapping steps, like the scales of some long, sharp-ridged reptile, and they gave a phantasmal look to the view, gruesome and sordid.

"But will they let you dictate terms?" she said.

"They'll have to—if one goes about it quietly," he replied.

"You don't think there might be a mutual understanding between the working classes and the owning classes?" she persisted.

"Ah Connie!" he said. "Don't go back over old ground. It's no good.— Any pretence at mutual understanding is just a bluff, to cover the tug of war. Somebody's *got* to be boss of the show,"

She plodded in silence by the chair.

"It seems hateful," she said at length, "that somebody must boss and somebody be bossed."

"It's a law of nature. You, as it happens, are born into the class that bosses—"

"But I *don't* boss!" she said vehemently.

"No! Because your servants know they've got to fulfil your requests.— It's a quibble, Connie! You belong to the bossing class, and you boss: even Mrs Bolton."

"I'm sure I don't boss her."

"Ah well! You ask her to do things, and she doesn't ask you to do things—put it that way. Bossing is a sacred responsibility, like fatherhood and motherhood. And if we don't boss the miners, the country will be brought to starvation. We mustn't let it be brought to starvation. Therefore we must boss the miners—wisely, but firmly."

In spite of herself, in spite of the fact that she knew there was a great deal of sound sense in what Clifford said, Connie felt her temper rise, and she hated the very sound of his voice.

"But is there no other way?—nothing but bossing or being bossed, and owning Wragby or living in a miner's dwelling? Can't there be something else?" she persisted.

"There can if you'll tell me what. Frankly, in this issue, I see nothing. The ownership of property has now become a religious question. Neither St. Francis* nor Jesus settled it. I own Wragby, and I have to square it with my own conscience. And I know I must and *ought* to own Wragby. Supposing I give it to the Colliers for a sort of club for Tedershall!—and I myself go and live down Beggarlee! Who's the better for it? Anybody? Isn't everybody the *worse*? Don't I *still* stand for a higher level of life? Hasn't Wragby stood to Teversall as a higher level of life, for two hundred years?—Wragby is the ship that sails on ahead in the voyage of discovery, ahead of all the rag tag and bobtail small craft of Teversall. And by God, she still sails on, and is going to!"

"And what does she discover?" asked Connie, awed for a moment.

"What has she discovered in the past? Who first emerged into the open waters of liberty: Wragby! Who sailed the high seas of poetry, of art, of thought? Wragby, houses like Wragby. No Teversall dwellings. Who gradually invented the piano? Wragby! And now every collier must have his piano.—Everything the collier has, Wragby has given him, really. And all he has done, is to dig in the ground. Left to himself, the collier could dig himself blind as a mole, and nothing would come of it. There's no inspiration in mere hewing of coal. Where has the inspiration come from, for centuries? Where does it come from now? Wragby! Wragby! Wragby! The homes of the aristocrat and of the enlightened middle class, the *owners*.—What stands for all the decency, dignity, and beauty that is left in life? Wragby, and places like it."

"Then why is Teversall so hideous."

"Because the colliers have hideous souls, and can't follow the lead even of the inspiration that's given them."

"Perhaps they could if they had the money."

"Then let them *get* money."

"Everybody can't."

"Then let them make some sort of an effort after decency, and dignity, and beauty."

"Perhaps they do."

"Damned little, as far as I see."

"And perhaps you don't want them to make the *real* effort after decency, and dignity, and beauty. After all, where would *you* be, if they made that their effort?"

"Where would I be? In Wragby! And with a handsome instead of a hideous Tevershall outside my park gates."

"But Clifford, you know that men who were making a real effort after dignity and decency and beauty wouldn't consent to work for you all their lives, down a pit. Would *you* consent to it?"

"The question is artificial. It is no question."

"But *can* colliers *know* they are condemned to work all their lives down pit, for very little money, after all, and *still* make an effort after dignity and beauty? Why Clifford, you *know* that as soon as they realised that they must make an effort after beauty and dignity, they'd throw you down the mine. Therefore, perhaps, they'd better not realise it."

"Your conclusion does not follow from your premiss," he said.

But, as they went down the red-gravelled path, on which the weeds were again encroaching, in barer places of the tussocky grass she noticed cottony young cowslips still tangled in their cotton-wool, in small bud. Something stirred strangely in her. They were so tender and unprotected. Yet they would swing their little yellow bells.

"No Clifford!" she said. "You can't ask men to live for beauty and dignity and even decency, and go down a mine every day, in order to earn fifty shillings a week. They wouldn't be men if they did it."

"Well, they are *not* men, in the beautiful or truly dignified sense of the word. They are the masses. And the masses live to eat. Therefore they must work."

"No wonder they hate you," she said.

"They don't hate me. They know it as well as I do. Where is their sense of beauty? where oh where?—And where is their dignity?—Get Mrs Bolton to gossip Tevershall gossip to you, and you'll know.—What it comes to, is that they are another *race*, the *plebs*, and they've got to be ruled and we've got to be content to rule them, however much we may dislike it."

"I hope you think you'll be able to do it," she said.

"I know I can do it!—And give me a child, and I'll train him up to do it too."

"Even if it's not your own child?"

"What difference does that make? It doesn't matter who begot you. What matters is, who brought you up!"

"Then the common people aren't a race, and it's all an accident of up-bringing."

"Whatever it is, we can't alter it. The thing is thousands of years old: old as man himself. We can only carry on the *best* of it to the best of our advantage."

"It sounds almost worse than starving."

"You've never tried starving, I believe," he said.

They had come to the gate of the wood. Inside the wood, Connie was determined not to argue. She opened, and let Clifford through. In front of them ran the open cleft of the riding, between the dense hazel walls and the gay grey trees. The chair pugged slowly on, slowly surging through the forget-me-nots that crowded the drive as if they were there, with their alert little eyes, to see the procession. Clifford steered as far as possible clear of the flowers. But Connie watched the wheels go over the wood-ruff, and the dark-blue bugle, the creeping-jenny of the soft clayey place, with yellow little cups, and the still unopened columbines. All the flowers were there, and the first bluebells in blue pools, like standing water blue with heaven.

"You are quite right about its being beautiful," Clifford said. "It is amazingly beautiful. What is *quite* as lovely as an English spring!"

Connie thought he spoke as if even the spring bloomed by act of Parliament. An English spring? The chair moved slowly ahead, over dead catkins of the hazel. And between the suave brown chords of hazel stems, clumps of sturdy bluebells, like wheat, stood up, and other great grey leaves spread themselves from their rosettes.

At a cross-path they left the hazel thicket and came to the open wood, and to the up-hill slope, where the trees had gone, and the light flooded in rather stark. But there the bluebells made bright blue places, sheering off over the curves in lilac colour and deep purple. And between, the bracken was lifting its many curled heads, like many drowsy snakes coming awake in the sun. Sheets and patches of living purplish blue swept away in pure clarity between the wreckage of old roots and ricketty young trees. The brow of the hill was sheer blue, and virgin.

Clifford had kept the chair going till he got to the top of the slope, for fear of getting stuck. Constance followed slowly behind, to be alone. The oak-buds had opened soft little brown hands. Everything was so tender and full of life. Why oh why need man be so tough, always tough and insentient, hard as iron gripping the wrong things, and missing everything! Why could human life never be soft and tenderly coming unfolded into leaf and blossom? If men were leaves of grass,* why was it never tender young green grass, new and soft with spring! Even the oaks, with all their craggy hardness, that had fought so many winters, even they took off their myriad myriad gloves, and spread their tender little brown paws to the sun. Why couldn't men be like that? Why not come out of the hard sheathing and into soft new leaf?

Clifford at the top of the hill sat and looked downwards, at the green interlacing boughs, and the lovely blue of bluebells that flooded right over the broad riding, on the down slope. Downhill, downhill, it lit up like a deep sky, and warmed the heart with warm blueness.

"It's a very fine colour in itself," he said, as Connie came up. "But absolutely no good to paint."

That, too, might be true for him. So many things are true and not true, in this composite world.

To the left, in the thicker forest, ran the path that went to the hut. But thank heaven, it was too narrow for the chair, only a one-foot track between trees and guelder-rose bushes.

"Shall I venture as far as the spring?" said Clifford.

"Yes! Try!" she re-assured him.

And the chair began slowly to advance down the long slope, in the broad, noble riding, slowly sailing as down the slope of a wave, and through the blue shine of the hyacinths, slowly downwards. Oh strange ship, surging through the hyacinthine shallows!—last pinnace of adventure, on obscure oceans, steering to the last discoveries of our civilisation! Quiet and proud, like the captain at the wheel of human adventure, Clifford sat and steered: in his old black hat and tweed coat, so motionless and cautious, in his slow ship! Downhill in the wake, along the wheeltracks, came Constance, watching, going slower than he, in her grey, finely-knitted dress, no hat on her brown hair. And the chair softly curved out of sight, as the riding swerved to the right, at the bottom of the slope.

And when it had gone, the keeper came striding with long strides down the hill. She heard his steps, and glanced round in fear. He gave a hasty half-salute.

"I heard the chair-motor," he said, in a soft voice. "Shall you come tonight?"

"Tonight?" she said, looking bewildered into his eyes.

"Ay! Come tonight!" His voice was low and infinitely caressive, and his eyes held her and had power over her.

"Yes!" she said faintly.

"An' I s'll wait for you at th' gate?"

"Yes!" she murmured.

He glanced quickly round. Then he put his fingers softly under her breast, and softly pressed her breast in the cup of his hand, smiling into her eyes, his own eyes softly dilating.

"I must go," she whispered.

"I shan't come to Sir Clifford," he said.

At that moment they heard Clifford's voice, away beyond the trees in the hollow, calling *Coo-ee! Coo-ee!*

"Coo-ee!" called Constance in reply.

Then the keeper said again:

"I shan't come unless he shouts for me—I s'll be at th' hut."

She nodded, looking at him over her shoulder as she ran down the hill after Clifford. The keeper watched her running, watched her hair shaking, and felt as if in his own body the shaking of her jolted breasts. Then he turned away down the track.

She found Clifford already at the spring, a little way up the opposite dark slope, where the larch-wood bristled with a burnt-out appearance, and yet was putting out tiny little green bursts, like the tiny emerald flames bursting from the striking of many tiny matches. Great leaves of grey burdock, that they call Robin Hood's Rhubarb, shoved out from the ghostliness of the larch-wood into the damp riding. Constance hurried up, following Clifford's wheel tracks.

"She only just did it!" he said, looking at his chair. "I hope she'll get home all right."

The spring was pretty, bubbling in its brilliantly clear little well, whose

CHAPTER 11

pebbles in the depths always wavered under the crystal. Bits of eyebright and cinquefoil showed among the grass, and oh, if the keeper saw it!—a mole actually worked up into the sun.

"I shall drink, I am thirsty," said Constance. "Will you?"

"I will, yes!"

She took the little enamel cup that hung on the tree, and drank, then filled it for him as he sat in his chair.

"So icy!" she said.

"Shall we wish?" said he.

"Yes, let us!"

"Have you thought of something?" he said.

"Yes! One mustn't tell!"

But as a matter of fact she wasn't thinking of it. She heard the distant tapping of a wood-pecker, and then the cry of a cock-pheasant. Then suddenly she became aware that a wind was blowing, soft but eerie through the larches. She looked up. There were clouds moving through the blue sky. The day was too-brilliant. It had to cloud over.

"The water is so cold," he said, sipping, "one has to wish in syllables.— I guess men have wished queer things, at this well! Don't you think?"

He handed her the cup.

"Any more?" she said.

"No more. I put the full-stop after my wish. Now you must drink another drop, to wash your wish down."

She stooped, rinsed the cup, and filled it. Then she thought to herself: No, I won't wish. I might spoil my destiny. I'll leave it to the unseen powers, and not interfere.—And so she drank.

"Did you wish again?" he asked.

"Yes!" she gasped, taking no heed of what he said.

She gathered a bit of wood-ruff, and watched the mole rising to the surface, swimming out of the soft earth with its broad little pink hands and waving little pink snout.

"See the mole?" she said.

"Where?—Ah there! Wonder Parkin hasn't had him!—What a life, eh, burrowing and worming your way down in that brown earth! Unpleasant little beasts!"

"You would think he could see with the pink tip of his nose!" said she. "Do you think he smells, or what does he do, waving his nose-end in the air?"

189

"Like a parson in a pulpit," he said.

She gave him the wood-ruff to smell.

"New-mown hay!" he said, with his ironic smile. "Oh ghosts of nineteenth century ladies!"

"Did they like it?" she said.

"I remember it in that dull Foguzzaro,"* he said.

She was looking up at the sky.

"I wonder if it will rain later!" she said.

They started home, Clifford steering carefully downhill, over the damp, clayey earth of the uneven riding. Then they came to the bottom of the hollow, and swerved to rise up the long slope, where the bluebells spread out like flood-water that is tilted but stands still.

"Now old girl!" said Clifford, starting the motor.

"I suppose she'll do it!" she said.

He did not answer.

The chair tugged slowly, unevenly up, with palpitating little jerks. She was not doing very well. But she came to the hyacinths that were blue around her, and with more jerks she struggled just beyond them. Then she stopped.

"You'd better call Parkin!" said Connie. "He will perhaps be at the hut."

"We'll let her breathe," said Clifford.

He waited a while, then started his little motor again. The chair made funny coughing noises, and reeled on a few yards, as if it were sick.

"Call!" she said.

"Wait!" he snapped.

And he had another go. With even worse results.

"Call!" she said.

"Hell! Be quiet a moment!" he said.

The chair made other efforts, more harmful than useful.

"You may just as well call, Clifford! Why waste your nervous energy!" she said.

"Any other time, the fool would have been poking his nose in," said Clifford crossly.

"Coo-ee! Coo-ee!" she called.

And almost in a moment, Parkin came striding down the slope. He saluted as he came close, then walked straight to the chair and stood with feet apart, looking down at it.

"I thought I heard trouble," he said. "Won't she do it?"

"Appears like it," said Clifford shortly.

Parkin crouched at the side of the chair, to look at the engine.

"You're sure there's enough petrol?" he asked.

"Quite! Field filled her up."

Parkin got up, leaned his gun against a tree, took off his coat, and sat down on his heels at the side of the chair, peering underneath. He touched various parts, poking awkwardly. Then he sat again on his heels, and pushed his hat off his forehead, rubbing his brow.

"It's nothing as I can see!" he said.

Then he lay on his stomach on the floor, and with his neck pressed up, fiddled at the engine, poking intently.

"I don't suppose you can do anything," said Clifford, looking down at the man on the floor.

"I don't suppose I can.—Connections seems all right!—" Parkin got up till he sat on his heels again, collier fashion. "Start her again, Sir Clifford!" he said.

Clifford tried her again—to no effect.

"Run her a bit hard, like."

Clifford made the poor little engine cough and buzz and snarl, then cough more violently; then she seemed to run free.

"Sounds as if she'd come clear!" said Parkin. "Start her."

But Clifford had already put the chair in motion. She surged feebly forward, as if she were dying.

"If I give her a push, like!" said the keeper, going behind.

"Wait a bit!" said Clifford, "Let her do it! She ought to!"

Constance sat on a bank and watched as the chair gaspingly edged a few inches further. As far as her-ladyship was concerned, there was only one course to take in the case of breakdowns: just go away and leave the men to it.

But she was amused once more by the busy, interested free-masonry of men, as soon as it was a question of machinery. Then indeed class difference broke down a little. Parkin was no longer a gamekeeper: he was much freer and more active, perhaps as when he was in the war, and drove a lorry. And Clifford was the officer, a little impatient with the Tommy, a bit out of temper, but not at all the *employer*.

The chair, as if dying of heart-disease, came to an end amid a peculiarly fine patch of blue-bells. There she leaned, like a derelict run aground in shallow water. Constance moved a stage nearer.

"She won't do it! She's not got power enough," said the keeper.

"She's done it before," said Clifford.

"I'm doubtin' she won't do it this trip, though. You'd best let me push her, Sir!"

Clifford did not reply. He began running his engine fast again, making a weird noise that must have gone to the hearts of the wild creatures of the wood. Then he put the motor into gear, with a jerk.

"You'll rip her guts out," murmured the keeper.

But the chair charged in a sick swerve sideways.

"Clifford!" cried Connie, rushing forward.

But the keeper had seized the chair by the rail. Clifford, however, putting on all his pressure, managed to steer into the riding, and with a strange tearing noise the chair was fighting the hill. Parkin pushed steadily from behind, and the poor thing laboured up.

"You see she's doing it!" said Clifford in triumph, looking for a second over his shoulder. There he saw Parkin's red face.

"Are you pushing?"

"Ay, she won't do it without."

"Leave her alone. I asked you not—"

"She won't do it by herself."

"*Let her try*—" commanded Clifford. "She's *got* to do it. "

The keeper dropped a pace into the rear, and turned back for his coat and gun.

The chair immediately seemed to choke. Clifford, seated a prisoner, became white with anger. He fought with the machine. Strange noises came out of her. She gave little lurches. Then she could move no more. Strange noises came out of the poor thing. Clifford moved little handles. But she did not budge. He stopped the engine.

"Ah, the cursed thing!" he said, glancing round.

Constance was there, seated on the bank, looking at the wrecked and trampled bluebells. The keeper strode up with his coat and gun. Flossie stood with her nose in the air, wondering. And Clifford asked Parkin to look at something or other in the engine.

Connie, who knew she knew nothing about motors, also knew she'd better *say* nothing. Parkin lay down on his stomach, his feet wide apart, and poked in behind the wheel in a busy way. Connie looked at his body lying there—was that how he looked when he lay with her?—and thought that somebody had to boss, and somebody had to be bossed.

It looked like it! she thought ironically. But Parkin managed to be very little bossed.

He got to his feet again, and said quietly:

"Try her again, Sir."

Clifford tried her, and Parkin went behind and gave her a gentle shove. She began to move. But Clifford glanced round, yellow with anger.

"Will you get off there!" he cried. Then he added, "How shall I know what she's doing—"

Parkin stepped smartly aside, like a soldier. Then, with an air of finality, he began to put his coat on. He was out of it.

The chair began slowly to move backwards.

"Clifford, your brake's not on!" cried Connie, again rushing to the rescue.

But Clifford had pulled a light lever, and stopped the chair. There was a moment's dead pause all around.

"It is obvious I am at everybody's mercy!" said Clifford.

But this too fell into silence. Clifford was yellow with anger, Constance was silent as was her wont on such occasions, and Parkin was slinging his gun over his shoulder, a peculiar little expression on his face. And the dog Flossie, sitting on her haunches behind her master, moved uneasily, eyeing the chair with great suspicion and dislike, and terribly perplexed among the three human beings.

In the silence, a cock-pheasant bolted across the riding absurdly, streaming his feathers and craning his silly neck. Everybody refused to speak. The *tableau vivant* remained motionless among the squashed bluebells.

"I'm afraid I rather lost my temper with the infernal thing!" said Clifford at last.

"It *is* annoying!" said Constance.

"Do you mind pushing me home, Parkin?" said Clifford. "And excuse anything I said," he added rather offhand.

"It's nothing to me, Sir Clifford!"

Even then, it was not easy to get the chair started, for the brake was jammed. They poked and pulled, and the keeper took off his gun and his coat once more. But Clifford said never a word. At last the keeper lifted the back of the chair up bodily, Clifford in it and with a sudden dexterous jerk, tried to loosen the wheels, unconscious of everything save his determination to get the thing free. Clifford clutched the sides of the chair in peril, as the chair tilted, but he did not look round. The veins in the keeper's neck were swollen, something seemed to be going to burst in his body, yet he kept the chair off the ground, and gave another snatching jerk at the wheel. The chair reeled.

"For God's sake!" cried Clifford, in agony.

But the wheel was free, the breath came out of the keeper's nose like a split tyre, his eyes seemed to be coming out of his head. He stood panting, while the chair leaned against him.

"Is she free?" asked Clifford.

"Ay!" came the gasp.

Then the keeper looked round. Then he looked at Connie.

"Bring me that bit of log," he panted quietly.

Constance brought the piece of tree-root, and he scotched the chair. Then he went and sat on the bank.

"I'll sit down a minute!" he said, his eyes unconscious because of the beating of his heart, his hands trembling.

Connie looked at him. But she sighed and said nothing. One must boss, the other must be bossed! There seemed a shameful irony in it.

All three were silent. Even the dog was motionless. The back of Clifford's head did not move. The sky was clouding over.

At last Parkin sighed, and getting a red handkerchief from his coat, blew his nose.

"It's a bit of a strain, holding that chair up," he said, as he rose to his feet.

"Quite!" said Clifford.

To Connie, it seemed wonderful that such sudden strength had come out of the keeper's body. He was not a powerful man: and lying flat on the floor, poking at the engine, he had looked a bit pathetic, not at all large and burly. Yet that sudden strength could come into him, into his limbs and breast and loins.

He slung on his gun without putting on his coat.

"Shall *I* carry your coat?" she said, holding out her hand.

"I can hang it here, my lady!" he said, in a low voice, pushing the coat into the handle of the chair. Then he stooped, and pulled out the scotch, putting his body against the chair.

"Are you ready then, Sir?" he asked.

"When you are," said Clifford.

The keeper put his weight against the chair: the thing was very heavy,

Clifford was a heavy man. But it moved slowly, and slowly, step by step, Parkin pushed it up the hill. He was rather pale, paler than Constance had ever seen him. Constance was angry with Clifford, for not having let him help the engine, while the engine still had *some* power. She did not like to see the sweat on Parkin's brow, and his face pale. She came suddenly to his side, and putting her hand on the back of the chair, began to push with all her woman's spasmodic energy. Parkin looked at her, and shook his head. But she nodded her head fiercely.

The chair ran swifter. Clifford looked round.

"I am helping," said Constance, in a hard voice, determined and dangerous. "I'm afraid Parkin has strained himself."

"No, I can manage," said Parkin. "I'd rather your ladyship left go!"

"I'll help to the top of the hill," she said, panting already, and shifting her hand till it touched his hand: that was brown, with the veins sticking out. And she thought fiercely: I'm going to sleep with him tonight!—And he, looking at her soft hand, gripped there beside his own, thought: I'm going to have her altogether tonight!—and a queer flamey strength seemed to move deep in his back, taking away his sense of exhaustion after effort.

Clifford sat still, and neither looked round nor spoke.

At the top of the hill, Constance was glad to let go. It made her heart beat. She walked apart. She had had visions of friendship between these two men. As leave think of friendship between fire and water, or iron and the living flesh.

In the park, Constance wanted to help push the chair again, but Parkin wouldn't let her.

"I'd rather you wouldn't, your ladyship. It runs easy here."

So she let him do it alone, sweating and panting, step by step. When the motor was running even a little, it made it so much easier. Now, it was a dead weight. And the sky was grey.

Parkin did not speak at all. Clifford made a little conversation with Constance, about Lady Eva, who was at Dieppe, and about Sir Malcolm, who had written to ask whether Connie would drive with him in his two-seater, across France, or should they go by train, or else get Hilda to drive them all the way, all three, in her larger car.

"I'd really rather go by train," said Constance. "I don't like motoring long distances. But I shall do what Hilda wants."

"She will want to drive her own car," said Clifford. "And your father will hate being driven—"

"I suppose that's how it will be," said Constance.

They came at last to the back door, and Clifford was helped into his house chair.

"Well thanks awfully, Parkin, I'm afraid it was harder work than you bargained for. I must have a different sort of motor to that chair. Go to the kitchen and have a drink of beer, won't you! Do!" said Clifford, but in a rather forced voice.

"No thank you, Sir Clifford! I'll be getting back to th' wood!"

He ducked out of his gun, put his coat on, ducked into his gun again, saluted, and was gone. Connie looked at him, but he never looked at her. But she was angry with Clifford, and went upstairs.

Clifford must have known what she felt, for at luncheon he said:

"I'm afraid I was a bit short with Parkin. But the fellow shouldn't interfere."

"He was only trying to help the chair," said Constance.

"But I don't want help that I don't ask for," said Clifford.

"Perhaps the chair did. And it would have been so much easier. I can't understand you."

"I know," said Clifford, "your sympathy is always with servants and underlings: perhaps because you can feel benign and godlike towards them. But it will do Parkin no harm to sweat a little. Take some of the modern impudence out of him."

"Weren't you impudent to *him*!" said Connie rudely.

"Not as far as I am aware. Of course you, in your zeal for the servant-classes—I had almost said the servile classes—may have detected ill-treatment of the poor downtrodden Parkin. But that is your one weak point."

"What is my one weak point?"

"Your feeling of sympathy and kinship with the servant class."

"And what is the servant class? Because Parkin sweated and nearly broke a blood-vessel and pushed you home, is he the servant-class?"

"Apparently—or he wouldn't be in the position of having to do it."

"He'd be sitting in your chair with paralysed legs, waiting for *you* to push *him* home!—I see *you* doing it, too!"

"My dear Connie, this promiscuous mixing-up of people's persons and personalities is at least a little vulgar."

"And your ingratitude is very vulgar."

"Must I be grateful? I pay the man. Is he to do nothing for me?"

"Not unless you feel a bit of human gratitude to him."

"But my dear child, I'm infinitely obliged to him, as I told him. Would you have me shed a tear over his horny hand, that kind of thing?"

"I'd have you be *aware* of people."

"And I'd have you a little *less* aware of that kind of people, and a little *more* aware of the people who are, after all, of your own sort and class."

"Who is of my own sort and class?" she said, rudely.

"That you must answer yourself, I suppose. As to myself, I tell you once more, I refuse to have personal emotions about people who do not concern me personally. Parkin is my game-keeper. Basta! Leave him as such. He is a good game-keeper. If I started having personal emotions about him, he would become a bad game-keeper. Therefore leave him alone."

"But he's a *man*."

"What does that mean? He is one of the modern working class, uneducated, of a very, very narrow range of intelligence, extremely limited in outlook, of a similar clumsy and narrow emotional range, in fact, incapable of being anything but what he is, a gamekeeper at two pounds a week. Believe me, a capable man earns money, and two pounds a week is apparently Parkin's value on the market."

"Life is not a market."

"Every living thing, and every dead one, comes at last to market and is priced," said Clifford.

"And how much would *you* fetch?" asked Connie in amazement.

"I? I think you know. I am worth about thirty thousand pounds in real estate, and—"

"Oh don't!" said Connie. "You estimate Parkin's price as he stands in his shirt, and you yourself claim all Wragby and the rest to give you value."

"My dear child, they are mine. They are my shirt, so to speak."

"No wonder you have no nakedness, and never did have," she said.

"I prefer you when you are not cryptic—but since it's one of your few vices—"

"And you don't rule!" she said. "People like you are only gaolers who keep people working with threats of starvation if they don't. I don't call that ruling."

He turned away, very angry. But she was perhaps angrier still.

However, she had promised to spend the night with the keeper; that was revenge enough. "Every living thing, and every dead one, comes at last to market and is priced."—And that settled it. The market value was absolute! The only point was that somebody set the price, and somebody paid it.—Well, she herself would pull the labels off. After all, she was not the doll in the song, to twist her neck to look at the fellow marked two-and-three, and despise the cheaper colonel on the tin gee-gee.*

Or was it that, having *got* the more ruling fellow, she now wanted to ogle the serving one? Clifford would have said so.

But she was not going to analyse herself. She had to make her plans for the night. She would have to steal away from the house like a thief, and act a lie, even if she did not tell one. But this did not trouble her. She had long since thought that out. It all was solved by the proverb: What the eye doesn't see, the heart doesn't grieve.

She really didn't want to hurt Clifford's heart. So she must spare his eye. Because after all, a feeling that comes just because you know something in your mind, is a spurious sort of feeling. If there had been any real bodily connection between her and Clifford, she could not have betrayed him. But there *was* no bodily connection, none, alas! Therefore why should she start false excitements in him, by telling him things?—or even by letting him suspect? It would be far more cruel to him, than quietly going her own way. Because he knew well, she did not believe in self-immolation, and was not going to practise it, beyond what was necessary.

And she had a real hatred of feelings and emotions which were merely provoked from the mind. If Clifford *knew* she was going to the game-keeper, what a night of fever, excitement, pornographic imaginings, and jealous torment for him! If he knew nothing, it would affect him not at all. Therefore let him not know. There is a time to chew, and a time to eschew, the apple of knowledge.—She made this joke grimly, in her own mind.

She went downstairs to dinner calmly, with her naïve, demure bearing. Clifford was reading Proust. It was not often he really read seriously any more, but when he did, it was the ultra-modern, so-called futuristic writers, who grouped round Joyce or Proust. In the same way, he no longer cared for his old favorite in painting, Renoir, but preferred younger men like Matisse. He called Renoir "sweet" and Cézanne "humanitarian".

Constance, on the other hand, found herself wearied by Joyce and Proust, and only very mildly interested in the clever tricks of Matisse, or, in music, of Stravinsky. There were amusing tricks: but they were still tricks. Clifford, however, being in a certain mood of roused alertness, was immersed in Proust.

"But doesn't he weary you at all?" she asked.

"Not at all! He stimulates me."

"But it is a false stimulant."

"Why so!"

"You said you were stimulated by *Ulysses*. But you were so drab and irritable later on, and it took all the work of the mines to get you out of it. It is a perverse activity of the will."

"My dear Connie, I know your nature is evangelical. Mine, on the contrary, is anarchic. Shall we leave it at that?"

"You! Anarchic! Why you hate the Russians—"

"As usual, you speak like an angel and an evangel. I did not say I was a *political* anarchist. If there is one thing I hate the thought of, it is social or political anarchy. In politics, I want *rule*, strong, firm *rule*, to keep the machine of the social order running smoothly. But emotionally, artistically, I am an anarchist; and I enjoy it."

"It makes you very dead, really."

"There speaks my evangelical little wife."

"Quite! There's no such thing as anarchy, really. It is only spite which makes you pull all the petals off the rose, and arrange them cleverly round a chicken-bone, and call *that* the true rose, rose of all roses."

He listened, and suddenly laughed.

"I like that!" he said. "The stem of the rose is a chicken-bone, and the heart of the rose is the knuckle of the bone, but the petals—"

"Oh, you stole those from a real rose. That is all that I can see in even the best of anarchistic art. It's all simulacra, and trimmings round a void, and clever furbelows on an empty skeleton."

"Why shouldn't we get pleasure, even out of that?" he asked smiling.

"Because you yourself become unpleasant, like the trimmed-up void."

"Or the furbelowed skeleton, or the rose on a chicken bone. If you were not an evangelist by profession, you would be an artistic anarchist by nature."

"Then I stick to my profession," she said, a little breathlessly.

"Oh do! We should feel very much like the naked chicken-bone, if you took away all the rose-leaves of your professional angelicism."

But he sent a chill to her inmost heart, a sense of dread also, as if the North Pole had drawn near, to silence all life. The cold, deliberate will which lies inside the emotional anarchist was horrible. It was like wrestling with a skeleton. Queer, that tonight, when she was going to her lover, she should find herself wrestling with the cold skeleton of Clifford's abstract will. She was in the arms of Clifford's skeleton will, and the cold void between the ribs of the skeleton was pressed on her heart.

She went upstairs early, took a bath, and lay in her bed awhile. At half-past-nine she got up, slipped a dress over her batiste night-dress, threw her pyjamas on the bed, as she did in the mornings, and went to the head of the stairs. The light was still burning in Clifford's room. She opened the door of the service stair-case. The servants had not gone to bed.

She went back to her room, put on rubber-soled shoes, a thin, dark coat over her dress, and softly went down into the hall. Marshall had not locked up. He made the round of the doors about ten o'clock. She softly opened the door of the hall, put her key in the yale lock, and closed the door without letting the catch click. Marshall would push the heavy bolts in a few minutes.

She was not afraid. If she had met anyone, she would just have said: I am going for ten minutes walk in the park, before I go to bed.—A half-moon was shining. No-one would be surprised. And in the morning, she would just walk in when the doors were unfastened, about half-past seven: or even go in through the kitchen: and say the same:—I went for a walk in the park.—She had gone out in the early morning before. She loved the hour. No-one would be in the least surprised. And her bedroom she had left exactly as she left it in the morning, when she got up. If the maid went in, everything was perfectly natural. The only possible risk was that something quite unusual would happen in the night, sufficient to make it necessary for her to be called. But that was a remote risk. She walked quietly across the half-lit park, with a certain hardness in her heart.

It was this that made her sad. The day had so hardened her heart, she could not unharden it. And it was the wrong heart to be taking to such a rendez-vous.

As she got close to the park gate, she heard him softly open it for her. So! he was there! She almost wished she could have been left alone, quite alone, tonight. Her heart was in the wrong mood.—But she had to submit to the chain of circumstance.

"You're well on time," he said quietly, as she brushed past him.

"Yes!" she said, looking at her phosphorescent watch: five minutes to ten. "It was perfectly easy."

He closed the gate silently, and strode after her down the broad riding, where a strip of light fell from the low moon. But she walked in the shade. And he walked at her side, not touching her, in silence. Neither of them could say anything. She was feeling a little hard, and a little hostile, as she tramped in the dew over the grass and flowers of the riding. The night was perfumed with flowers, though it was too early for honeysuckle.

As she went up the slope beyond the long dip, she suddenly asked him:

"Do you feel all right? I was so afraid you'd strained yourself this morning, lifting that chair."

"No, I'm all right," he said. "I'd forgotten it was only this morning. It seems a long time since, doesn't it?"

"Years!" she said.

They trudged on again in silence. She seemed to hear all sorts of sounds in the wood.

"There are strange little noises!" she said, standing still to listen; and he stood also.

"It's the trees, expanding or contracting, and rubbing against one another," he said. "They're always moving and easing themselves. You could sometimes say they was talking."

"How queer!" she said, moving on again.

At length she saw the yellow light of the cottage, and again she stood still.

"Did you leave a light?" she said.

"I allers leave a light at night," he said. "Then nobody knows if I'm in or out. But I blow it out when I go to bed."

She felt curiously detached from him, and from his voice. And he, in his quiet, almost correct speech, seemed to know it.

He quietly unlocked the door, and bolted it when she had entered. There was a red fire, a singing kettle, and the table set with plates and tea-cups and a white cloth.

"Shall you eat something?" he asked her.

"No thank you! But you eat."

He stood hesitating.

"There's pork-pie, and cake, and cheese—" he said.

She looked up at him. He was a little pale and remote.

"No, I won't eat anything," she said. "But you eat."

"Not if you don't," he said, going to the pegs to hang up his coat and his hat.

"I shall take off my shoes," she said. "My feet are wet with dew, in these canvas shoes."

She sat down in his arm-chair, and slipped off her tennis shoes, putting her feet on the shining steel fender. The room was warm, after the chill night outside. She still had on her coat.

He sat in a small chair back against the wall. Above his head was the big sheet of the parish almanach, nailed up where the "likeness", as he called it, had hung.

"But *you* eat!" she said. "Do have something! I'm sure you eat at this time, don't you?"

"A bit of bread and cheese, maybe," he said.

"Well, do eat it now."

He seemed to think about it. Then he said:

"Nay! I don't feel like eating, if you don't."

She looked at him. Why should her not eating prevent him? But she left it.

She was getting hot. She stood up and slipped off the thin coat, then looked again at the parish almanach. He, in his shirt-sleeves, had bent over and was unfastening his leggings.

"Tell me," she said. "Tell me, if you don't mind, what made you marry your wife!"

He lifted his face, flushed with stooping forwards, and looked at her with puzzled eyes.

"What made me marry her?" he repeated vaguely.

"Yes!" And she looked into his eyes. "You didn't really *love* her when you married her, did you?"

He met her searching eyes for a moment. Then he took his two leather gaiters, put them together, and laid them by the wall at the side of the chair, saying as he did so:

"I don't know as I ever loved anybody—or ever knew what it meant, if it comes to that."

Then he stooped and began unlacing his heavy boots, that looked so ponderous beneath the legs in their dark worsted stockings.

Connie pondered a minute. Perhaps she did not know either.

"But you didn't even like her, did you?" she persisted. "At the time you married her, did you even *like* her?"

There was something insistent, almost magisterial, in her question. He put the toe of one boot to the heel of the other, and shoved this boot off.

"Why!" he said. "It's all bygone, an' can't be helped nor altered now—" He spoke with a queer unwillingness and apology. "What does it matter, now?"

And he stooped to unlace the other boot.

"It matters," she said. "Your wife is the third party. You haven't forgotten her. And I don't understand. I should like to understand what was between you."

He pulled off the second boot, and set it beside the first. Then he went to the scullery, fetched the coal-shovel and a piece of sacking, and taking his boots, began carefully to free them of mud and clay, scraping the dirt into the coal-shovel.

"Do you think you need bother yourself about it?" he said, looking up at her with the same unwilling eyes.

"I should prefer to know," she said; "because it puzzles me. But I don't want to if you'd rather not tell me—"

The dog rose from a shallow box where she had been quietly lying, and came softly, gingerly across to him, stood looking up at him. He looked down at her abstractedly. She vaguely waved her tail, still looking at him.

He lifted his head and said to Constance:

"It doesn't matter to you, does it, why I married or didn't marry?"

"Yes!" said she, frowning slightly. "I think you must have had such an awful boyhood, with your mother and that father who wasn't even your father! ghastly!—And then to marry that woman who was older than yourself, and must have been instinctively much *lower* than you were—"

He had let his hand slip from his thigh, and hang at his side. The dog softly intruded her nose into the hollow of the fingers, and softly put her head sideways, as his hand unconsciously closed round her brown face, in a motionless caress. And so the gentle bitch sat still, with her cheek nestling against his hand. Till his fingers softly began to touch the silky mat of her hanging ear.

He lifted his eyes again and looked into Constance's eyes.

"Who's been talking to you?" he said.

"Oh, I asked Mrs Bolton. But I *asked* her! Naturally I wanted to know about your life."

"You'd hear nothing rosy from Mrs Bolton," he said, with slow irony.

"Rosy! No indeed! Dreadful!—But it seemed so queer, that you married that Bertha Coutts."

"Why queer to marry her, more than anybody else?" he said.

"I don't know! I got an impression of her—and of Beggarlee and the Couttses—all rather awful. I think you had a *very* hard childhood—" she lingered and paused.

"It might seem hard to one of your sort, maybe," he said. "It was no harder than anything else. It would be harder for me to have to live in Wragby. An' I'd as leave marry Bertha Coutts as Sir Clifford, comes to that. It's the way you look at it."

"Perhaps!—When you were a boy, at Beggarlee, did you know her then?"

"Yes, I knew her. The Coutts lads, Dan and Jim, was my chief pals. They gen me my tea i' *their* house, many a time, when my mother wouldn't have us in."

"And they were very common—*low*?"

"They might'a bin! But they was as good as me. An' they'd give yer as much bread-an'-drippin' for your tea as you wanted: which was more than my mother ever gave anybody."

"And how much older was she than you?"

"Five years."

"And how did she treat you when you were a little boy?"

"I don't know as she iver took much notice of me. And I took none of her."

"Didn't you like girls?"

"I kep' away from 'em."

"But with low boys like the Coutts boys—?" she said.

"What?" he asked.

"Didn't they go with girls? Weren't they rather horrid, with girls?"

"Oh, they talked a lot of dirty talk. They said fuck! an' shit! if yer said anything to 'em. An' I did same. But they had no more idea of girls than I had, afore they went to pit an' began to get on towards being men."

"And did they go with girls then, or with women?"

"I don't know. With what they could get, I suppose. That is, sometimes! Once in a blue moon."

"And did you do the same?"

"No! I kep' clear of women."

"All the time till you were married?"

"Yes."

"Were you virgin when you married Bertha Coutts?"

"I didn't know as men was iver virgins."

He twisted the dog's ear round and round.

"But you'd never been with a woman?" Constance insisted.

"No!"

"Why not?"

"I didn't want to."

"But you *like* women—or you like *woman*—" she emphasised.

He did not answer this.

"And did you never go with a woman before you went with Bertha Coutts?"

"No, I never did."

"Then why did you go with her?"

"'Appen she made me," he said, with the faint twist of a smile. His face was pale and strained. He looked down at the dog, which looked up at him.

"Dost want thy supper?" he said to Flossie, in an artificial voice.

He picked up the shovel and went into the scullery, the dog at his heels. In a minute Connie could hear the dog lapping something in the darkness. But he was slow returning.

When he came back at last, silent in his stocking feet, and sat in the chair away against the wall, carefully wiping and drying his boots, Constance returned to the charge.

"Tell me how she made you take up with her," she said.

He looked up, his face hard.

"Have I got to tell you?" he said, queer and hard.

"Yes, do tell me. I feel it is important."

"Why?" he asked softly, almost mocking.

"If you and I are to be more than just mixed up in an affair—and I think we *are* more than that—then it is—it is important to me."

He stared away into the air for some time in silence. Then suddenly he said:

"Ah well, I told *her*, an' she was the first. I might as well tell *you*, as is the second." He paused, and Connie waited. "When I was a lad of about eleven or twelve," he said, "I went in their house one night, winter-time, for Dan an' Jim. An' there was nobody in only her—"

"Bertha?" said Constance.

"Bertha! An' I dunno what she said. On'y I know she lifted her clothes up an' showed me—you know what.—They wore them split drawers then, girls did."

He came to an end.

"And what did *you* do?" said Constance.

"I did nothing."

"What did she want you to do?"

"She wanted me to come an' feel. But I never knowed afore then, as women had hair there. Black hair! An' I don't know why, it upset me an' made me hate the thoughts of women from that day."

"But what did you do? What did you say?"

"I don't know. I suppose I ran off."

"And did she never say anything to you again, then?"

"No!—She went to Sheffield a bit after."

There was a pause. Constance pondered.

"And you hated the thought of women because they have hair the same where men do?"

"Yes! I know now I was a fool. But that was it."

"And you went on hating the thought of them?"

"Yes."

There was a long pause.

"And then when she came back—how old were you?"

"When she came back afore we got married? I was just twenty-one."

"And she was twenty-six?"

"I suppose so."

"And how did you come together?"

"Well! When she looked at me, I knew she remembered. And she knew as I'd never been able to forget. So she sort of made up to me. And so we got married. I was in th' blacksmith's shop then."

"And when you were married, didn't you mind any more about the black hair?"

He was silent. The dog came padding to him.

"Go an' lie down!" he said to her softly. And softly, she went.

Constance waited for an answer.

"Yes!" he said at last. "I couldn't touch it. I couldn't do nothing to her."

"And what did she say."

"She said, wait a bit. An' we waited. An' then she asked me about everything, an' I wouldn't tell her. But she never got mad with me, an' never threw it up at me. She seemed as if she wanted me to be all right. So in the end I told her: an' she cried.—She cried a' one night. Then in the morning, she said, if I shaved her. An' so I did, an' she laid there so still. An' then it come up in me, an' I wanted her—"

He came to a stop, there was silence.

"And you loved her!" said Constance, in a low voice.

"Ay—for a time," he murmured.

Again there was a long pause.

"Then why did you leave off loving her?" said Constance, still rather dully.

"Why—!" he said, rather bitterly. "I suppose I was so pleased with myself, and with her for having me, I made myself a bit cheap to her: I let her do as she liked with me. An' then she began to play tricks on me—an' wouldn't cook my dinner—an' wouldn't sleep with me—an' when she did sleep with me, she wanted it all her own way, I was nowhere: as if she was the man, an' me the woman. I came to hate her. And because I wouldn't give in to her, an' had a right set-to with her once or twice when she let me come home to no dinner—though she was as strong as I was, if it comes to that—she went off to her mother's an' left me alone in the house. But I made shift for myself. After that, whenever she got worked up, she went off to her mother's an' set Dan an' Jim against me, swearin' they'd break every bone in my bloody body— —"

He ended in reminiscent bitterness.

"But there was a child?" said Constance.

"Ay! That come the year o' th' war, when we was living here.—She'd come back quieted down, after she'd been off to her mother's—I never told nobody. An' she'd sort of make a set at me again. But I got sick, body-sick an' soul-sick, so I joined up to get away—An' while I was in the army I sort of got myself clear of her. When I come home, in 1920, it wasn't home, it wasn't nothing. She kept threatening to go off. And when she went, I was glad to be at peace, an' be myself again, like I was when I was a lad. I always felt like somebody else when she was about—"

There followed a long silence.

"So you never really loved her," said Constance at last.

"No, I never did. An' she always said it. But I was gone on her that first year, she knowed that. She did as she liked with me, turned me inside out like a glove. And I let her. That's what I had to pay for ever after."

"But she loved *you*!"

"No no! No no, she never cared about me! No, she only cared about having her own way with me, an' then wipin' her feet on me because I'd let her have it. No, she cared about nobody, not even the child. Herself, maybe!—nobody else!"

Constance felt very unhappy.

"But she may want to come back to you," she said.

He slowly shook his head.

"I think not!" he said. "I think not. She's had out of me all she'll ever get—an' I sort of don't know her any more. She's gone out of me, we've come apart, an' I feel as if I'd been asleep, an' wakened up. She's gone dead out of me."

"And do you think you've gone dead in her?"

"Oh, I think so. I think I was dead in her when the child was born, comes to that!"

Constance pondered, unconvinced.

"Yet she was good to you," she said, "when she first married you."

"Ay! she was! she was! she was good to me! An' that made me a fool over her, I was so glad to be all right with a woman, an' to have a woman— you know as wanted me as well. I'd have given her the soul out of my body. 'Appen I did, for that matter. 'Appen that was what made her start wipin' her feet on me. It was my own fault. I know it. That's why I wish her no harm. I wish to God the other man could make her content. With me she was never content. Yi, I hope she's content."

"Do you think she is?"

"Maybe she is! She's got a sort of life that suits her better. I never could stand her goin' to th' pub. An' I never went with her. An' for years, I'd nothing to say to her. Seemed as if there was nothing to say. Oh, she's better off with him, you back your life. An' I think she knows it."

She could hear in his voice the dazed relief at being rid of the woman who had oppressed him for so many years. It amused her, and angered her a little.

"I wouldn't trust her, though," said Constance. "She might just turn up because she knew you didn't want her."

"She might. But that would upset her game wi' th' other fellow, who's got a grand idea of himself So I don't think she will."

The clock on the wall struck eleven. Constance looked round the bare little room, that seemed so cheerless, save for the fire and the copper kettle, the white hearth, the steel fender. This was where the other woman had lived! Upstairs she had borne the child.

"Do you sleep in the same bed where she slept?" she asked him.

He looked at her quickly.

"Ay! There's no other."

Constance sank into a muse. He put his boots on the rack of the fireplace, to dry: and put up hers too. Then he found his slippers, and went out of doors to bring in the big lump of coal, with small coal for backing, with which to rake the fire, to keep it in till morning. Connie watched him carefully pressing the big lump, called the raker, down on the red coals, then packing the slack behind it. It was a task he had done every night, since he had had a house of his own. Then he washed his hands, and looked at the porridge in the double cooker, setting it on the hob above the oven. After which he opened the stair-foot door, and went up the creaking stairs.

He came down in a moment, saying:

"I've lit the candle."

Constance was staring at the fire, extinguished by the coal of the big black raker, dismal.

"And did you think," she said, looking up at him as he stood on the hearthrug with one foot on the fender, and his hand on the mantel-shelf above his head, "did you think you'd never have anything to do with women any more, when your wife was gone?"

He looked at her steadily.

"I thought so," he said.

"And wouldn't you, do you think? but for me?" she asked.

"Eh, don't ask me! I know nothing," he said, with a certain helplessness.

"But you're not sorry you have me?"

"No!" he said, with a queer smile.—"It'll probably end in more trouble.—But it's 'appened, so no use talkin'. An' if I've got me a woman—eh well!—I'd rather have a woman an'—what should I say?— good fuckin',—an' get shot for it after, than not have a woman, an' no fuckin', an' not get shot—"

"Well, you've not had many women!" she said with a smile.

"One!" he said.

"Two with me," she said in irony.

"Ay! Two with you."

He still hung with his hand on the high mantel-shelf, his face looking down at the blackened fire, his foot on the fender. She still sat in his chair.

"And are you sure you even want me?" she said.

He looked down at her, his eyes stirring and dilating.

"Ay, I'm sure as I want you, as far as ever I s'll get you.—Are *you* sure you want me?"

"Sometimes!" she said softly.

He lifted his chin with an odd tossing motion.

"Ay, *sometimes*!" he said, smiling. "I'd forgot that."

He rested his head on his arm, and she saw the little quivers of restrained desire chasing over his body in light shudders, stiffening the muscles oddly.

She looked up at him pleadingly.

"Would you love me?" she said.

He looked into her eyes, with a sort of smile.

"I'd love you if you wanted to be loved," he said quietly.

And she dropped her head.

She heard him sigh, and looked up. He met her eyes.

"Shall you go upstairs?" he said.

She rose, with a certain unwillingness: unwilling, really, to give herself. He saw it. And she knew he saw it.

"I don't want to force you in any way," he said.

She looked back at him from the stairfoot door.

"Come too!" she said, a little pathetic.

He blew out the lamp, and closed the stairfoot door after him, as he slowly mounted the stairs behind her. The candle shone through the open door of the bedroom, on the tiny landing at the top of the stairs. The other door was shut.

The bedroom was small, with a whitewashed sloping ceiling, and stuffed with cheap furniture, pushed under the slopes of the roof. The big iron bedstead stood in the corner by the door, facing the gable window. Under the roof slope by the window was a yellow-painted dressing-table with swing mirror, but with no cloth, nothing on its bareness. There was a yellow-painted washstand, with basin and ewer decorated with chrysanthemums, under another roof-slope, and across from the bed, a chest of drawers. So there was hardly a yard of empty space in the little room.

Constance stood on the strip of matting by the bed, and looked round. On the wall were two cheap pictures. The candle flickered on the chest of drawers. The big white bed stood untouched. He stood in the doorway. Then he entered and closed the door.

"Shall you sleep inside?" he said.

"I suppose so!" she replied.

She sat on the bed, while he stood at a loss near the door; then, pulling off her stockings, she hung them over the bedrail. Then she slipped out of her silk washing-dress, and stood bare-armed in her almost transparent night-dress. As she hung her dress over the bed-rail, she saw her own queer, fixed face in the swivel mirror, and she was startled. Then she looked at him. He was watching her with bright eyes, as he stood waiting near the door.

"Are n't you coming too?" she said, glancing at the bed.

He nodded. And as she was getting into the bed, suddenly his hands were clasping her body, closing on her hanging breasts, and he was putting back her night-dress to kiss her body, with sharp kisses, then pressing his cheek against her warm flesh.

She turned and took his head between her arms, holding it fast to her breast. She daren't let him look at her.

"You're sure you'll love me?" she quavered.

"Ay, I'll love you," he said, from her breast.

"I want you to! I want you to!" she whispered wildly.

And she slipped into the bed, away from him.

He quickly pushed off his stockings and breeches, and dropped his waistcoat, and turned to her, in his flannelette day-shirt.

"Take your shirt off too!" she said.

"Then you take off that nighty!" he replied.

Obediently she began to pull the frail thing over her head, and he watched, watched her long breasts shaking as they emerged. Then he turned his back to her, to take off his shirt, with his rapid, slipping movements. She reached out from the bed and laid her hand on his warm, white-skinned body, at the waist. She felt his body wince.

"Turn round to me! Turn round before you blow the candle out," she said quickly.

He turned slowly, in the unwillingness of his roused, exposed nakedness. He saw her looking at his phallus, then up into his eyes, with big, strange blue eyes.

"Tell me it isn't only fucking," she said, pleading.

He was breathless for a moment. But the tense phallus did not change. It was like another being.

"I don't know what you mean by only!" he said, baffled.

Only the erect phallus seemed sure, cocksure, a strange, wildly alert proud presence between the two beings.

"How strange it is!" she said.

She put her arms round his waist, and her swinging breasts touched the summit of the erect phallus in a sort of homage. He managed to twist, reach over, and knock out the flame of the candle, then he got into bed and went straight in to her.

"What is there more? What is there more than fucking?" came his puzzled voice like an unknown voice out of the night.—And for the moment she submitted, and was gone.

Afterwards, he slept, with her left breast cupped in his right hand, for she had her back to him. And she knew that he must have slept with his wife like that, in the first years: Bertha Coutts! Because his hand came with a strange blind instinct and gathered her breast and held it as in a cup, in a sleep. If she moved, and shifted his hand away, it came back by itself, stirring, groping, till it had her breast again softly enclosed, while he slept. And she lay encircled in his arm, feeling as if her very soul were cupped in the soft hollow of his hand.

It was a kind of prison: a prison! Yet she knew she could break it. So she lay perfectly still, as in a kind of inertia, in the circle of his arm, letting her breast rest like an egg in the strong, warm cup of his hand. Her heart was sad, and wouldn't let her sleep. And something flickered like a spark of irritation in her mind.

It was what he had told her, about Bertha Coutts and about himself. She found nothing extraordinary in it. Yet her heart hurt her, because she had felt the bitterness and the hate in him. His desire for sex intercourse, and his hatred of sex! His desire for woman, and his hatred of women! This made a gnawing soreness in her heart.

Now, he slept absolutely motionless, keeping her within the circle of his arm, her breast like a fruit on the tree, in the hollow of his hand. And now; he seemed really at peace, he seemed to have achieved his own peace, perhaps at the expense of her own. While she would lie still and submissive in the circle of his enclosing arm, he was at peace, and his wounds were closed. But the moment she broke away, he would wake, and memory would open like a wound.

She could feel the slow, strong thudding of his heart, as he held her against him. And it made her think of that other strange creature in him, the erect, sightless, overweening phallus. A little frightening that had been, in its erect, blind overweening. And somehow she realised that it was the soul of his phallus, the overweening blind male soul in him, that had been wounded all his life, wounded through his mother and his step-father from the beginning of his days, and whose wound gaped with the pain and hatred of sex. Because, his phallus was rooted in his soul, and rose erect from the soul's deeps, in naïve pride of creation. And it was this queer, sightless, mindless phallic nature that had been hurt in him all his life, and whose wound only closed now, in sleep, while she lay submissive in the circle of his flesh.

Vaguely, she realised for the first time in her life what the phallus meant, and her heart seemed to enter a new, wide world. Between the two hesitating, baffled creatures, himself and her, she had seen the third creature, erect, alert, overweening, utterly unhesitating, stand there in a queer new assertion, rising from the roots of his body. It was like some primitive, grotesque god; but alive, and unspeakably vivid, alert with its own weird life, apart from both their personalities. Sightless, it seemed to look round, like a mole risen from the depths of the earth. The resurrection of the flesh, it was called in joke. But wasn't it really so? Wasn't there a weird, grotesque godhead in it?

And this godhead in him had always been wounded, yet even now was not dead. In most men it was dead. To most men, the penis was merely a member, at the disposal of the personality. Most men merely used their penis as they use their fingers, for some personal purpose of their own. But in a true man, the penis has a life of its own, and is the second man within the man. It is prior to the personality. And the personality must yield before the priority and the mysterious root-knowledge of the penis, or the phallus. For this is the difference between the two: the penis is a mere member of the physiological body. But the phallus, in the old sense, has roots, the deepest roots of all, in the soul and the greater consciousness of man, and it is through the phallic roots that inspiration enters the soul.

Vaguely, she realised it. Vaguely, she knew now what he meant when he said: "I don't know what you mean by *only*." To him, there could never be "only fucking". Because his phallus rose in its own weird godhead, with its own swarthy pride and purity, and "fucking" went to the phallic roots of his soul. It was not just sensational excitation, worked from the ego and the personality. His phallus was not the vulgar organ, the penis. And with the life or death of his phallus, he would live or die. That too she realised, Men like Clifford, and a vast number of modern men, lived in the petty triumph over the phallus. They have a nasty penis, with which they play about like dirty little boys. But when it comes to the act, in spite of all the gush about love, it is merely fucking—the functional orgasm, the momentary sensational thrill, the cheap and nasty excitation of a moment.

She herself was enclosed in the phallic circle of flesh, and her female nature set in the socket of the male clasp. For the moment. But this night; at least, she submitted. She did not feel a prisoner. She felt enclosed, and safe, and her heart at last was still, had lost its tightness. She was no longer afraid. Always, all her life, she had had a seed of fear in her heart, that could suddenly grow like a grain of mustard-seed. Fear of what? Of nothing, and of everything. Fear of life, fear of society, fear of what would happen, fear of what would not happen. The war had ratified the fear, once and for all. And to conquer the fear, she had wanted to be free, and free, and more free. And the freer she was, the deeper the fear sent its root in her soul.

Tonight she realised. The root of the fear had been fear of the phallus. This is the root-fear of all mankind. Hence the frenzied efforts of mankind to despise the phallus, and to nullify it. All out of fear. Hence the modern jazz desire to make the phallus quite trivial, a silly little pop gun. Fear, just the same. Fear of this *alter ego*, this homunculus, this little master which is inside a man, the phallus. Men and women alike committed endless obscenities, in order to be rid of this little master, to be free of it! Free! Free! Freedom! Oh tale told by an idiot!*

Tonight she submitted. Tonight she would be enclosed and encircled within the phallic body, like an egg set in a cup. Tonight her freedom should be within the folds of the embrace. Tonight for once she would be without fear. The only thing which had taken her quite away from fear, if only for a night, was the strange gallant phallus looking round in its odd bright godhead, and now the arm of flesh around her, the socket of the hand around her breast, the slow, sleeping thud of the man's heart against her body. It was all one thing—the mysterious phallic godhead. Now she knew that the worst had happened. This dragon had enfolded her, and its folds were pure gentleness and safety. There was something that danger could not touch: one thing and one only: the perfect sleeping circle of the male and female, phallic body.

For once, her heart yielded, yielded and passed out. What did it matter who he was, in the daytime world! Now he was the silent male who enclosed her in the phallic circle, and she was like the yolk of the egg, enclosed. She wanted only, only to be perfectly enclosed, to be perfectly comforted, to be put perfectly to sleep.

She slipped round in his arms, and clung to his body, pressing her body to his, in the nakedness. And she felt the mysterious change in his flesh, the beginnings of the inrush of power, the subtle potency that accompanies the rousing of the phallus. And her own flesh quivered and seemed to melt, in wave after wave of new moltenness, as he entered her and melted her in successive sharp, soft waves of unspeakable pleasure, molten and forever more molten, while her voice uttered sharp, strange cries, till she reached the climax and was gone, in the pure bath of forgetting and of birth.

Then at last she nestled into him, and slept as he had slept, in the new sleep. And her breast lay in the socket of his hand, and she was unaware of it. She was only the yolk in the egg.

He woke at dawn in the morning. But he lay still, thinking. It was so good to lie like this, so still, within the inner circle of the angels, beyond all fear and pain. She slept, and his soul slept with her. Only his eyes watched the light through the window-blind, his ears heard the voices of birds, the moving of Flossie downstairs. If one could remain forever so, naked in the stillness, with the sleeping, naked woman! On the edge of his consciousness pressed the day, with its fear, its evil problems. But he remained within the inner circle of the phallic angels, with the woman.

And at last she stirred too, woke, with a certain wonder, and turned round to meet his wide-open, quiet eyes, that gazed at her.

"Are you awake?" she said to him.

He smiled a little with his eyes, but did not answer. And again her breasts and all her body yearned to him with the great yearning. And she clung to his firm, live body, as he softly stroked the silky, voluptuous arches of her waist.

"Let me kiss you!" she said, suddenly kneeling in the bed and bending over his naked breast, kissing the male nipples.

"Look how pretty the brown hair is on your breast!" she said, ruffling it with her fingers. "How could anyone think it not nice! You don't think the hair on my body is nasty, do you? You don't wish it wasn't there?"

She kneeled naked before him. He put his face to her belly, and rubbed his nose among the sharp hair of her body, kissing her gently on the gentle mount of Venus, letting the little hairs brush his mouth, while his moustache brushed her body and made her laugh.

"You don't want me shaved or anything, do you?" she said.

"No-no!" he said, in a low voice.

And he suddenly kneeled in front of her and folded her close, rocking her in a queer rhythm, while the phallic sway enveloped them again.

And then again they both dozed. He was awakened by her soft, long breasts dangling against his face as she reached over to see what time it was by his watch on the chair. He laughed, and caught at the breast with his teeth.

"What is it?" he said.

"Only a quarter to seven," she said.

"You'll have to go," he said.

"Ten more minutes!" she said, nestling down into his arms.

"Was it as lovely for you as it was for me?" she whispered

"Ay!" he said. He hated her to talk.

"Do you love me?"

"Yi!"

"Do you know what love means? Tell me you do!" she said wistfully.

He held her close in his arms, and said in dialect:

"Tha knows what Ah know an' what I dunna know! Dunna keep axin' me! Tha'rt 'ere, aren't ter? Tha can feel me! Tha knows, doesn't ter? What dost ax for?"

"No, I won't ax then!" she said, with a comic mocking of the dialect.

He laughed.

"Don't yer like it when I talk broad?" he asked.

"I love it!" she said, suddenly nestling down over his face and smothering him. "I love it when you do it out of niceness," she said. "Sometimes you do it out of nastiness, don't you?"

He wriggled his face clear of the soft pressure of her breasts.

"Maybe!" he said.

"Why?"

"I dunno! What art axin' for again? Tha allers says *why*?—"

"Because I don't feel sure, and I want to feel sure," she said.

"Sure o' thysen, 'appen? That's what tha'rt niver sure on," he said.

"And *you* feel sure of me, don't you? Kiss me!—Say you do!"

He kissed her, and said seriously:

"Ay, I feel sure o' thee at this minute. If I axed thee for owt, tha'd gi'e 't me, shouldn't ter? This minute?"

"Ask me for something then!" she said.

For reply he held her fast in his arms.

"Tha'rt wi' me at this minute, aren't ter?" he said, in a little voice, half pain. "Even if ter leaves me, tha'rt wi' me at this minute?"

She clung to him convulsively, and did not answer.

"An' I've got thee for this minute, 'aven't I? for this minute tha howds nowt back, does ter?" came the voice, like a lonely little bell clanging.

She could feel vivid passion mount over her.

"Take me!" she whispered. "Take me!"

She gave herself, and it was the best she had known.

When he lay in the strange stillness, that always overawed her a little, she said:

"Was it all right?"

He lifted his head, looked at her, and kissed her. And she hid her face in his shoulder, hid from all consciousness, for some minutes.

They heard the far-off hooters go, for seven o'clock. He still lay motionless, with her in his arms, for a minute or two. Then kissing her quietly he released her, and got out of bed, going to the window in his whiteskinned nakedness. He drew the blind and looked out.

"Is it a fine day?" she said.

"It will be," he replied.

And he turned again to her, not ashamed now in his nakedness, the phallus little and sticky. She leaned out of bed, and touched it delicately.

"How strange it is!" she said, with a certain awe. "So little now, like a bud, and innocent! Little and innocent! What a queer character it's got, don't you think?"

He laughed.

"A bad character, eh?" he laughed.

"No, a good one, a lovely one!" she said.

He laughed, and picked up his shirt, getting it over his head.

"You must get up," he said softly.

"Yes!" she said, reaching for her nightdress. He handed it to her, and stooped for his breeches.

In a moment he was dressed, had tied the garters round his stockings, and slung on his waistcoat. Then he looked at her as she sat up in bed in her nightdress.

"You must be quick," he said gently.

"All right!"

And with another quick look, he went downstairs.

She got up, and went to the dormer window, opening the sash wider. The wood stood there, hoary and still, showing in the haze of morning the fleece of half-open leaves, and a blue mist of hyacinths, almost identical with the haze of day, deeper in beyond the hazels. As yet the sun was not clear, yet the sky was blue overhead. The world was very still, not yet roused from its dream. The dream is very old, yet hyacinthine every spring.

She washed herself in the ugly basin, decorated with brown chrysanthemum transfers, and thought vaguely of Bertha Coutts. And as she combed her hair with the little black comb he had laid on the bare dressing-table, she thought how many times the swivel mirror had reflected the face of the other woman. Ah well! Bertha Coutts had had her chance with a sensitive, passionate man, and she had thrown it away, in her violence and her coarse egoism. Now, probably, she regretted it, with the same egoistic violence. Remembering him in his naked quickness, Connie pitied the other woman a little. But also she disliked her deeply. It was such coarse egoism in women that ruins the world for women.

He was in the scullery when Connie came down the steep little stairs, and she heard the splashing of the water over his face. She slipped on her tennis shoes, and went to the inner doorway. He was wiping his face and neck on the roller towel that hung behind the back door. He looked at her out of the towel, giving it a jerk so that the roller rattled, to bring it to a dry place.

"Don't bother to come out with me," she said. "I must go."

"Shan't you have nothing to eat nor anything?" he asked.

"It's twenty-past seven! I'd better go."

"I'll come with you to the green riding, then?"

He hastily combed his brown hair at the little mirror that hung low, by the window, so that he had to stoop. Then taking his coat and hat, he went with her into the still, fresh morning.

"How lovely it is here!" she said, as they crossed from the little white gate of the front garden, over the rough grass, to the hazel thicket. There was just the narrow track which his feet kept worn. "This is one of the loveliest places in the world."

"Should you like to stop, to live here?" he asked.

She pondered a moment.

"If the world was different, I should love it," she said, "to stay here with you and have your children. If the world were only different."

He strode in silence, through the wet grass of the woodland path.

"Ay!" he said at last. "The world would have to be different."

And they both walked in silence, in the freshness and the stillness of the half-awake wood, whose trees stood around like presences, like witnesses, among the mist of bluebells. There was something of the phallic stillness and power in them too, as they stood deep-rooted. And the birds darted among them, in little flashes.

In the green riding, the forget-me-nots were fluffing up. The greenway made a cleft through the wood. The sun was delicately beginning to shine, among the tree-trunks, frail and tentative in its new beams. And a new glow rose from the greenway.

"There!" she said to him. "Don't come any further! You haven't eaten yet: and I'd best go alone."

"Ay!" he said. And he made her an odd, slight salute, turned, and was striding away.

She went on slowly down the dip, watching the heavenly blue of the flowers on the upslope opposite. Slowly, in the soft, full life of the body, she climbed the upslope among the bluebells. They too knew it, the fulness of the beauty of being in the flesh. She could tell, by the way they hung their purple bud-cluster, and starred out their azure bells. There was a hint of night in them too, and in their bodily blossom, fulness from the night.

She felt still and full and hyacinthine as they were, on the cool stem of flesh. The body! It was a greater mystery and complexity than anything. It was not even physical. It was like the hyacinths, a thing of bloom, the love-body. A thing of bloom.

12

A T WRAGBY, THE DOOR WAS OPEN, and nobody was about. She went to her room in silence. And it was the same.

But she did not bathe. She changed into fresh clothes, slowly. But she did not want to disturb the touch upon her flesh. Later, this evening, she would bathe.

She went up to her room, her sitting-room, when the maid tapped. This too was a new arrangement. Coffee was brought up for her on a tray to her own room, Clifford had his in his room. Breakfast had become a slight meal for him. So they did not meet, often, till lunch.

There was a letter from Hilda on the tray. "—Father is going to London this week, so I shall call for you on Thursday week, 7th June, and we will go on at once. I shall probably stay the night with the Coxleys at Retford, and start early in the morning for Wragby, so I should be with you for lunch—Thursday. Then if you are ready, we could start about tea-time. There is no need for me to spend an evening at Wragby, with Clifford trying to show how much he dislikes me and how he can ignore my existence. I know he loathes me for taking you away, so the quicker we go, the better. Send your trunk to London, to father, in time for him to give it to his man to bring along. Let me know you are expecting me on the seventh—"

So! In a week's time she, Connie, would have to be off. So it was! As sure as she did not want to go, she must. She must go. She felt it inevitable; it was her destiny. And her heart clung to the wood at Wragby, to the keeper's cottage, to the naked man of last night.

Yet she knew she would go. After all, after all, it was but a month. And things would come clear, in her own soul most of all, in the interval. She would go, if only to test her own experience.

For some reason, she put off telling Clifford. He was in a mood that irritated her: a sort of silent overbearing, silently putting people down. It was almost like a game with him. Whoever came near him, he would try, in silence, to make feel small. He had done it in the past with her, and for a long time she had been puzzled by her own feeling of subjection, almost of fear. Till at last she realised that Clifford tried to do it to her, almost deliberately. When he felt she was too uppish, too much herself, he would play the silent trick on her, of silently *willing* to make her feel small: using his will against her.

She had never been able to decide whether he did it in full consciousness, or whether it was an instinctive retaliation of his wounded egoism. Anyhow the result was the same. And in the past, it had succeeded with her. She would feel a nameless fear, a nameless guilt, a nameless necessity to cringe to some god, perhaps a god of hate. Now, however, she knew what it was. It was Clifford setting his will against her. So she avoided him, and shook off his influence.

He then tried the trick on Mrs Bolton, on Linley, the pit-manager, on the engineer—on anybody who had to come near him. Silently putting them down and robbing them of their own life. He would ring for Mrs Bolton: then when she came, ignore her presence entirely.

"Did you ring, Sir Clifford?"

"Oh! Did I? Yes! I suppose I did."

"Was there anything I could do?"

Then he would look at her, in the eyes, with his cold, devilish look, till she had to turn her face aside.

"Do you mind seeing if there is a bottle of fountain-pen ink anywhere," he said calmly, as if she were at the other end of a telephone, and not in the room at all.

"I have a bottle of my own in my room. I'll fetch it," she said, flustered.

"Er—! No thanks! Go upstairs and see if her ladyship has any."

"Very good!"

But Mrs Bolton went out of the room furious. She felt deliberately insulted. "I'm hanged if I'll go up two flights of stairs," she said to herself. So she went into her room, and sat there for a few minutes, with two red spots of anger on her cheeks.

Then she took her bottle of ink, tapped at Sir Clifford's door, entered and set the ink on the table within his reach, turning at once to go.

He picked up the ink-bottle as if it were some marine specimen, and looked at it.

"Er—!" he said, when she was at the door.

She stopped, turned, and said:

"Yes?"

"This is her ladyship's ink, of course?"

The woman stood dumb, for a second. Then she replied:

"The moment her ladyship wanted it, it would be."

And the red spots of colour flew brighter in her cheeks. He looked at her with a faint smile of contempt.

"You are very kind, I'm sure!" he said, with a sneer.

She still stood motionless at the door.

"Is there anything else?" she asked.

"Nothing thanks!" he said, in his most courteous voice, but with the most perfect contempt.

And poor Ivy Bolton went round all day, feeling as if she had been caught in some dirty, dishonourable deed, and privately exposed. It was as if she could not get her head erect.

He had another go, at Parkin, when that individual came to report the case of the two poachers, who had been before the magistrate.

"Good-morning!" said Clifford, when Parkin saluted. "Which of the rooms have you left your dog in?"

"I've tied her up by the back door."

"Ah!—Well?—What is it?"

"Them two poachers as was 'ad up at Uthwaite yesterday—"

"What did they get—?"

"They got off—"

Clifford looked at his man in silence, but with queer smiling hate. He hated the fresh red face, that showed so little subservience. For a long time, he said nothing, just fixed the game-keeper with his light-blue, gimlet-sharp eyes, and stared him out of countenance. But Parkin, who was hard on his guard, stared with concentrated attention at a new, futuristic picture which Clifford had hung in his room. He stared with such strange, animal fixity, that Clifford had to glance to see what he was staring at.

Then he said:

"Who was the magistrate?"

"Mr Merfin."

Now Mr Merfin had never forgiven Clifford for a certain snub that young gentleman had given him.

"You gave evidence?" Clifford said at last. "What did you say?"

"I towd 'em where I catched 'em, an' what wi'—"

"What did you catch them with?" asked Clifford, with a slight sneering smile.

"I catched 'em with two rabbits apiece on 'em," said Parkin, sharp and hard.

"And what then?"

"Then Joe gave evidence—"

"Towd 'em where you catched 'em, like?" said Clifford, who could imitate the dialect with disastrous effect.

Parkin glanced at him quickly, to see if he were jesting. But on Clifford's face was only the faint, subtle sneer.

"Summat same!" said Parkin—"Anyhow Mr Merfin knowed what he meant."—he added in perfect good-humour.

"We'll give him the credit. Go on!"

"Then he axed if it wor t' first time they was 'ad up."

"And you said it was the second or third?"

"No! I said I'd catched 'em, the same two fellers, twice afore. An' they swore as I hadn't, 'cause they'd nobbut just come from Ilson road: which was a lie anyhow.—Anyhow Mr Merfin let 'em off with a caution—"

"Did he tell you you were a bright man—?"

"No, Sir Clifford. He said I had to do my duty by my employer, like any man in any other employment."

"And the court, no doubt, gave you three cheers."

"They might ha' done, only they didn't," said Parkin, with a faint smile. His eyes were very bright.

"Good-morning!" said Clifford, with sudden bland abruptness.

Parkin stared at him, and asked quietly, very slowly:

"Did you mean as I was to go, Sir Clifford?"

"You've hit the nail on the head," said Clifford, who had already turned away and was pretending to sort some papers.

"I give you good morning, Sir Clifford!" said Parkin, with a stately sort of slowness. But he added mentally: "An' lucky for you as it wor nobbut th' nail I hit on th'ead!" Clifford ignored him entirely, so he left the room, giving a glance at the broad, hulking shoulders of the cripple, leaning forward over the table.

And this time, it was Clifford's turn to feel small.

Constance, who had heard Flossie yelp, was out on the drive. Parkin saluted as he came up. She saw his bright eyes.

"What was it?" she asked, in a low voice.

"I was only telling Sir Clifford as them two poachers as was 'ad up at Uthwaite yesterday had got off with a caution."

"It's just as well," said Constance.

He gave a queer tip of his head, looked into her eyes with a faint yet glittering smile, saluted, and went on.

So that evening Constance told Clifford of Hilda's letter.

"Well!" he said calmly. "I suppose you're going?"

"I suppose so," she replied.

He turned to his book in complete indifference: or with that appearance. Constance knew it meant anger, and resentment. But she went upstairs, and began sorting out her clothes. She had nothing new at all. But she could get something in London and Paris. She went slowly over her wardrobe.

Clifford said nothing for a day or two, neither did she. Then he asked, casually:

"Your sister Hilda comes on Thursday?"

"Yes! Thursday morning."

"And how long does she propose to stay here?"

"Just for lunch. She says we may as well go straight on."

"The same afternoon?"

"Yes."

Then he said ironically:

"She stoops to pick up the pet lamb, and away—!"

"If there is any pet lamb," said Constance.

"Surely you are that, to your family—" he said.

But she refused to be drawn.

"And you will be back, when?"

"In a month or five weeks, as I said."

"That is, if you come back at all."

"Why? Why should I not come back?"

"The hand of God, I suppose. There might be an earthquake."

"There might," said Constance.

"Or a heart-quake! Is your sister Hilda going to look for a new husband for herself, as well as for you?"

"I haven't asked her."

"Ah! The plot only concerns yourself?"

"There is no plot."

"You dear innocent! Do you think you are going to trust to luck? Not while your sister Hilda is about."

"Luck for what?"

"Don't you remember, you were going to pick up a baby—or the wherewithal of a baby—on the trip?—by family advice, and with your sister's assistance."

Constance was silent.

"It depends," she said at last.

"I should say so!" he replied. "Do you mind hearing my stipulation?"

"Why should you stipulate anything?"

"I shall be the legal and acting father of the babe. Had it slipped your mind?"

She did not answer this. But she said roughly:

"What stipulation?"

"The child shall be English by both parents: and of at least *decent* descent on the father's side."

She pondered a moment, then replied:

"I have never been able to fathom your idea of decency."

"That, no doubt, is because you are a deep sea fish. It is just the commonplace idea."

"Very well!" she said coldly.

She went quietly about her business. Clifford continued to be ironical and superior. A change had taken place in him, for good. He was always inwardly watchful, suspicious, and resentful. Perhaps he had got what is called an inferiority complex, a very subtle and deep-reaching disease. He had somewhere inside him a deep, compelling grudge, a grudge against the entire creation.

Being clever, he was more or less aware of it; and more or less aware, now he was nearly forty, that he had always been so. He had bluffed himself for a long time. He was clever, subtle, and with keen aesthetic perceptions. He had managed for many years to persuade himself that he was happy, and successful, one of fortune's favorites. Even after the war, he had tried to keep up this idea of himself. But gradually, it had become too great an effort.

He felt that, in the universe, he was a thing apart, and that all the other things in the universe were probably taking away a portion of life he himself might have had. The expansive yellow face of the dandelion irritated him, with its crude yellowness and its exposed foolishness.

He preferred the nipped bud, in the rain. Mrs Bolton's slightly effusive goodwill annoyed him, and he wanted to hurt her. Parkin's fresh, out-of-door healthiness and solitary perkiness, like a cock chaffinch, exasperated him. The fellow ought to be put down. And Constance's vague unawareness, added to the freshening of her beauty and her look of "maidenliness," filled him with rancour. He himself was at a disadvantage, while all these others, all inferior to himself, flourished sickeningly.

He felt superior to them all. Secretly, inside himself, he felt superior to everything on earth. He could not help it. It was part of his psychic condition. It was deeper almost than instinct. He just *felt* superior, and there it was. And he had a shrewd idea that everybody else, in their private mind, felt the same. Even Mrs Bolton! Even the housemaid Alice! Every individual is to himself a nonsuch, and the supreme pearl of existence.

This was Clifford's idea, arguing from his own experience. And the idea is certainly not entirely fallacious. Nearly every man, and still more nearly every woman, is to himself or herself the supreme pearl of human life, incomparable, and subtly *superior*. It is the illness of the housemaid as much as of the duchess. And in a world of such abounding superiority, Clifford was determined not only to hold his own, but to win out.

He had now forgotten the other condition of grace, wherein neither superiority nor inferiority enters. So long as the heart retains its warmth and its gentleness, the question of superiority or inferiority does not enter. The hateful discord of superiority and inferiority only arises upon challenge, and upon some assertion or some defection of the individual ego.

But now the madness of secret superiority infects the world, and carries with it the rabies-germ of secret inferiority. Because, a man who is really a man, and not a sterile assertive ego, is no more conscious of superiority or inferiority than a thrush is. Superiority and inferiority are a disease of the consciousness, an illness of the soul.

But Clifford now saw nothing else. He was, of course, a gentleman, and had his code of honour as far as behaviour went. But his feelings were beyond his control, and they were a private anarchy all his own.

Constance instinctively avoided him, and avoided even sounding her feelings with regard to him. She had a secret dread of him, and of his inner anarchy. If it was a conservative anarchy, then she would be aware only of the conservative-behaviour part of it, and she would let the anarchy remain unknown and unfathomed.

Yet at times, the anarchy of his feelings poked out a serpent head, and struck at her.

"You entertain, of course," he said to her two days before she was leaving, "the possibility of your being swept away by love?"

He said it with complete ironical contempt.

She looked at him with her wide blue eyes, frightened, but subtle and guarded as he was.

"Swept away where to?" she said.

"The answer is obvious! The arms, and the bed, of the man who is going to make a mother of you."

"What man?" she said.

"You are going to find out," he said. "You take a flight into Egypt* to *get* a babe—"

"I don't—!" she said.

"You mean you don't intend to find a lover, nor to allow yourself a lover, nor even to have a lover thrust upon you?—Why isn't that the purpose of your journey? Or is there a *volta face*?"

She looked at him steadily.

"I don't want you to talk to me like this, Clifford," she said. "Have you no proper feelings at all?"

"A great many, I assure you. One of them is a serious concern for you in this little adventure."

"You needn't think about it."

"Need I not? Are you the absolute power that dictates the necessity of thought?—Or shall I say, I have very substantial *feelings* about the matter, since feelings appeal to you?—and that therefore I must think!"

"But you needn't talk at me."

"I only wish to warn you. May not the tide of sexual love sweep you away, not only to the arms and bed, but even to the permanent domicile of some other man?"

She had to unravel what he said. When she had got it, she replied:
"And what if it did?"

"Exactly! That is the point we must consider. You would expect a divorce, no doubt—"

"Yes."

"Quite! Then I have to look what cards I have in *my* hand—"

"Why don't you wait till I ask you for a divorce, before you talk about it?"

"Because I don't care to be jumped into anything. I am a reasoning human being, and like to use my reason—"

There was a pause.

"Well! I suppose you would divorce me if I really wanted you to," she said.

"I am not so sure," he replied, with a faint smile.

"Why? What good would it do you—?"

"Not to divorce you?—That is not the aspect I shall consider. I shall have to figure out what *harm* it would do me if I *did* divorce you."

"It couldn't do *you* any harm."

"You really think so! What a charming idea you have of our innocent marriage!—But I want you to look before you leap! That is all! Count the costs before you make the bargain."

"Do you mean, count the costs with you?—Then tell me what the costs are."

"I have not made out the entire bill.—But I should probably *not* consent to divorce you, upon request."

"Very well! Wait till you are asked!—And what else? Perhaps you will take the initiative, and divorce me if you think I *don't* want you to?"

"No! Perhaps not that!" he said slowly. "Yet I wouldn't promise, even that. It depends on how you play about with my name."

"I'd better travel *incognito*," she said. "But I wish only one thing of you—"

"And what is that?"

"That you wouldn't think about me *at all* in these connections. It is just indecent."

"My dear child, the wind bloweth where it listeth,* especially through the mind. Do you want me to promise not to *dream* of you?"

"Do as you like!" she said. "Think what you like, dream what you like. And if you drive me away, do what you like."

"*I* drive you away! I see myself in the stern rôle."

"Well! Don't talk to me about it. I loathe talk."

"You are all for deeds and derring-do! Good luck to you, and especially in the derring-do!—What shall we call the child? Eureka? Bentrovato?* Little Benny—?"

But Constance went away from him. She was really afraid of him, though she would not admit it to herself. He dominated her in some way: perhaps her mind, or her will. She was afraid, if he really set his will against her going away with Hilda on Thursday, probably she would defer to him, and not go. And perhaps, if he had resolutely set his face against her having a lover, she would never have had one. She would not have made the one supreme effort of going dead against him, against his final will and wish.

Why? She asked herself why? Why would she not have made the one last effort of opposition?

She did not answer the question. She evaded it. But she knew, in her heart, that it was because she did not want finally to break with him. If ever she deliberately broke through his wish and will concerning her, and acted dead against him, their relationship would be broken, finished. And she did not want it finished.

That was why she did not go, for several days, to see Parkin. To be sure, the gamekeeper had been away in Uthwaite one day, and a timber-man had been in the wood another day. But when she might have gone, she did not. Because she did not want finally to break with Clifford. And she did not want to have to tell Parkin so. For her instinct made her know, that she would have to tell him this.

"In your present frame of mind, you do *intend* to come back to Wragby, after your jaunt? don't you?" Clifford asked at tea-time.

"Yes!" she said, looking at him. "I shall come back."

"That is at present your intention?"

"Yes! Of course! Of course I shall come back! Don't you want me to?"

"Yes! I think I do. But I am such a cynic about feminine freedom.—

When lovely woman stoops to freedom*
And finds she's safely got away—

Anyhow, I'll finish that couplet later—"

She listened without heeding very closely. Then she asked:

"Do you want me *not to go*?"

She looked at him openly. And he moved uneasily on his chair.

"No!" he said. "I don't want you *not to go*.—I don't want to play dog-in-the-manger, as your family think I do."

"With me?—They don't think it!—But you don't really want me to go, do you?"

Again he hesitated uneasily.

"If it only depended on me," he said, "I should say, I don't want you to go. But since I believe every individual must live his own life: and since the dog in the manger will have to eat the hay himself, if he won't let the hee-haws and the jack-asses and that sort of cattle come near it: and since it would stick in his throat: I think, on the whole, the hay had better get out of the manger, and walk towards the young bulls, or the old asses—"

"And I'm the hay?" she said, laughing.

"You're the hay.—

The wench is a bundle of hay
Mankind are the asses that pull,
Each pulls it a different way—*

And that quatrain I'll finish when you get back.—"

"Very well!" she said. "It'll give you something to think about."

But somehow, she felt she had scored. And he, because he was pleased with his own wit, felt that *he* had scored. So they could both be in a good humour.

Also, she felt he really wanted her to go. He wanted to think all sorts of things about her.

And further, she was really more afraid of Parkin, or of herself under Parkin's influence, than she was of Clifford. Therefore, she left it till the very day before she was leaving, before she went to find him in the wood.

It was raining, though the wood glowed with flowers. The bluebells were intensely blue, the guelder-rose spread its circles of cream. In places, forget-me-nots were knee-deep, all with wet faces, and the pink campion was showing its touch of rose. It was beautiful, still and mysterious in the quick pattering of June rain.

The hut was silent, closed. She went indoors. It was tidy and vacant-seeming, as if no-one had been busy there for a long time. She took the hatchet, and chopped a piece of wood on the block. It was good exercise, so she went on chopping. There was a little fireplace in a corner of the hut, she could even make herself a fire. This amused her.

Just as her fire was crackling up, in the little grate, Flossie ran in at the open door, and he followed, in a short oilskin coat, like a chauffeur. She smiled at him as he entered. And he said, rather restrained:

"I thought you'd gone lost!"

He eyed her with a queer sort of suspicion.

"No, not lost!" she said. "But I've been busy. I'm going away for a month to France, with my father and sister."

"When are you going?"

"Tomorrow."

He stood silent, watching the little flames crackling in the fire. And she felt the peculiar warm power of his presence.

"Tomorrow!" he repeated.

"Yes! My sister will come for me in the morning, and we shall start off in her car in the afternoon."

He was silent and inscrutable, watching the fire. Then he crouched in front of it, poking in the little red embers with his finger.

"How wet your knees are!" she said.

She laid her hand on the hard, bent knee, where the rain had wetted the cloth. And she felt the warmth come through.

"And where are you going to, like?" he asked, in a guarded voice.

"To London, then to Paris. Then to the border of Spain, to Spain."

"Nowhere where the war was."

"No! Down south, to the sea, to the Bay of Biscay."

"And Sir Clifford's not going?"

"No!"

"What does he say, to you leaving him?"

"He doesn't mind.—Do you?"

He rose, and straightened his shoulders.

"What'd be the good of me mindin'?" he said.

His trouser-knees were smoking with damp.

"You'll catch rheumatism!" she said. "Couldn't you change?"

"Eh no!" he said contemptuously. And he stared at the fire.

"But it's only a month," she said.

"Oh, ay!" he replied, meaningless.

"And you'll be glad to see me back, won't you?"

He looked at her with his faint, mocking smile.

"Let's hope so," he said.

She fetched the stool, and sat down.

"You see I think I ought to go away for a while," she said. "I've been here for four years without a change."

"Ay, it'll do you good," he said.

She could get nothing out of him. She felt hot, from the fire, and from walking in her mackintosh. The rain, which had abated, suddenly came peppering down, as if it had a touch of thunder.

"I want to run in the rain!" she said, her eyes glowing.

"To get wet?" he asked ironically.

"With nothing on! I want to feel it!" she said.

And in an instant, she was stripping off her stockings from her ivory-coloured legs, then her dress and her underclothes, and he saw her long, pointed, keen animal breasts tipping and stirring as she moved, while he stood motionless by the little fire. Then naked and wild, ivory coloured, she slipped on her rubber shoes and ran out with a wild laugh into the sharp rain. He watched her run with her arms extended, queer and pale and bright, in the sharp rain, across the open space and to the trees, her soft waist full and yielding, her haunches bright and wet with rain, leaping with queer life of their own, as she became more shimmery and indistinct in the rain. Flossie ran after her, with a sudden, wild little bark, and she turned, holding off the brown dog with her naked arms, visionary and bright in the distant rain.

The wonder changed to a faint, defiant smile on his face. He unfastened his boots, and threw off his clothes in a heap on the floor, and as she was running breathless back to the hut, he ran out naked and white. She gave a little shriek, and fled, Flossie gave a yelp, jumping at him, and he, catching his breath in the sharp rain, ran barefoot after the naked woman, in a wild game. She could not run for glancing in wild apprehension over her shoulder, seeing the ruddy face almost upon her, the white, male figure gleaming in pursuit just behind her, The strength to run seemed to leave her. And suddenly his naked arm went round her soft, naked-wet middle, and she fell back against him. He laughed an uncanny little laugh, feeling the heap of soft, chill flesh come up against his body. But he gathered it in, voluptuously, pressed it all up against him, the heap of soft, female flesh, that became warm in an instant, and his hands pressed in on her lovely, heavy posteriors.

She for the moment was unconscious, in the beating overtone and the streaming privacy of the rain. He glanced at the ground, tipped her over on a grassy place, and there in the middle of the path, in the pouring rain, went into her, in a sharp, short embrace, keen as a dagger thrust, that was over in a minute. He got up almost instantly, drawing her up by the hands, and snatching a handful of forget-me-nots, to wipe the smeared earth off her back, as they went to the hut. And she too, abstractedly, caught at the campions and the forget-me-nots.

He shut the door of the hut, and dried her upon an old sheet which he had put with the blankets on the shelf, and she rubbed him down behind, the glistening, healthy white back. Then, still panting, they slung a blanket over their shoulders, and sat before the fire, warming the front of their naked bodies, and panting speechless. The brown dog shook herself like another sudden shower, and he shouted at her, in a queer wild voice, to get back.

Turning round to the dog, he had noticed the torn handful of wet flowers on the bench. He took them up and looked at them.

"They stop out-doors all weathers," he said.

She sat with her knees open, receiving the fire-glow on the soft folds of her body. He looked at her with interested scrutiny, and at the fleece of brown hair that hung in its soft point between her thighs. Suddenly, he leaned over and threaded a few forget-me-not flowers in this golden-brown fleece of the mount of Venus.

"There's a forget-me-not in the right place," he said.

"Doesn't it look pretty!" she said, looking down at the milky, odd little stars at the lower tip of her body, among the hair.

"The prettiest part of you!" he said, smiling.

And he laid his hand, brown and warm, upon the ivory, silky inner thigh of the woman, stroking it softly.

"You must have a flower as well," she said.

And reaching over, she threaded two pink campions in the bush of red-brown hair above his penis.

"Charming!" she cried. "Charming!" Then in the darker hair of his breast she stuck a spray of forget-me-not.

"Now you've got a forget-me-not in the right place, as well!" she said.

He laughed, and the flowers shook on his body.

"Wait a bit!" he said.

He got up, and quietly opened the door. The sudden rain had abated, the mysterious twilight was gone. He stepped out quickly in the soft rain, and she saw his white figure among the leaves, stooping and gathering flowers.

He came back with a mixed bunch of forget-me-nots, campions, bugle, bryony, primroses, golden-brown oak sprays. She watched him running towards the hut with this bunch of herbage, his knees lifting wild and quick, his red face glistening with an inward, intent look, and again she felt a certain fear, as of the wild man of the woods whom she remembered in old German drawings.

He shook the flowers and laughed at her, showing a slight flash of his teeth, as he shut the door.

"You want to be dressed up," he said.

Coming to the fire, he sat down and turned towards her. He put sprays of fluffy young oak under her breasts, and the weight of the breasts held them there. Then among the oak-leaves he put a few bluebells. He twisted a spray of bryony round her arm, poised a primrose in her navel, and put primroses and forget-me-nots in the hair of the mount of love. There she was, with odd sprays of flowers and leaves on her naked body.

"Now you'll do!" he said.

And he stuck flowers in the hair of his own body, with a childish interest. She looked at him in wonder and amusement, the odd intentness with which he did things. And she pushed a campion flower into his moustache, where it dangled under his nose.

"Now you've got a nose ornament as well!" she said.

He put more sticks on the fire, so that it blazed up. Outside, the morning was coming clear.

"We might as well make hay while it rains," he said, "if other folks makes it while the sun shines."

"Wouldn't it be nice," she said, "if there weren't many people in the world, and this wood was a forest as it used to be?"

"Ay!" he said softly. "Wouldn't it be nice if we could squash it all up, Tevershall an' Sheffield an' all the rest?"

"And Wragby!"

"Ay, Wragby!" he said with contempt.

He was silent for some minutes, looking at the fire.

"You feel sometimes," he said, looking at her, "as if you could start out with a hatchet an' begin smashin' the whole place up. Sometimes, when I'm at top o' th' hill i' th' wood here, something comes up inside me, an' I feel my heart 'd fly out o' my body, wi' rage, an' because I fair hate it all, all there is outside this wood."

She was silent, with a sense of foreboding.

"The world is so big!" she said. "And it spreads over everything. The best is to dodge it, and forget."

"Ay!" he said. "Dodge it. But when you're dodgin' a man who's after

234

you, you don't half hate him. An' now, you have to dodge everybody, an' hate everybody—"

He went into a silence, the old silence of fear.

Suddenly he held out his arms to her, and his knees.

"Come here a bit!" he said. "Come an' sit with me!"

He was seated on a low log before the corner fire. She came and squatted between his thighs, leaning back on his naked body. And he pressed her between his thighs, with uncanny quivering power.

"If they knowed we was like this," he said, "they'd want to kill us. If they knowed you had forget-me-nots in your maidenhair, they'd want to kill us."—He pressed his powerful thighs on her, and held her close. "Should you like to go away wi' me to Canada or somewhere?" he asked.

She curled over and laid her face on his thigh, feeling his penis move curiously, with the little life of its own, against her back.

"The world is all alike, all over," she said. "It would be the same in Canada."

He was silent, unwilling to accept this.

"It might be," he said slowly. "An' it mightn't."

"Ah!" she said "You can't get away from it. The world is the same all over. Or at least, our world has got all the rest of the world in its grip, right to the north pole. You can't get away."

"But nobody would know us," he said.

"They soon would. And it would be the same."

He felt it was true, so he sat silent. Outside, the morning was brightening, the sun was going to shine.

"Sit in my lap," he said. "Sit in my lap."

He closed his thighs, and she curled up in the hollow of his body, his head bent over hers.

"They won't leave us alone, you know, not for long," he said.

She received this in silence. Then she said, in a low dull voice:

"No! I know!"

There was silence. He glanced at the brightening day outside.

"You wouldn't like me to get a little farm," she said, "and you live on that, and work it? I've got enough money of my own. And you'd be your own master!"

"And what about you?" he said.

"I don't know. Perhaps I'd come and live with you."

"We should both have to get divorces."

"Yes, I know.—But we could find a little farm somewhere—and you could start it, no matter where I was—"

"How much money have you got?" he asked her.

And even she hesitated before she said:

"I don't quite know. But I have between four and five hundred a year."

"Between four and five hundred of your very own? every year?"

"Yes! From my mother."

"You're all right then, for money!" he said. "I thought I was well-off, wi' two hundred pounds to my name, let alone four or five hundred a year."

She was silent. She felt him, for some reason, withdraw a little from her, now she was rich in his estimation.

"Would you like a farm?" she said. "My sister would help me to get it. She's very practical."

He was silent for some time. Then he answered slowly:

"I don't think I want a woman to set me up in business, like. I don't think I do."

"But I'm not a woman, merely: at least, not to you. And it wouldn't be just setting you up in business. You could start. And then I could come and live with you if—if we both got divorced, and we wanted to live together. And anyhow, I could come and *stay* with you sometimes."

He answered only the first part of her proposition.

"You'd never want to live wi' me on a little farm," he said. "You'd never want to be Mrs Oliver Parkin."

"Why not?" she said. "I think I should. We should be independent. And at least we could see how things worked out."

"With who?"

"With you and me—and Clifford—and your wife. We could see if we *wanted* to get divorced and marry again. Perhaps you wouldn't any more than I should. Perhaps less. Perhaps it is you who really hate marriage, not me."

He pondered this in silence, without reply.

"I think," she continued, "you like to be alone most of your time. I think you only want me sometimes. I think you don't want me always there. I think you'd find me a burden and a strain on you, if I was there morning, noon, and night."

Still he pondered in silence.

"I believe in marriage," she said. "But I don't believe in living together. At least I think I don't believe in it. What ruins marriage is that the man and woman always live together, on top of one another. If they lived apart, in separate houses, they'd be able to go on liking one another. And if not, it wouldn't matter very much.—That's why I think it would be nice if you could have a little farm, and I could come and see you sometimes, and we needn't burden one another with marriage. I've been saddled with one marriage. So have you. And I don't believe either of us wants another, not with anybody on earth. If we were two angels, I don't believe we should want to put the burden of marriage on one another. Do you?"

"No!" he said. "No! I don't! The minute you marry a woman, she's spoilt for you. She becomes a part of the whole my-eye bossing business as makes a man's balls go deader than sheep's kidneys."

"And the woman hates it just as much," she said. "So why don't you let us find a farm where you can live and make a living, and I can come and be your wife sometimes, like it is here, in the wood?"

"And you'd go on living wi' Sir Clifford?" he asked.

"For the time being, at any rate," she said.

He was silent. A shaft of sunlight fell into the hut. He glanced uneasily at the window.

"The sun's out!" he said. "Anyhow, we can be thinkin' about it while you're gone. No need to fix nothing. But they wouldn't let you, you know, live wi' Sir Clifford an' come an' be my wife sometimes. They wouldn't let you."

"Who wouldn't? They wouldn't know."

"Everybody! They'd find out, some road or other."

"Everybody's nobody!"

"Ay! That's what they say! Well, Sir Clifford wouldn't. He might let you go on the randazzle for a bit. But he'd put a stop to it after a while. He'd be your boss."

"Oh no! Surely you know you've no reason to be jealous of poor Clifford."

"Poor Clifford if you like! But if you live with him, he's your master, say what you may."

"Is he my master at this minute?"

"You'll have to mind to get home in time for dinner," he said.

"And if I lived with you, would *you* be my master?" she said.

"In a way! If we was married. In a way!"

She sighed with impatience.

"I don't *want* a master, of any sort," she said.

"Nay, an' I don't want to be one, neither. Neither do I want to be bossed, not by anybody, man nor woman. But folks won't let you be. Especially if you get married."

"We aren't married, are we?" she said, clinging to him.

"No!" he said. "There's a lot between us an' marriage."

"Let's not think of it!" she said. "Kiss me, and let's not think of it."

She lifted her face, and he kissed her. The flowers had fallen from her breasts and her navel.

"If there weren't so many beastly people in the world!" she said.

"Ay!" he replied. "But there they are."

"Never mind!" she said, clinging to him. "Love me while you can!" She clung to him, and caressed him, and felt his phallus rise against her.

"I love it!" she said, quivering, and feeling the rapid thrills go through her loins. "I love it when he rises like that, so proud. It's the only time when I feel there is nothing *really* to be afraid of, from all the world of people. They seem so insignificant. I love it when he comes in to me!"

She clung to the man's shoulder, in the wild thrills of forgetting.

They went out, dressed, into bright June sunshine.

"I'll come to you tomorrow night!" she said. "Shall I? Shall I? And Hilda can wait for me in the morning at the end of the lane. Shall I?"

And that evening, the last before Connie's departure, Clifford read out to her a bit from the end of a book he had been reading. He was still concerned with his own immortality, he still read every new book about God. And this last one seemed to please him.

"Listen to this, Connie," he said. "If only we were an aeon or two ahead, you'd have no need to go out looking for a Holy Ghost on two legs. Listen to our latest famous philosopher.—'The universe shows us two aspects: on one side it is physically wasting, on the other side it is spiritually ascending—'"

"How does he know?" said Connie. "Does he take its weight every day?"

"I don't know. He's a great man, and a vogue. Listen!—'It is thus passing, with a slowness inconceivable in our measures of time, to new creative conditions, amid which the physical world, as we at present know it, will be represented by a ripple barely to be distinguished from non-entity!'"

"Oh, he only knows he's going to die!" said Connie. "I suppose he will leave behind a ripple scarcely distinguishable from non-entity. But who cares?"

"Listen! Don't interrupt the great man in his last solemn words!—'The present type of order in the world has risen from an unimaginable past, and it will find its grave in an unimaginable future. There remains the inexhaustive realm of abstract forms, and creativity, with its shifting character ever determined afresh by its own creatures, and God, upon whose wisdom all forms of order depend.'*—There! How's that!"

"Amen! Selah!* Hallelujah and all the rest to him!" she said. "He's another windbag, talking about unimaginables. I expect he's one of these intellectuals with a dead body, so he wants to kill everything and have a universe of abstract forms."

"I thought it would get you," he said, amused.

"Men who talk about God nowadays," she said, "must be half-defunct. They go on about unimaginable futures and pasts! If they had ten drops of blood in their bodies, they'd hold their tongues."

"Tell me how *you* expect the unimaginable future will work out," he said, looking at her excited face and glowing eyes.

"I don't have futures if I can't imagine them," she said. "And anyhow, I don't pretend they're unimaginable, and then stuff them full of abstract forms."

"No! But don't you imagine any unimaginable future?"

"Oh, I do! And it's so *physical*! Such amazing physical awarenesses! and marvellous delicate contacts, touches, between men and women who still keep apart. I can imagine men and women with quite different sort of consciousness from ours: silent, and intuitive, and physical like perfume."

She looked at him with brilliant, excited eyes, such as he had never seen before.

"And will these delicate physical beings have guts?"

"Oh yes! If there is a God, he has guts."

"And occasional indigestion?"

"Yes! If there is God, he has occasional indigestion."

"In fact, he is capable of all the marital services."

"Why yes! How could there be a god who left it out?"

"Tu l'as voulu, Georges Dandin!"* he said, with a grin. "A God who occasionally smells?"

"Why not? else a civet cat would have the better of him."

"And a skunk might lift its tail and turn its rear at him, and be his boss!—Why not? Quite!—They are part of creation, and creation's order. Quite! God must have an oesophagus and an alimentary canal, I suppose, so long as we've got one. But if we evolve beyond it, presumably God will have done the same. Or is God still an ichthyosaurus? I suppose he must contain the principle: of the ichthyosaurus and the dodo. Everything that has passed away can't have passed because it was evil, can it? Since creativity is change.—You are right, God must be everything that is part of the creative order: and so he must have guts and testicles. You are quite right. But he must also be pure spirit, and I prefer that aspect."

She looked at him in wonder.

"I never heard you be so clever, Clifford," she said.

"Really! But I'm joking. Wherein do you see cleverness?"

"That god must have bowels and testicles!"

"And that he must urinate, and have occasional flatulence?"

"Yes! Of course! *Now* at last I love him!"

"My dear, you would! *Cherchez l'homme!**—But I am jesting."

"No you're not! You're serious! And for once, *for once*, you've really spoken the truth."

"But my dear, you *know* I believe that God is eliminating the guts and testes part, and passing on to pure spirit."

"Never! You don't believe it! God is just waking up the guts and testes to real creativity."

"My dear, you are a female Don Quixote! Avoid everything but trying to come face to face with your Dulcineo del Toboso: your Don Dulcineo!* since you are the Doña Quixote de la Wragby!"

"You are so witty tonight, Clifford!" she said.

"And you, my dear, are flashing with lightning like a hot summer night. You look like a Bacchante just off to the hill, with the *Iacchos*! cry ready in your throat!"

"How clever of me to look all that!" she said.

"But you are so glad to be going!"

"Yes!" she said, with a flash. "I am glad to be off! I *do* feel thrilled! Is it horrid of me?"

"Not at all! You communicate your thrill to me, and I'm thrilled that you're going. I feel my heart jumping like a fawn, and saying: How wonderful! She's really going! She's nearly gone!"

She watched him with glowing eyes.

"It *is* wonderful, don't you think?" she said. "Every departure snaps some bond, don't you think?"

"Possibly! The old sentimentalists used to say *heart-strings*: like Romeo and Juliet, whose heart-strings were torn when they parted.—But we say bonds! I suppose that's how we feel it. The lust to say *farewell*!—But every new meeting puts on a new pair of hand-cuffs, remember that."

"I shan't let them snap them tight," she said.

"Don't boast too much, while the gods are listening," he said.

"Yes!" she said, pausing. "I suppose they are listening."

And she was more cautious.

But she was strangely, wildly excited: to be gone! Strange gusts of electric energy swept through her. She could hardly sleep at all. And she felt as if, by some magic touch, she would make Wragby crumble into ruins as soon as she had left it. As soon as her presence was withdrawn.— "Leaving a ripple barely distinguishable from nonentity!"*—Who would care to distinguish it from non-entity, either, at that pass!

After a feverish morning, towards noon, she heard Hilda's car. Hilda was as quiet, as grave and demure as ever. Both sisters had this odd, maidenly demureness. Perhaps it was something Scotch in them. Anyhow quite a number of devils could hide behind it.

Hilda washed her face and combed her nut-brown hair, that was soft and loose, so like Connie's.

"Are you ready to go?" said Hilda.

"Pining!" said Constance. "But!—do you mind?—I want to stay the night *near* here! Quite near!"

"Where?" said Hilda.

"You know I've got a man I'm in love with?"

Hilda looked at her sister in a wise steadiness.

"I *suspected* it, from your letters. But no more.—Do you want to tell me about him."

"Yes! He's our game-keeper!"

Hilda's face took on a look of distaste.

"Your game-keeper! Is it worth while?"

"He's lovely as a lover," said Connie.

Hilda was silent for a time, in disapproval.

"But won't you regret it later?" she said, with a tone of distaste, even of contempt.

"I don't think so," said Connie, labouring under a feeling of distance between herself and her sister. "You know sex never really meant anything to me before. Now it's—wonderful."

Hilda's calm blue eyes looked at the glowing, excited eyes of confession that Connie lifted to her.

"But does it *matter*—in the long run?" said Hilda, with a slight weary impatience. She herself was through with sex.

"It matters fearfully, for the time," said Connie.

"Well!" said Hilda at last, a little petulantly. "I think it's unwise—a mistake!—it's so much easier to have an affair with a person on one's own footing. But I suppose you'll get over it.—Where do you want to go, for the night?"

"Only to the keeper's cottage."

Hilda seemed more out of patience.

"Don't you think it's very rash?" she said.

"No! Why? I've been before."

Hilda disapproved, but she agreed to drive off with Connie that afternoon to Mansfield, where they would stay to dinner, and she herself would stay the night. But she would drive Connie back at dusk to the lane-end at the bridge over the railway-cutting, on the side-road to Crosshill, nearly three miles from Wragby park gates. There would be little risk. And the following morning she would pick up Connie again at the lane-end, at half-past-eight.

So Connie hung out a green shawl from her bedroom window, as a signal to Parkin that he was to wait for her at the lane-end by the bridge, at dusk. Green was Mohammed's colour, and the Prophet had houris in paradise. And Connie had a bright green shawl, which suited her warm colouring.

Clifford and Hilda were polite and almost friendly. They got on quite well together, and had a long talk after lunch. And Clifford decided that Hilda, after all, had more brains and more stability than Constance, and that if he had married the elder sister, instead of the younger, perhaps——!"

There was an early cup of tea in the hall, whose doors were wide open to let in the sun. Constance and Clifford were both thrilled, as if parting were a real adventure to each of them.

"Good-bye, Connie girl! Come back safely."

"Good-bye, Clifford! Yes! I shan't be long."

"Good-bye, Hilda! Take care of her, won't you?"

"I will! And I'll bring her back," said Hilda.

"It's a promise!" said Clifford.

The suitcases were in the back of the car, Hilda and Connie sat in front. They were off. Mrs Bolton waved, and shed a tear. Mrs Lecky at the lodge waved, and shed a tear likewise. Hilda steered out of the park gates and round on to the Crosshill Road.

"It's a pity we can't go clear off!" said Hilda, impatiently. "We could have slept at Grantham tonight."

"It *is* almost a pity!" said Connie, half regretting, in Hilda's presence, that she was delaying her freedom for a man.

"I suppose you can't let him know you've changed your mind about tonight?" said Hilda.

"Well, hardly!" said Connie, who, once she had made up her mind, was as difficult to move as the star Aldebaran.*

So off they went to Mansfield, where Hilda took her room, and they both dined. The evening was wonderfully bright and clear and long-lingering. It would be half-light all night. So back they sped towards Crosshill, just after sunset. And Hilda *hated* going back on her steps. But to Connie, the warm luminous twilight, the sense of light lingering and sighing in the world, into the night, was wonderful.

"Oh Hilda!" she said. "It's so wonderful to *live* and to be in the middle of all creation!"

But she regretted it, the moment she had spoken. One should hold one's tongue on these matters.

"I suppose it is, if one *is* in the middle of creation. But every mosquito thinks the same, if it thinks at all."

"I don't begrudge it it," said Connie.

Hilda had on the head-lights by the time they passed Crosshill. They ran along by the railway cutting. Hilda had looked at the bridge and calculated the turn, in the daylight. She slowed up at the bridge, and curved into the lane. A man's figure moved in the outer dusk. Connie's heart gave a jump.

"There he is!" she said.

But Hilda was absorbed, or pretended to be, manipulating the car. She backed, and made the turn, before she let Connie get out. Then she switched off the lights, and they were all in the dusk.

"Did you wait long?" Connie said to him, as he stood under a tree.

"Not so very!" he said.

They both waited, for Hilda to get out of the car. But she sat on, and shut the door.

"This is my sister Hilda! Hilda, this is Parkin!" said Constance, going to the side of the car.

Parkin raised his hat, but came no nearer.

"Why don't you come down to the cottage with us?" said Connie to her sister.

"What! Leave the car here?"

"People leave them in the lanes."

Hilda looked round.

"Can I back just round that tree?" she said, in a soft voice like Connie's, but more masterful.

"Yes!" said Parkin. "I should think you could."

He didn't want her to come to the cottage, and she knew it.

Hilda backed the car, and got down. The three set off in silence down the overgrown lane, that led only to the cottage, between high hedges at the wood's end. The dog Flossie ran ahead. The three walked in silence, Constance carrying a little silk bag. There was a whiff of honeysuckle, the first bit! And a heavy scent of hawthorn, which Connie could see glistening in the warm, eerie twilight. And still no-one spoke, though it was about a mile to the cottage, between the dark hedges. Parkin had a flash-light torch, for the bad places. And at last Connie saw the lonely little yellow light, that made her heart beat faster.

They went into the warm room, where the fire was burning with a red glow. He turned up the lamp. The table was set, with two plates and bottled beer.

"Shall yer drink a glass of beer?" he asked.

"I will if I may," said Hilda.

She had pulled off her hat, and was looking round the cheerless little room. He poured out the beer.

"An' shall yer eat a smite o' ham?" he asked. He was reverting, a little stiffly, to the dialect. "There's ham, an' there's a pickled walnut," he added, standing flotsam in the middle of the floor.

"Yes!" said Connie, as she drank the fresh, sharp beer. "I should like it."

He went to the pantry with a candle, and brought the bread, butter, ham, cheese, jam, and pickles, setting them on the table. Then he took his coat off, apologising.

CHAPTER 12

"Sit down!" he said. "I'll take my coat off, if you don't mind."

Hilda was going to sit in his chair, against the wall at the window corner. But Connie said:

"That's his chair."

"Sit wheer yer like—it matters nowt ter me!" he said, in broad dialect, now he'd got his coat off, and had metaphorically rolled his sleeves up to them.

But Hilda took another chair. He sat in his shirt-sleeves, very clean, clean-washed-looking, as working-men look.

"Yo' mun 'elp yerselves!" he said. "Dunna wait f'r axin'."

And he sat with his hands motionless, with a queer distance and sang froid, under cover of the dialect. And Hilda noticed, that though the aspirate of the *h* was dropped, the dialect used the French stopped *h*.

He watched her, and she sometimes stared with a soft, queer stare, at him. She was handsomer than her sister, larger, more like a large-featured, warm-coloured Pallas Athene, regular and almost always in repose. But he judged her harder, with that hard opposition inside her, which modern men know so well in modern women. No, he wouldn't want *her* for a lover. She could never curl up soft, all curved in a man's arms, as her sister could. She seemed shy, demure, modest. But he felt she was hard, with a heavy, dark hardness like mysterious flint whose fire is sparks, never flame.

The three ate in silence.

"Ta'e what ter wants," he said to Connie, who was hesitating with her fork. And he knew Hilda's flesh shrank from the intimacy of the *thou*.

"But you've had hardly any," Connie expostulated to him.

"I ate afore this. This wor a' for thee!" he said. "So now it's for thee an' thy sister."

"Hilda!" she said giving him the name.

"Ay!" he said, comforting her, because she was a little ill-at-ease.

"Do you keep house for yourself?" Hilda asked him, all at once.

"Ay!" he said. "'Xcept f'r th' bit as my mother does, a-Sat'days."

"But do you go shopping for yourself? Did you buy this ham and this beer?" she asked him.

"Yes!" he said, with a smile.

"You don't mind?" Hilda persisted.

245

"Nay, what's there to mind i' that? I'm by mysen', so I mun fend for mysen'. No, it non troubles me."

She finished her food in silence. He was fully armed for defence.

"Do you think it's safe for Connie to come here?" she asked him.

He seemed taken back for a moment. Then he said, in that queer voice of indifference which Connie could not quite understand:

"As safe as owt else, I s'd think, if she's a mind to't! It's not as if the German guns 'ad got us located—"

Hilda looked at him, puzzled. Then she said:

"She's my sister. It would be very awful if she came to any harm."

Again he put up his eyebrows in the odd look.

"Ay!"—he said. "I know it! 'Er's non my sister, but 'er's what 'er is.— What d'yer want me ter say? Anythink?—'Er comes as long as 'er's a mind to come! when 'er doesna want to, 'er wunna. What else?"

"I only hope," Hilda faltered, "you'll take care."

"Care, ay! Care! Care killed t' cat,* as 'ad nine lives. Ay, I'll take care! But what by that?"

Hilda frowned with sudden impatience.

"It would be horrid if there were a mess, a scandal."

He was silent. Then he said:

"I know it! It wouldna do *me* no good. Shall y'ave some more beer?"

"No thank you! I must go!"

She rose, and picked up her hat.

"Would you like to go with Hilda to the car, and leave me here?" Connie said to him.

He stood still, holding his breath, looking at her.

"You'd better let me go alone," said Hilda.

"Nay!" he said quickly: in both directions.

"I'll come," said Connie.

They walked again in silence down the dark, eerie, overgrown lane. Half way, Hilda suddenly said:

"I only wonder if it's worth it, that's all. I don't blame anybody, or think anybody is wrong. But I do wonder if it's worth it."

Her voice came out of the night into the silence, and was received in silence. Nobody answered. They walked in silence, while an owl softly hooted. Then suddenly he stopped, and looked at the little stars of summer beyond the high edge. The air was scented with a midsummer night.

"Is folks very different, or aren't they?" he asked. "There's a few stars. When I look at 'em, it seems *to me* worth it, over an' above. What do *you* think? Is it worth it?" He looked at Connie.

"You know what I think," said Connie, a little self-righteously.

"Yes," said Hilda. "But we live in the world, not in the stars."

"We live under 'em!" he said. "But I know. It's the same when I look at the Daily Mirror, or the Illustrated London News. All them royalty and Lords an' Ladies an' people who've got divorces or been had up for something! You think to yourself: My Christ, I'm puttin' my foot i' th' man-trap!—is it worth it?—But then nothing's worth nothing, at that price. So I put th' newspapers on th' fire-back, an' forget 'em an' a' th' faces in 'em."

"But you can't put the world on the fire-back," said Hilda.

"I canna. No! But if I could, I'd kick it in th' face—all of 'em, an' the faces they show!—But what's the bother! There's stars i' th' sky, an' leaves on th' trees, mayblossom an' dog-roses into th' bargain. An' I'm a man. What am I a man for! What's a woman a woman for? What are you a woman for?"

"Not merely for lovemaking, certainly," said Hilda softly.

"Nay! But for love-makin' if yer get a chance: an' same for me, if I get a chance: what else am I a man for? If I get a chance!—An' I've got a chance. Would y'ave me wear my breeches arse forrards?"

There was a curious hostile sarcasm and human hopelessness in his voice. Connie felt, how alone he was, and how wary of a hostile universe. How afraid! but also, how fixed and inimical! There was something hard, fatal, dangerous, in his spirit. Yet she knew, he felt himself in tune with the natural things of the night, stars and hidden leaves. It was only humanly he felt the hard hopelessness, the eternal hostility.

"Still," said Hilda, "we must consider how it will end."

"What's the good! How will anything end? How did the war end? How will you end? Any of us! I leave it."

"Yes," said Hilda. "*Laisser-faire* and *laisser-aller*!"

"I dunno what that means: Lacey fair and Lacey alley."

"It means nothing, anyhow," Connie interposed.

The car was there all right—getting dewy. Hilda got in, and started her engine.

"Then I'll be here at half-past eight in the morning," she said.

"Right!" said Connie.

Suddenly Hilda leaned over the side of the car, holding out her hand.

"Goodnight, Mr Parkin!" she said. He strode up, and took her hand.

"Good-night!" he said.

"If you feel you're right—" she said, "I suppose nobody has any business to interfere."

"Nay, I don't say as I feel I'm *right*. But if an apple falls on my head, I eat it. I like what I like, an' gimme lashin's—"*

Hilda, who was hardly listening, flashed on her head-lights. There was a blare of white light, frightening every natural creature. And the hulk of the car swayed and slowly eased out of the lane, mounted the bridge, and slid away into the dark country.

Connie and he stood under a tree in the night. She turned to him. She felt a bit miserable.

"Kiss me!" she murmured, lifting her face to him.

"Nay!" he said impatiently. "Wait a bit! I don't feel like it. I'm put out."

Instead of being angry, she laughed.

"But you'll give me your hand, won't you?" she said.

He held out his hand to her, rather crossly. She took it and nestled her own in it. It was so warm! the warm life! That was really all she wanted from him, the warm physical contact. But as they walked home, he was so silent, she asked him at last:

"What were you thinking about?"

"Nothing!" he said.

Yet when he was home, the door was locked, and he had taken off his coat and was unfastening his boots, he said:

"It strikes me the Bolshevists was about right, to smash 'em up. What good are they?"

"Who?" she said.

"Folks!"

She was silent, feeling her heart sink. Then at last she asked:

"But didn't you like Hilda?"

"Ay—ay—all right!"

"Then why do you talk about Bolshevists?"

"Eh well! I don't!"

"I think Bolshevists are such dreary, uninspired people, just smashing things and creating nothing."

He received this in silence. But as he pushed off his boot with his other foot, he said:

"It's us or them. One or t'other's got to go smash."

"Who? Us or who?"

"Folks! Other folks!" he said.

"But that's everybody except you and me!" she said, laughing at the idea.

"'Appen so!" he said complacently.

There was a funny sort of anger in him. But it wouldn't prevent his making love. It was an anger that amused her and made her want him. It was a queer, atmospheric anger that she wanted to feel in her body. Perhaps it was part of her own revolt. She wanted it to be let loose in love.

It was a night of sensual passion, in which she was a little scared, and almost unwilling. But she let him have his way, and the reckless sensuality shook her to her foundations, and made another consciousness wake deeper in her. It was not love, in the emotional sense. And it was not voluptuousness, nothing so soft and gluttonous. It was sensuality sharp as fire, burning the soul to tinder.

She had always wondered what Abélard meant, when he said, in the long fragment of his autobiographical letter, that in their year of love he and Héloïse had gone through all the stages of passion, and had known all the refinements of passion. She had always wondered what they were, the stages and the refinements of passion. Vaguely, she had imagined it meant some sort of emotional, perhaps sentimental development.

Now, however, after this night, she knew it meant stages of sensual intensity, and degrees of refinement in the different practices of sensuality. In this one short summer night, a new range of experience opened out to her, frightening, but acute as fire, and necessary. She had never known it was necessary, till she had it. And now at last she felt she was approaching the real bed-rock of her nature, her intrepid sensual self. She thought she would have been ashamed. But she was not ashamed. She felt a triumph, almost a vainglory. So! That was what one was! That was it! There was no more to suppress.

But what a reckless devil the man was! One had to be strong to bear him! She felt that she was mated. And that was what had been at the bottom of her soul all the time! the hunger for the daredevil, sensual mate! What liars poets were!—at least for her. Communion of love, and all the rest! When the bed-rock was sharp, flamey, rather awful sensuality. And the man who dared do it, without shame or sin or abating his pride. If he had been ashamed, it would have been awful. But now, in the morning light, he slept with the innocence and also the mystery of the full sensual creature. As a tiger sleeps, with its ears half pricked.

She leaned against his firm, warm, living body, and dozed to sleep again, in complete confidence. And till his rousing waked her, she was aware of nothing. When she did open her eyes, he was sitting up in the bed, looking down at her. A queer, fluid maleness seemed to flow out of his eyes into hers, and she stretched voluptuously. Oh, how voluptuous it was, to have limbs and a body half sunk in sleep, yet so strong with life.

"Are you wake?" he said.

"Yes! Are you?"

"Ay! I woke at half-past five, as usual."

"What time is it now?"

"Nigh on seven. I'd better go down an' get breakfast. Flossie's whimperin'.—Should I bring it up here, on a tray?"

"Oh do!" she said. "Then I can stay in bed! It's so lovely!"

He smiled a slight smile, and got up, quick and alert as ever.

"Pull the blind!" she said.

He drew up the blind and opened the window wide. The sun was shining already on the tender green leaves of morning, on the wood that stood a little way back, across the clearing. She sat up in bed, looking out of the low dormer window.

"Where is my nightie?" she said, looking round.

He pushed his hand into the bed, and produced the flimsy silk nightdress.

"I knowed I could feel it under my ribs—summat silk!" he said. "Did it rip, though?"—and he held it in the air.

The night-dress was torn almost in two.

"Never mind!" she said. "I've got others. I can leave it. It's not a smart one."

"Ay! Leave it!" he said. "I like the feel an' the smell of it. I can put it between my legs for company, at night sometimes! There isn't any name nor nothing on it, is there?"

"No!" she said carelessly. "It's just a plain one that anybody might have."

She slipped on the torn thing, as she sat in bed, and was perfectly content, looking out of the open window. It didn't even occur to her that in about an hour's time she would have to depart. She was content. She could hear him starting the fire and pumping water. And by and by she could smell bacon frying, which made her feel hungry.

At last he came slowly up the stairs, with a huge black tray that would only just pass through the door. She made room on the bed for the tray. He poured out tea and set the tea-pot on the floor, then sat on a chair by the bed, his plate with egg and bacon on his knees.

"How good it is!" she said, as she sat squatting in bed in her torn night-dress, and eating voraciously. "How good to have breakfast in bed, for once!"

"Don't you have it in bed?" he asked.

"Never! I don't want to, just myself!"

He ate in silence. He was already thinking of the departure. This made her remember it too.

"How I wish you were coming along with me!" she said.

"Ay!" he said.

"Would you like to?"

"Me?"—He thought about it. "Yes, I should—if it worn't for a' t'other people," he added, with a slight ironical smile.

"One day—soon!—we'll *really* have a time together, quite together! Shall we?"

"It'd suit me!" he said; "when it comes off!"

"Yes, it'll come off. I *really* feel married to you, as much as a woman ever need feel married to a man, in her real feelings—not just social. Do you feel married to me?"

He looked at her with queer eyes.

"Married! No! But that's how I don't want to feel.—I feel all right with you!"—He added this last in an odd, easy, indifferent voice, that amused her. She gave a quick laugh.

"I should think you do!" she cried.

But he suddenly started and lifted his hand. Flossie had given a short bark, then three sharp yaps. Silent, muted, he put his plate on the floor and hastily went downstairs. Constance heard the gate click, and a knock at the door, then the door open and Parkin's voice, frank and cheerful:

"What have you got for me this time?"

251

"Letter!"

"All right! I'll keep it in mind."

"Right-o! Mornin'."

She heard the gate click again, then silence. In a minute he came upstairs with a letter in his hand.

"Post-man!" he said, in a low voice.

"He's very early."

"It's th' rural round."

"Do you think he heard?"

"I s'd think not. A bicycle comes so quiet, else Floss would have heard him sooner." But he was angry, none the less.

"Anyhow he wouldn't know anything."

"No!"

But he seemed troubled, gloomy. And before he let Connie go out, he went and looked round outside, with his dog.

"Nowt's safe!" he said gloomily, as he came in again.

She was ready. He took her in an overgrown path through the wood, rather than go by the lane.

"Lucky he didn't come just when the car was there!" he said. "Or when we was walking up.—I don't have a letter more than twice a year, I should think. But it's sure to come on the day you don't want it."

"Is it a nice letter?"

"I've not read it! It's from a cousin of mine in Canada. I wrote to him as 'appen I might go out there."

"You won't though, will you?"

"Not this summer, anyhow," he said.

She walked a way in silence, then she said:

"You must stay for me, now. I really do feel married to you, so you mustn't leave me.—Don't you think one *lives* for times like last night?"

He walked on in silence. Then he said:

"Ay, one lives for that! But in between, you've got to keep your pecker up. That's what a man lives by."

"Is that what a man lives by?—keeping his pecker up?—Then I think you'll be all right!" she said, with an easy laugh.

He walked in silence, oppressed by the noise. The path was overgrown and difficult, and he went quickly, she had to hurry and she felt hot. He was silent, shut up. Sometimes he spoke a low word to the dog.

At last he said to Constance:

"Wait here a minute!"

He strode off through the brambles to the right, and through a thick screen of hazel. Then he came back.

"Car's not there yet!" he said, in an undertone.

She looked at him curiously, he seemed so depressed.

"Is it time?" she said.

"Hark!"

His ears had caught the distant sound of a car. They waited. The sound drew nearer, the car was on the bridge, slowing down.

"There she is!" said Constance.

"Wait till she's turned!" he said quickly.

They heard the car buzz, and whirr, and then there was silence.

"She's backed into th' lane!" he said. "I shan't come out.—Mind th' brambles!"

She followed him through the undergrowth to the thick hazel screen, into which he had wound his way. She followed. But he stood still.

"Go on!" he said. "Go! I shan't come out o' th' wood."

She looked at him in sudden dismay. She had not realised to this minute that she was parting from him.

"Go!" he said fiercely, with a flash in his eye. "You don't want that car standing there!"

"Good-bye!" she faltered, gazing into his face.

But with a fierce motion of his hand he made her go, creeping through the hazels, till she came to the nettles at the edge of the lane. Hilda was just getting out of the car.

"Hilda!" said Connie softly.

"Goodness!" cried Hilda with a start. "Were you waiting!—There's been a bicycle down the lane."

"Yes! The postman! He didn't see anything!" said Connie, as she got in the car and slammed the door violently.

Hilda was busy starting the car. It gave a heave of motion. Connie looked back into the lane. Nothing! not even Flossie. Nothing! She waved her hat, tears blinding her eyes. And the car leaped over the bridge.

"You know it's not worth it, Connie!" said Hilda vexedly, as the car sped away.

But Connie was gone in bitter tears. She had never realised it was parting. And death might come like that, unbeknown.

13

T HEY WERE IN LONDON BY TEA-TIME, staying in a little hotel near the Haymarket. Sir Malcolm was at his club, but he came to take his daughters to the theatre. And there was a certain family thrill, for all three of them, that they were together, and apart from all other people for the time being. They were a little clan in themselves. And Connie realised, rather unexpectedly, how strong the family bond was in her. She had so often denied it. But now, being out with Hilda and her father, and away from every other connection, again she realised the sense of ease and gratification. It was something in the physical vibration. They vibrated, the three of them, more or less with the same wave-length, from the blood, and that was a substantial relief and gratification.

Connie found that her family feeling did not at all interfere with her feeling for Parkin, as it had done with her feeling for Clifford. In the past, when she was with her people, she felt inside herself an instinctive, or at least involuntary hostility to poor Clifford, amounting almost to malevolence. But now she sat between the burly, well-groomed Sir Malcolm, and Hilda, who looked distinguished without trying to, and she felt that both of them were bulwarks to her passion for Parkin. She was safe between two rocks.

To be sure, Hilda disapproved of the tiresomeness of the *mésalliance*. But she was in instinctive sympathy with the passion itself. And now that Connie was safely under her wing, she had nothing to complain of.

Sir Malcolm was in ignorance of his daughter's connection. But the vibration of his blood seemed to know, and seemed pleased. He was happy as a young man, out with his daughters, and his tenderness for Connie, in her soft, attractive vagueness, stimulated him and filled him with new energy. With his sensitive nostrils, he sniffed a genuine sensual passion, and took heart. And Connie, looking at the round, well-nourished thighs of her father, in the fine black cloth, realised that underneath him too was a Parkin, but a Parkin that had never been hurt so much, and in whom the passion was more of an easy heat, than a hard fire. Still, there it was, basic: the son of Adam. Clifford had always been different: as if he had never had a really physical father, had never been born of the blood, only of the nerves.

CHAPTER 13

They were a few days in London, shopping and seeing the dentist. Connie still vaguely, in the depths of her, lamented and wailed at being far from Parkin. She did not want to be far from him. Yet she had a strange superficial submission to circumstance, as if it were fate. She wrote two letters, nice and chatty, to Clifford. To the other man she did not write at all. She didn't even want to. What was the point of writing!—And she did the things her father or Hilda suggested, acquiescent, and quite pleased. She saw a few people. But they were all vague to her, quite nice, but vague. Her nervous social consciousness was in abeyance.

In Paris, she was happier than in London: she felt nearer to the man. It was not miles that mattered: it was the psychic influence. In London, at the theatre or at people's houses or even in the street, she felt the whole influence of all the people dead against her own rhythm, her own slowly-pulsing but vital passion. They seemed dead against it, and she had to sink deep, deep down into herself, to escape them: leaving her social consciousness floating like shallow scum on the surface, for other people.

London was far, far worse than the Midlands, than Uthwaite or Tevershall, in spite of the ugliness of these latter. The noise of London, and the endless chatter, chatter, chatter of the people seemed like a death's-head chattering its teeth in a sort of cold frenzy. So many dead people! So many dead ones, masquerading with life!

But in Paris, she felt a certain tenderness again. In the restaurants, where the well-nourished men ate their food with a long-refined passion of the stomach, and then cast glistening eyes at the young woman, as if she were some soft persimmon just in perfect condition for dessert, she had to laugh. She didn't resent it. She didn't mind the so-called lustful glances of the men. They didn't do her any harm. Not like the cold, analysing eyes in London.

And in Paris, the lewd people, and they were plenty, did not frighten her like the lewd people of London. The sensual lewdness is not so terrifying as the mental, spiritual lewdness of the north. And there were many men, workmen, students, all kinds of Frenchmen, who reminded her a little of Parkin. Only they hadn't got his deep defiance. They were willing, in the last issue, to have the phallus, the phallic man, despised and done to death, crucified in ignominy so that the mental-spiritual man might rise from the corpse. This, to her, was the feebleness of the French. The women lived for money, and the power of money. And the men, half-worshipping the phallic principle, were willing to betray this principle with a kiss, to the Judas* of woman-mammon. The woman-mammon in the shops and the streets, the woman who is female-mammon, with money or property or material power, for her ultimate significance, struck Connie as barren, and rather repellant. Though even then, less repellant than the mental female-mammon of England.

And the men, the true Frenchmen, a little pathetic! often very attractive, but a little pathetic, so willing to sell the phallic man in themselves, to the female mammon. There they were, all self sold, one way or another, to the mammon, usually female. Never being able to muster themselves to fight for the phallic man in themselves. Like Abélard, a thousand years before, undergoing the final mutilation, because they would not openly stand by their own phallic body.

But they left Paris, and drove south, through Chartres and down the Loire. Gothic, however, though she still saw its beauty, no longer moved the soul of Connie. She preferred the empty, open spaces of the country, the sense of the past, the queer bleak past, filling France up again, gradually. Yet even the past did not really interest her. She felt the present moment swaying with silent momentousness, inside herself. And France, with its shadows of woods, and lonely hillsides in the sun, its flat places so still and void, passed like the dream it is, the old past slowly filtering back and taking possession.

But it was pleasant, motoring slowly along, and stopping often. The people were nearly all quite nice. They liked Sir Malcolm, who was at home in France. And to Connie they were gentle and friendly. To be sure, they all accepted money. But who doesn't, in this world! So the family got on very well. They were rich enough, and they were Scotch. "Ah, Monsieur est Ecossais! Très bien! Et la jeune Madame est belle comme la reine Marie Stuart!"

It was not true, however, that a woman in love is a prey to all other men. Connie found the men very nice and attentive to her, running round for her. But they were not pressing or insolent. And she felt a certain gentleness for them, because they were men, sexual men. But this gentleness, this queer sympathy that had a touch of compassion in it, for the odd generosity and the equally odd cold selfishness of the Frenchman, did not expose her at all to familiarities. On the contrary, the men seemed to like her with *real* warmth, because her woman's humanness was *not* flirtatious, *not* suggestive. There was no sexual end in view. It was the simple human sympathy of a woman who was sensually wrapped up in her own man, and so was never naked to other men, yet had the basic sympathy for them. And she was amazed how they responded the same to her, kind and warm and glad, really, not to have to force the sexual game.

At last, however, they crossed the frontier and came to the Villa Natividad. It was some distance beyond Biarritz, above a little bay, and the mountains went up steep behind it. The sun poured on it, yet the air was fresh. And it was a lovely place, a villa built in the Spanish style, built square round a patio, or courtyard, in the midst of which was a fountain and tubs of flowering oleander. The façade, rather showy, faced west, facing the sea. But Connie had a room on the east side, where the hot sun poured in for only a brief while, and she looked at the dark mountains. Hilda and she had a little sitting-room between them, and a very modern bathroom, and were altogether comfortable.

Their host was an elderly Scotchman who had made a decent fortune in Spain before the war, and who became very rich indeed, during the course of the war. His services in that period were rewarded with a knightship, and he was altogether rather pleased with himself. He was a big, heavy, rather coarse man whose conduct, however, was exemplary, and he had a quiet, sly English wife who had been a governess, and who had a long, sharp nose and an intense desire to be the power behind the throne: her husband being the throne. She also painted "sweet" water-colours, and had a very "successful" exhibition in London, where she made over a thousand pounds.

But then, of course, the hospitality of the Melroses was proverbial: and ex-guests could not but buy! Who was there, that was anybody, who had not made use of the Casa Natividad: or the Villa, as most English people called it! Sir Andrew loved to entertain. He loved to say: "When the Duchess of Theddlethorpe was here last spring!—" or else: "I am giving you the rooms that my friends the Conde and the Condesa de la Huerta have just left—" Still, he was not really a snob. Titles somehow thrilled his coarse soul, but he was a man who had struggled long and hard in a difficult country, and titles therefore never blinded him to the individual inside the name. And he judged individuals by their toughness and their power of resistance—even to himself and his wife. For Lady Melrose was a snob. She had never got over her original inferiority, so she had very many quite clever tricks, to make people feel small, and herself aggrandised.

However, with their pleasant rooms to themselves, Hilda and Constance hoped to live more or less in their own way. There were seven other guests, besides themselves and their father. One was a young Spanish Count with an American wife and a modest income. There turned up, after a few days, an old friend of Connie's, Duncan Forbes, a modern and rather impecunious painter. He was returning from Madrid. He had known Connie and Hilda in the Scotch village where their mother's father was the laird and Forbes' father was the minister. So they were glad to see him. There were two elderly ladies of means but not fortune. And there were two Americans. But the company changed every day or two, and practically every day somebody came over from Biarritz for lunch, tea, dinner, or all three. It was something like living in an hotel, except that one was introduced to everybody, and didn't get a bill.

The house, however, was spacious, and nobody met anybody till luncheon, unless they wished. And some of the guests always lunched out, on a picnic or a jaunt. It was on the whole easy. Yet Lady Melrose's eagle eye—or sparrow-hawk eye—gradually made itself felt, and her tough will, which at first seemed non-existent, gradually exerted its pressure. She little by little bent her guests and forced them in some direction or other. And though she was discretion itself, still she managed to know everybody's private secrets, and to make it *half*-apparent that she knew them.

Connie thought of Clifford, who expected her to have *affaires d'amour* in this house. Ghastly thought! with Lady Melrose's sharp nose smelling out the rat. A rat it would be, too! And Sir Andrew giving one the leer, or tipping one the wink, of a man who isn't going to be a spoil-sport, not he!

It is curious how a personality pervades a house. Ostensibly, the Casa Natividad was Sir Andrew's creation: the rather luxurious furniture, slightly vulgar: the carved oak, the suits of armour, the private chapel—episcopalian—so comfortably fitted up, but so small an altar space that chaplain's feet—there was a private chaplain, but he lived in the village and "visited" the visitors—stuck out beyond the altar rail when he kneeled down before communion. The billiard room was like that of a good hotel. The library was a smoking-room with a few English, French and Spanish books.

Altogether, it struck one as rather like a private hotel run by Sir Andrew. But gradually Lady Melrose's water-colours, so sweet, almond blossom under a blue sky, delicate sea between the arms of a bay, flowers among pale rocks!—gradually they made themselves felt, upon the walls. Even Sir Malcolm hated them. And gradually the more tasteful chintzes of the long sitting-room, and the Dresden of the little green room began to hint at her ladyship. And gradually the smooth-faced butler and his two swarthy, but clean-shaven footmen, who bowed so quickly at Sir Andrew's hearty voice, were seen to bow much more nervously, and to glance much more apprehensively at the sound of Lady Melrose's voice. They were afraid of her: And it was a queer sight to see her pale, set face sweep the table at dinner-time, to see if everything was impeccable. And the servants waited nervously for that glance, and for the stony impassivity that followed when there was no fault. But if something was wrong, she would say in a queer, hard, jocular sort of voice, to her husband:

"Are we a cover short, Sir Andrew? Or am I bad at arithmetic?"

And Sir Andrew, glancing at the table, would say shortly, with command, but not with ill-humour, in Spanish:

"Another cover, Manuel. We are eleven!"

But it was her ladyship who fixed the smooth-faced Basque with her eye, as he turned quickly to the side-board, muttering to one of the footmen. The cover appeared in a twinkling: the house was well-run. But the prick of the goad had been felt.

The "refined" Lady Melrose was in the end more objectionable than the crude Sir Andrew. He was a bully, in his own way: which was the way of a man used to having work done at his order. But she was a bully by suggestion. Connie came to hate the sight of her, even when she saw her starting off in the morning, in an impeccable Paris coat and skirt of delicate stone-coloured linen, and a wide hat, to go painting, a maid going behind her with a cringing, slinking sort of motion, carrying a board and small easel and folding stool. Lady Melrose's face was pale and fixed, and she steered silently ahead like a torpedo destroyer, the maid seeming to ramble in her wake like a towed oar-boat. But the eyes in the pale, forward-steering face saw sideways, and almost backwards.—She was a woman who could never get over her craving for perfectly-tailored coats and skirts, even in the most bare-armed period.

Connie, Hilda, and Duncan Forbes made a trio by themselves. They bathed at their own hours: to the silent fury of Lady Melrose, who liked a bathing party, and who did not quite know what kind of figures the sisters had, and who did not quite know which sister was the mistress of Forbes, but suspected Connie. They played tennis together, usually with a queer little musician called Blood, the last name for such a creature of nerves, who had no money and travelled with a valet who looked as if he had a job in the City. The rest of the visitors they refused to know, except just casually. They did not play golf. They refused to take part in tennis tournaments or swimming contests: said they were not good enough. And they refused to sit in the music-room when the wireless was on, they refused to be interested in cross-word puzzles, they slipped away when parlour games were mooted—Sir Andrew had a weakness for them—and, last and worst, Connie refused to dance, and Hilda would only dance with Forbes. She could not bear to be held up against Sir Andrew's stout coarse body. Altogether, after the first week or ten days, there were various little rifts in the lute. Hilda, however, was superior to the tension. She loved the situation of the house, the bathing, the comfort, the walks and drives into the mountains, the foretaste of Spain. During her married life, she had got hardened to dinner-parties. She managed to go her own way and despise her hostess' manœuvres, and make use of her host's hospitality, jesting with him good-humouredly.

Sir Malcolm was frankly content. He had luxury around him: he had good golf, good swimming, a good club to go to, good bridge, and good-looking women to think him handsome and feel flattered if he drove them in his car. And he had his two daughters there with him in the clover, so to speak.

But an uneasiness, almost a fear, gnawed at Connie's heart. She had, at first, to say she was happy. The weather was perfect, brilliant sun, yet a fresh little breeze that made the olive-trees silver. The mountains folded steep and mysterious, the sea was fresh, invigorating, there were many, many mountain flowers still, though the roses were passing. It was holiday. It was "care-free".

But underneath the "care-free" atmosphere—how she hated the word!—was care, or else a tough resistance. The queer, rubber-necked toughness of that social world made her now want to cry. She used to take it for granted. Now she could not. It seemed inimical to her, to be destroying something in her. She came to hate the meal-times with loathing—those bright holiday faces round the board, the genial sense of plenty of money, the flippant assertion of care-freeness, the hard, insentient chatter of people enjoying themselves by will to do it, and the exasperating but never-ending attempts to be funny, to be witty, to be humorous! Oh humour! Oh that deadly cog-wheel sense of humour which starts so many automatic little souls spinning with a sort of self-satisfaction!

After she had been at the Villa Natividad for a fortnight, Connie was pining to go away, to go back to Tevershall, which was by no means care-free, thank God! But she dared not suggest it to Hilda, and it would have been sheer unkindness even to hint it to Sir Malcolm. He thought everyone was really disporting on the hill o' beans.* But Connie did manage to get a trip of a few days with Hilda and with Duncan Forbes, across the base of the Pyrenees. Forbes was supposed to be taking the train to Paris. He said goodbye! to his host and hostess. But he made this little trip with the two sisters, before he shipped himself back.

When she and Hilda returned to the Villa, Connie found two letters from Clifford. She thought of him with affection, in her new surroundings. Whatever he was, he was not a shallow, complacent little fool, he was not small beer in a champagne glass. He wrote quite good letters: and she diligently answered. There was no news of Parkin. And, being caught up in the wrong spirit, she did not think of him. Only some sense of loss gnawed in her soul. She felt she had lost some treasure out of her being, and she wanted to hurry back on her steps, to look for it, to find where she had dropped it.

She began to suspect, also, that she was pregnant. She could not, of course, be certain. But she waited in a queer suspense, almost certain. And that made her uneasy too. She had thought she would be glad. But she wasn't. She was uneasy. She would almost have liked to put it off. There, in that tough society, she felt afraid, as if she were putting herself in some nasty jeopardy. And she felt again as if she would never get out, never escape. It was "the world".

She no longer wondered why she had married Clifford: He was golden, by comparison, being much better bred and more intelligent. But perhaps he was the same, in having the tough indiarubber bowels these "care-free" people seemed all to have. They were hard inside as golf-balls.

Then came a letter from Clifford containing an unexpected blow: a horrid blow.

"We too have had our mild local excitement," he wrote. "Parkin's wife came back to him unexpectedly, two days ago, and, it seems, was unwelcome. He turned her out of the house and locked the door, but when he came back from the wood, report has it he found the lady in his bed, *in puris naturalibus,* not so much as a shift to cover her rather battered nudity. The intimate facts of course I don't know: but it appears he retired to Teforshall, to his mother's house, for the night. The wife, however, says she has come to stay: I believe she is still at the cottage: and Parkin, I believe, is domiciled with his mother in Teforshall. I shall not send for him until he comes to me.

"I have this bit of local garbage from our particular garbage bird, our scavenger crow, our sacred ibis, our intimate buzzard, Mrs Ivy Bolton. I would not have handed it on, had not she exclaimed: What *would* her ladyship say!

"I like your picture of Sir Malcolm in the sea, with his white hair washed over his forehead, like a bonny babe in a bath. He is the most mortal of mortals: one might almost envy it him. He washes off any smear of immortality every time he takes a bath, and emerges a rosy incarnate mortal of mortals who may really live for ever, there is so little reason why he should die. I suppose mortality is a gift: or would you call it an acquirement? or an attainment? I think it is a gift. To be immortal requires some effort, but—"

Connie read no more. She only glanced to see if there was any further news. Nothing. So she was left to swallow the bitter pill of Parkin and Bertha Coutts. And she had to dress, for it was dinner-time. She had to go down among the guests—there would be heaven knows how many new ones—and renew the subtle fight for prestige, which is the essential game of society, now and always. What prestige amounts to, nobody knows. But it is the essential, and if you are in the world, you must use your elbows and fight for it. It is something like getting first on to the bus.

But Connie was feeling angry, very angry. From being sad and melancholy, she was filled with anger. She was angry with Parkin, because Bertha Coutts existed, and because it was *possible* for "that woman" to force her way back into the cottage. That she should force her way in, and take possession! And that he should meekly abandon the field to her! Rage filled the female soul of Lady Chatterley.

Connie retired early, and sat silent and motionless by her window. Hilda could feel the vibration of the storm in her sister. She asked anxiously:

"Is anything wrong? Have you had any news?"

"No!" said Connie.

And Hilda retired, to leave her to it. But Connie could not sleep. She tossed and tossed in her bed, consumed by an anger that felt like fever. She hated the villa, she hated the life there. It was a nasty substitute for life, as margarine is for butter. At the same time, she no longer wanted to go back to Wragby. She felt a violent repulsion from Wragby and all its environments.

With the first dawn, she got up and wrote a note to Mrs Bolton, casually asking for particulars of Parkin's affair. As soon as she heard the first servants, she went downstairs and out to the post. She hated the mountains going up so steep and theatrical against the early sun: mere theatricality. She hated the sight of the sea in the bay, like a great bath-tub laid out by the servants for the "visitors". She hated the sound of the first motor-car going down with a bunch of before-breakfast bathers, the energetic type. She hated the idiocy of holiday in the coming blaze of the day.

When she got back, she found Hilda looking for her.

"Do say if anything is wrong, Connie!" her sister urged.

"Nothing is wrong! Things are never more than idiotic!" said Connie, handing Clifford's letter to her sister.

Hilda had a look of distaste on her face as she read. For some time she said nothing. Then at last she remarked:

"Yes, it is annoying. But after all—if you have the child—perhaps it is the best finish to the intrigue, if he takes his wife back."

The intrigue! If he takes his wife back!—the child! *the* child!—Every phrase was a mortal insult to Connie. The child indeed: *the* child! Why, she didn't know if it was even conceived. And if it was, she felt she almost hated it in advance, for foisting itself on her. The child! It would be another *substitute*. It would once more be the margarine, when she asked for butter. And everybody, her family even, and Clifford, would think that now, now, with the child, the margarine for the rest of her days, she should be purely satisfied. How they loved to force substitutes on to one: all of them!

Hard and angry, she waited for the letter from Mrs Bolton. Her heart had shut against Hilda. And in her queer rage, she found a certain sympathy in Archie Blood, the grey-faced little musician. He was a man, a bachelor, of nearly fifty, but he seemed also like a petulant boy. He composed rather charming Elizabethan sort of music, very old English in taste—and he played the piano very well. He earned his hospitality playing occasionally to the other guests, and hating them for listening so stupidly.

She found him in the late morning sitting alone in the music room, in absolute despondency.

"Aren't these places awful!" he said as she sat by him. "Of course I'm going mad."

"You mean these holiday places?" she said.

"No! These rich, made-over villas! I'm going perfectly mad, from staying in them."

"Then why do you stay in them?"

"What else am I to do, with an income like mine, when I *must* have a certain amount of luxury. I *know* it is *manie de la grandeur*,* and perfectly ridiculous. But I must have it. It is part of the first stage of my insanity."

"But you can't be insane, if you know it."

"On the contrary, not only do most insane people know it, but they are proud of it. They are proud of their insanity. It is part of the disease."

"You *are* cheerful!" she said, a little relieved to find someone in a worse condition than herself.

"We've got cold feet," he said. "You know how the Americans say: And then he got cold feet!—That's what's the matter with us."

"And do cold feet affect the brain?" she laughed.

"Assuredly! after a while! They say Schiller used to sit with his feet in a tub of cold water, when he wrote his immortal works."

"I wouldn't be immortal at the price," she laughed.

"Quite! Well, I think I do the same, here. I'm an insignificant person, really. That's why I must have a valet de chambre.—Only I think my music is good. But I'm an insignificant person, really. That's why I *have* to stay in a house with six footmen, and perhaps sit next to the Duchess of Toadstool at dinner. I'm *furious* if I don't sit next to the duchess. Yet all the time I am sitting with my feet in a tub of cold water. And not even creating anything as good as *Don Carlos*,* at that."

"Then why don't you go away?" said Connie, laughing.

He looked at her with queer, rather beautiful, haunted pale eyes.

"Because I'm insignificant. And because I'm going mad. I've got cold feet. All of us in this house have got cold feet. Like lobsters and crabs, which crawl about eating putrefaction. We should all go scarlet if we were boiled."

"And look as handsome as cardinals!" said Connie.

"Quite!"

He lapsed into inscrutable silence.

"Some of the people here seem to enjoy themselves," said Connie.

"Pah! Eating putrefaction! Their loathsome happiness! They're as cold-blooded as crabs! They're crustaceans. There's not a mammal among them. Even tigresses have milk. But crabs have only crab-juice, like these people here."

"It seems a pity," said Connie.

Suddenly he looked at her, really alert.

"It's because we are really all proletarian," he said. "A German once made that plain to me. The proletariat is a state of mind, it's not really a class at all. You're proletarian when you are cold like a crab, greedy like a crab, lustful with the ricketty egoism of a crab, and shambling like a crab. The people in this house are all proletarian. The Duchess of Toadstool is an arch proletarian. It's obvious. And the Bolshevists are proletarian. The proletarian *haves* against the proletarian *have-nots* will destroy the human world entirely. A coal-miner is a proletarian *have-not*! Sir Andrew here is a proletarian *have*! They are the two halves of the scissors that will shear off the head of the human race."

"And then what?" said Connie.

"There'll be no human race."

"Perhaps it will be a good thing."

"Oh, assuredly.—But I, being one of the lice in the head of the human race, see my own extinction absolute."

To Connie, however, there seemed a real truth in what he said. There was no longer any such thing as class. The world was one vast proletariat. Everything else had gone. The true working class was gone, as much as the honorable bourgeoisie, or the proud aristocracy. Bolshevist or Fascist, the world was proletarian, a vast homogeneous proletariat made up the whole of humanity.

But the homogeneity of the proletariat was divided between haves and have-nots, owners and wage-earners, capitalists and workers. It was a polarised homogeneous proletariat. It was all Robot. And it was the suicide of the human race.

"They're individualists, they're egoists, and they are cold-blooded. Their righteousness and their unrighteousness alike are cold-blooded. And when the Lord sent to Sodom and Gomorrah for ten righteous men,* he meant ten warm-blooded, hot-hearted men. And he didn't find 'em. The Sodomites and the Gomorrahites were cold-blooded to a man. So the Lord dropped the curtain of fire.—Myself, I see the extinction of the white race in sixty years: because by that time, the last warm-souled man will be dead, and the last gentle, warm-bodied woman."

A new truth seemed to have entered Connie's soul, when she realised that there was no real class-distinction any more. In spite of herself, she had been obliged to think in terms of upper and lower class. And Parkin had been lower class, she herself had been upper class. And unconsciously, she had been forced to feel a certain class hatred. The ugly humanlessness which was killing the world, she had been forced, with helpless automatism, to identify with the lower class, the working-class, the so-called proletariat.

Now she suddenly realised what the little man Archie Blood said: that the proletariat was a state of mind. Even Clifford, with his central insistence on the mines, and on his own position as employer and boss, was really proletarian. That was why his immortality troubled him: and his happiness. To trouble about happiness or immortality was a proletarian symptom, because the proletariat has neither immortality nor happiness, being in essence Robot. And Mrs Bolton was proletariat: so were most, perhaps, of the colliers.

But Parkin wasn't. He was hot-blooded and single, and he wasn't at all absorbed in himself. She had held back from him with a certain grudge, because he was lower class. Now the barrier broke, and her soul flooded free. Class is an anachronism. It finished in 1914. Nothing remains but a vast proletariat, including kings, aristocrats, squires, millionaires and working-people, men and women alike. And then a few individuals who have not been proletarianised.

Ah the mistake, the mistake she had made! She had held herself aloof, just a little contemptuous of Parkin, because he was lower class, a working man, and therefore she had identified him with the proletariat. Now she realised, the proletariat was a state of mind, embracing Clifford and the gambling Lady Eva, and Mrs Bolton and the beastly Bertha Coutts, but missing Parkin, and missing herself. She had been merging into the proletarian frame of mind. But thank God, she had escaped!

She felt a great relief, when she was no longer forced to think, and feel, in terms of class. The warm-blooded were the warm-blooded, they were sons and daughters of god,* in all the world. And the cold-blooded and the cold-willed were the proletariat, the world over, from colliers to kings. A release flooded her heart and her bowels, as she felt her soul flow out towards the warm-blooded-ones in all the world. Against the proletariat she could bear to fight. But her heart-flow must flow somewhere.

And at last it flowed free to Parkin, to the thing he was, in his solitary self, and the thing he stood for. She had a great yearning, now, to unite herself to him in some way: not necessarily to live with him, but to be married to him forever, in an intrinsic marriage. She was weary of the trammels of extrinsic marriage. But she wanted to meet him, and pledge her heart to him, finally, forever.

She would have to leave Clifford. This, too, she realised.

She had a letter from Mrs Bolton:—"You will be pleased I am sure, My Lady, when you see Sir Clifford. He has made great strides, and seems greatly improved in health and strength, and looking forward to seeing you among us again. It is a dull house without My Lady, and we shall all welcome her bright presence among us once more, as I can truly say for all at Wragby, from highest to lowest, for you are quite loved by everyone. Everything has gone on very quietly. Sir Clifford has been very busy at the mines, in fact it is wonderful what a lot of work he gets through, and he has had consultations with several experts and other gentlemen about the new plant, which he will start on in the autumn. I am sure, I wish him every success, for he deserves it. The new work means the life and death of Tevershall, and I'm sure the miners ought to be very grateful to him. But one must not look for much gratitude on this earth, and Sir Clifford knows it.

"About Mr Parkin, I don't know how much Sir Clifford told you. It seems his wife came back all of a sudden one afternoon, the miner at Stacks Gate having thrown her out. So Mr Parkin found her sitting on the doorstep when he came in from the wood. But he wouldn't have her in the house, and she went to her brother Dan's, at the Crosshill turnpike, though Mrs Dan Coutts didn't want her either. However, it was a force-put, though Mr Parkin had offered her money to pay for lodgings for herself, but she wouldn't take it. She said that was her home, meaning the cottage. But he wouldn't have her in. So she went to her brother Dan's, and Dan said she could stop, but Dan's wife didn't want her. Well they thought she'd gone to bed, but she came down with her things on, and said she was going out, and it appears what did she do but walk to the cottage in the dark, and start knocking at the door. It must have been late, because Mr Parkin was in bed, but he shouted who was it, and she said it's me, and she'd nowhere to go, Dan's wife wouldn't have her, and Swain had turned her out. Well Mr Parkin said he wouldn't have her neither, but she went on knocking and crying, and the dog barking and yelping, so Mr Parkin got up and slipped out into the wood by the back door, and left her to knock, as it was a fine night. Well, when he got back in the morning, he could see she'd got in. She'd broken a pane in the back-kitchen window, and got in that way, but there was no signs of her about. So he went upstairs, and there she was in bed with no nightdress on nor nothing. I don't know what happened, but she says he got in bed with her, and he says he didn't. Anyhow he went and fetched his mother to make her go. But old Mrs Parkin couldn't do anything with her, and noone could have thrown her out, short of killing her, for she's as strong as a bull. She swore Mr Parkin had been in bed with her, and he swore he hadn't. And she swore he'd been having women in the cottage, because the post-man had heard something, and there was a smell of scent in the bedroom, and his things were scented, and *he* never used scent. Anyhow there she lay in bed with not a stitch on her, till old Mrs Parkin said it fair made you sick, and there was nothing to be done. So Mr Parkin and his mother took all they could carry with them, his things and food, what there was in the house, and he unscrewed the handle of the pump so she could have no water, and they left her in bed, lying there without a stitch on, and a bare house, and both doors locked on her. But I suppose she must have got up sometime, for she was at her brother Dan's in the afternoon, and swearing and raving and carrying on, calling Mr Parkin all the blaggards and the bs, and saying he'd been in bed with her, and she'd have the law on him. Then she went to the police-station, to kick up a shine there, so they threatened to lock her up. Then she changed her tactics, and went to Mr Burroughs, who is J.P. now, pleading with him to make Mr Parkin take her back, and crying and weeping, and saying she only wanted to be taken back and live a straight life. Mr Burroughs sent for Mr Parkin and asked him if he'd take her back, and he said he wouldn't, he'd die rather than live with her again. So Mr Burroughs said why hadn't he got a legal separation, and protected himself that way, and he said he never wanted no legal separation, he wanted to be rid of her. So Mr Burroughs said he must apply for a divorce, and he said he would. And she said she'd show him up, afore he ever got a divorce, as he'd been in bed with her and was carrying on with other women. So Mr Burroughs asked her, was she destitute, and she said she'd money of her own enough to keep her, she wasn't beholden to a dirty game-keeper. But her home was her home, and nobody was going to turn her out. So Mr Burroughs said Mr Parkin had better apply for a divorce, and live at his mother's, and let her provide for herself. This was a week last Wednesday, and Mr Parkin's been at his mother's ever since to sleep. But he says he'll have to leave, so Sir Clifford is looking for another keeper. Mr Parkin has put in for a divorce, and his wife goes about saying the most awful things about him, but awful, you have to stop your ears. And she kept on going to the cottage to sleep, and managing goodness knows how. But Sir Clifford put a stop to that. Old Mrs Parkin took a cart and two men, and fetched away all the furniture and things, and Sir Clifford had the house sealed, and let her know he'd have her arrested for house-breaking, if she got in. So she went and got lodgings with a woman down Beggarlee. But she's like a mad-woman, and keeps going to the wood for Mr Parkin, raving at him and weeping and carrying on, till he threatens he'll shoot her. But Sir Clifford got the policeman to tell her he would take her up for trespass and interference with a man's duty, if she was found in the wood again, and the only place she seems to fear is the lock-up. She even came weeping and wailing to the Hall, to get Sir Clifford to make Parkin take her back. But Sir Clifford wouldn't see her, and he was quite right. He sent word he'd have her arrested if she trespassed on his property or interfered with his servants. So since then she's been more quiet, but she spends her time at the *Three Tunns*, and does nothing but talk and get the men to sympathise with her. The things she says about Mr Parkin are something awful, the things he did to her when they were married, why it's shameful for a woman to open her mouth about such things. And yet she says she was a true and faithful wife to him, and never even thought of another man, till he drove her to it, and told her to go, and made her go off with this Swain. When everybody knows Swain wasn't the first, by any means. The way she carried on with those wood-men during the war, who were taking timber for the trenches. Why even Sir Geoffrey had to tell her he wouldn't have her in the wood round the men. But the worst is the things she says about Mr Parkin, because they're awful, and some of it's sure to stick, and everybody looks on him quite different from what they did. I think he's quite right to go away from these parts. She isn't allowed in the *Three Tunns* any more, since Mr Burroughs warned Mrs Anthony, the landlady. But she goes around, living a life of ease, dressed up to the eyes, and telling everybody about Mr Parkin, till he's almost worse looked on, nowadays, than she is. I'm sure everybody seems to think her badness is his fault. And her brother Dan is that worked up, he says he'll break every bone in the little b's body, for the things he did to his sister. She vows if Mr Parkin goes for a divorce, she'll tell the judge all she knows about him. But Sir Clifford says she won't be allowed to open her mouth as wide as she likes, to vilify anybody, in court.

"I'm sure, My Lady, you are lucky to be away from this scandal, for it's upset me more than I can tell you. There's more talk in Tevershall than ever there has been, as long as I can remember, and all so nasty. As for the woman, she is evil-mad, and as I tell them, it is her time of life. A woman who has lived in a wrong way, as she has, almost always goes wrong when her change of life comes. These low sexual women, who always have low things on their mind, even when they don't do them, they always seem to go evil-mad when they get between forty and fifty. It is a kind of hysteria, no doubt, but to my mind it is more evil than anything, and comes from having lived wrong—"

Connie read this long letter with a sinking heart. How squalid! oh how awful and squalid! Why on earth had he ever taken up with such a woman!—Yet, as a woman herself, she knew well enough. It was a passion, even if an impure one, that had existed between Parkin and Bertha Coutts. But how squalid, how awful! She felt, for a time, that death is the only clean thing, for human beings.

And herself! As far as she could make out, her name had not been suggested in the scandal. Which seemed to her, now, a mercy, and almost a miracle. Hilda was right: *how* careful one had to be, in this world of hyaenas! He seemed to have been careful. There was no mention of the torn nightdress. And the perfume was her own folly. She herself had put scent on his three or four handkerchieves, in the little drawer of the dressing table.

She was depressed utterly, and didn't want to think. He seemed to have stirred up so much mud. Yet when she shut her eyes to sleep, she saw the image of him, naked white and with tanned face and hands, a tiny image, small as a flake of bright light on a convex mirror, but vivid and untouched. That was still pure, among all the impurity.

She had to fight hard to rise above her jealousy for Bertha Coutts, and to master her hate of him, for being connected with Bertha Coutts. What made it worse was her fear, amounting almost to hate, that the other woman loved him, and perhaps had a right to him: and that perhaps she herself had no right to his love. This thought lay icy in her soul. Bertha Coutts would not hate him so, like a mad dog, if she had not cared for him, if she had not felt her whole being possessed by him. Poor woman! the extent of her reckless defamation, and the fact that she talked about her indecent conjugal intimacies with him, showed the extent of her morbid love for him. It was a love gone mad. But it was like a dog with hydrophobia, insane at the sight of water for which she has been thirsty.

Why? Why had Bertha Coutts lost his love? Because Connie knew she had. His heart was dead, as far as his wife was concerned. It was exhausted and dead. Poor Bertha Coutts! what annihilation for her. No wonder she was evil-mad.

Yet she had brought it on deliberately. She had deliberately fought against even the love in her own soul, and had taken a long, evil pleasure in humiliating him. He had never fully respected her, never felt his heart at one with her, in destiny. So she in revenge had tried all in her power to humiliate him. Because he had never felt that he and she shared, in some way, a destiny.

Yet surely, in the beginning, there had been the beginnings of a mutual destiny, even between Bertha Coutts and him. But Bertha Coutts had already formed the habit of behaving more ignobly than was her real nature; and once having put herself in the wrong, she had run on to frenzy in her wrongness, always, from worse to worse, behaving more ignobly than the best spark in her nature. Till she had come to this madness, and there was nothing but death and madness for her ahead.

For him, too, unless something was done. Connie felt that, just as he had denied a mutual destiny with his wife, because she behaved perversely, so was she herself inclined to deny a mutual destiny for herself and him, because he was not of her world. And she realised, with the sternness of fate, that no man and no woman can have a full destiny alone. There are men and women, plenty, destined to be alone. But for them, a certain fulness is denied. For warm-souled men and women, the lonely destiny is death. Real men and women are destiny to one another.

Connie realised that she had been trying to avoid her destiny with him. She wanted the selfish pleasure of the contact, but not the submission to the subtle interweaving of her life with his, in creative fate. She had wanted to have her cake, and to eat it. She had wanted to keep Clifford and Wragby and her-ladyship, and take the contact with Parkin as cream to the pudding. Now she realised, that she could keep Clifford and Wragby and her ladyship, if she liked. But Parkin would not be the cream to the pudding. He would be the pivotal point of her life. Clifford, Wragby, and her ladyship were circumstances, and circumstances are a vast concatenation over which the individual has not very much immediate control. When circumstances and destiny do not pull in the same way, then it is no use tearing oneself in two. The thing to do is to follow the resultant of the two forces, and swerve in the unknown curve that will emerge from the diverse pull of circumstance and of destiny. If there *has* to be a break, break with circumstance rather than with destiny, even if you are left a cripple. But if there is an honest resultant of the forces of fate and things, then follow that.

Connie wrote a letter to Parkin, enclosing it in one to Duncan Forbes, who was back in London. She put only Forbes London address—and she began without any preliminary:—"Clifford and Mrs Bolton have written to me about your trouble with Bertha Coutts. I am awfully upset about it. You mustn't altogether blame Bertha Coutts, perhaps in her way she loved you more than you loved her, and so she despised herself for being the one who had to love more than she was loved, and she went wrong, trying to get even. But now it is terrible, and you are quite right to go away and to try to get a divorce. One must not let oneself be dragged back, if one wants to go on. But remember there is something between you and me, which I hope will never break. I hope you feel the same. I hope you want me to stay in your life always. I want you to stay in my life till I die, and I want to stay in your life till you die. But we needn't try to force anything. Write to me to tell me how you feel. I shall be home at the end of next week, but there is time for you to write a letter, if you write at once. Write to me. I will do whatever you truly wish me to do, because I would always trust you, when you sincerely wished anything. It is different, when one is just hasty. Try not to go before I come back. I can't be back before the end of next week. And I do trust you. So write to me, and tell me.—C."

After having sent this off, Connie sat and wept awhile, and then felt better. After all, if one stuck to what one most sincerely felt, and if one were not afraid, and if one put one's chief trust in the destiny of oneself and the man, one need not be lost. It was a great relief to her that that vague, yet very profound class-mistrust which had lain like a negating serpent at the bottom of her soul, was now gone. Vitally, organically, in the old organic sense of society, there were no more classes. That organic system had collapsed. So she need not have any class-mistrust of Parkin, and he need have none of her.

And following this came the new hope and the new relief, of an undefined, unknown, yet sacred mutual destiny between him and her. One could not be immortal, alone. If, in the beginning of time men and women had been joined together in one body, as Aristophanes said in Plato,* and only later time had cleft them in two, then somehow, in the immortal they were one again: there was no I: there was no he and she. The two came together and formed one immortality, in which the I, the wearisome solitary individualistic I, disappeared and became a whole. She felt so acutely, and so achingly, the fragmentariness of the I. She was sick of single individuality.

But she felt, tentatively, and timidly, a mutual destiny between herself and Parkin, because of the kindling together of their bodies. Bodily, and in the passionate soul, they were the makers of one destiny between them. The rest was circumstance.

Circumstance was a strange clutch one had to submit to. Even if he had got into bed with Bertha Coutts—the thought rankled, though she did not believe he had—but even if he had, it was the chain of circumstance, and not the dim breeze of destiny.

She saw herself and him like two sailing vessels crossing a sea to the same port. They were not steamers, to churn the same wake. The steamers are the proletariat. But she and he were like two sailing ships. Each captain handles his vessel in a different manner, and the ships stay apart, for their own safety. Only in a smooth sea can the jolly-boat row from one to another. And after a squall, the morning finds them blown far apart, out of sight, so they seem lost to one another, in the empty seas. But steering always to the same point in the west, the one rises over the horizon to the other, and they go on.

So it must be: a voyage apart, in the same direction. Grapple the two vessels together, lash them side by side, and the first storm will smash them to pieces. That is marriage, in the bad weather of modern civilisation. But leave the two vessels apart, to make their voyage to the same port, each according to its own skill and power, and an unseen life connects them, a magnetism which cannot be forced. And that is marriage as it will be, when this is broken down.

She had a letter from Clifford: "I am delighted to hear you are actually leaving that place. Once you set your face north, I shall feel you are really coming. We miss you, Wragby misses you. You are an essential here, for some reason which not even you could explain. Of course I don't for an instant complain of your absence. I have been looked after most assiduously by the excellent Mrs Bolton. But it is a grey day, while you are away: and the house is like a room with no fire in it.

"Mrs Bolton is a queer cut. The longer I live, the more I realise what very strange *animals* human beings are. They are weird, some of them might just as well have a hundred legs, like a centipede, or six, like a lobster. The human consistency and unity which one has led oneself to expect from one's fellow man seem not really to exist. One doubts if they exist to any startling degree in oneself.

"I am regaled with a great amount of Tevershall gossip. Mrs Bolton *must* talk. She reminds me of a fish, which seems as if it were breathing silent speech, endless speeches. And like a fish, she takes all water indiscriminately through the sieve of her gills. Nothing really surprises her or shocks her. She only gets pleasantly excited at times. She takes the offensive Mrs Parkin Junior as calmly as she takes you or me, in spite of her exclamations of horror, and the secret misdeeds of Parkin himself, though she does not mention them to me, provide her with merely a slight mental thrill. I did not know that people were essentially unmoral, and that practically all their morality is worn as a street costume. After an hour of her gossip, I find myself slowly rising to the surface again, to the comparative paradise of Plotinus or of Hegel,* even. And there I breathe again.

"It seems to me absolutely true, that our world, which appears to us as a surface, is only really the *bottom* of a deep sea;* all our trees are submarine growths, and we are weird, two-legged submarine fauna, creeping like shrimps. Only occasionally the soul rises gasping through the fathomless fathoms under which we live, far up into the other world at last, where there is true air. I verily believe the air we normally breathe is a form of water, deep sea water at that.

"But sometimes the soul comes up from below like a kittiwake, that shoots into the air with ecstasy, after having preyed upon the submerged fishes. It is our mortal destiny, I suppose, to prey upon the awful subaqueous fauna of the human submarine jungle. But our immortal destiny is to escape, once we have swallowed our catch, up into the bright ether, bursting out from the surface tension of old Ocean, into real light. And then one realises.

"When I talk to Mrs Bolton, I feel myself plunging down, down, seizing the wriggling fish of the human secret; then up, up again, out of the liquid into the ethereal, where one *knows*, and is calm. It is a great game. To you I can tell the whole process. But with Mrs Bolton I only feel the downward plunge, down, awfully, among the sea-weeds and the pallid monsters of the very bottom. And till she has gone, I can't come up again. I cannot rise. If she were always physically present, I should suffocate like a diver whose air-tubes are tangled and stopped.

"We have had a great lashing of little monsters in our own particular pool of ocean. I mentioned the Parkin scandal to you. I don't know if I told you how the truant wife came back to him, or rather, came back at him, to use an Americanism, and lay stark in his bed like a succubus, when he came home from the wood. He beat a retreat, after we know not what scrimmage, and has since lived more or less in retirement behind his mother. The truant wife fortified herself in the cottage, but I had her evicted. Since then, she has been sleeping somewhere or other in Teetershall, and spending her waking hours raising Cain.* She besieged old Mrs Parkin's house one day, and seized upon her own daughter, as that chip of the female block was returning from school. The little one, being true kitten of the cat, bit her mother's hand with such force that she received a smack in the face which sent her into the gutter, whence she was rescued by the indignant grandmother. The village women turning out in force, Parkin's gentle spouse beat a retreat.

"She has, however, blown off so much steam, as the colliers say, in her own defence, that a good part of the village is disposed to look on her as the poor victim of her husband's enormities and mal-practice. She has, apparently, aired in minute detail all those incidents in her conjugal life which are usually buried, by married couples, in the deepest grave of decent silence. But she has chosen to exhume them, after ten years time, and a weird sight it is, an extraordinary recital. Of course I have nothing of this from Mrs Bolton, who only says 'it is too shameful to mention.' But Linley, Burroughs, who is now J.P., and the rector have all been to me about the business. They want to get rid of Parkin, and to close the mouth of his wife. A dozen years ago, of course, the decent colliers and the decent colliers' wives would have suppressed such talk effectively: But there is no body of public decency of that sort any more. Everybody listens: as I do myself. Nevertheless, it is deplorable, highly so. Dr Smith, who is a humorist in these matters, has brought me most of the tit-bits. I must confess, I find them rather funny, like some of the *Cent Nouvelles*,* and some of the modern dirty French stories. It is a curious, almost mediaeval assortment of sexual extravagance and minor sexual perversities with which I suppose every enquiring mind is familiar, but which is not often made a subject of popular gossip. I pretend to be shocked, but I find I am more amused. These minor sexual perversities are of all time and circumstance, like fleas or bald heads. They even enter the animal kingdom. But I had thought the colliers were too entirely unimaginative to diverge from the straight and narrow path of sex. They always seem to me like the stud bull, who jumps in and out, and it is over.—So we have at least to credit our friend Parkin with some imagination, even if it is a dirty one. I had thought him too commonplace for such transgressions, or digressions, whichever you will. But apparently he has in him a touch of the great Rabelais.* Nemmeno male!*

"I have had to interview him several times about this uproar, and now I find him a curious specimen of subaqueous monster. He goes about with his old air of insolent I-care-for-nobody,* but I think he feels somewhat like a dog with a tin can tied to its tail: a plucky enough dog, that since he can't escape the tin can, pretends it isn't there.—Of course all Tevershall look upon him as a monster, and mothers draw their children from his approach as if he were the Marquis de Sade* in person. He pretends to bluff it out, and to despise them in turn. But as I say, the tin can is firmly tied to his tail, and I think he feels like Don Rodrigo in the Spanish ballad, when the serpent of infernal vengeance seized him: 'Ah, now it bites me where I most have sinned!'*

"But as I say, he braves it out, with impudence, though I am not sure he doesn't run some physical risk of tar and feathers, or a sound drubbing. Anyhow, in our interviews, though I have heard some faint tinkle now and then, of the tin can tied to his tail, I pretend I hear nothing. When I told him I heard there was a lot of talk buzzing in the village, he said:— Ay, maybe there is! Folks should do their own fuckin', and not listen to clatfart about other folkses!—Which, though coarse, is perhaps just.

"I have sent him to Pilbeam, as a good lawyer, and he will make proper application for a divorce from the offending wife. But meanwhile I am afraid I shall have to look for another game-keeper. Burroughs and the rector are determined to silence the woman, if it means a few months gaol for her. But they insist also that the man had better go away. Of course I wanted to keep him, for the affair amuses me, and he is a good keeper. But he himself is determined to leave. I said to him: 'You shouldn't let a little talk drive you away,' whereupon he replied: 'Neither am I! But I'm going, and I wish you'd tell her ladyship same.'—I asked him: 'But if you're not ashamed, why are you going?'—He replied to this: 'I'm not ashamed. Fuckin's fuckin', an' every man should stan' by his own.—But I'm goin' because I don't want to live here any more.'—I said nothing to this; but I suppose I must have been smiling at his aphorism, because the next thing he said was: 'Nay, Sir Clifford, it's not for a man in the shapes you're in, to be laughin' at me for havin' a cod atween my legs.'—He said it in a nettled tone, and I considered it impudence. I said to him: 'Any man who walks with his shirt hanging out, let alone his cod, will find himself laughed at.' And he replied: 'Ay! Yo' mun button your breeches buttons, but you can't button the mouth of a bad woman. An' them as listens shows a dirty shirt-tail, ask me anything—' And at that I stopped him and sent him off, reminding him that no-one had asked him anything. But he gave me a nasty look. He is a born bolshevist, so perhaps it is as well he goes. But he must, or I must, find another keeper first. The callow Joe I am afraid is inadequate, as the job is a pretty tough one.

"Well, I have spilled enough ink over this squalid affair. But we are deep-sea-monsters, and even a lobster stirs up mud, when he takes a walk—"

The peculiar cruelty which came out of this letter pierced poor Connie's heart, which was feeling particularly tender at the moment. She was angry, and she wept, and she waited sullenly to depart. In three days she would be gone.

Mrs Bolton wrote rather hastily:

"I saw Mr Parkin yesterday, looking rather poorly. I had to go to his mother's, to give him your message, and I found him up, but sitting in a chair saying nothing. I gave him your message, but he made no answer.

"I suppose you heard the latest! I'm sure it's shameful! Mr Parkin was passing the Three Tunns on Saturday afternoon just at turning-out time, and the colliers were standing about as they do, when they're not at work, which is the best place for them. That great hulking Dan Coutts was there, among a set of his pals, having drunk himself nasty. It seems he stopped Mr Parkin and told him to take his jacket off, as he was going to give him a dusting. Mr Parkin said, why what's amiss with you?—You know they used to be very thick together, as boys. However, Dan Coutts told him to shut his measly face, and take his jacket off, or he'd take it off for him. So it seems they went back into Slater's brick-yard and had a fight, stripped to the waist. That Dan Coutts is about twice the size of Mr Parkin, and punished him cruel, though I hear Mr Parkin broke his nose for him, so he'll bear the mark, as well he ought. But Mrs Slater came down from the house, fetched by one of the children, and she said it was an awful sight, both of them all over blood, and those hulking colliers standing round. And then Mr Parkin got a blow that sent him backwards with his head bang on one of the iron rails of the little railroad. She said she made sure he was dead, and ran for the policeman, and Sergeant Bower came himself. When they got back they found Mr Parkin on his feet as white as death, ready for another round. Sergeant Bower told them to stop it, and go home, but Coutts told him to s—t! So Sergeant Bower sent a boy for the Constable, and he told them again to stop it. And Coutts said: 'Not till that b. goes on his knees,' and he squared up again, and Mr Parkin too. Then Sergeant Bower said he'd arrest them if they didn't put their shirts on, and Coutts said S—t! again, and they began to fight. The sergeant was in a rage, and seized hold of Coutts, who gave him a hit in the jaw, and there seems to have been a free fight, till the Constable came, and Mr Parkin and Coutts were marched off and locked up in the police-station. Well then it seems Mr Parkin started retching and vomiting, and retching something awful, and it went on all afternoon, till Mrs Bower ran for the doctor. It seems there was a slight concussion of the brain, and the doctor said they'd better send him home, or to the hospital at Uthwaite. So they had a talk, and decided to take him home, so they carried him on a stretcher, retching and not conscious. I went to help his mother that night, Sir Clifford let me go, and it was hours before we could get the retching to stop, and get his eyes right. And a pitiful sight he looked, with his face all bruised and swollen, and mouth cut, and two teeth gone, and his eyes so *queer*. Really, I thought sometimes he was going. But at last, in the night he went quiet, and then went to sleep. So we let him sleep while ever he would, and he didn't wake till next day at tea-time. The doctor said he'd be all right now, but oh dear, it was a time. So when I went the next day, I found him up, and sadly disfigured, sitting in the arm-chair and saying never a word. I could tell he was feeling bad, so I didn't bother him. I just gave him your message, that you'd be home at the week-end, and he just looked at me.

"That Dan Coutts is sent to Uthwaite gaol, for assaulting the Sergeant, and we hope that Coutts family will have a stopper put to it.

"I hope you'll get this before you leave, to prepare you for the worst. Indeed I hope the worst is over, for we've had enough of this affair. It will seem like peace and happiness again, to have you back, and everything settled down once more—"

The next day, Connie was leaving. She waited for the mail to come in. And it brought her a note addressed by Duncan Forbes. But the handwriting inside was ill-formed and aslant: "My Mother opened your letter, the day I was bad, when I knocked my head. I have got over it all right. I shan't go till Sunday night, then I am going to Sheffield to work. I shall stop at Bill Tewson's. I hope you will have a pleasant journey, and all will be very pleased to see you back. But I am leaving Tevershall. Hoping to see you again, Yours sincerely O.P.—My Mother didn't make anything of your letter.—"

Connie put this letter in her bag, and went down to the car. But she found the physical effort of smiling her last goodbyes almost did something to her face: as if, as children say, it would set.

14

CONSTANCE AND HILDA DROVE AWAY ALONE, their father had chosen to go by train. They took the road to Bordeaux and Tours, intending to go straight to Dieppe, omitting Paris. Hilda drove quickly, they travelled far in a day. And the country rushed by, almost unobserved. Hilda suddenly was anxious to get back to her children, and Connie, too, was pressed.

It was full summer, end of hay harvest, almost time to cut the corn, but the grapes were not yet dark under the leaves. But in some places, apricots and peaches were ripe and warm from the sun. France was almost always strange and remote, holding aloof, as ancient Gaul must have held aloof. Sometimes when Connie and Hilda ate in some inn where the peasants and workmen sat drinking their wine, talking in their guttural dialect, sitting with strong knees apart, and open, sleeping thighs, having a sleeping, half-clenched fist lying on the board, Connie would be overcome with the nostalgia of the old life, that is not nervous nor mechanical. But the new life was coming over these peasants and sea-folk, like an electric glare, to make them ghastly. Soon, the warm life would be dead in them. Man is a column of blood; or else a column of bitter thin brine, netted with nerves and mechanically muscled.

"It's so different," said Connie to Hilda, "*knowing* life, and *being* it."

"In what way?"

"Look at those sailors in jerseys: they are alive, and they don't know it. And people like Clifford know life so well, yet they aren't really it."

Hilda watched the sailors, laughing over a game.

"Yet you marry a Clifford," she said coldly.

"I wouldn't again," said Connie.

"You would never marry one of these sailors, no matter how alive he was."

"Why not!" said Connie. "Parkin is almost like one of them."

"You haven't married him," said Hilda coldly.

"I want to."

Hilda, annoyed, was silent for a time. Then she said:

"I doubt it. I see the attraction of him—or of those sailors. But it doesn't attract *us*. We only think it attracts us. We never have one of those men for a lover."

"Why don't we?" said Connie. "I'm sure they'd be much nicer than our own sort."

"They have no meaning for us, when it comes to actual contact," said Hilda, in a dull voice.

"Then it's our own fault," said Connie. "I'm sure they're nicer than men like Clifford, or your Everard, or even Duncan Forbes or Tommy Dukes."

"Yes! But you see, these sailors are all just workmen, under somebody's authority. And Clifford and Everard and Duncan and Tommy are all in authority themselves. They are all masters, and these are just hired men. And a woman is always ashamed if she takes a hired man. She must take a master, somebody in authority, she can't submit to a man who is under another man."

Connie received this piece of truth as if it were new to her. Of course, it meant Parkin. He was a hired man. He was not a master among men: not even by birthright nor money-right nor intellectual-right. He was just one-who-must-obey. The thought made her angry.

"And yet," she said, "the real phallic man doesn't care. It doesn't enter there—into the love-activity."

"Doesn't it! I should have thought it did!" said Hilda. "If what you call the real phallic man is always an underling and a hired worker, then he'll have to look for different women from us: at least, for wives. We may take him for a time as a lover—But we only marry men who are, in some way or other, men of authority."

"But!" said Connie slowly, "Parkin is as good a *man* as father, for example."

"He would have to take father's orders, never-the-less, while father was at Wragby. And a woman always loves half-pitifully a man who is a servant or an underling. You have a lot of pity for Parkin in your love for him: and a lot of self-superiority. You feel you could buy him his freedom.—It's all very well for a short time. He's got a nice body. But you can't go down among those who have to be servants, or wage-earners, and who are under all the rest of the bosses. Parkin is far away down below Mr Linley—and Mrs Linley;—they'd both order him about, and he'd more or less have to obey.—How could he be your husband? Supposing you heard Mrs Linley giving him orders—"

Connie had to admit to herself that it was impossible. It produced a great sense of frustration and anger and anarchic confusion in her.

"Yet!" she said, "he is so wonderful! There's something a bit starry about him."

"What?" said Hilda. "What is starry?"

"His body! even his penis! You don't know, Hilda, how strange it is, like a little god. Surely, surely it is more sacred than Clifford's being a baronet, or father's being an artist, or that awful Sir Andrew being so stinkingly rich. Surely it *really* means more—"

"It may to you, at the moment. But even you'd get over it, and realise that Parkin's penis doesn't rule the world, whereas Clifford's baronetcy and Sir Andrew's money does,—father's art too."

"But Hilda, I don't care."

"Yes you do. Everybody does. Every woman does. A woman falls for the ruling man—he can rule in what way he likes, as a saint or an aristocrat or an artist or a brewer with money or even a politician or a journalist—and women will fall for him. Whereas a woman will despise herself for being the wife of a mere servant or a man who only takes orders, and never gives them: whether his penis is like a little god, or whether it isn't."

"But I'm not like that."

"Yes you are! If your Parkin, or your phallic man as you call him, asserted himself and made himself a ruler, practically any woman would want him. But it's the ruling spirit, or the authority, a woman yields to, in a man. If your Parkin was master of *anything*, except just his dog and his penis, he might stand a chance. But as it is, you won't marry him. Or if you do, it will only be because you have an income, and can still live in your own way, and stay in the ruling class, the class that gives orders, rather than takes them. You couldn't take orders from anybody—"

"Why should I?"

"Quite! Every reason why you shouldn't! But Parkin has to take them from Clifford, and from you: and he used to have to take them from the bosses at the pit. If his penis is a little god, I'm afraid it's a fallen idol, as far as power goes."

This made Connie very angry. And yet she could not contradict it. The thought weighed on her all the afternoon, and oppressed her in the evening, when she came to the sea and saw the stars shining above it.

"I don't care!" she said stubbornly to Hilda at bed-time. "I know the penis is the most godly part of a man."

"Of a man like Parkin, who has nothing else, maybe! But other men have minds, and creative power, and power to command or control. And then the penis is *not* the most sacred part of the man."

"Then it should be!" said Connie. "I *know* it is the penis which connects us with the stars and the sea and everything. It is the penis which touches the planets, and makes us feel their special light. I *know* it was the penis which really put the evening star into my inside self. I used to *look* at the evening star, and think how lovely and wonderful it was. But now it's in me as well as outside me, and I need hardly look at it. I *am* it. I don't care what you say, it was the penis gave it me."

"Well!" said Hilda. "I suppose you're in love, that's all. It's a pity your Parkin doesn't manage to make himself a captain of some sort. As it is, the penis is like the grass that withereth, and the place thereof shall know it no more."*

With this final shot, the sisters parted. Connie took the early morning boat over to Newhaven, and Hilda had to wait till the night boat: because of the car.

There was a fog on the Channel, and the boat thumped slowly forwards in the nothingness of yellow-white mist, bellowing and hooting. Everybody was nervous, in a state of tension. There was nothing to be seen, nothing to do but to sit still and breathe vapour. Connie sat inert, and the hours dragged out, the engines sometimes went a little faster, sometimes seemed to stop altogether. So they edged their way through the nothingness of things, as if it were the end of things. Connie felt that if it were, she wouldn't greatly care. There was a great dismalness everywhere.

They landed at last, however, and Connie wired to Clifford, before getting into the train. In London she crossed straight to St. Pancras, and got a late afternoon train. The fog did not affect the land, but the day was grey. She watched the familiar landscape go by.

At Uthwaite she looked out, to see if Field were on the platform. And the first thing she saw, so that her heart jumped almost out of her breast, was Clifford, standing on crutches leaning back against an iron pillar. He saw her at once, and made a sharp little salute. How well he looked, ruddy and alert! But the sight of him on crutches was a great shock.

The train stopped, Field came running to the door, she got out and went towards her husband. But she could hardly bear his light-blue, keen, abstract eyes staring at her face. They seemed almost more electric than human.

"Why Clifford!" she said, in a breathless voice.

He leaned forward slightly and kissed her forehead.

"How are *you*?" he asked, watching her with those keen, cold eyes.

"Perfectly well!" she said. "But it's you! How wonderful that you are here! Can you really *walk*? It's a miracle!"

He laid his hand on her shoulder, the crutch under his arm-pit.

"I can't exactly walk," he said, "but I can *go*, after a fashion."

How strange his hand on her shoulder! She wanted to crouch and shrink away from under it. How strange, his naked face near hers! She had forgotten him, physically, while she was away, and his physical actuality came as a shock to her. It frightened her too.

He also realised with a sudden change of temperature, what strangers, alien to one another, he and she were. They had come apart.

"But how did you learn?" she asked in wonder. "How did you begin?" Her eyes, however, avoided his face.

"Mrs Bolton put me up to it! She's a determined woman, in her own quiet way. I think she wanted to give you a surprise."

"I must say, she has done! It's perfectly wonderful! And aren't you a bit nervous?" she asked, solicitously. But in her mind she was thinking: That's it! He's gone completely into Mrs Bolton's hands. That's why he seems so strange!—And thinking this, she let her old, habitual effusion of intimacy towards Clifford sink down and die out. He was Mrs Bolton's man! Very good! Then she herself need not trouble.

She was silent, having nothing to say to him. He was looking round for his man Field. Connie saw that square, stout, powerful young man bustling up the platform towards them, watching them, and waiting to salute.

"Why Field!" said Connie. "How do you do? All right? Isn't Sir Clifford too wonderful!"

"Was yer surprised, my lady?" said Field, smiling a broad smile. Yet his rather small, light-blue eyes were quite keen and subtle.

"Amazed!" said Connie. "And a bit scared! Is it really safe, really?"

"Oh ay! We get on fine!" said Field. Then he added to Sir Clifford, in that queer tone of respectful distance and benevolent protection, which Clifford used to resent: "Are you ready, then? Shall we be goin'? Th' bags is in."

"I'm ready," said Clifford.

Field took his master round the waist, and carefully held him balanced, while Clifford took the first leap. There was a queer look in Clifford's face, like some weird bird making one of its flights, a look of excitement tinged with fear and exaltation.

Then with a strange swift plunge of his crutches, he was off, and poling himself with long, anxious strides of his crutches along the platform, his body swinging huge and loose in weird pendulum-strokes, the inert legs coming to earth and holding long enough for another strange wing-sweep of the crutches, as on he went, with a sort of wildness, like a wounded huge bird flapping along. Everybody made way, and Field trotted at his side, watching him sideways with that alert, almost maternal watchfulness of a male nurse, Field too looked an odd figure, squat and broad and very active, trotting there absorbed in Clifford's motion, his fat, fresh-coloured face turned in steady attention, the light-blue eyes with colourless lashes looking as keen as a young pig's. Queer he was, and of some old, earth-bound aboriginal race.

Constance followed breathless. She was frightened, and a bit awestruck. Life seemed so weird.

She emerged from the station in time to see Clifford with his hands on the side of the open car, the crutches fallen to ground, and Field lifting his master bodily into the automobile, when Clifford let himself subside carefully into the seat. Then Field picked up the crutches and placed them by Clifford's side. Such a quick, squat young man, with such amazing strength in his fat body. He turned with perspiring face and beaming smile to Constance as she approached, holding the door for her.

"We've managed it then!" he said, with that broad quick smile of his, speaking with the dialect twang.

"I think it's marvellous!" she said.

"Do you! Sir Clifford's such a clever balancer, he times himself that well," said the chauffeur, in a low, confidential sort of voice. He was infinitely proud of the new achievement, as if it were *he* who was lame. And Connie was amazed at the power of gentleness there was in the broad, fat body, and at the utter willingness to serve.

"Well!" said Clifford, looking at her benignly as the car moved off. "You look blooming! Is it very hard to have to come back to these regions?"

"Not at all!" she said, shrinking still, with odd dread, from his physical nearness. "I was quite ready to come home."

"Ah! You don't find the district *too* ugly, then?"

"It *is* uglier than I thought," she said, looking round at the great iron-works and the rows of workmen's dwellings. "It *is* ugly. And it *is* unnatural. But for all that, I don't mind coming back. It is—I don't know how to put it—part of one's destiny."

"You feel that, do you!" he said.

"And one gets fearfully fed up with trying to enjoy oneself. I begin to loathe what they call *being happy* and *enjoying oneself.* I prefer infinitely to be humdrum," she said.

"Ah!—Well, you have ample opportunity to he humdrum at Wragby!" he said, in his well-bred, self-assured voice.

"But you are the wonderful one," she said, looking at him yet shrinking away from him. "Tell me how you did it."

"What? Going on crutches? I tell you, I yielded to Mrs Bolton's urging: and she declared how pleased *you* would be. So there is the circle, as usual."

"But how did you do it? Where did you first try?"

"Where? Oh, in the hall. Mrs Bolton got the crutches, and we got in Field."

"But didn't you feel awfully scared, the first time?"

"I did rather. It was like a second infancy. It made me realise what a lot of courage must lie behind a new evolutionary stride.—But I soon learned to trust to Field."

"He is amazingly good," said Connie.

"He really is," Clifford admitted.

The car was running on through the well-known landscape, in the grey, cool evening of July. It all seemed strange to Connie. She felt herself such a stranger. She looked at it all as if from a far distance. It was unreal. Everything was unreal, Clifford, the dull-coloured hills, the pits, the rows of dwellings, the low, grey, darkening sky, the weird, ghoulish country, it was all unreal. And the very thought of Parkin was unreal.

In spite of herself, the sun and the old clarity of southern Europe were reality to her, and once more, the grey, weird ghoulishness of this middle of England seemed unbelievable, as if it were a phantom of a world, and everything that happened there were phantasmal.

Mrs Bolton was on the steps at Wragby, almost like a hostess welcoming Connie home. Her long, pale cheeks were flushed with red spots of excitement, her eyes were flashing.

"Welcome home, my lady, welcome home!" she cried, almost hysterical.

And Wragby lay there sombre and gloomy, spread out in the twilight, the great trees in front massive in full foliage.

It was so queer to sit tête-à-tête with Clifford again, in the dining-room with the dark Dutch pictures. The sunlessness! this was what entered Connie's soul with such a shock: the eternal sunlessness of it all! From the beginning of time it had been in shadow, nearly always in shadow. It was a land that the great globe tilted away from the sun, thrusting it into an almost perpetual twilight. And in the twilight it had grown great, and learned weird and potent secrets. And now the world had grown weary of it. The secrets must be carried into the sun, the world of the twilight must die. It was passing into real ghoulishness and the after-death, this realm of twilight and the mystery of iron, this disembowelled earth of coal and steel and steam, and the glare of red fire and of shadow. It was becoming a region of dread dreams.

The next world, the electric world, would be short and sharp, and would lead back into the sun again. Back into the sun!

She sat like a strange bird from the sun, in Clifford's parlour, where the red fire glowed. And the red fire of coal made her feel uneasy, frightened her a little as it frightens wild animals.

"Are you really at all glad to be back?" Clifford asked her again, as he sat in his chair with his glass of liqueur.

"Yes!" she said, looking at him evasively. "I wanted to come back. I'd have come sooner if I could."

"That's good hearing," he said.

Nevertheless, he felt puzzled, and a little thrown out of gear.

"But I hope you had a good time?" he said.

"Yes! Very!—But it felt like holiday, and one gets impatient of a holiday feeling."

"I suppose one does! Though a holiday from oneself might be a very pleasant change. For me at least.—But I think we might go away together for a little spell one day—What do you think?" He looked at her uneasily.

"Of course!" she said. "Other men travel who have been wounded! You are so *healthy*! Of course you could go anywhere."

"Another year, we'll think of it," he said.

He was excited, and he kept her up a long time, talking, talking. He was queer, so interested in everything, drawing everything out of her. The thought of the south suddenly seemed to have cast a spell on him too. He could see the sun in her. And it seemed to him like new life. And he thought it meant love, some other kind of irresponsible passion, all mixed with sunshine and roses. An elation, and a sense of illusion came over him. He drew her forth, her feelings, her impressions—and she told him about all the people, and the natives of the country, and the few Basques she had met, and the French—the feeling of other races, nearer the sun. And it had for him the glamour of illusion. He knew, in a sense, that it was all illusion: that passion and sunshine and roses and sea-surf was an illusion one had at a distance, that the reality was quite different. Yet the illusion held him. He was in the spell of unreality. And she talked and talked as if her suppressed, pent-up life were streaming out of her in talk. All the time, she hated doing it. Yet she went on till past midnight. And then the flow choked.

She went to bed feeling dazed and unreal, as if she had lost herself, lost her real virtue. And her soul loathed the process of talk.

And in the morning, when she came down, she was shocked at the change in Clifford. He lay in bed inert and, as it seemed, almost in a state of coma.

"He's a little tired after the excitement of meeting you yesterday," said Mrs Bolton, speaking of him tenderly, as if he were a patient entirely in her charge.

"Was it too much for him?" asked Connie, fear-struck.

"Oh, I don't think so! But he suffers from these lapses of energy. You remember he always did. It seems as if men do suffer that way since the war, even men who were never touched, or never even in the war at all. But their energy collapses, without anything being wrong with them. So we mustn't wonder at Sir Clifford, must we? He was a little too excited yesterday. He has energy like that, in rushes. And then it leaves him. But he'll be feeling better tomorrow."

Connie was frightened. It seemed as if the bottom had suddenly fallen out of life. Clifford seemed as if his very soul were paralysed; and he knew it, his eyes were haunted with fear and irritable horror. He hated Connie to see him like that. She had to leave him.

It was Sunday, and a warm, dull morning.

"Is there anything new in the Parkin scandal?" she asked Mrs Bolton.

"No my lady! nothing new!—I believe Mr Parkin's wife has gone away somewhere. And Mr Parkin has finished here. He's going away too—or else gone. To Canada, they say."

"But when did he finish here?"

"Yesterday! At twelve o'clock! He came and saw Sir Clifford, and it was all finished. I believe the new man is already in the cottage."

Connie said no more. Everything felt burdensome and heavy. But she had said she would see him again, so she supposed she ought to make the effort. She felt, at the moment, in the dislocation of her return, as if nothing mattered very much.

However, she summoned up her energy, and walked out to Tevershall. The bells were ringing in Tevershall old church, pealing away with that forlorn sound which no longer fits our life. And at the Methodist Chapel, the one bell was going tang-tang-tang! She loitered, to let the church-goers get inside their places of worship before she passed. Up at the church, the pealing had stopped, the one bell sounded the last minutes.

Colliers, pale-faced and underworld, a little distorted, stood about in their Sunday clothes, or in their clean shirt-sleeves. They looked at her, but did not salute her. Young men were buzzing away on motor-cycles, others were walking briskly, as if to some appointment, others were strolling in little gangs, purely aimless, some were walking with young women dressed up in the latest fashion, high heels and bare arms and little hats pulled-down over their eyes. The place was half-deserted, the shops shut, and the streets curiously alive with people dressed up and strolling about. Everybody watched her as she passed, and, she knew, made comments. But in that place which was her home now, nobody spoke to her or saluted her. She didn't know the ordinary people. Neither did Clifford.

Motor-cars, motor-cycles, motor-buses went rushing by. It was quite a business to cross the road. But it was Sunday morning. As she passed the Methodist Chapel, they were singing shrilly:

"I need thee, Oh I need thee
Every hour I need thee!
Oh bless me now my Saviour!
I co—ome to—o thee."*

The sound made her shiver: so queer and wild and demonish in its howl.—And as she went on up the hill, the miners who were standing or squatting on the pavement turned after her their pale pit faces, watching her. They were not unkindly or unfriendly: but uncanny, unearthly, or under-earthly. And their bodies too were uncanny, distorted with an under-earth distortion, one shoulder a little higher than the other, legs oddly screwed.

Mrs Parkin lived in one of the old cottages, the end one of a row. It had a little brick yard with the tap outside, and no garden. The door stood open, and she saw the old woman at the table rolling out paste for a gooseberry pie: there was a pie-dish of greenish gooseberries on the table, as well as paste-board and lard and flour.

Connie tapped, and the old woman turned to the door. She had sharp hazel eyes, and tight grey hair, and still a good deal of her old, hard energy and quick, fierce, violent movements. Her face was flushed with heat.

"Lady Chat'ley!" she said in some surprise, and then she waited for Connie to speak.

"Is Parkin in?" said Connie, on the door-step.

"You mean our Oliver? He's in bed. He's not got up yet."

Connie didn't quite know what to say.

"Isn't he well?" she asked.

"He's better than he was. But he was out most o' th' night; in th' wood, I suppose. He's finished his job with Sir Clifford, you know."

"Yes!" Connie hesitated. "Is he going away?"

"He's going tonight."

The little woman's sentences came out sharp and short, like a rap on the knuckles.

"Could I speak to him?" said Connie.

The old woman eyed her with those shrewd, hard hazel eyes.

"D'you want me to call him?" she said.

Connie still stood on the doorstep, the old woman, in a white apron and with floury hands caked with paste, stopping the way.

"Would you mind? Would he be getting up soon?"

"I s'h'd call him for his dinner, anyhow. Come in! Though you'll be broiled to death, I'm just cooking Sunday dinner. Sit down, and don't notice the pig-sty I'm in. You can't keep clean an' cook and do."

The place was small, hot, crowded, and vigorously clean. The linoleum on the floor was polished bright, and white hearth was speckless, the old fireplace was like black velvet, the copper kettle like new gold. Everything was rigidly in its place. Only the table had a litter of pastry-making.

Connie sat on an edge of the sofa, and the old woman clumped into the back room, which was the little sitting-room out of which the stair-foot door opened.

"Oliver! Oliver!" came the old woman's hard, shrewd voice.

There was a sort of grunt from above.

"Get up then! You're wanted."

Connie heard his cross voice, in broad vernacular, upstairs:

"Who wants me?"

"Get up an' see," said the old woman, shutting the stair-foot door and returning to her pastry.

Connie heard the thud of a foot on the floor overhead. How near everything was! How terribly close and on top of one another! Every sound that anybody made, audible to everybody else!

"It's that hot you can hardly breathe!" said the old woman, suddenly snatching the iron screen, that was like an iron shield, polished glossy black, and hanging it on the fire-bar, in front of the glowing coal fire.

Connie heard his footsteps, in stocking feet, cross the floor overhead and descend the creaking stairs. She gazed sideways in a sort of fear, at the inner doorway, to see him come through, as she sat on the sofa at the side of the door.

He came stooping a little through the low doorway, not seeing her on the first instant. But she saw his face, still slightly bruised, his moustache ragged, and his cut mouth not quite healed: and on his face the dogged, expressionless look of an animal. At that instant his eye saw her, and he stopped as he passed her. He was wearing navy-blue trousers, and a clean shirt. He glanced at her, holding his face aside.

"There's Lady Chat'ley come for you!" said the mother roughly, rolling out her pastry with a certain ferocity.

His eyes met Connie's, and she felt a vivid pain at her heart. She saw the peculiar little patches of dead pallor, on his cheek-bones, caused by acute misery, and the abstract tension of his eyes. His mouth was still swollen out of shape.

"I got back last night," she said, in her soft, breathless way.

"Yes! I 'eered," he said.

He was aware again of his mother. He went across the room, stooped to a little cupboard, moving the arm-chair before he could open the door, and took out his slippers. Then he put the chair in place, put on his slippers, sitting down in the corner by the cupboard and the window.

"You are going away?" said Connie, across the room.

He held his face lowered, to hide the disfigurement. The light was behind him. But his voice came harsh and strong:

"Yes! Tonight!"

"Where?"

"To Sheffield."

"Have you got other work?"

"Yes."

There was a sort of thick lisp in his speech.

"What kind of work?" she said.

"Labouring! in Jephson's Steel Works."

His voice was so harsh and distant, and his tongue seemed so queer, she would hardly have known it was he speaking.

"I thought you wasn't tellin' nobody!" snapped his mother, in censure.

He looked up at her sharply.

"I'm not talking to you, am I?" he said.

The old woman made no sign of having heard, whipping the paste-crust on to the pie, and trimming the edges with sharp movements. There was silence for a moment. The room was very hot.

"Can't yer leave that a bit?" he said to his mother.

"Why what d' yer want?" she snapped at him. "No! I can't leave it."

"Go up an' ma'e my bed," he said.

"Ay! An' leave my cookin' in th' middle! I sh'd think so!" she retorted obstinately.

He waited a minute, while she finished the pie. Then he repeated, in hard, broad vernacular:

"Tha can leave it now. Goo up an' ma'e my bed."

"Interferin' nuisance!" she muttered, as she whipped out of the house to the tap, to wash her hands, then returned, wiping her hands hastily on her coarse white apron.

"An' if you get your dinner at two o'clock, don't blame me," she said, as she went with that odd, rushing impetuosity into the inner room and up the stairs. On the stairs she called back:

"Look at th' meat!"

"Ay!" he said, short.

Then they heard her footsteps overhead, heavy and pegging for a little woman.

He opened the oven door. There came a smell of beef roasting, and a faint sound of sizzling. He looked in apathetically, yet attentively, then shut the door again.

"I'm afraid you had a bad time," said Connie to him.

He glanced at her across the little room, and smiled with faint indifference, but said nothing.

"I wish I could have come back sooner," she said.

"It wouldn't ha' helped none," he said.

"Not if you'd had me there?" she enquired wistfully.

He glanced at her again, but said nothing. There was something unyielding in his eyes and his body, but also, something dead. A pain went through her bowels. She saw, in some way, death in connection with him.

"Look, I brought you a hanky," she said, tears filling her eyes, as she looked in her little bag and got out the gaily-coloured silk handkerchief He was watching her. She held it out to him, and he rose suddenly and came across the room to take it. But his face did not change from its stiff, deadened look.

She caught his hand and held it, looking up into his eyes. In her own eyes the tears had risen again, seeing the queer white, dead places on his cheek-bones, and the unseeing of his eyes.

"I'm so sorry!" she faltered. "You won't blame me, will you?"

He looked down at her almost irritably.

"You? What for?" There was only a pain and a hardness and an irritation in his eyes.

"You won't, will you?—And you'll talk to me before you go away? Will you come to the hut this afternoon, so that we can talk things over?" she said.

"I wasn't going to the wood no more. Albert's in the cottage," he said, averting his face. But she saw a gap in his mouth, where it seemed a tooth was gone.

"But you can come! Will you? After lunch? Will you? And let us talk?"

He was silent, but she clung to his hand. Then he looked down at her and shook his head slowly.

"You shouldn't run no risks," he said, dully.

"There's no risk. Where's the risk? You'll come, won't you?"

She gazed up at him with the tears in her eyes, and in her distress she was very beautiful, at least to him. He swallowed, and a pressure lifted from his face.

"I'll come!" he said. "It seems I always do the wrong thing."

"Not the wrong thing!" she pleaded, cheering up.

And suddenly she put his hand to her cheek, then kissed it furtively, quickly. Then she looked up at him, to see the first sharp little lightnings of passion stirring in his eyes, and his chest filling again. He was like a flower that revives in water. And she was pleased.

They heard his mother stamping across the floor upstairs. Connie let go his hand, and rose to her feet. He stood on the hearthrug near her: looked at the handkerchief, then stuffed it in his trousers' pocket.

"I shall come after lunch," said Connie, in her soft, breathless voice, looking at him. He met her eyes, and nodded. He was listening to his mother coming downstairs.

The little woman darted into the room, rushed at the oven, looked at the meat, turned it, shut the door, snatched the screen from before the fire, set it aside, and taking the poker, eased the red fire carefully near the oven, so that the black coal above began to smoke dense yellow under the bonnet, then leaped into flame. Whereupon the old woman set the screen before the fire again, and immediately darted the lid off the iron saucepan, peering into the steam. And all this time she had not even noticed the presence of her son and of Connie: or had refused to take notice. Then she kneeled to remove from the white hearth the crumbs of black coal that had rolled out from the fire.

Connie moved to the door.

"Good-morning Mrs Parkin!" she said. "I must go now"

"Good-morning Lady Chat'ley," said the old woman, not deigning to look at her, from the hearth where she kneeled.

Connie glanced at him. He was looking down with a queer, half tolerant, half weary look at his mother. Then he glanced at Connie in the doorway, and faintly smiled. But there was a touch of genuine amusement in the smile, and Connie went off, cheered.

Nevertheless, as she walked down the hill, she was aware of one predominant thing: and that was, that he might fairly easily die. He was not tough. She saw in him, she knew not how to describe it, but she saw in him the danger of death. She felt it with her heart, as children sometimes do. And it touched her with acute pain, such as she had never known before. No, he was not tough! Nothing can be more easily wounded, in our day, and mortally wounded, than the passionate soul. It is the passionless soul which is tough and rubbery, almost indestructible. The survival of the fittest.

The day was hot, and smelled of Sunday, roast beef and spring cabbage cooking, a host of Sunday dinners still in the oven, and everybody's waiting. The roast beef of Old England mostly came from the Argentine, or from Australia: but what's in a name!*

She went in the hot afternoon across the park to the hut. It was the last time she would be going to meet him there. A certain anger filled her, against the stupidity of circumstance. Really, life itself was now almost entirely at the mercy of the ugly concatenation of circumstance, dragged along a helpless victim. Oh, if somebody would only start to break the mesh of chains!

There was still no one at the hut when she arrived. She opened the door, and saw the place very tidy, the traps and work-bench and tools all in order, but all the odd little things of Parkin's own, were gone. This place too had died for her, in the clutch of circumstance.

She wandered disconsolately, and presently heard voices. Flossie came running joyfully to her, and she welcomed the brown dog with a pang of pain. Then two men emerged from the path, Parkin, in a navy-blue Sunday suit and a black soft hat, and Albert, the new gamekeeper.

Albert was a colonial, a tall, stringy fellow, clean-shaven, with a close-pressed mouth and hard, keen blue eyes that had seen all round the world without having seen much in it. He was dressed in a khaki cloth shirt and black tie, belted khaki trousers and leather leggings, and an old brown hat: and a gun. He was at once spruce and careless, watchful and indifferent, unsure of himself, and yet cock-sure: a real colonial. Seeing Connie, he lifted his hat a little, not quite knowing how to behave, watchful, yet with the backwoodsman's curious self-assertion in his bearing.

"This is the new gamekeeper, my lady! Albert Adam!" said Parkin.

Albert watched to see if she were going to shake hands. She was not.

"How do you do?" said Connie. "You are living in the cottage?"

"Yes Mam!"

"Do you think you'll be all right?"

"Fine!"

"And will your wife like it, do you think?"

"Oh, it'll suit her fine. Just what she's been craving for, to be back on the old place."

"She's a Tevershall girl—was in service in Wragby before the war—afore she went to New Zealand," said Parkin.

It was queer, the difference in the two men's speech: Albert so prompt and distinct, with an American twang, Parkin seeming by contrast so much softer, vaguer, but to mean more.

"Oh, you are a New Zealander?" said Connie to Albert, who stood easy in front of her, resting his long, wiry length on one leg, and leaving the other knee loose.

"Yes Mam! But I've spent a lot of my time in California, so I'm half an American, so to speak."

"What did you do in California?"

"I was mining most of the time: cattle-punching some of it."

"And then you went back to New Zealand?"

"Yes Mam. I joined up in 1915. And at the end of the war I married my wife, who's given me no peace till I've brought her back to the old place."—He smiled a slight complacent smile.

"I suppose England will seem very small to you!—and this wood quite tiny!"

"Oh, it's not such a bad little bunch o' trees! I got used to Europe in the war, you may say."

"And will you like it, do you think, being here?"

"Oh, I can contrive to get along, anywhere. It takes a lot to make me feel uncomfortable."

He laughed in an easy-going, yet self-conscious way. Tough as he was, he seemed all the time to be putting up a front against possible criticism.

"I hope you'll be all right!" said Connie. "You know I have a key to the hut, don't you? I sit here sometimes."

"Yes Mam. Mr Parkin here has told me that. Oh, it's a dandy little shanty: make a cute little home for a man, out west among the timber, if you put a stove in!"

He spoke with such curious precision, and sounded his "h's" so distinctly, he might almost have been a gentleman by education. And yet his manner was so unattractive, and somehow ill-bred. It was nervous without being sensitive, punctilious without ease.

Parkin meanwhile had stood by passive, in his Sunday suit. He would no more wear the velveteen corduroy coat with baggy skirts, nor the breeches and leggings, nor carry the gun. He was a little artizan in navy-blue with a dark red tie. And Albert, as a colonial, would not condescend to the velveteen coat either. In fact he wore no coat at all, but a cloth hunting-shirt with pockets on the breast, khaki-coloured and spruce: and a black silk tie. He had a certain stringy elegance.

Flossie was roaming round in nervous excitement.

"I expect you'll find th' milk by th' warren gate by now," said Parkin in an aside voice, to Albert. "They milk early, Sundays.—An' if you'll call Flossie, we'll make her follow."

"Well, I'll say Good-day!" said Albert, lifting his hat to Connie. "Goodbye then!" he added to Parkin, shaking hands with him. "Thanks for putting me in the know here. And good luck, you sure can do with it!"

"Ay!" said Parkin. "I s'll come over an' see how yer gettin' on."

"Fine! Fine! You know where you're welcome! Well—"

"Ca' th' dog!" said Parkin.

Albert gave a short, sharp, imperious whistle. Flossie looked round, and immediately cringed to the ground, as if her bones had gone soft. Albert strode off to the path, and whistled again, looking round. Flossie, as if smitten with paralysis, was creeping along the ground towards Parkin.

"Go!' he said fiercely, pointing towards Albert.

The dog only collapsed on to the earth entirely, and lay pretending she could not move, only watching Parkin with her yellow eyes.

"Get up, you fool of a bitch!" he said angrily.

Albert whistled again. But the dog lay motionless.

Parkin strode up to her rapidly. She winced down on to the earth, but it was obvious she would rather take a beating than follow the other man.

"Go with him!" said Parkin, standing above her and pointing fiercely at Albert. But Flossie only lay inert, her yellow eyes fixed on her master's face, her silky hair glistening in a heap.

"Of all the damned and blasted fools!" he said, in a little voice of angry pain.

And suddenly, while she lay absolutely motionless, he stooped and picked her up and swung her after Albert. She fell in a flurried little heap, and he, running with sudden frenzy, seized a thick oak stick and rushed towards her. Casting an eye of real terror behind her now, she loped with a cringing run, her hind quarters dropped and her tail pressed under her belly, into the path after Albert, still looking behind her. Parkin waited there, with the stick in his hand, white with anger and emotion, ready to fling the stick at her if she returned. But she did not return. They heard the voice of Albert speaking to her in the distance, with that colonial geniality which has no warmth. Then Parkin flung aside his stick and pushed back his hat.

"Poor Flossie!" said Connie, with a little blurt of laughter that was almost tears. It was indeed pathetic and ridiculous at the same time. "Couldn't you have kept her?"

It was some moments before he replied, in a blanched, small voice:

"How could I!"

He knew himself he had cared too much for his dog. And he knew he was ridiculous.

Connie felt a certain resentment against him. He should have managed better, about the dog.

"It will be nice for *me* to see her," she said. "I shall have her for a friend."

"You might keep an eye on her," he answered, his voice still anxious.

"Oh yes! And if she's not happy, *I'll* take her."

He pondered this for a time.

"Ay!" he said. "If yer'd have her."

He was evidently terribly downcast about his dog. It irritated Connie a little. Parting with Flossie upset him more than parting with herself.

"I think Albert is quite nice," she said.

"Oh ay!"

"Not interesting, but nice. One will feel safe with him. Is his wife pleasant?"

"Yes, she seems a nice enough woman."

There was a long pause. It was still and hot in the wood, and the flies were a pestering nuisance. Under the oak-trees, the bracken spread like a sea, reflecting a dullish light on the great fronds. All was green, and dense and still, with a scent of bracken.

"Let us go and sit somewhere in the wood—not here!" she said.

They walked slowly to the hazel-thicket, then he wound through the hazels to a place where the bracken rose high, and the great oaks were undisturbed.

"Here?" he said.

"Yes!"

He threw off his coat and hat, and they sat down under a big oak-tree, with the huge bracken sloping over their heads.

"Yes, it's lovely here!" she said. She was thinking how he would miss the wood, that he knew so well.

Everything was green, green, with arching, over-riding vegetation of branched fern, and the smell of fern-seed. It was like being in a sea whose waves branched overhead. He sat motionless and silent, in a moment of acute depression. They were deep in the wood.

"You mind going very much, don't you?" she said, taking his hand.

He did not answer. His heart was dead, for the moment.

"Look at me!" she said. "Why do you always turn your face away?"

He glanced at her, but turned his face aside again, flapping away the flies, which irritated him.

"Have you got friends in Sheffield?" she asked him.

"Yes! That's why I'm goin'. I've got Bill, as was my pal in th' war."

"Is he married?"

"Wi' three children."

"And will you stay with them?"

"For a bit. I s'll have lodgings there."

There was a curious thick lisp in his speech.

"Have you lost a tooth?" she asked him.

"Yes."

"Let me look!"

She put her hand on his chin and turned his face to her. Then she pushed back his swollen lips, and saw where two of the front teeth were gone from the lacerated gums. It was a nasty, disfiguring mess.

"What a shame!" she said, as anger rose in her heart. "But never mind, it's not really hurt you. You can easily have two teeth put in."

He did not say anything.

"Kiss me!" she pleaded.

"Why—" he said. "I've got no kisses in me, just now."

"Why not? Why not? Are you cross with me as well as with everything else?—Be cross with everything except me—" she coaxed.

But he did not answer.

"I want to tell you," she whispered. "I think I'm going to have a child."

He looked at her sharply.

"Have yer told Sir Clifford?" he asked.

"No! Not yet! I don't want to tell him yet."

"An' what when yer have to?"

"He'll think I had a lover when I was abroad."

He turned and looked at her, with a faint smile of derision.

"An' he'll take it on, will he?" he asked.

"Yes!" she said. "Do you despise him for it? Would you like him better if he wanted to cut me off from life altogether?"

He pondered for a while.

"No!" he said. "Seeing things is as they are, I expect he's right.—Yer won't tell him whose child it is, though, shall yer?"

"I don't think so."

"If yer did, he'd never swallow it," he said, with another cruel smile.

"Why do you hate Clifford?" she said.

"I don't."

"Yes, you hate everybody," she said, miserably.

He did not answer for a while. Then he turned to her:

"I hate everybody just now, you're right," he said. "An' I feel as if I'd swallowed poison, and had a bellyful of it."

"How horrid!" she said.

But he turned his face aside, and did not answer.

"But it's so horrid of you to hate me as well."

"I don't! Only I've got a bellyful. I expect I shall work it off."

His face shut again.

"Do you hate going to work in Sheffield?"

He did not answer for a time. He hated being catechised. She waited.

"Yes, I hate it."

"Would you have liked to stay here?"

He pondered awhile, sullenly. She knew quite well he would have liked it.

"I knowed I couldn't. I always knowed this 'ud come to an end. I always knowed I should get chucked out o' this wood. It couldn't last."

"But listen! Why don't you let me get a little farm, and you work it for us? And I could come and stay sometimes. Don't go to Sheffield and be a workman, a labourer! It's not right for you. It's not your nature. Don't do that! Let us look for a little place, that would be our own."

He pondered this for some time.

"Why—" he said. "It doesn't seem to me right for a man to make his life off a woman!"

"But how! In Jephson's steel works you'll have to make a living off the company. There's my money. Let us use it. You're not afraid, are you?"

"No!" he said stiffly. "I'm not afraid. Only let me try what I can do by mysen. An' if I canna ma'e no headway—why, I maun come to thee." He said it with real resentment.

"How much will you earn in Sheffield?"

"Seven-an'-six a day! And I have to gi'e my mother fifteen shillin' a week, for th' girl.—But Bill's goin' to try an' get me a lorry-driver's job, an' then I get three pound a week start."

"It does seem awfully little," said Connie.

"If you've been used to more, it does," he said.

She was thinking how awful it must be, to be cramped forever within three pounds a week, and never any hope, never any getting out, chained down to a job, for three pounds a week!

"I'm so afraid," she said. "You'll just be miserable and out of place, being a workman like that, and then you'll have a collapse of some sort."

His ominous silence showed that he feared the same.

"Well—we can but see!" he said, obstinately.

"And you promise me—you promise—look at me!—you promise, if you're really unhappy, you'll let *me* find some way of making a living. Thank heaven I have that money of my mother's!—You promise, don't you?"

He looked her in the eyes for a moment, and his body relaxed with infinite sadness.

"Yes!" he said. "It's better to be beholden to a woman, than live a life o' misery. I'm not like other chaps: I'm miserable when I can't be by myself. My mother allers said as I was on'y ha'ef a man. 'Appen I am! 'Appen I am! An' if I am, I mun manage at that."

"But why *should* you be like other men?" she cried. "They're only stupid. Why *shouldn't* you be different, and more lonely! *Don't* try and force yourself to be just like other men, will you? Promise you won't! You'll only ruin what you are."

"It's no good if I do!" he said. "I'm never no better, so I needn't try an' force myself. If I've got too much of a woman in me, I have, an' I'd better abide by it. And if I can't fend for myself, I'll come to you—"

He spoke with intense bitterness. The idea that he was too womanly was terribly humiliating to him: and manliness meant stupid, unimaginative insentience to him.

"Why do you mind?" she said, tears coming to her eyes. "It's foolish! When you say you have too much of a woman in you, you only mean you are more sensitive than stupid people like Dan Coutts. You ought to be proud that you are sensitive, and have that much of a woman's good qualities. It's very good for a man to have a touch of woman's sensitiveness. I hate your stupid hard-headed clowns who think they are so very *manly*—"

She was angry, angry at the implied insult to womanhood, and at his stupidity regarding himself.

"Ay!" he said. "I know—Ca' it sensitive, ca' it what you like, I canna get on wheer other chaps gets on. I canna get on wi' other chaps—I want ter be by mysen. I dunna want to work, neither at pit nor nowhere. This job suited me, so I knowed I should get sack.—But if I'm handicapped,

I'm handicapped. Sir Clifford's handicapped another road. I sh'd 'ave liked to go to Canada—to get away, an' 'appen make somethink of my life—out there. On'y you don't want to go—an' you don't want me to go—just yet?"

He looked into her face with tormented, unyielding eyes.

"No!" she said hastily. "Don't go to Canada yet! You won't, will you? Trust me first, won't you? I've been to Canada and America, and I *know* I don't want to live there. You wouldn't like it. Perhaps you'd be able to be alone—but you wouldn't like it. It would kill something in you—the most sensitive bit of you, it would kill it. I know! You have got a gift—a gift of life. Don't spoil it. And don't take it away from me. You've got to help me to live, too. Don't have silly ideas about being manly. You've got a gift of life, which so few men have. Don't destroy it. Do trust me! We only want to live. It's not a question of *making* something of your life. It's a question of living it. Look at all the colliers!—they don't live. They only exist in a sort of greyness. Promise me not to spoil the life in you. Promise me you'll trust me. Promise me faithfully you'll come to me, before you let yourself be really damaged. Oh thank God I've got that money of my mother's! Promise me you'll never be obstinate. Promise me that!"

He hung his head in silence for a long time. Then he said quietly:

"Ay! I've got nowt but my life, when a's said an' done. An' if I hire it to Jephson's for seven-an'-six a day, I could hire it to you for less. If I do game-keepin' for Sir Clifford, I could do farm-labourin' for you, an' feel none the worse. Work's work! I don't mind workin'—but the thought of workin' at a job is like death. I want to be by mysen, on my own.—An' if you bought a farm, or rented one, I could work it for you, 'appen, without feelin' as if you'd rented me as well. I've got no money, an' I've got to live an' to keep my child. If I've got to work for a capitalist, you might as well be th' capitalist as any other. Only f'r a' that, I wish I could be independent, an' earn my living by myself—"

He looked at her still with a touch of resistance.

"I don't *care*!" she said. "I'll give you all the money tomorrow, and let you buy what you like, if you'll take it."

"No no!" he said, sinking into sullen silence. Then he looked up suddenly, beginning in a harsh voice, then breaking suddenly into broad dialect: "I love—Ah luv thee! Ah luv thee!" He took her hand and pressed it against his belly. "But tha wunna want ter ma'e me feel sma', shall ter? Let me be mysen, an' let me feel as if tha wor littler than me! Dunna ma'e me feel sma', an' *down*!—else I canna stop wi' thee. Let me luv thee my own road, let me, I canna be no diff'rent an' be right. I've *got* ter feel as if I was bringin' the money 'ome, I canna help it. Tha can laugh at me—but dunna want ter ma'e me feel sma'! Laugh at me—I like thee ter laugh at me! But be nice to me, an' dunna be big! For I feel I've got no place in the world, an' no mortal worth to nobody, if not to thee. An' I dunna want ter hate everything. It ma'es me feel as if I'd swallowed poison, an' had a bellyful. I dunna want to hate even Bertha—nor Sir Clifford. I do hate 'em, in a way. But I don't want it to lie in my belly an' I can't get rid of it. No no! Tha'rt good to me, an' that frightens me a bit. But I'm neither made clever nor rich. I'm not even a good cricketer like my own father. Yet I feel I'm not a liar, an' that's a' as I can say I am. An' I believe I should soon be dead, even then, but for thee just now."

He held her hand close against him, and suddenly she turned and clung to his breast. It was true, he was nothing but a man. And if his dignity as a man was really hurt, he would die. She didn't care much about anything, however, except his physical presence. That was essential to her.

"I'd better work i' Sheffield while I get my divorce," he said, after a pause. "An' then see—"

"When will that be?"

"It doesn't come on till September. An' if it goes through all right, it's another six month after that afore it's final—End o' March o' next year, you may say—"

This seemed to her a long time.

"Do you care so much about a divorce?" she said.

"Yes! Yes! I must get clear o' Bertha. I must! I must be clear of 'er, if ever I'm to breathe."

"So you'll have to be careful, till there's a decree absolute,"* said Connie, with some indifference.

"Yes, I s'll have to mind."

She put her arms round his waist and clung to his body. That was what she chiefly wanted: to feel him alive and breathing, close to her. He held her folded, quietly. She could tell he was still tormented: his heart seemed to beat sadly.

She suddenly lifted her head and looked up at him.

"Take me if you want me," she murmured, her eyes glistening.

He looked into her eyes and shook his head slowly.

"You don't want me," he said.

Her face fell a little. It was true.

"Why don't I?" she said, half anxious.

"Maybe you're thinking of the child," he said quietly.

She buried her face against him, and clung to him fast.

"But I care more about *you* than the child," she murmured in confession. "I want *you*, more than a child."

He drew her a little closer, warmer, and softly kissed her hair as she clung to his breast.

"Ay!" he said. "Well, I can wait."

"But you love me?" she said anxiously, looking up.

He bent and kissed her face, and her eyes.

"Ay!" he said, in the soft, low, free voice, that at last was without care.

She clung to him, and wept. He held her tighter, and she could tell he was frightened.

"I'm only crying because it feels better between us," she stammered between her sobs.

"Kiss me then!" he murmured, in a whisper.

She lifted her face, and he kissed her eyes and her wet cheeks, wiping her wet cheeks with his own cheeks, because his hands were fast, holding her. And she laughed with a sudden catch, because he wanted to dry her face with his.

He held her very close, and very still, covering her from the flies with great fronds of bracken, that sheltered him too. And she clung to him in an intense and healing stillness, that was passion itself, in its pure silence. And so she seemed to sleep, and he too, in the silence of the wood, buried among the bracken, while the afternoon passed away.

At last she said to him suddenly:

"And I'll come to see you in Sheffield, shall I? Shall I come to Bill's house? We can say we're friends."

"I'll ax 'em," he said slowly.

"And you'll write to me? Write to me to my sister Hilda, and she'll send it to me. Will you?"

"Ay!—I can ax Bill an' his wife when they'd like you to come. An' then I'll write to you."

"You promise! And if anything goes wrong, you'll tell me?—I should never forgive you if you didn't trust me—if you let anything bad happen to what is between us. Promise me you won't betray what is between us! I don't mind what you do. I don't even mind so *very* much if you go to other women, since you can't have me—if only you won't damage what is between you and me. Promise me you won't! Promise me you'll be true to the feeling that is between you and me. And if you do ever go to other women, go nicely and gently, and be grateful to them. And don't tell me. If you keep your heart gentle, I shall know I haven't lost you. The other won't matter, if you need it."

"I shan't need it," he said, in a stilled, low voice.

"I don't want you to promise that. I want you to promise, if ever you do go to another woman, to be gentle with her, and feel grateful to her, and to remember, it's *me* you really want."

He kissed her gently.

"Nay-nay!" he said. "Be still! I'm not a baby. I've done without women when I had no woman. I can wait. I can wait."

"You will, won't you?" she said, clinging to him. "You *will* wait for me!"

"Yes-yes!"

"But I don't want you to promise to be faithful to me. If you *do* want another woman, then have her, never mind. But love me with your heart, won't you?"

"Ay! Be still! Be still!—Shall you love me with *your* heart?"

"You know I shall," she said.

"And lots besides," he said, smiling.

"No! No! With the heart that loves you, I shall only love you—other things will be different—not such a warm heart.—And you won't love anybody with the same heart you love me with, will you? I don't mind if you love them with another heart."

"No," he laughed. "I doubt I shan't love anybody, with any heart of any sort, warm nor cold."

"Yes you will!" she said. "You love Bill a bit, don't you?"

He pondered.

"Ay!" he said. "If you may call it love."

"And perhaps you'll love his children a bit—and his wife, just a bit. If you live with them, you ought to. Think how you loved Flossie!—too much, really."

He winced.

"Ay!" he said. "Then she pays for it—an' me."

"Love them a bit, but don't love them too much, will you!" she pleaded.

"Shall you measure for me?" he laughed.

"Yes! Yes! I'll measure for you, if you'll let me.—Now give me your pocket-book, and let me write Hilda's address, and you write yours."

He got his coat, and found the little memorandum book. Connie wrote Hilda's address, and he read it. Then he wrote Bill Tewson's address, and gave her the leaf.

"And we won't say goodbye!" she said. "Because you love me, don't you?"

"Yes! I'll say it again. *Yes!* Will that do?"

"And you'll write to me *soon*, won't you?"

"Soon!" he said.

"If you don't, I shall just come. And promise me you won't be miserable."

"No no!" he said, kissing her with sudden quickness. "Tha's cured me! I'm a' right!"

His voice was soft and grateful, and tears flew to her eyes.

"So remember!" she said, beginning to cry, and laughing at the same time, as she drew away. "I want to go now. I want you to stay there, till I'm gone. Don't say goodbye!" At each sentence, she drew a little further off, and sticks cracked under her feet. "But *remember*!" she said, looking back again.

"I shan't forget," he said gently.

And she hurried away into the hazel thicket, crying her tears in a sort of relief.

He watched her go, till she was far gone. Then he sighed, and put on his coat. After all, nothing mattered very much, if one kept peace in one's heart, peace for the woman and peace for oneself. He realised this, and for the moment kept true to the peace, and let the circumstances wait.

15

CONNIE FOUND IT HARD TO SETTLE DOWN again in Wragby. She could not get back inside the life. She realised that she was outside, and that to pretend she was inside didn't work any more. Clifford recovered from his inertia, and had a certain access of energy. But he had ceased to be a man to her. He was a circumstance, not a man. He wasn't even a creature: he was something circumstantial and not quite natural.

The whole place was like that: indeed, the whole of the Midlands. Since she was back, she could not get into it again. She stood mysteriously outside, looking at it all from the outside. And it gave her a sense of sadness more acute than anything she had ever known. It was a sense of doom. Doom, doom, impending, inevitable doom! this she saw in the Midlands' sky, and on the Midlands' earth. It looked at her out of all the faces, Clifford's, Mrs Bolton's, the colliers', the rector's—they all walked with unconscious and impending doom upon them. It was worse than Aeschylus, worse than any House of Atreus.* Even the fat, energetic Field, with his quick smile and his comfortable appearance, had a look of innocent apprehension, a furtive dread of something, in his small blue eyes that were like the eyes of a sprightly young pig, only not so hysterical.

It was as if the place had died, in some mysterious way. The whole terrible region of the Midlands of England seemed to her like a heart that has stopped beating, in a body warm but dead. And especially the colliers seemed like ghosts, ghouls, not men. They were passing back into the strange life of elementals, the elementality of lemurs* or of angels. Angels, thrones, ministers and powers!*—she could not remember how the heavenly hierarchy was arranged. But there was an infernal hierarchy to correspond. And these people were part of the infernal hierarchy, something that frightened her, as being elemental, and *less* than a created being.

Clifford seemed to her really weird. He now had Mrs Bolton behind him, as a man has his daimon or familiar spirit behind him. And he was quite unaware. He was quite unaware how he was no longer an individual, how he was part of a weird duality with Ivy Bolton. He thought he was the master, Sir Clifford, and she was the servant. But it was not so at all.

Mrs Bolton had in some way fused her strange, pale, revengeful soul with his. She was as unconscious of it, *almost*, as he was. And she was certainly unconscious of the *drive* she lent him. A weird, but powerful impetus came out of the pair of them. It was an urge and a force and a direction derived from the unison of their two souls. And it drove Clifford into "business", weirdly.

Connie held her breath to see the curious intensity with which, when he roused again from his depression, he entered into the serious business of rejuvenating the mines, *to make them pay*. He seemed to lose his consciousness of everything else. Even himself, his health, his own egoism, he lost in the strange intense *raptus** of "business". He was gone, he was no longer a human being, but an elemental, caught up in a weird inspiration, a *raptus*. The exhausted mines were going to be made to *pay*. And his soul, fired by the strange pallid breath of Mrs Bolton, had passed into a weird permanent ecstasy, the long-enduring ecstasy of the struggle with uncanny Matter. It was as if he fused himself into the very existence of coal and sulphur and petroleum and rock, and lost his humanity, as the trolls have lost theirs, in iron. It was not the human mind triumphing over matter, as in real science. No, he had gone beyond that. It was the human soul worshipping in ecstasy at the mystery of Matter, to draw out the very blood of Matter, gold. It was an intense and ecstatic form of idolatry. A great portion of his consciousness seemed to have lapsed out, like a flame blown out. And what remained of him was this idolatrous ecstasy at the shrine of Matter.

Connie suddenly understood the hatred of "inspiration", in Plato.* In the days of Socrates, men must have been very frequently in this state of awful intoxication, when they were not themselves, but mere instruments of the howling elements. Raving poets, raving orators, raving bacchanals, raving oracles, none of them in possession of themselves, but possessed by some non-creative frenzy, like machines running out of control: it must have been awful. She saw now the greatness of Socrates with his dictum "Know thyself". He meant,—Possess thyself, don't be possessed by some mere raving force.

That had been the danger of the Greeks: to lose themselves, and be possessed of some raving force. They too had the mad egoism, and the insane love of money. And here it was again, after three thousand years of idealism, the same loss of self, the same "inspiration", the lapsing into the possession of the raving materialist forces.

And yet one must not possess oneself either, too absolutely. There were these elemental forces which possessed people and made them weird, the infernal hierarchies. But there *was* also the God-mystery, the breeze of God, with which one must travel. One had to know the distinction, even here in the great invisible influences.

But Clifford had lost the power of distinguishing. He had gone over. He was in the intoxication of the material forces, the *raptus* of mechanical inspiration. He had launched into extensive business activities, raised large sums of money, Wragby was mortgaged as far as it could be: and the most elaborate, expensive, and ultra-modern plant was being set up not only at Tevershall pit, but at New England, High Park, and Crosshill. The four pits were to be worked in conjunction, under an intense pressure. And they were going to pay. In this, their last lap, they would make Clifford's fortune, a modern fortune. And after that, let the skies fall if they wanted to.

He was so sure of success, that he spent almost lavishly on himself and on the household. He bought a new car, and gave Connie the old one: which after all was only a few months old. He talked of hiring a second chauffeur, for Connie. But she wouldn't have it.—He had a man-servant to wait at table and do foot-man's duties. He contemplated the repairs for Wragby. And he raised Mrs Bolton's wage.

He was, in fact, carried away into business, as into a rapture. He spent many hours at the mines, and was gone for hours to Sheffield, Nottingham, even Leeds, on "business", taking with him only the faithful Field, who served him as valet and nurse, gentle as any woman, but a little doomed in his willingness.—And when Clifford's energy fell, and "business" went out of him, then he would sit for hours, vacant as an empty whelk-shell, listening to the radio. With a blank, absorbed face, almost like a cretin who might have been a prophet, he would sit motionless, listening to the loud speaker. Connie refused to have the thing going at meal-times. So he would rush through his meal, no longer noticing what he ate, no longer anxious about "nourishment", bolting his food in a blank absorption, to get back to the radio. And there he would sit, like an empty shell, with the noise of the thing rattling through him.

He would have bursts of talk: politics, especially politics which touched on property, wages, mines, and he talked with a weird inspiration, as if property itself were talking. If the pit could have uttered speech up its vast throat, and the great fan-wheels, like two lips, have softly, rushingly spoken, they might have said what Clifford said. Property must be kept alive, men must adapt themselves. Men must adapt their very souls to coal; minds and souls as well as bodies, for coal is not adaptible except in a very small range.

Another change in him was that often, in the night, instead of gambling—though he and Mrs Bolton gambled a certain amount every day, or every night—he would have Mrs Bolton read aloud to him. The card games, foolish little gambling games like pontoon, were an old institution between them. It excited Mrs Bolton intensely. The red spots glowed in her cheeks, and she would sit up till the small hours of the morning, in the dead silence of Wragby, exchanging sixpences with him, as they played the cards, he lying in bed. Pontoon is a quick game, and some evenings she would lose eighteen shillings, even more, to him. Which for a woman in her position was impossible.

"You're a lucky devil!" she said fiercely, as she flung the money on the bed. For she would always pay up on the spot.

And he was not offended, so deep was he in the game, and in the night.

Indeed he was rather lucky than unlucky, so she was the loser. So he made a bargain with her.

"Look here!" he said. "You can't afford to play pontoon and lose. I'll tell you what I'll do. I'll give you twenty pounds every six months, for being my partner. And if I can win it back from you, I will."

"I shan't have it," she said.

"Then I shan't play with you—I'll play chess again."

She loved the gamble as much as he did, so she gave way, and the two gamblers went at it with renewed zest.

But then, as a variation, he got her to read to him. And she would read such books as *Jane Eyre* or *Wuthering Heights,* or a best-seller like *The Steadfast Sylph.** And he, his critical faculty entirely in abeyance, would lie and listen with the same blank-absorbed face as when he listened to the loud speaker. Constance saw him once: though usually the pair neither played cards nor read aloud while she was about. But once she saw him, with the extraordinary vacant, unconscious look on his face, as he unconsciously listened, and fear overcame her again. He looked a mixture of an idiot and a corpse: something essentially dead, yet idiotically alive. And it shocked her so much, she had to hide the memory from herself.

In the past, a book like *Jane Eyre* had just seemed to him ridiculous, and *Wuthering Heights* just a morbid affair with not an idea in it. But now he listened with a kind of babyish relaxation, and in a queer, absent way was tickled, or thrilled. He was not really *interested*. It was more like a pleasant tickling, that enervated rather than stimulated him. He could not bear to be stimulated. He could not bear to have to pull himself together. He wanted to relax and relax and relax, and then to be carried away in the weird rapture of "business". *That* was orgiastic to him.

And now, he was afraid of Connie, of her criticism, of her look. So he was either vacantly humble or irritably sulky with her. He was terribly conscious of her. He always wanted to know where she was.—"Where's her ladyship?" was his first question, when he had been out, or anyone had called. And Mrs Bolton had to tell him. As soon as he knew, he was content. But he had to know that Connie was somewhere about.

He did not want her actually present. In fact, he preferred it now when she was *not* actually with him. She strung him up, and he didn't want to be strung up. He wanted to relax, and relax, and relax, under the influence of Mrs Bolton and of Field: and then gather himself up, like some sudden boneless octopus, to grapple deep underseas with "business".—So he was always uneasy when Connie was actually there, for fear she should "say something to him". He didn't want to have anything said to him.

Yet when she was out of the house, and he didn't know where she was, he was tortured with anxiety. She saw now, it was even the torturing anxiety of her absence which had made him risk the going on crutches. He had done it, he said, for her sake. And Mrs Bolton likewise had urged him to it, because "her ladyship would be so pleased." Even this ecstasy of business, he had gone into it for Connie's sake. And Mrs Bolton stimulated him by saying: "It *will* be nice for her ladyship when she isn't quite so tied for money!—It *will* be nice for her when she can have her own car and driver!—It *will* be nice when she can travel with her own maid again!—It *will* be nice when she can keep up all the style in Wragby that she'd be so clever at!"

Poor Connie! All this, the last thing on earth that she really wanted, was for her sake. Mrs Bolton and Clifford were like a couple of fiendish conspirators, conspiring to throw the golden net of Mammon over her, and hold her down. At first she was puzzled, and touched. It did seem unselfish of them. And when Mrs Bolton said: "It's a different house when your ladyship is away. The soul seems fair gone out of the place when you're not there, and as if there was nothing to live for—" then Connie knew that the woman was sincere. She was not putting it on.

Both Clifford and Mrs Bolton *needed* Connie in the house. They were both alike, both were best pleased when she was safe in bed, or safe in her room up two flights of stairs. They didn't want her actually with them. But she *must* be in the house. That made them feel safe, and free to play their own little game. When she was gone, they felt frightened, and in some way, guilty. They felt a sort of nakedness, and a sort of helplessness, like shell-fish that have lost their shells. But when she was there, they were as happy as molluses covered by the sea.

She had at first been caught, and had felt grateful to them. But then a deep depression, a sense of deathliness and ghoulish despair had come over her, and she had reacted. She reacted in revulsion, and found both Clifford and Mrs Bolton deeply repulsive to her. And she knew she would have to depart, to leave Wragby for good. They wanted to prostitute her very soul, drag down her real woman's soul and choke it with a slime of money. She would have to go. The atmosphere of the place was awful and obscene. She must go, for her own sake, the sake of her own decency. Parkin or no Parkin, child or no child, she must go. If she were penniless, and had to go and be a servant or a waitress in a tea-shop, she must go. She knew it, and gradually, in silence, began to free herself.

But of what she felt, the other two were now quite unconscious. It was enough that she was there. She had come back. And they had got her. They would not mind what she did, *in private*. And they trusted her not to make any public splash. For the rest, neither Clifford nor Mrs Bolton cared a rap, how "immoral" she might be. In fact, they both liked the idea that she was immoral. They wanted her to be immoral. That would make them safer of her. But of course, she would keep up appearances.

And she knew, when Clifford asked her so particularly what men had been at the Villa Natividad, and all about them individually, he was seeking to find out if she had had a lover, or lovers, and who. He wanted to know *secretly*. If he knew openly, he would have to get into a state about it, he wouldn't know where he was. He wanted her to give him a hint. But she was cold as ice, and as far as the moon from letting him pick any suggestion from her.

In the same way, Mrs Bolton watched her and tried to spy her out, to find out if there was anything in her physical condition. Connie knew almost certainly that she was with child, now; that probably the child was conceived in her, in May, and it was now August. But knowing it made her the more desperately anxious to hide the fact from the others.

It was not so easy, because in the last weeks she had got a little fatter, and her flesh had taken that delicate softness and slightly animal, milky bloom that sometimes comes in the first months of pregnancy: a softness which is no longer fired by desire, a milkiness that is already touched with maternity. Of course Mrs Bolton noticed this, and watched for further signs. But Connie, as far as she could, hid them from her rigorously, and pretended rather the opposite. And she was furious when Mrs Bolton came up to her room in the morning, bringing the tray, instead of the maid Annie or the footman Ernest.

She would have to go! She would have to clear out of Wragby in good time, otherwise she would never get away. These two, Clifford and Ivy Bolton, by the very pressure of wanting her, seemed to weight her down: by their very deference to her, their yielding before her, their apparent giving up everything to her, cast a net over her, fine and silken, almost invisible, but also, almost unbreakable. Ah, Parkin did not know what danger she was in! He thought she was so absolutely well off, in Wragby Hall. Whereas she herself knew she was in the most subtle danger, the danger of being dragged under water by these two uncanny creatures, and made to produce children to keep their uncanny game going on in the next generation. The grisly game of mammon, the game of the infernal ministers, possessed by *material* inspiration.

No, Parkin was not good to her! He ought to *know* that she must be taken away from Wragby! He ought to *know* that something dreadful would happen to her if she was left there. Instead of that, he thought she was in a sort of earthly Paradise of wealth and well-being, and he was the poor sufferer, having to work. But he did not know! No, he wasn't good to her, he abandoned her to the subtlest danger. He was selfish, like all men, and only aware of himself.

She wept, and fretted, for she was now really afraid of Clifford, of Wragby, of Mrs Bolton, of all these Midlands of England. She was afraid, and her horror was, lest she should never escape. She *must* escape.

Clifford asked her if she would put her money into his business. But her money consisted of property in Scotland, and certain good investments. Well, would she sell out, and invest in his business? He would pay her the same interest: nay, he would pay her a better interest. She would make seven hundred a year on it, instead of five.

She felt his voice going hot and strange, with the weird power in it that came when he talked of business. It had an almost mesmeric effect on her, as he sat there, talking, opposite her, with his eyes abstracted and excited, his voice like a hot wind blowing over her, his will pulling her down in a sort of net. How strange, how strange and ghoulish and *cruel* he was, when it came to that mystic rapture of "business," of "money". Money! Money! Money! The air whispered it.

But her money was all her own. He had settled nothing on her at her marriage. He had given her only a few jewels. And she had brought nothing into the marriage settlement. Nevertheless, he would have won over her, if she had not felt a queer feeling, like retching, in her womb. And suddenly, like a heroine in the eighteenth century, she swooned, and he yelled out for somebody to come, and was yellow with ghastly terror, when she recovered. Abject, almost gibbering with terror, he was.

"It's nothing, Clifford!" she said. "Only liver! You know I get liver sometimes."

But he was terrified in his soul, what soul he had. His life depended so abjectly on hers, for its coherence. And if anything happened to her!

Later she said to him: "Let me think about the money, Clifford, will you? You know how bad I am at understanding those things! I want you to have it, if you need it. But I'd like to understand. Do you mind waiting a bit, while I ask I Hilda and Father?"

"Oh, I don't want it, I don't want it! I can manage quite well without it," he said, in heavy haste.

But she knew, in her soul, that he had fixed his business mind on it.

And it was already August. Parkin had been ten days gone, and he had not written. She was feeling gnawed and anxious, the terrible gnawing anxiety, the fear of everything, that came over her often in Wragby. How awful the future was! She could think of nothing, but just to go to Hilda.

Then came a letter from Sheffield.—"Dear Lady Chatterley, Excuse me for writing to you. You will know who we are, from Mr Leivers. He has taken his own name now, and dropped the other. He said that perhaps you might like to come and see us one day, and we should be very pleased to see you on Monday, being Bank Holiday, and we're not going anywhere this year, being just back from a fortnight by the sea, which has done us all a lot of good. So if you would care to come to tea, we should be very pleased, and, of course, highly honoured. You mustn't take any notice of the poor little place we live in. Mr Leivers would have written himself, but his hands are in rather a poor shape, so he got me to do it. Please excuse my letter, and believe me, yours respectfully, Lilian Tewson."

This too was rather annoying, as Connie had kept her Saturdays free, but on the Bank Holiday people were coming to Wragby. She had to write by return, to ask if she could come on Tuesday instead of Monday, to Blagby Street: it would not matter if she came after tea instead of before, for just an hour.—She had a reply from Mrs Tewson, who was sorry Lady Chatterley couldn't come Monday, but if she would come on Tuesday at five o'clock, the men would get home from work as early as possible. To this Lady Chatterley agreed, finding all this arranging rather irritating.

On Tuesday afternoon, therefore, Connie set off with Field. She told Clifford not to mind if she were a little late home, as she was going to call on some acquaintances, elderly ladies fairly well known in the English-Buddhist circles, whom Constance had met abroad. And Clifford, in return, asked her to bring him something or other for his radio, and be sure to get just the right thing.

In town, she did her shopping, and drove to the Miss Conibears. They were at home: so she dismissed Field, and told him to wait for her at the garage between six and seven. She stayed half-an-hour with the Miss Conibears, who were intelligent, really refined women, kindly and free from the *lowness* which one finds so often in the world. But their atmosphere was a little too rarified. She couldn't stand it very well, and imagined Parkin saying "Balls!"—However, the ladies promised to call at Wragby.—And so one goes on tangling oneself in the net.

It was nearly five o'cock. She pleaded an appointment. The servant got her a taxi, and she gave the address, 57 Blagby Street. The driver looked a little mystified, but drove out of the substantial, middle-class street slowly. Then he stopped, and leaning back, opened the door of the car.

"Do you happen to know just about where it is, Mm?" he asked. "Blagby Street?" He looked as if the place didn't exist.

"I'm sorry, I don't know at all," said Connie.

So the taxi edged slowly on, towards a stand.

There the man pulled up again, and asked discreetly:

"Eh Jim! Know where Blagby Street is?"

"What?"

"Blagby St?"

There was a blank, while the words "Blagby Street" were re-echoed among the chauffeurs. Connie sat marooned. At last a seedy fellow shouted:

"Blagby St? Ay! Up St. Ann's Well! Next after King Alfred—or next but one! D'yer know where the Cross Keys is—?"

The driver received the information curiously, as if he had been directed to the middle of Africa, and the taxi ran on through the grey August dismalness of the town, past huge hoardings and chocolate-coloured chapels and miserable black dwellings. Driving slowly round a corner, Connie saw on a church notice-board the huge words: *"No Reduction in Wages!"*—In view of the strike that was then on, startled that a church should make such an announcement, she looked closer, and saw underneath the first words, in smaller letters: *The Wages of Sin is Death*. There it was, the Midlands in one breath!

NO REDUCTION IN WAGES
THE WAGES OF SIN IS DEATH.

Thus spoke the voice of the church, in ghastly irony, considering the cruel tension of the strike.

Blagby Street was one of those streets running steep uphill, almost like a precipice, paved with granite setts, and bordered by mean, rigid stone dwellings, blank on the pavement, with jutting-out door-steps. The car had a great struggle getting up the very steep incline, on the granite setts, and the children playing on the pavements all stopped to look. Up this street no traffic came, the ascent, or descent, was too precipitous. Connie was afraid the car would not make it. The children played about as if in some isolated region not yet touched by petrol and steam. And at the advent of a car, they held their huge slices of bread and jam to their mouths and stared transfixed, as no yokels stare any longer. Meanwhile the driver peered at the mean, rigid dwellings, the mean doors and mean windows that repeated themselves identically so rapidly, in the utter aridity of stone and black pavement. And the car ground painfully, slowly up.

At last it stopped, and went back on the brakes with a little jerk.

"Number fifty-seven," said the driver, opening his door.

Connie glanced at the awful door, up two steps, and got out. She gave the driver a shilling tip, conscious of his utter resentment at having come up such a place. He looked uphill and down, to see which was worse, and determined to go on uphill now, the little distance to the brow.

Connie stood on the stone doorstep and knocked. She waited. Then she knocked again. And at last the door was being unbolted and unlocked from inside. It opened, and Parkin stood there, in his shirt-sleeves, grimy as he had come from work. He looked queer and smallish and peaked, rather insignificant, a little workman.

"You come to th' front door!" were his first words to her, as if in reproof.

"And oughtn't I?" she said, as she climbed the step.

"Ay! If you like! Only everybody goes to th' back."

He spoke a little drearily. She stepped into the room, and he closed and locked the street door again. She found herself in a small parlour, crowded with a "suite" in dark rosewood and green cotton-velvet brocade, a dark and glossy piano, various stands with ferns, a bronze fire-screen, and huge vases on the mantel-piece. Everything was very close to everything else. On the floor was a deep Wilton carpet—the room was so small, it only needed a tiny one—and near the bronze fender-curb was a huge-seeming hearth-rug of black curly-silky sheepskin. She stood in this deep and embarrassing hearth-rug, and looked in dismay at the four close little walls, papered in browny gold.

"Shall yer sit here a minute while I go an wash me?" he said gloomily. "I've only just got in."

"You sit down too, a moment," she said.

She took one of the big green-velvet arm-chairs, and he sat on a smaller chair at the small, dark rose-wood table or "stand", resting his arms on the edge of the polished wood, careful not to touch the velveteen poker-work cloth it was adorned with. And even sitting down, she dislodged one of the imitation bronze fire-irons, which rolled with a clatter on the hearth of small, shiny, peacock-blue tiles. Poor Connie started, afraid that all the huge vases and knick-knacks would come tumbling round her ears, if she moved another inch in that dressed-up little hole. It was awful!

He sat there, diminished and in silence, seeming more conscious in his hands than in his brain. She saw his hands, and it was a shock. They were swollen, deeply grimed, and gashed with ragged, dark-red slits with blackish edges. She would never have known they were his at all! He had had such sensitive, live human paws, rather small and lovable.

"Your hands!" she said, shocked.

He opened them, and looked at the swollen, inflamed callouses.

"Ay! That's where it catches you," he said dully.

He was dulled, stupefied, almost extinguished. She would never have believed he was the same man.

317

"Has it been very horrid?" She asked in dismay.

But he would not look at her. He stared dully at his hands.

"It takes a bit of getting used to," he admitted, drearily.

She gazed at him. Where was he? He was not there? This was not the man she had known.

"But why should you get used to it?" she asked, in her soft, breathless voice.

He looked up into her face now, as if in resentment.

"It's what other men has to—pretty nigh every other man."

She was puzzled. Every other man! In her experience, no man got used to such things. What did she care about the millions of working-class men!

"But *you're* not other men," she said. "Why do you do it."

He did not answer, only dully picked at a half-healed wound in his thumb. He was scarcely conscious. And she became aware that his hands trembled with aching and with pain, that his arms and his shoulders hammered his brain with their overtaxed aching. She remembered his white, silky, rather slender arms, and the delicate white male shoulders, and the man's belly, so sensitive and white and slightly rounded. Now, stupefied with brutal fatigue, he picked blankly at the wound in his thumb.

"Don't do that!" she said softly, and he suddenly lifted his head, startled like a schoolboy caught in a misdemeanour.

"Why should you do this awful work?" she said.

He glanced at her, in the aching stupor.

"I'm a working man, like a' th' rest," he said.

"Why are you? You're not! Why should you do heavy work that is beyond your strength? You're not big enough."

Even this only made him feel inadequate.

"I s'll be all right when I get a driver's job," he said.

"When will that be?"

Again he was very slow in answering.

"You never know. 'Appen in th' New Year. There's plenty after a' th' jobs now."

She did not know what to make of him. He seemed so sunk, so deadened. He had fallen to picking his thumb again, with overwrought, helpless irritation.

"I went to the doctor here," she said.

He glanced up at her sharply.

"*You* did?" he said. And by the intonation, she realised that he too had been to the doctor, or had thought of it.

"Yes! He says he thinks the child will be due in February."

He stared at her fixedly, half-comprehending.

"You mean your child?" he said, stupidly.

"Ours!" she said. And she watched the strange cloud, like some thing far off, go over his face.

"Ay!" he said at last.

It already seemed so remote and unreal to him, *that*.

"Have you told Sir Clifford?" he asked, as an after-thought.

"No, I shan't tell him."

He was silent, not knowing what to say. Then he remarked:

"I have to go up again about my divorce next week."

"Will it be heard before September, then?"

"No! It's on'y th' lawyer who wants to see me—or something o' that sort."

She realised how this business preyed on his mind.

"I wish it were all over!" she said fretfully.

"Ay!" he said slowly.

Well, it was no good! she could do nothing with him.

A voice said insinuatingly, behind the inner door:

"I've mashed th' tea, if you'll come."

He rose to his feet in silence. Then he looked back at Connie.

"Are yer comin'?" he said.

She too got up from her chair, a little nettled by his immediate obedience to the voice behind the door.

"Are you sure they want me?" she said.

"Ay! It's all ready"

She followed him into the small passage-way, where it was dark, and the stairs went up steep and dim as Calvary,* and from another dark doorway a few steps went down to the pantry under the stairs. To sheer away from the gulf of this doorway, Connie found herself running into the coats that hung from the pegs on the wall of the passage, and a hat, a bowler hat, fell with a rattle. She picked it shame-facedly up, hung it on the peg again, over the coats, and emerged into the living-room.

This was slightly larger than the parlour, but it was full, not only of furniture, but of a large, brilliantly spread tea-table and what seemed like a crowd of people, though it was only a family.

Connie found herself in front of a thin, freckled, pale woman in a fashionable putty-coloured silk dress.

"You are Mrs Tewson," said Connie, holding out her hand. "How do you do! I'm afraid I give you a lot of trouble."

"No trouble at all, if you can put up with the poky places we have to live in," said Mrs Tewson, shaking hands.

"And this is Mr Tewson," said Connie, to a big, pasty-faced man with dust-coloured hair and rather nice eyes. He shook hands with her, gripping with his big, hardened hand, but it was his wife who said:

"That's right! That's my 'usband, Bill. But we usually call it Towson, though I know it's written Tewson. But folks mostly says Towson."

"Ay, Towson, that's right!" said Bill, adding with uncomfortable heartiness: "Pleased to see you! Hope you can make yourself comfortable. You must make yourself at 'ome."

"Now where shall you sit?" said Mrs Tewson. "Oliver—" she turned to the scullery—"are you goin" to wash yourself first?—I'm sure you ned n't bother. Nobody'll mind, will they?"

"Not I!" said Constance, rather bewildered.

"I shan't be a minute—you c'n start without me," said Parkin from the scullery. And there came a sound of water splashing.

"Well let's sit down," said Mrs Tewson.

"You haven't introduced me to the children," said Connie, seeing a little pale boy of about eight, and a freckled, pink-checked girl of about six sitting side by side on the sofa against the wall, while a little girl of two sat in a high chair at the table, next the sofa.

"I haven't, have I!" said Mrs Tewson. "I did my best to get shut of 'em, but they wouldn't be shunted off Come, Harry! come an' shake hands with the lady. Come Dorothy!"

The two children suddenly slid silently down under the table, like letters into a letter-box, and emerged crawling among the chair-legs on the other side.

"Oh, you shouldn't have moved!" said Connie. "How do you do, Harry! Are you the eldest?—How do you do Dorothy! You *are* a nice little girl with rosy cheeks!"

The children gave their hands shyly and awkwardly.

"And the little one's Marjory. Shake a dandie with a lady! Give lady a dandie, Marjory-love!" said the mother.

Marjory-love banged the tray of her high chair with a spoon, and Connie patted her cheek, laughing.

"Perhaps you'll sit next to my husband," said Mrs Tewson, adding, to him: "Sit down, then, Bill, an' make yourself shorter."

Bill sat in the chair next to Marjory-love, and Connie sat next him, round the corner. On her left was Parkin's vacant chair. Mrs Tewson had all the tea-cups, and one side of the table, to herself.

"How do you like it?" she said to Connie, as she began to pour the tea.

"Rather weak, please," said Connie, dreading the strong Ceylon tea.

"Weak did you say? Shall I put a drop of water in then?—Bill, bring th' kettle, there's a good lad!"

Bill went to the scullery for the kettle, and murmured something to Parkin. Connie looked at the table. There were tinned peaches and tinned pears, slices of ham and slices of tongue, water-cress, cream-cheese, plum-cake, little cakes, plates of brown and white bread-and-butter, and a plate of tartlets. The glass dishes sparkled, the embroidered cloth was snowy but crowded to invisibility, knives, forks, spoons glittered, though the latter were only "metal", and the china was fine and quite pretty, with poppies on it.

But what a spread! It took one's breath away. The Tewsons, however, sat before it expectantly, ready to fall to. Connie was forced to help herself to tongue, while Bill helped the children to pears or peaches. It was bewildering. Connie was so afraid she would smash something, for there was not an inch of room on the table. But the family took it calmly, and Marjory-love dipped her fingers in pear-juice on her little plate with utmost *sang froid*, the other two children calmly tackled their huge half-peaches.

"Well 'ow do you think Mr Leivers is lookin'?" asked Mrs Tewson, when she had poured her own tea.

"Who? Oh!—Not very well," said Connie hastily.

"He's *not* well!" Mrs Tewson confided, in a suddenly lowered, intense voice. "He's not at all well. He doesn't eat. And he's had a sprained shoulder.—I'm not at *all* satisfied with 'im."

"Work's a bit too 'eavy for 'im," said Bill, also *sotto voce*.

"That's it!" hissed Mrs Tewson secretly. "He's not strong enough for it. But 'e won't be told. You can't tell 'im anything."

"He's strong enough for a man of 'is build;" said Bill, still in a low tone, so that Parkin should not hear. "But he's built too light. His bones is light, he's not got resistance enough for handlin' them iron bars an' lengths."

"That's it!" hissed Mrs Tewson. "But 'e won't 'ave it! He won't listen to reason. He says other chaps no bigger than him does the same work.— Yes! I say. But they've been used to it all their lives, an' they're wiry ones, which you aren't!—Oh, he's knockin' himself up. It fair worries me and Bill."

"Can't he do anything else—something lighter?" said Connie.

"Every job's full up, an' twenty men waitin' for th' next, what with this strike an' unemployment. Bill's tryin' to get 'im on to a lorry—but it's not easy, you know. An' we thought if only he could get into th' tool shed! Bill's goin' to go on trying. Else I'm sure he'll be knocked up, he *can't* stand it.—But men's that obstinate."

"Why need he work at all, for the time being?" said Connie desperately.

"Well I suppose he's got his living to earn, and child to keep, like every other man," said Mrs Tewson rather coldly.

"Yes, but—" said Connie impatiently.

"I'm goin' t'ave another go at Mr Fellows to get 'im in th' tool shed," said Bill. "That's the place for him. It's not heavy work, an' wants a light touch. An' he's done sharpenin' an' settin' on Te" "Tevershall pit-bank.— Only he's an outsider, an' they won't make an exception for him."

"Wouldn't they if you paid them?" said Connie, with a woman's callous anarchy.

"*Paid* them?" said Bill, looking at her strangely.

"If you said: Here's five pounds, or ten, if you'll get Parkin into the tool shed!—" said Connie, looking back at him calmly.

A slow smile spread over Bill's face.

"Well, I've never 'ad five or ten pounds to try 'im with," he said slowly. "An' afore t'war, you'd ha' got sack for tryin' it on. But you never know nowadays. Things is so different.—I should like to see Alfred Fellows face if I told him I'd make it worth his while, up to five or ten pounds, to shift Oliver over."

Bill's own face was a study: he was shocked, amused, uneasy, and malicious all at once.

"Doesn't he go to church? Doesn't he have missionaries or something to collect for?" said Connie.

CHAPTER 15

"No!" said Bill. "He's more or less of a socialist. But he *is* secretary for our club, an' he does have a bit of work screwing funds out of us boys."

"Then can't you say you'd hand him on five pounds, or what he wants—from a friend of Parkin's?" said Connie, anxious and unscrupulous, her face bright.

"I might sort o' hint it like," said Bill.

"Money'll do anything—lucky them as has it!" said Mrs Tewson abruptly.

"I'll send it in a letter," said Connie.

"Wait while I feel my way, an' I'll let you know," said Bill. "I wouldn't do it for anybody but Oliver. But a pal's a pal—especially one as was in France with yer—"

"Well, if you can do it that way—if Lady Chatterley doesn't mind—I don't see why *we* should," said Mrs Tewson. Nevertheless, she seemed annoyed. And she looked at Connie with a certain hostility.

Parkin came in with his face washed and pinched looking, and his hair combed. He squeezed past Mrs Tewson to get his coat out of the passage.

"Come on, lad, your tea'll be cold," Mrs Tewson said to him with brusque solicitude.

He got rather painfully into his coat, because of the sprained shoulder.

"Now if yer'd let Bill help y'on!—" said Mrs Tewson. "But yer that stubborn!—If yer tea's not sweet enough, say so. 'And 'im the 'am an' tongue, Bill."

Parkin used his knife and fork clumsily, with swollen hands and was silent.

"How's yer cup?" said Mrs Tewson. "I can see my 'usband lookin' at 'is. Let me give y' another—The men won't 'ave these little cups ordinary. They both want big ones, swilkerin' over.—You ma' drink up slow today, ma lad," this last to her husband.

She poured out the tea quickly. Everything she did, she did with a kind of sharp, efficient haste, rather jarring.

"Bill, *can't* you see to that child! Marjory-love, not on mother's clean table-cloth! No!"

Marjory-love was reaching over and spooning a mixture of tea and fruit-juice on to the table-cloth.

"A-a! A-a!" said Bill, in a queer sound, to his infant daughter. He took

323

the spoon from her, so she immediately began to kick the tray of her chair, with all her might. Bill gave her the spoon back, and she started ladling out her tea again.

"Draw her back a bit from th' table!" said her mother. "That's naughty, Marjory! Marjory, that's naughty!"

Marjory-love, drawn back from the table, made pools of tea on her tray, and splashed them with her chubby fist, so that the drops flew around.

"Marjory! Will Mamma have to get up an' whip you! Marjory!"

There was a crisis coming. Bill removed the tea and slopped food from the child's tray. Marjory-love, without a sound, sent her spoon flying across the table, where it hit her brother Harry on the head, and bounced off on to the table. Harry laughed sheepishly at this lovable little exploit, but Mrs Tewson repeated, with a curious ugly intonation:

"Marjory! Mamma will get up an' whip you! She will!"

It was almost as if she looked forward to a little excitement.

"'Ere! Ta'e that, an' be good!" said Bill, giving the child a lemon-curd tart. She immediately squashed it up into a mess, and demanded water-cress. He gave her water-cress. Her mother was eyeing her with dangerous eyes, the woman's pale face lengthening.

"She's a bonny child!" said Connie.

"Ay, an' a bad one! That's 'cause we want her to behave. She can be a good as gold when she likes."

The mother eyed the child fixedly, the child bent her head in obvious impudent defiance, and scrubbed her sticky board with water-cress.

"She doesn't shame 'er cupboard, does she!" said Bill with pride.

"It's 'er father as spoils 'er," said the mother.

And the battle of wills continued, between the woman and the girl infant.

"Oh Marjory!" said Connie. "Does your mother say you're spoilt?"

Marjory-love had a faint self-conscious look on her face, half shy, half defiantly amused.

"Ay, an' her Dad says so an' a', doesn't 'e!" said Bill, softly pinching the fat little cheek.

"You're makin' no tea at all!" said Mrs Tewson to Connie, turning from the sight of her husband and the child. She was a jealous woman, jealous even there.—"Now what shall y'ave! You must eat, or we s'll think it's not good enough for yer."

"It's much too good!" said Connie: and she took a bit of currant loaf.

She could feel Parkin inwardly squirming, at her elbow. But he was eating tinned peaches and thickened cream.

"How are yer gettin' on at Tevershall, like?" said Bill. "I've been over there. I stopped a night in th' cottage wi' Oliver—didn't I lad?"

"About a year sin'," said Parkin.

"I s'd think it is," said Bill.

"Really! I didn't see you," said Connie.

"No! But I seed you an' Sir Clifford in th' park.—You didn't know Oliver so well at that time, like."

"No," said Connie.

"It was raisin' th' young pheasants this spring as started you talkin' to me a bit," said Oliver, cold and quiet, turning to her. She looked at him, and saw he resented their knowing much of his relationship with her.

"Yes!" she said softly.

"An' you got almost friendly this summer, did you?" said Mrs Tewson, fixing her brown, searching eyes on Connie.

"Quite friendly," said Connie, looking back at her.

"Fancy now! Well, I suppose people can be a bit of friends, no matter how different you're situated in life.—But it doesn't do to brood over it, for all that. Does it?"

"No!" said Connie, accepting the innuendo.

"Do you mind," said Bill, shifting uneasily in his chair, "if I ask you a question? a plain question?"

"Not at all," said Connie, wondering what was coming.

"Now you won't mind, will you, if I'm a bit plain-spoken?—No!— Well, what I want to know—Do you think it *is* possible for people in a very different walk of life to be friends—really friends—?"

Connie looked at him. His pale face was quite earnest, and his grey eyes were rather nice. But there was a certain underneath toughness, insentience in him, He had the modern emotional incompleteness.

"I don't think you can generalise," said Connie. "If you mean me and Parkin, I think we're quite good friends."

"Well, I didn't mean that altogether. I meant *generally*—"

"Friends across a distance, like!" put in Mrs Tewson, with a slight sarcasm. "You aren't friends with Mr Leivers—Parkin, as you say!—like we are, as one of us-selves." She was very biting.

Connie looked at her, rather puzzled. She didn't realise that to Mrs

Tewson, for a woman to call a man merely "Parkin", was as good as an insult.

"Leave that!" said Bill.—"You see what we are—working people; decent working people, it's no good pretending anything else—" he added deprecatingly,—as if he *might* have been mistaken for an archangel in disguise. "An' you know your own class: the upper classes. Well, what I want to know, is it possible, is it likely that there could be a real friendly feeling between the two? I don't mean patronising, mind. I mean a real feeling of friendliness, like what we feel for one another: me an' Oliver, for instance."

It all seemed very vague, to Connie.

"But I don't know the working classes," she said innocently. And Mrs Tewson scored another black mark against her, and was deep offended, but coldly, biding her time. "I only know one or two—a little—and they're not really working class—"

Connie ended vaguely, not knowing what to say.

"That's it!" said Bill. "That's it! That's where it is. You don't know any working people, an' we don't know any of the nobs. Some of them comes an' speaks to us from the platform. But I mean—that's not knowin' them. They're no nearer to us, when they're on the platform, than they are when they're in their homes, with all the servants to wait on 'em. What I mean to say, we never come into contact with them—"

He had laid his workman's hand on the edge of the table, and was leaning forward, gazing at her with those clear, wide-open, anxious eyes which puzzled her so. He stared too hard, too abstractedly.

"How could you," she said, "come into contact with them?"

"No!" and he emphatically slapped the edge of the table. "That's where it is, how *could* we!—We seemed to, a bit, in the war. Some of the officers was very friendly, like, sort of a bit pally. But you knew it wasn't going to last. You knew they were goin' back to their own lives, an' we were goin' back to work, an' it'd be same as before. Worse! I allers knowed they laughed at us, for the way we talked. You know how chaps says 'that', at every verse-end.—*Ay lad, it is that! Does thee like this French bacca?* I do *that*!—" he imitated the rough men who were a shade or two lower in the social scale than himself.—"Well!" he said. "Th' officers made a big joke out of that.—"

"People are so silly," said Connie. "But the working men should be proud of speaking dialect. Anybody can talk ordinary English."

"Ay! You think so! Ay! 'Appen so. But everybody wants to talk fine, everybody as wants to get on. An' as for th' other chaps—!—But that's where it is. We never meet the nobs, an' they never meet us, so how can we get on together?—What I should like to ask you—they don't *want* to meet us, do they? They don't *want* to know us?"

"Perhaps not," said Connie.

"It's natural!" said Mrs Tewson, with a sniff. "Them as is up doesn't want to lower themselves. An' them as is down doesn't get a chance o' risin' very far, considerin' th' money they earn—"

Connie hated the way she said "money". She pronounced it "munny", with the Italian *u*, and the word sounded even more loathsome than usual.

"But *aren't* people very much alike, everywhere?" Bill persisted, while she shrank in a kind of fear from his pale, forward-thrusting, wide-eyed face that glowered into hers so insensitively. "What I mean to say, *is* there very much difference between me an' the kind of folks you mix with, the nobs, except in money an' eddication? If I'd been brought up an' eddicated like Sir Clifford, for example—shouldn't I be about as good a man as he is? More or less, you know! You know what I mean."

"Yes, no doubt," she said. "I don't think *real* difference goes by class."

"You don't, eh? You don't think so? You don't think they're any superior to what we are, except for the chances they've had?"

"But the chances make a great difference," said Connie.

"Ay! *There*! *There's* where it is!" he roared, slapping the edge of the table. "There you've said it! Ay! *That's* the point! The chances *do* make a lot of difference! A world of difference! An' that's why we shall never get 'em. There'll always be a world of difference while some has chances which the others can never get.—An' do the upper classes realise that they're sitting on all the chances of life? Do you think they do?—An' don't they feel guilty about it?"

"I don't think they feel guilty" said Connie. "Would you, under the circumstances?"

"Ay!" he ejaculated, with profound assertion. "I'm sure I should. I should think of all the chaps I've left behind, slavin' their guts out an' rackin' themselves to pieces, like Oliver here, as is my pal; for a dirty bit of a wage; an' I *sure* I should feel guilty. I'm pretty *sure* I should."

"Perhaps they can't help being upper class, any more than you can help being lower," said Connie.

"No!" he roared. "I know that. They can't help it, to start with. But what I want to know, do they feel any *sympathy* with workin' men as has nothing but work before them, till they drop. Do they *sympathise*—"

"But do you sympathise with them?" said Connie.

"Eh? What? Sympathise with *them*? Who?"

"The upper classes. Do you sympathise with them?"

"What for? They don't want sympathy. They've got everything "

"Perhaps they haven't. And in any case, sympathy *can't* be on one side only. It must be on both sides. Both sides must be in sympathy with one another, if there's to be any sympathy."

"How? Why how? If l give a blind man a penny, I don't expect him to sympathise with me. He's not got anything to sympathise with me about."

"But you're not a blind man, are you?" she said.

"Compared to the rich, I'm as bad off," he said.

He jerked his head, and sat up in his chair, his face like a mask of pale and weird passion. It was as if a gun had gone off in the room, and this silence was the after-vibration. Bill's passion seemed to have exploded from him in smoke and noise, and now his consciousness was a blank cartridge.

"What's the good o' talkin' about it!" said Parkin testily. "Leave it alone! You get no forrarder, more you talk."

"Eh! Get no forrarder?" said Bill, jerking forward to attention again. "Yi we do, lad!—Oh yi we do!"—He gave a hollow, roaring laugh. "We should understand a lot, if we could only get *at* the people of Lady Chatterley's class, an' have a straight talk with them. But we can't get at 'em! They're too close. They never come within a mile of us, as you may say.—Mind you," he turned to Connie again, "I'm not speaking personally!—What I should like to know is, if they have any feelings as a *class* with us chaps as does the dirty work: an' we're a hundred to one!—Now I understand a lady like you. Your father was a painter, a great painter,—" Hear, oh Sir Malcolm!—"and artists *are* more free, like, than the nobs. I can understand you might like a bit of straight talk with Oliver, or even me, sometimes. An' I can understand you might like to come 'ere, an' see us in our 'omes. Something new for you, like!—But take Sir Clifford. Would he go even as far as that—?"

The pale-grey, bright eyes glared with question into hers.

"Perhaps not," she said.

"Ha! perhaps not!"—He gave a blurt of laughter. "You mean certainly not. Certainly not! It's a dead cert you wouldn't catch him 'ere, 'aving tea with us, no matter what sort of tea we offered 'im. Would you?"

"No!" said Connie, who felt she was being put on a very precise shelf of class-distinction, a little lower than Clifford.

"No! You ma' bet your bottom dollar. Yet why?—We aren't fools altogether, even if we're not that smart. An' we're men, aren't we? We all went through th' war. We're all English. If we go smash, we all go smash together, don't we?—Then why aren't we good enough to speak to? Why can't a man like Sir Clifford come an' sit down an' talk to a man like me? What 'arm would it do him? His isn't the only life on the face of the earth—"

He sat erect and stared at her with a strange, pallid-gleaming challenge. His spirit seemed so pallid and weird, even in its intensity: so little human.

"I suppose he would feel uncomfortable," she said.

"Feel uncomfortable!" he repeated. "Does he think other people feels comfortable all the while—?"

He glimmered in a pallid flame of intense irony, then leaned back in his chair, his face very pale and spent, yet rapt.—So this man too had his weird *raptus*!—Then Bill quickly shoved his dust-coloured hair from his forehead, turned a bewildered sort of face to Parkin, and gave a quick little bark of a laugh, saying in a roguish voice:

"It's what tha towd me, lad."

"What did he tell you?" said Connie.

There was a pause.

"I said as a man like Sir Clifford was frightened to come off his perch, and speak out to a workin' man. He's too frightened to do it," said Parkin unwillingly.

"Perhaps he thinks it's no good," said Connie.

There was a pause, after which Parkin admitted:

"'Appen it isn't."

"Well now!—" up flickered the whitish flame in Bill's face again.

"Oh Bill, for goodness" sake shut up, we've 'ad enough o' your blather.—Can't yer get Lady Chatterley t'eat somethink, an' eat somethink yerself, an' shut your mouth?"

"I've finished!" he said with decision, sweeping his cup further aside. Then he remembered sufficiently to ask, with some politeness, of Connie: "Shan't y'ave something else? Have y'ad enough? Sure?"

"'Ave a drop more tea now!" said Mrs Tewson. "I've got 'alf a potful."

But Connie refused. Bill accepted, and swallowed it in a mouthful.

"Well then, if we've all finished, I think we'll let th' children go," said Mrs Tewson. "They've been very good! Harry an' Dorothy, you ma' leave the table.—An' shall you mind Marjory while mother washes up?"

The two elder children had sat so mute and patient on the sofa, during all the talk, Connie had sympathised with them deeply. They slid under the table, and out by their mother's chair.

"Mind mother's dress!" Mrs Tewson admonished.

"Well you *were* good children!" said Connie. "Come and let me give you a penny."

"Oh, you shouldn't bother!" said Mrs Tewson.

Harry received half-a-crown, and Dorothy a florin, as there wasn't another half-crown.

"There now!—What do you say!" admonished the mother.

"Thank you! Thank you!" murmured the children, sidling to get away.

"Wait for Marjory! Come Marjory-love, let mother wipe your face. Bring th' flannel an' towel, Harry! Come love! Are you going out with Dorothy an' Harry?—Now mind 'er, you two, an' see as she doesn't get into any danger—"

Marjory-love had her face and hands wiped and dried, and she howled with impatience.

"There!" said Connie, offering her also a florin. "There's one for you too."

The child took it in a chubby fist.

"Oh you *shouldn't*!" said Mrs Tewson. Then to Marjory-love: "Say thank you! Say thank you to the pretty lady! Thank you! Thank you!— There, there's a love!"—The child had coyly murmured her *thank you!* which her father echoed with a little blurt of a proud laugh, while the mother kissed her with a smack of gratification.

"Let mother take a pretty penny, an' put it in Marjory's money-box. Let mother take it an' keep it for her—put it in Marjory's money-box. Will Marjory put it in?—Harry, get 'er money-box off parlour mantel."

Oh the sound of that word *munny-box*!

CHAPTER 15

The children departed, Mrs Tewson put an apron over her smart silk dress, that was very short in the leg, and began to collect the cups. Bill, who had waited, wound-up, for the hubbub to settle, said to Connie:

"You don't think the upper classes feels guilty, then, at having ten times and a hundred times more than their fair share of all the advantages?"

"Now Lady Chatterley!" said Mrs Tewson. "Don't you pay no attention to these men. They'd talk the leg off an iron pot. An' since Mr Leivers is 'ere, Bill's worse. It's politics from morning to night—"

"Now my dear!" said Bill to his wife. "This is a special occasion. Let me alone a bit.—You're sure you don't mind?" he added, turning suddenly with naïve gravity to Connie.

"Not at all," she said.

"Ay well!—You don't think, then, they feel a bit guilty, like?"

"I don't really know," said Connie. "They may feel a little uneasy sometimes. But I wouldn't call it *guilty*!"

"You wouldn't!"—He stared at her with strange intentness. "You don't think they feel there might be a need to even things up a bit: let a bit more come *our* way, for example?"

"I don't really know," she said. "People never like giving up what they've got."

"Not till they're forced to," said Bill. "They say as our rich people feels much more kindred feeling with other rich people, whether they're Americans or Germans or Russians or Jews or anything, than they do with us, their own countrymen. It isn't *Germans* they're holding out against, and afraid of: it's us working-men, who are Englishmen the same as they are an' in a big majority, when it comes to."

Connie was silent. Parkin broke the pause.

"What I say is, there's only two sorts o' folks on the face of the earth, them as 'as got money, an' them as is after it. What's it got to do with nations? Men's all alike—an' so's their wives. When anybody's different, they get trod on," said he, in his harsh, vibrant voice, that had a curious twang of cat-like, sardonic contempt in it.

"An' me an' thee, lad, we belong to them as is after a bit more o' the dirty stuff,—eh boy?" said Bill, with his queer mad guffaw.

"I want to eat," said Parkin dismally. "I've got to keep myself 's all I want."

"Ay, 'appen so! But tha'd like to keep thysen a bit more easy, like, eh?" said Bill.

331

"But *you* don't think the upper classes are responsible for all the evils on earth, do you?" said Connie, turning to Parkin.

"Me! I'm always sayin' it," he replied, "everybody's alike, money smells to 'em like toasted cheese does to a mouse, an' they go for it, if it's fifty thousand mouse-traps. An' that means rich folks an' poor, just alike."

"Includin' thysen, lad!" Bill said, in his teasing, roguish way. "Tha'rt after thy own bit."

But Parkin did not answer.

"I really must go!" said Connie, rising. "I suppose I shall find my way to York Road."

"Oh, Oliver'll go with you," said Bill, surprised.

"Perhaps he doesn't want to be bothered," she said, turning to look at him.

He met her eyes, startled.

"Why?" he said.

"Do you?" she said.

"If you'll wait a minute for me!" he replied—and he went upstairs.

"Well!" said Bill, rising and stretching himself. "It's been rare havin' a talk with somebody from up above, like. You're a bit of a socialist yourself, aren't you, like Lady Warwick? So you won't take any notice of what we say!—Shall we be seeing you again, do you think?"

Mrs Tewson came in from the scullery, taking off her apron.

"Shall yer 'ave to go!" she said. "Well, I'm sure we're very flattered to 'ave 'ad you. I hope you didn't mind the poor poky way we live in, but it's all we can do, on what a man's able to earn with 'is hands. We should be very pleased to see you any time you'd like to come, if you'd let us know. I'm sure it'll cheer Mr Leivers up a lot, you 'avin' come. Men does love talkin' these politics, don't they? especially with one who is a lady born! It flatters them, you see."

"Quite!" said Connie.

"An' Mr Leivers is a bit down on 'is luck just now!—But I mother 'im all I can, an' I think 'e feels at 'ome with us."

"I'm sure he does!" said Connie.

He came downstairs, and in silence they departed, walking side by side down the steep stone slant of the hideous street. He looked a poor little working-man: and she knew he felt it. But she did not feel equal to any more efforts on his behalf.

In the tram-car that served this poorish quarter, he sat silent, with his damaged hands curled against his body, for comfort. Only he got the pennies out of his trousers pocket, to pay the fares, like a man. And Connie looked at the depressing ugliness of the other passengers, poorish working class, without colour, grace, or form: or even warmth of life. It was too gruesome.

"Write to me!" she said, as she left him.

"All right!" he answered.

16

THE NEXT DAY BUT ONE, she had a letter from him, not so very badly written.—"Bill told me about bribing Fellows to get me in the toolshop. But don't do it. I'm leaving anyhow. I knew what you were thinking, Tuesday. So I went to give my notice in this morning, and they letting me off on Saturday, So I shall have to look round for something else. I shan't stop in Sheffield anyhow. I shall go round the country, and try and get some farm-labouring, and I ought to find some, with corn harvest coming on. I can't go far, because of my divorce hanging over me. But I give up trying to work with a lot of other chaps. I can't stomach it. I have to be doing something where I can be by myself I'm sorry as Bill talked so much on Tuesday. I'm sick and surfitted of talk. I don't care what other folks does, I only want to be by myself. If I get a farm-laborers job, I shan't get more than thirty shillings a week, so my mother will have to come down a bit. But I should be learning, for if ever there was anything in the future. I feel I care about nothing on earth, except to get away from folks, and perhaps if we had a farm in the future. I thought you were looking harrassed on Tuesday over something, but I expect it was my imagination. Don't think as I don't remember the wood and the cottage and everything. I would give my head if it could but have lasted, but it couldn't. You say you don't believe in living together if you are married. Then there is nothing for it but living alone. I don't seem to be much use on the face of the earth, I must say. But I don't even feel I want to be. I shall go on quite quiet, and wait, it is all there is to do. I can make my living, and I care about nothing in the world, except I ache for the wood and the cottage these last few months, as if something was drawn out of me. I get a bursting sometimes inside me, till I feel I can't hear them talking much longer in this house. I can't breathe easy with other folks. I suppose it is my own fault. But it is no use talking. When a man has no money and no special qualifications for anything, he is not much cop. He just has to learn to contain himself. But I hope there is not anything fretting you at Wragby. You have to live easy and be contented now. I shall write to you when I get a place. Think of yourself, and don't trouble about anything. O."

The same day that Connie received this, he had a letter from her. But he did not get it till he came home in the evening.—"—I was sorry to see you looking so ill and depressed on Tuesday, you seem to be only half your natural size. I'm afraid that work is bad for you, but I know it is no use my saying anything. I asked Mr Tewson to use every effort to get you into another department, where the work will be lighter, and I do hope he will be successful.

"I want to tell you that I have decided I must leave Clifford. It is not really on your account. But I feel I am living here on false pretences; I am in a false situation, I feel false all the time, and I can't bring a child into the world like that. I am sorry for Clifford. He doesn't really want me, except for a background. But I think it will be rather terrible for him if I have to give up being a background for him. But I must, I feel so false, so false to myself, and especially to the child, which is yours and mine, but which is also itself, and I mustn't put my falsities over it, if I can help it. I should like you to be its father, as it grows up. Then it would have *some* freshness in its soul. People have no freshness in their souls. You still have some, if it isn't soon killed off.

"I wasn't very happy at Mr Tewson's. Perhaps we could meet somewhere else, before I leave. I shall go to my sister in Scotland, and perhaps winter abroad, if I am to be alone.

"You must let me know when you are willing to try a little farm somewhere. We must talk it over in private. Will you meet me somewhere on Sunday afternoon, perhaps at Stanton. I shall expect to hear from you.—C."

He replied to her by return, writing in the Mechanics Hall, where there was a free club-room.

"—I can understand what you feel about Wragby. I feel a bit that way about Bill's house, I can't breathe in it, something shuts me up so I can't breathe. But I'm sorry you feel like that at Wragby, you will be so homeless, if you go. A sister's home isn't like your own. But then I think sometimes a dry ditch is better than a bed in people's houses. Shall you go to Canada with me? I'll go next week, if you will. I've a cousin there as would help me. I'd go anywhere with you, except stop round these parts. That is, if you wanted me. Bill had no business to talk so much. I am fair heartsick of talk, everybody has got so much to say, and where does it leave you. I wish you and I was on a desert island. I don't think I should soon wish myself off it. I've only tomorrow and half-day Saturday at Jephsons. Shall we say Hucknall on Sunday? I've got one of my own uncles, my father's brother, who lives out Annesley Woodhouse way, and keeps a grocery shop. I could wait for you at Hucknall church, any time after two. They've got Lord Byron's heart buried there, though there's nothing to see. But we could walk through Annesley park. I shouldn't care if the bolshevists blew up one half of the world, and the capitalists blew up the other half, to spite them, so long as they left me and you a rabbit-hole apiece to creep in, and meet underground like the rabbits do.—"

And by return, he had her answer.

"I'm so glad you are leaving Sheffield. I was so afraid you were just going to deteriorate into a socialist or a fascist, or something dreary and political.

"You shouldn't trouble about money. You know I have enough. I have even saved some since I have been married, though I spent most on housekeeping. I *can't* think it matters if you use my money. You don't really care about it any more than I do.

"I wish you said you loved me. I think you do. But I don't feel certain. I am afraid I love you too much.

"Shall we meet at Stanton on Sunday?—"

They both had their letters on Friday. And both replied hot haste. He wrote:

"I wanted not to say things in a letter. But if you don't feel certain, I'll tell you. I really don't know what love means. I don't feel like they do on the film. But I love you, whether or not. I don't think much about you, because what is the good. But—" here were words scratched out. "Nay, what can I say? Don't let us say things. You are home to me, I don't care about houses. When I think of you—but I don't think if I can help it, if a man starts thinking, the fat is in the fire. Everything is a prison, I know that. You are the only bit of freedom I've ever had. I've never felt free, I've always felt cooped in and small, except with you, and with you I'm all right, you open all the world to me. When I think about how you opened

335

to me, nay, I don't care what happens. But I don't think if I can help it. We've got to live our lives, you yours and me mine. Best never think, something's bound to happen. And the day will come again, and happen the night, when we've got the world to ourselves. What do I care about anything besides! I don't really care about money, though I'll earn my living somehow. But if you can set me up, next year, so that I can be my own boss, and keep to myself, I'll take it from you, and be thankful, and I know there won't be anything lost, because I trust you, and I'll work for it. Which is about all I know about love.—If you don't change it, I'll wait by Hucknall Church, out of sight so Field shan't see me. And tell him to meet you again at Annesley lodge gates, by the hall. But if you change it, I shall bide by what you say.—"

She wrote very briefly:

"I will be at Hucknall soon after two on Sunday. We can talk then. I am glad you sound better in health and spirits. I don't think we should either of us be really happy in Canada. But we can talk it over. I have written to Hilda telling her I want to go to her in September, but not the details as yet. I can understand better how you feel about a divorce. One does long to be clear. It ought not to matter, yet it does. What a curious trap marriage is, if one ever wants to get out!

"Be sure you are there on Sunday—"

Sunday was a grey but warm August day. Clifford wanted Field, because he had promised to call that afternoon on another mine-owner, to look over his new plant. So lunch was early, and Connie had a hired man from Uthwaite. That suited her very well.

Hucknall she found a very dreary, depressing little mining town, squalidly ugly, and sunk in a grey kind of doom. There was a sense of energy, nevertheless. The people had a weird sort of energy simmering and bubbling inside them. But it was the energy of a steam-boiler, a matter of internal pressure and desire for explosion. It was quite different from the calm, soft, swaying energy of a tree, that is full of life as soft as sleep, and in the end, more resistless than any pressure of steam or iron.

To Connie, the wood where she had known Parkin in the spring had become the image of another world. It was full of trees, silent individuals themselves full of life, but not talkative, and full of sap, but not friction. She realised there were two main sorts of energy, the frictional, seething, resistant, explosive, blind sort, like that of steam-engines and motor-cars and electricity, and of people such as Clifford and Bill Tewson and modern, insistent women, and these queer vacuous miners: then there was the other, forest energy, that was still and softly powerful, with tender, frail bud-tips and gentle finger-ends full of awareness. She herself was seized by both kinds of energy. With Clifford and Mrs Bolton, and at Bill Tewson's house, and with her sister Hilda, even, strange frenzies of the explosive energy came over her, she felt herself full of force. Sometimes this seemed to her the utmost desirable. But lately, she felt a great desire to escape it. That sort of energy, that sense of force and power was accompanied by a craving restlessness and unsatisfaction, something seething and grinding deep within, that she longed with all her soul to escape. She had tasted the other, the fulness of life, which is so different from the frenzy of energy. "Then shall thy peace be as a river."* She knew what it meant. It meant the wood where she had been in stillness with Parkin. It meant the fulness of life that trees have, which never want to wander away to somewhere else.

And Parkin stood to her for this peace. Then lately, in Sheffield, he too had lost it. And this had thrown her out of her reckoning. She was almost afraid of meeting him: that pinched, rather insignificant little working-man of Blagby Street.

She walked into the dreary sort of Square where the church of Hucknall stands so extinguished, holding the heart of the seething Byron, who had no peace. "There's not a joy the world can give like that it takes away!"* Why do poets say these things, and then not be true to the joy the world can only destroy, if you let it?

Parkin came forward out of a squalid street, to meet her, taking off his hat. She looked at him almost in dread. His face was still pale and pinched looking, but it had come clear again. It had been as if a wire net was over it. Now it was clear, and had its own light, a little pallid, but not unjoyful, and its own courage again.

"Shall you go in?" she asked, nodding towards the church.

They went into the dark church together. It was empty. And she looked at the little slab behind which rests the pinch of dust which was Byron's heart: in that thrice-dismal Hucknall Torkard. The sense of the greatness of human mistakes made her want to cry.

She sat in a pew, and Parkin sat beside her. He was very still, and she did not know what he was thinking. She herself felt a little raw and lost. She groped for his hand, and it closed over hers for a moment with that sudden soft, strong grasp of trust, then relaxed and lay still, while she held it in both her hands, clinging to it for safety. She felt the roughness, the callouses, the shapelessness, and the ugly little jagged cuts on it. And yet it was warm and still and softly heavy. And from his body came the physical effluence of life which has its own peace, of passion which identifies itself with life, faith in life itself, in the soft splendour of the flesh, in the bigness of destiny, which is so much beyond the carping of human knowledge. In the stillness of his body, she felt again the unconscious faith in life, faith in his own living sex, faith in his own purity. He had got it back again, whereas she was still jangled.

"You *mustn't* go away from me!" she whispered pathetically.

But he said nothing, and was quite still. She felt she could not really find him. She would have to touch him, or she was lost. She put her fingers to his face, and he turned his head and kissed them softly, laying his hand with sure instinct on her belly, where the fret was, and the coming child. Softly he seemed to gather her belly and her womb into the safe warmth of his hand, that pressed so still across her navel. And it was like the sudden warmth of the sun, after a bitter winter. She put both her hands over his hand, and peace began to come into her again, in the dark church, where is the pinch of dust that was Byron's heart.

"Don't leave me!" she murmured. "It makes me so unhappy"

His hand still lay warm and cup-like, over her navel, below which the child that would come lay unseen like a pinch of life.

"Ay! It does me!" he said.

"It is harder for me than for you," she said. "It is easier for you to get out of the old life, you haven't so many things holding you down. You must help me to get out. You don't know how miserable I've been this week."

He edged a little closer to her, and his fingers pressed comfortingly down, to close the crying lips of her sex.

"What would you like me to do?" he said.

"I want to be with you," she said.

He was perfectly still. She never knew what he thought.

"You don't want to go to Canada, do you?" he said.

"No! The thought of it is cold to me."

"Nor Africa nor Australia?"

She thought about it. She had an unconquerable aversion from leaving Europe. She had been overseas. He had not. She knew what it meant. She did not want to break with the past, even for her child's sake. She had no faith in the newness of new countries. It was exile, always exile.

"No!" she said. "Not to the colonies. You wouldn't be happy, either."

He was silent, waiting for her. She rose suddenly.

"Let us go into the light," she said. "Let us get out."

She hurried from the gloomy church, and they walked towards Annesley, in the Sunday afternoon with all the colliery population in their smart Sunday clothes, among the unspeakable ugliness of the streets and railway-lines and pit-hills. What was the point of dressing up, in such squalor! Yet everybody was dressed up, dressed to kill, latest fashions.

"Take me somewhere where you can hold me in your arms!" she said.

And he took a footpath that led round past the deserted kennels, towards Felley Mill. It was more lonely here. And in spite of the risk of gamekeepers' sending them away, they went into a little hollow of a wood, and sat under the trees, hidden behind the great bramble and rose-bushes, in the tall bracken.

"I must touch you! I must touch you, or I shall die!" she said.

"Ay! Touch me then!" he said quietly, unfastening the front of his trousers and pulling away the shirt from his body. She slipped her arms round his naked waist, curling her face against his belly, and he put his hands under her dress, till he patiently found her naked body. Then he stroked her with infinite soothing, to himself and her.

"Oh hold me! hold me!" she moaned. And he drew her a little closer. Till his hands seemed to go to sleep on her naked body, and she dozed into peace again, against his flesh. And once more her womb was soft with peace and that queer, sap-like happiness over which one has no control, save to kill it.

His quick ears were startled by a sound. He looked up, and saw a keeper, a big-face, middle-aged man, striding round the brambles and dog-rose thickets. Swiftly he put down her dress, and as she began to lift her face he murmured:

"Keep still! There's keeper! Dunna move!" And he held her closer.

"Now then!" said the burly keeper, in ugly challenge, and Parkin felt all her body jolt in his arms. He pressed her closer. The keeper was smiling an ugly smile.

"Let us be, man, can't you!" said Parkin, in a soft, quiet voice, looking into the light-blue, half-triumphant eyes of the other fellow. "We're harmin' nothing. Have yer niver 'ad a woman in your arms yourself!" The perfect quiet rebuke of his voice was in key with the steady, unabashed rebuke in his eyes. But he remained still and defenceless, his clothing all undone, the woman hiding her face against his naked body, under his turned-back shirt.

The keeper looked at the clinging woman hiding her face, and at her legs in their silk stockings. Parkin had pulled her dress tidily down. Only himself was all undone. The fat keeper slowly looked away, and the nasty smile went off his face. He took a few steps past the great bushes, and looked out of the copse, down the wild slope of tussocky grass. Then he looked again, fascinated, at the woman clinging motionless to the other man.

"Ay!" he said, in a changed voice. "But Squire an' some of 'is folks is walkin' a bit down th' coppy." He spoke dully, with a dull resentment against the squire and his folks.

"They aren't comin' this road, are they? Nobody can see us in here," said Parkin.

"I seed yer come, though. An' if Squire sawn you, he'd let you know! He 'ates couples," replied the man.

"Ay! let 'im!" said Parkin. "E's 'appen not a man 'isself."

"Nay! On'y yo' colliers, yo' all ower t' place!" The man was neutral, really bored by his job.

"I'm not a collier, anyhow.—Eh well!—Let us be, eh?" said Parkin softly, and for the first time Connie heard his soft cajoling to another person, not herself.

"You won't stop long, though?" said the keeper, looking curiously at Connie, who lay with her face hidden against Parkin, her arms round his body, under his shirt, motionless. A queer sight, as she clung to him, covering his nakedness. The keeper was fascinated. He wanted to see her.

"No! There's no chance o' bein' in peace anywhere, for long!" Parkin said, formally.

Still looking sideways at the clinging figure of the woman, with its hidden face, the keeper moved slowly away. He wanted so much to see her.

Parkin softly stroked Connie's hair, and murmured, in broad dialect:

"Niver mind, 'e's gone! Dunna bother about it, it's nowt, 'e's not a bad sort a chap. What's it matter! What's it matter! There's folks ivrywhere!"

She lifted her face to him blindly. She was really almost blinded, pressing against his body, and her face was red and sightless.

"Kiss me!" she whispered. "Kiss me.—I know the old squire here—"

He kissed her many times, she was so queer and sightless.

"Ay well—he won't see you," he said.

Then she softly rearranged his clothing, kissing the last glimpse of white flesh below his breast, and pushing down the cotton shirt. For once it was not flannelette. And she rose, and they went slowly back to the path where long ago Byron must have limped* in his unhappy inability to feel sure in his love. The path, the whole hillside is a desert now, given over to rabbits and strolling colliers. In a sense, it is dead. The kennels are grown deep in nettles. Dead as Nineveh!* The Chaworth girl*—perhaps she was wise not to love that fat lad.—And they were all long dead. "There be none of beauty's daughters with a magic like thee"—*

Connie and Parkin went slowly down the tussocky hill, above the grey-green country. Across was Haggs Farm. Beyond, Underwood, the mining village, and the mines, The old, old countryside where Byron walked so often, and Mary Chaworth. Now colliers straying with their lasses, from ugly Underwood, from Eastwood, from Hucknall. And the mill-ponds at Felley lying so still, abandoned, abandoned like everything that is not coal or iron, away below. The dead country-side!—and the grisly live spots, the mining settlements!

"If I really want you to do anything, will you do it?" Connie asked him. "You mustn't think you can just leave me. Will you come to me if I need you, even if you never get your divorce? If I can't bear it, will you come and live with me—even next month? We can go to Italy if you like."

"If you feel it's the best, I will. I'll do anything you like, for the best. I don't reckon it's any good layin' the law down, not for myself or anybody—But I can go on looking for some farmin' work, like, an' then—"

"You'll come to me if I can't bear it?"

"Yes," he said.

(End)

Note on the Text and Illustrations

The text in the present volume is that of the 1999 Cambridge University Press edition, edited by Dieter Mehl and Christa Jansohn, with minor corrections based on D.H. Lawrence's manuscripts. The author's spelling mistakes, punctuation and inconsistencies have been preserved.

The photograph of the *Second Lady Chatterley's Lover* manuscript is reproduced courtesy of the Harry Ransom Humanities Research Center, The University of Texas at Austin. The photographs of D.H. Lawrence, Lydia Lawrence, Jessie Chambers and Frieda Lawrence are reproduced with kind permission from John Worthen. The stills from the film *Lady Chatterley* are reproduced courtesy of Artificial Eye.

Notes

p. 11, *toile de Jouy*: Printed decorative wall hangings, which originated in the eighteenth century from Jouy-en-Josas in France.

p. 14, *corona*: An expensive brand of cigars.

p. 17, *to make sure of it*: The source of this quotation has not been identified.

p. 17, *dog-biscuits... Atalanta*: According to Greek and Roman mythology, the entrance to Hades was guarded by the three-headed dog Cerberus. Those entering Hades got past him by feeding him cake, as Aeneas does in the *Aeneid*. Atalanta was a huntress sworn to chastity, who repelled suitors by forcing them to race against her – a race which she invariably won, until one of these suitors was given help by Aphrodite. He won by distracting Atalanta from the race with golden apples. Lawrence here conflates these similar myths.

p. 44, *Lead kindly light*: 'Lead, kindly Light, amid the encircling gloom' (1836) was a popular hymn by John Henry Cardinal Newman (1801–90).

p. 44, *Les Liaisons Dangereuses*: The notorious novel was published in 1782 by Pierre-Ambroise-François Choderlos de Laclos (1741–1803).

p. 46, *Hajji Baba*: *The Adventures of Hajji Baba of Ispahan* (1824) by James Justinian Morier (1780–1849) was a popular story set in Persia.

p. 49, *tendre*: "Soft spot" (French).

p. 52, *A woman had written a book*: The book referred to has not been identified.

p. 53, *Cherchez la femme*: "Look for the woman" (French).

p. 55, *Noli me tangere… voli me tangere*: "Don't touch me… do touch me" (Latin). The first of these is taken from John 20:17 – words spoken by Jesus after his resurrection. The second is a play on the biblical quotation.

p. 55, *Delenda est Cartago*: "Carthage must be razed" (Latin). The saying was attributed to Cato the Elder (234–149 BC) by Plutarch (*c*.45–*c*.125 AD).

p. 57, *the body of the new life*: A reference to the Christian belief that the afterlife will supply everyone with new bodies in place of their earthly ones.

p. 58, *the descent into hell*: A reference to Christ's harrowing of hell.

p. 60, *The hymn says it*: A reference to the popular hymn 'Onward! Christian Soldiers' by Sabine Baring-Gould (1834–1924).

p. 61, *Dorothy Perkins rambler rose*: A popular kind of rose.

p. 61, *gathering roses while she might*: A reference to the poem 'Gather Ye Roses' by Robert Louis Stevenson (1850–94).

p. 62, *Queen Alexandra*: Alexandra of Denmark (1844–1925), the Queen Consort to Edward VII.

p. 64, *Lord Palmerston*: Henry John Temple Palmerston (1784–1865), the twice-serving Prime Minister.

p. 65, *this Ethel M. Dell touch*: A reference to the popular novelist Ethel M. Dell (1881–1939).

p. 66, *pink*: This refers to the coats worn for fox-hunting.

p. 73, *the song… Touch not the nettle… ill to loose*: A song from 1840; the words are by Sir Walter Scott (1771–1832).

p. 74, *the great I Am*: An Old Testament name for God: see Exodus 3:14.

p. 75, *desire has failed*: See Ecclesiastes 12:5.

p. 77, *Thou hast conquered, O pale Galilean*: See 'Hymn to Proserpine' by Swinburne, l. 35. These words were the final ones spoken by Julian the Apostate, the last pagan Roman Emperor, according to Christian tradition.

p. 86, *Thou… Greek vases*: The quotation is from 'Ode on a Grecian Urn' (1820) by John Keats (1795–1821).

p. 94, *j'adoube*: "I adjust" (French). The phrase is used in chess by a player wishing to correct the position of a piece on its square without playing it.

p. 95, *wedding present for the Princess Mary*: Princess Mary (1897–1965), married Henry George Charles Lascelles (1882–1947) in February 1922. The wedding presents were put on public display for two months at St James's Palace.

p. 100, *golden apples… apples of Sodom*: Golden apples occur a number of times in Greek mythology. For the meaning of the "apples of Sodom", see Genesis 13:10 – before it was destroyed, Sodom was fertile land.

p. 119, *Bacchae*: Female followers of Bacchus.

p. 119, *Iacchos*: Bacchus.

p. 119, *Man is… says Byron*: See *Don Juan* II, 179: "Man, being reasonable, must get drunk; / The best of life is but intoxication."

p. 137, *A Woman's Love*: The title may be an invention of Lawrence's: it hasn't been identified with any film.

p. 139, *Eleusis*: A reference to the city in ancient Attica which was the home to annual fertility rites in honour of Demeter and Persephone.

p. 141, *stately homes of England*: A reference to the poem 'The Homes of England' (1827) by Felicia Dorothea Hemans (1793–1835).

p. 144, *A cold wet… hay*: A proverbial saying.

p. 146, *roman de la rose*: The famous medieval French poem, started by Guillaume de Lorris (*fl.* 1230) in around 1230 and completed by Jean de Meun (*c.*1250–1305) in around 1275, was an allegorical work dealing with love in courtly society.

p. 147, *au grand sérieux*: "Very seriously" (French).

p. 155, *the snake itself*: See Genesis 3.

p. 156, *woman who touched Jesus*: See Mark 5:25–34.

p. 168, *Polly-anning*: A reference to the heroine of the children's book *Pollyanna* (1913) by Eleanor Hodgman Porter (1868–1920). The name was used to describe someone as cheerfully optimistic and trusting, although it was also extended to have the derogatory meaning of a naive optimist.

p. 173, *Heloïse loved Abélard… mutilated*: Peter Abélard (1079–1142) and Héloïse (*c.*1098–1164) were famous lovers in the Middle Ages, whose affair was frustrated by Héloïse's uncle. Abélard was castrated by Héloïse's relatives.

p. 174, *Hamletising men*: Men who adopt the posture of Hamlet.

p. 182, *Stone walls... a cage*: A quotation from 'To Althea, from Prison' by Richard Lovelace (1618–58).

p. 182, *two-horse chariot*: See Plato's *Phaedrus* 246a–c and 253c–254e.

p. 184, *St. Francis*: St Francis of Assisi (*c*.1181–1226), the founder of the Franciscan order of friars, famously devoted himself to a life of poverty.

p. 187, *leaves of grass*: See Psalms 90:5–6, 103:15–16 and Isaiah 40:6–8.

p. 190, *Foguzzaro*: Antonio Fogazzaro (1842–1911) was an Italian novelist.

p. 198, *doll in the song... gee-gee*: The song referred to has not been identified.

p. 214, *Oh tale told by an idiot*: See *Macbeth* Act v, Sc. 5, l. 26.

p. 227, *flight into Egypt*: See Matthew 2:13–14.

p. 228, *the wind bloweth where it listeth*: See John 3:8.

p. 228, *Bentrovato*: "Well found" (Italian).

p. 229, *When lovely woman stoops to freedom*: A reference to *The Vicar of Wakefield* (1766) by Oliver Goldsmith (*c*.1728–74), which contains the couplet "When lovely woman stoops to folly, / And finds too late that men betray".

p. 230, *The wench... different way*: See *Epigram* (1821) by Lord Byron (1788–1824): "The world is a bundle of hay, / Mankind are the asses who pull; / Each tugs it a different way, / And the greatest of all is John Bull."

p. 239, *our latest famous philosopher... The universe... It is thus passing... The present type... depend*: The quotations are from the final pages of *Religion in the Making* (1926) by Alfred North Whitehead (1861–1947).

p. 239, *Selah*: A Hebrew term which occurs frequently in the Psalms. It indicates a musical, liturgical or possibly interpretative instruction.

p. 239, *Tu l'as voulu, Georges Dandin*: "It's what you wanted, Georges Dandin!" (French). The line is taken from *Georges Dandin* (1668) by Molière (1622–73).

p. 240, *Cherchez l'homme*: "Look for the man" (French).

p. 240, *female Don Quixote... Don Dulcineo*: See *The Female Quixote, or The Adventures of Arabella* (1752), by Charlotte Lennox (*c*.1730–1804), a humorous take on *Don Quixote de la Mancha* (1605, 1615) by Miguel de Cervantes Saavedra (1547–1616).

p. 241, *Leaving… nonentity*: The source of this quotation has not been identified.

p. 243, *star Aldebaran*: The brightest star in the constellation of Taurus.

p. 246, *Care killed t' cat*: See *Much Ado About Nothing*, Act v, Sc. 1, l. 127.

p. 248, *gimme lashin's*: "Give me plenty of it" (dialect).

p. 256, *a kiss… Judas*: See Matthew 26:48–49 and Luke 22:47–8.

p. 261, *disporting on the hill o' beans*: Enjoying themselves in good humour and prosperity (American slang).

p. 264, *manie de la grandeur*: "Megalomania" (French).

p. 264, *Schiller used to sit… Don Carlos*: Friedrich Schiller (1759–1805), German poet and dramatist, was the author of *Don Carlos* (1787), a historical drama in five acts. The source of the story that he wrote with his feet in cold water has not been found.

p. 266, *when the Lord… ten righteous men*: See Genesis 18:20–19: 25.

p. 266, *sons and daughters of god*: See Genesis 6:2.

p. 273, *men and women… joined together… Aristophanes said in Plato*: See Plato's *Symposium*, in which Aristophanes develops the idea of a hermaphrodite race, which, when each of them are split in half, constitute one man and one woman separately.

p. 274, *Plotinus or of Hegel*: Plotinus (*c*.204–270 CE) was the founder of Neoplatonism. George Wilhelm Friedrich Hegel (1770–1831) was one of the main thinkers in the movement of German Idealism.

p. 274, *our world… the bottom of a deep sea*: See Socrates' description of the earth in Plato's *Phaedo*.

p. 275, *raising Cain*: See Genesis 4.

p. 276, *Cent Nouvelles*: *Les Cent Nouvelles Nouvelles (The Hundred New Novellas)* (*c*.1460) is an anonymous collection of stories in French, most of which have erotic or obscene subject matter.

p. 276, *Rabelais*: François Rabelais (*c*.1484–1553), a French writer, wrote *Gargantua* and *Pantagruel* (1532–34), works which are notorious for being exceptionally grotesque and obscene by the standards of his time.

p. 276, *Nemmeno male*: "Not at all bad" (Italian).

p. 276, *I-care-for-nobody*: See the refrain "I care for nobody, not I, / If no one cares for me", from the popular song 'The Miller of Dee'.

p. 276, *Marquis de Sade*: Donatien Alphonse François de Sade (1740–1814), a French novelist, was the author of pornographic works which often included philosophical ideas and violence.

p. 276, *Don Rodrigo… ballad… most have sinned*: "He eats me now, he eats me now, I feel the adder's bite, / The part that was most sinning my bedfellow doth rend" (ll. 50–1). A two-headed serpent eats Roderigo's heart with one mouth and his genitals with the other at the same time: see 'The Penitence of Don Roderick' in *Ancient Spanish Ballads: Historical and Romantic* (1823) by John Gibson Lockhart (1794–1854) .

p. 282, *like the grass that withereth… more*: See note to page 187, and Job 7:10.

p. 289, *I need thee… thee*: This is the refrain from 'I need Thee every hour' (1872), a hymn by Annie Sherwood Hawks (1835–1918).

p. 294, *what's in a name*: *Romeo and Juliet*, Act II, Sc. 2, l. 43.

p. 303, *decree absolute*: A stage in divorce proceedings at which the divorce is made final.

p. 307, *Aeschylus… House of Atreus*: Aeschylus (*c.*525–456 BC) was a Greek writer of tragedies. The house of Atreus was a family doomed to tragic misfortune, whose members were central to Aeschylus's plays.

p. 307, *lemurs*: In this case, the word is used in the original Latin sense of "spirits of the dead".

p. 307, *Angels, thrones, ministers and powers*: These are traditional terms for the divine hierarchy, mostly taken from the Book of Revelations; see also John Milton (1608–74), *Paradise Lost* (1667) V, l. 600.

p. 308, *raptus:* A Latin word occasionally used in medical psychology to describe an overwhelming fit, whether of rapture or depression or obsession.

p. 308, *the hatred of "inspiration", in Plato*: See Plato's attack on poets and artists in *The Republic*.

p. 310, *Jane Eyre… Wuthering Heights… The Steadfast Sylph*: *Jane Eyre* (1847) by Charlotte Brontë (1816–55) and *Wuthering Heights* (1847) by Emily Brontë (1818–48) were coming to be recognized as the classics they are today when Lawrence was writing *Lady Chatterley's Lover. The Steadfast Sylph* is a parody of *The Constant Nymph* (1924), a popular novel by Margaret Kennedy (1896–1967).

p. 319, *Calvary*: Mount Calvary was the site of Christ's crucifixion, also known as Golgotha – see Matthew 27:33.

p. 326, *bacca*: "Tobacco" (colloquial).

p. 337, *Then shall thy peace be as a river*: See Isaiah 48:18.

p. 337, *There's not a joy the world can give like that it takes away*: See 'Stanzas for Music' (1815), l. 1 by Byron.

p. 341, *Byron must have limped*: Byron had a club foot.

p. 341, *Dead as Nineveh*: The Assyrian city was destroyed by the Medes and Babylonians in 612 BC.

p. 341, *Chaworth girl*: Mary Anne Chaworth (1785–1832), who Byron fell in love with in his youth.

p. 341, *There be none... magic like thee*: First two lines of Byron's 'Stanzas for Music' (1814–16).

Extra Material

on

D.H. Lawrence's

*The Second Lady
Chatterley's Lover*

D.H. Lawrence's Life

David Herbert Lawrence was born on 11th September 1885 in *Birth and Early Life*
Eastwood, a small colliery town just outside Nottingham. He
was the fourth of five children – three brothers and two sisters. His father, and most of his other relatives, were involved
in some capacity with work at one of the collieries, including
labour at the coalface.

His mother Lydia had once had ambitions to be a teacher,
but the poverty of her parents had thwarted her earlier aspi-
rations. However, she still took an interest in reading and in
intellectual matters. She tried to contribute to the Lawrence
family income by running a small clothes shop from the
ground floor of the family house – a financial venture which
was never very successful. Lydia tried to encourage all of her
children to save money and study, but Arthur, her husband,
would go out drinking most evenings, leading to arguments
and tension.

The boys in the local school were almost all destined to finish up down the mine, while the girls also would work in the
colliery canteens and laundries. However, from an early age
the Lawrence children seemed to aim for higher things, and
took their school studies extremely seriously. Furthermore,
they regularly attended the local Nonconformist Christian
chapel, and all took the pledge early in their lives not to touch
alcohol.

A major dramatic occurrence in D.H. Lawrence's early life *Bereavement and Illness*
was the death in 1901 of his elder brother Ernest from ery-
sipelas. After this traumatic experience, Lawrence developed
severe pneumonia and nearly died. This may have been a con-
tributing factor to the tuberculosis and general ill health which
dogged his later years, and which finally caused his death.

Lawrence was at the time reading omnivorously in the local municipal library and at school. In 1902 he became a pupil teacher at a senior school in Eastwood – a common arrangement at the time. Some of the more promising older pupils were given lessons by the headmaster early in the mornings, and then they proceeded to teach the other pupils, usually for nothing or a nominal sum, since the personal tuition they received was meant to constitute their reward. Lawrence's token recompense was £12 per year. He took the opportunity of spending some time each week at what would now be called "teachers' centres" in Nottingham and at Ilkeston in Derbyshire, which ran training courses for other people in his situation living in the area; this led to a huge expansion of his social and intellectual horizons.

After two years as a pupil teacher, Lawrence successfully sat the King's Scholarship Examination in 1904, which gave him entry to a teacher-training college, or even, if he so wished, the opportunity to study for a degree at a university – almost unheard of at the time for anybody from a lower-class background. Interviews with this "working-class boy made good" were subsequently published in the local press and in the national teachers' magazines *The Schoolmaster* and *The Teacher*.

Although success in the examination conferred access to higher education, it gave little financial assistance, and so Lawrence and his family now had to decide whether he should do the degree full-time, supported by his family, or part-time, working to finance himself, as there were no student grants at the time.

It was finally decided he should spend a further year as a pupil teacher at a salary of £50 per year before going to university to do his teacher training. He entered the teacher-training department of Nottingham University in September 1906, but between the scholarship examination and entry to higher education he had started to write. He experimented with poetry, and in 1906 began writing *Laetitia*, the earliest version of his first published novel, *The White Peacock*.

Jessie Chambers Lawrence was by now spending a considerable amount of time in the company of a young woman he had met some five years earlier, Jessie Chambers. They read together and discussed literature, philosophy and other intellectual subjects. His sisters and mother were worried that this blossoming relationship would be a distraction to "Bert"; they wanted him and Jessie either to get engaged, or meet less frequently. Lawrence took all this to heart, and told Jessie they must cut down the number of their meetings drastically for the time being. She was deeply hurt, and this was the first of numerous occasions on which he treated Jessie, and other women, with seeming insensitivity and selfishness.

At teacher-training college, Lawrence met socialists and *Early Writing* freethinkers, and his whole universe expanded. He spent a great deal of time writing and revising his novel. He found the course boring, but ploughed ahead with it and finally gained his teaching certificate in 1908. He also wrote more poetry and experimented with short-story writing. He submitted three stories to a competition in the biggest Nottingham newspaper, and one of these – 'The Prelude' – submitted for him by Jessie Chambers under her own name – won the prize for best story in its category and was printed in the paper. Lawrence also apparently sent some work – possibly one or more essays or sketches – to G.K. Chesterton, then literary editor at the *Daily News* in London, but these were returned with such negative comments that he nearly decided to give up writing altogether.

Lawrence was still living at home but, under the influence of the new ideas he was encountering at college, he began to react against his narrow upbringing, particularly the world of the Nonconformist chapel his parents attended, and religion in general. Unlike his fellow graduates, Lawrence was prepared to bide his time waiting for a good job to turn up – which might, besides providing him with a reasonable salary, enable him to escape from home. In the meantime he did jobs including farm work and clerking until he obtained a position as a teacher at a boys' school in Croydon, a working-class area of South London, just after his twenty-third birthday.

He started work in London in October 1908 and moved *London* into rooms in a family-run private house nearby. This was the first time he had lived away from home for any extended period, and working at the school proved extremely demanding, as he found it difficult to enforce discipline. However, in his leisure time he went up to central London to attend concerts and plays, and visited art galleries and bookshops. He continued his reading and writing, including further revisions to *Laetitia*.

Literary Breakthrough   Lawrence's breakthrough into the literary world came with some of his poems, which he sent initially to Jessie Chambers – still in Nottingham – for comment. Without his knowledge, she submitted them in September 1909 to Ford Madox Hueffer (later known as Ford Madox Ford), the illustrious critic and editor of the recently established radical journal *The English Review*. Hueffer decided to print a few of them and encouraged Lawrence to send him any further work of his, whatever the genre. Hueffer knew all the major London literati, and invited Lawrence to artistic gatherings, where he met, among others, Wells, Yeats and Pound.

Because his journal pursued a radical line, Hueffer was especially interested in promoting Lawrence as an "author from the collieries", and suggested that Lawrence should write about the life of the people he was familiar with. Accordingly, Lawrence's first two plays, written around this period (*A Collier's Friday Night* and *The Widowing of Mrs Holroyd*), were concerned with the life of mining families and partly written in the Nottinghamshire dialect. In December 1910 he sent the manuscript of *Laetitia* to the London publisher Heinemann, accompanied by a letter of recommendation from Hueffer. Heinemann asked for some cuts and alterations – which Lawrence made, including renaming it *The White Peacock* – and accepted it for publication.

Love Life   Despite his efforts, Lawrence had failed to forge a physical relationship with any of his various female acquaintances. Around this time, he suggested to his long-time intellectual companion, Jessie Chambers – still living in Nottinghamshire – that they should become lovers. Jessie agreed, but Lawrence did not wish to be tied down by one woman, and the affair was extremely unhappy and bitter. In August 1911 the sexual side of the relationship ended, and two months later Lawrence's mother became seriously unwell, possibly with the first signs of the cancer that would ultimately kill her.

All the following year his mother was in increasingly severe pain, and he was now without Jessie. In this sense of isolation and sadness he embarked on the composition of a new novel, largely drawn from his own experiences at the time. He was at this period re-establishing contact with a friend from his adolescence, Louie Burrows, then living in Leicester. She was apparently not as intellectual as Jessie Chambers, but very loving and fond of Lawrence. Possibly on the rebound from Jessie Chambers, Lawrence proposed marriage to Louie.

Just at this time *The White Peacock* appeared in print, and Lawrence personally put the first copy of it into his mother's hands. His mother would die later that year, on 9th December.

Lawrence's second novel, entitled at this point *The Saga of Siegmund*, was rejected by Heinemann; they suggested numerous revisions and a change of title. Accordingly, Lawrence reworked the novel, which would appear as *The Trespasser* in 1912. At the same time as composing the later stages of *The Saga of Siegmund*, he had started on a third novel, which he planned to entitle *Paul Morel*. By now he had begun to realize his engagement to Louie had been a mistake – since she could not provide the lifelong intellectual companionship he desired – and agonized over ending their relationship. He became very depressed, and in November 1911 developed a severe, near-fatal case of pneumonia – which may have been an early symptom of the lung problems which would plague Lawrence throughout his entire life. He spent a month convalescing at a hotel in Bournemouth, making the final revisions to his second novel and progressing with *Paul Morel*. He gave up teaching on the advice of his doctors and returned to Eastwood in February 1912. There he completely rewrote *Paul Morel* – Jessie Chambers reading all his drafts and making suggestions – while living in his childhood home with his father and two sisters.

It was at this time that one of the major events of Lawrence's *Frieda* life occurred: he met the woman with whom he was to spend most of his life – Frieda Weekley. Née von Richthofen, she was the daughter of minor German aristocrats from the Metz region. She was the wife of the Professor of Modern Languages at Nottingham University, Ernest Weekley, whom she had met and married at the age of nineteen. The couple lived in a respectable suburb of Nottingham with their three children. Lawrence first met her when in March 1912 he came to their house to enquire about the possibility of finding teaching work in Germany. He immediately fell passionately in love with her, even though she was eight years his senior. Since she reciprocated his feelings, he convinced her that she was wasting her best years in her current, comfortable way of life and persuaded her to start a relationship with him.

In May 1912 *The Trespasser* was published, to reasonably favourable reviews, and on the 12th of the same month Frieda left her husband and travelled with Lawrence to Metz. Ernest Weekley immediately asked for a divorce, stipulating that she should never see the children again. While in Germany staying with her relations, Lawrence made his final revision of *Paul Morel* and sent it off to Heinemann. The publisher rejected it as being poorly written and too sexually explicit. However, Edward Garnett, the reader for Duckworth publishers, assured Lawrence that if, under his guidance, he made a large number of alterations, he would recommend the novel for publication. Lawrence and Frieda undertook a walking tour of Germany, Austria and finally Italy, where they intended to stay for some months as it was much cheaper than Germany and they were short of money.

In Italy, in rooms near Gargnano, on the Lake Garda, Lawrence made the requisite alterations to *Paul Morel*, renaming it *Sons and Lovers* in the process. He sent the novel off to Duckworth and, after further negotiations, the novel was accepted for publication. Lawrence now worked intensively on poems, plays and ideas for possible future novels, finally settling down to a project he provisionally entitled *The Sisters*, which would ultimately, over the next seven years, become *The Rainbow* and *Women in Love*. In June 1913, the couple finally returned to England, since Frieda desperately wanted to see her children again before consenting to a divorce which would forbid her access to them. *Sons and Lovers* had by this time been published to mixed but generally favourable reviews.

Frieda did not succeed in seeing her children, and was threatened with legal action if she attempted to do so again. The couple returned to Italy, this time to Lerici, near La Spezia. There Lawrence produced the first section of a completely revised version of *The Sisters* – which detailed the sexual relationships and emotional development of two sisters, Ella (later Ursula) and Gudrun Brangwen. Having sent this draft to Garnett – who lambasted it as very badly written – Lawrence set about a further revision. However, following the success of *Sons and Lovers*, other publishers were now making overtures to Lawrence, some offering him lucrative contracts for the novel – which by this time had been renamed *The Wedding Ring*. Garnett once again criticized the new version heavily, and in March Lawrence returned to London to negotiate a possible deal with another publisher: Methuen outbid Duckworth and were promised the novel. Finally, in April 1914, Frieda gained her divorce, and Lawrence married her in July of that year. Things seemed to be looking up on all fronts for Lawrence.

Then war broke out and the couple faced enormous problems in returning abroad. The war also hindered the possibility of getting further novels published, since there was a paper shortage, and the entire economy was now geared towards providing for the military effort. Furthermore, Frieda was regarded with suspicion because of her German origin. Lawrence – profoundly disillusioned with the war – felt that the conflict was barbaric and that the entire British national and racial consciousness had been polluted. *War and Rejection*

Suddenly Methuen returned the manuscript of *The Wedding Ring*, claiming the subject matter was too risqué, and that publishers' lists were being cut back drastically because of the war. Lawrence and Frieda were once again without money, so they moved to a small cottage in Chesham, Buckinghamshire. He rewrote *The Wedding Ring* between November 1914 and March 1915, splitting the novel into *The Rainbow* and what was ultimately to become *Women in Love*. However, *The Rainbow* became even more sexually explicit than the previously rejected drafts.

During these years, Lawrence had begun to enter new literary circles. Among others he had become acquainted with Lady Ottoline Morrell, the aristocratic society and artistic hostess. At her receptions he met famous intellectuals, such as E.M. Forster and Bertrand Russell. Lawrence's letters from 1914 and 1915 – principally to Russell – show the evolution of his ideas on the best way to live one's life and to develop one's real inner self. At first, Russell was highly impressed by Lawrence, but then became deeply disturbed by what he saw as the authoritarian character of his personality and beliefs, which he later characterized as "leading straight to Auschwitz".

The Rainbow was published in September 1915 and received vicious reviews. Bookstalls and libraries refused to stock it, because of what was perceived to be the pornographic nature of its material. Finally, in November 1915, the police seized all unsold copies and the book was prosecuted in the law courts for obscenity, the magistrates ordering all copies to be *The Rainbow Controversy*

357

destroyed. Although some of Lawrence's artistic entourage protested against this censorship, it was generally the idea of censorship itself they were criticizing: most in fact detested the book as an aesthetic creation.

Move to Cornwall   Lawrence now seriously thought of emigrating permanently to America with Frieda to set up an artists-and-writers' commune in Florida, encouraging their various acquaintances to come and join them. However, Lawrence could only acquire a passport if he declared himself ready to be summoned for military service at any time, which he could not bring himself to do. If they could not leave Britain, they decided to move as far from the centre of war activities in London as they could. Accordingly they hired a cottage in Cornwall, where they lived by growing their own vegetables, settling there in December 1915. In this cottage, Lawrence produced books of poetry and reminiscences of his time in Italy, as well as reviews and other pieces of writing that procured them a very meagre income. Although Lawrence was often ill with colds and pulmonary complaints – perhaps because of the winds from the sea and the moors – both he and Frieda enjoyed the open countryside and often entertained guests from London in their cottage.

Lawrence now began to recast the material left over from *The Wedding Ring*, using that work's original title, *The Sisters*, for the first draft of this reworking. After several revisions the manuscript went through the usual round of publishers, who all rejected it – one even asked if it was really finished. In addition to their reservations about the content, they were probably frightened off by Lawrence's reputation and the police prosecution of *The Rainbow*. Lady Ottoline Morrell had caught a glimpse of the manuscript, thought herself slandered in the person of the novel's society hostess Hermione, and consequently severed all ties with Lawrence.

Because of his weak lungs, Lawrence was rejected for conscription on medical grounds in June 1916, and the locals in Cornwall became suspicious and irritated at this non-combatant writer living with a German wife, and spread rumours that they were spies. They would sometimes be stopped by the coastguard while out on their walks, and return to their cottage to find it had been broken into and searched.

Return to London   In September 1917 they were finally served with a legal order
and Derbyshire   excluding them from Cornwall altogether, so they moved back
358   to London, staying in a series of cheap lodgings. In London

Lawrence attempted to settle down to writing his next novel, *Aaron's Rod*, but progress was slow due to their precarious living conditions and the fact that he was at the same time trying to eke out a living by writing poetry, reviews and essays. In May 1918, they moved back to the Midlands – to a cottage in Middleton-by-Wirksworth in Derbyshire – because it was so much cheaper to live there than in the south. Although he was now closer to his family, Lawrence felt himself to be "lost and exiled", sinking into severe depression and growing extremely pessimistic as to his future prospects.

In September 1918 Lawrence was compulsorily examined for military service: by this time the British Army was so desperate for manpower for the war effort that it was willing to conscript almost anybody. He was enlisted for "light non-military duties", a decision which drove him into a fury: "I've done with society and humanity. Labour and military can alike go to hell. Henceforth it is for myself, my own life, I live." He was never actually called up, since war ended in November 1918. In February 1919 he went down with a serious bout of influenza, and nearly died – the disease was then killing millions of people worldwide.

The armistice meant that Lawrence and Frieda could finally *Leaving England* obtain passports, and they decided to abandon England for good. In December 1919 they moved to Capri, and then to Taormina in Sicily. Lawrence now concentrated on his work, *Psychoanalysis and the Unconscious*, followed by his next two novels, *The Lost Girl* and *Mr Noon*. *The Lost Girl* was published in Britain in November 1920 but, because of his reputation, many bookshops again refused to stock it. His publisher demanded both major revisions to this novel and further alterations to *Women in Love*, since the composer Philip Heseltine (better known by his pen name of Peter Warlock) had perceived himself as portrayed and libelled in the novel's character of Julian Halliday.

As a result of all this, the Lawrences grew utterly fed up *Australia and New* with Europe, and decided to renew their attempt at moving to *Mexico* the US, as Lawrence had been invited at this time to set up residence in Taos, a colony of writers and artists in New Mexico. Disillusioned with society, humanity and the artistic life, he and Frieda set off to the States. En route to New Mexico, they spent short periods in Ceylon and New Zealand, and six weeks in Australia, where Lawrence met the Australian writer

359

Mollie Skinner, and collaborated with her in producing *The Boy in the Bush* – probably the least didactic of his novels and the one most similar to an ordinary adventure story. He also began to draft his next novel, *Kangaroo*, also based on Australian life. The couple finally arrived in San Francisco in August 1922, then making their way down to Taos, establishing themselves on a ranch on Lobo Mountain. Lawrence was overwhelmed by the primeval beauty of the landscape opening up around him. At Taos he completed *Kangaroo* and earned a slender living by journalism, reviews and a book of essays on American literature.

Mexico and Return to Europe   In March 1923, Lawrence and Frieda visited Mexico and, by the lake near the settlement of Chapala in the south-west, Lawrence began work on his next novel, *The Plumed Serpent*, which dealt with pagan Mexican religion and political insurrection. Before taking up residence permanently in America, they decided to pay a brief visit to Europe, as Frieda in particular desperately wanted to see both her German and English families again. However, just before they were due to sail, the Lawrences had a huge row, the causes of which are unclear. Frieda sailed to Europe alone, and Lawrence returned to Mexico. It's possible that Frieda may have wanted to return to Europe permanently, whereas Lawrence detested the old Continent so wholeheartedly that he was determined this was going to be his last visit – the shorter the better.

Frieda did not return and, at the end of 1923, he finally wrote to her offering a separation, with the provision of a regular income. She begged him to return to Europe, and other old friends also expressed their desire to see him. Finally in November of that year he set off with the greatest reluctance. He wrote: "I don't want much to go to England – but I suppose it is the next move in the battle which never ends and which I never win." As soon as he reached England, he was confined to bed with a severe cold and, although he visited friends and relations, he declared openly that he now loathed London and the entire country. He once again appealed to friends to come back to America with him and set up an artists-and-writers' commune, but only the artist Dorothy Brett would commit to doing so. At a farewell party, Lawrence drank too much and vomited over the meal table – this traumatic final event in England symbolizing all his loathing for European culture.

Lawrence, Frieda and Dorothy sailed back to the States in March 1924, and they all moved to a ranch just two miles away from their previous residence on Lobo Mountain. Unfortunately, his American publisher now went bankrupt, depriving him of a great deal of expected royalties. However, Lawrence at last seemed to have found some slight measure of happiness there, writing and living the simple life away from the civilization he so detested. The only major drawback was that he suffered from serious chest ailments, and began spitting blood – possibly as a result of the altitude of 2,600 metres. In Autumn 1924 came news that his father had died at the age of seventy-eight, but he did not return to Europe to attend the funeral.

Return to America

In order to complete *The Plumed Serpent*, Lawrence felt he needed to spend more time in Mexico to imbibe the atmosphere, so in October he, Frieda and Dorothy travelled down to Oaxaca, which seemed a warm paradise conducive to the subject matter of the book and to sustained writing. However, tensions were now surfacing between Frieda and Dorothy, and Dorothy returned to America after just ten days. Lawrence finally finished the book in late January 1925, and immediately went down with a combination of influenza, typhoid and malaria which nearly cost him his life. Although he survived, his lungs were fatally damaged by these illnesses, and he was finally diagnosed with tuberculosis. He was given at most two years to live, and decided to return with Frieda to his ranch in the US. The doctor at the border initially refused Lawrence re-entry, as he now showed obvious signs of tuberculosis, a dangerous and contagious disease, but they were eventually granted a six-month residency.

Tuberculosis

Once back at the ranch, he recovered somewhat, and began writing again. In September 1925 – the six months having expired – the now forty-year-old Lawrence sailed back to Europe. The couple once again visited Lawrence's family, Frieda taking the opportunity to see her now adult children, before moving on through Germany and down to Italy, to a villa in Spotorno, a Ligurian town on the coast. Lawrence took up writing again, and started work in 1926 on his final novel, *Lady Chatterley's Lover*. Although Lawrence's health was generally stable, he still had bouts of blood-spitting, and felt his general condition slowly deteriorating. They then moved to a villa in Tuscany; Lawrence thought briefly of returning to

361

America, but realized that in his sick state he almost certainly would not be allowed entry, and that the strain of the long journey would exhaust his body still further.

Lady Chatterley's Lover   Lawrence was occupied with completing *Lady Chatterley's Lover* from October 1926 to summer 1928. The manuscript underwent countless radical alterations throughout these months, and during the final stages of revision, Lawrence was writing up to four thousand words a day. Although he had few hopes of its publication, because of its sexually explicit subject matter, he had discovered that it would be possible to publish the novel at his own expense on the Continent. 1,200 copies of the book, which he had arranged to be printed privately in Florence, finally appeared in June 1928. *Lady Chatterley's Lover* was an instant commercial success, and Lawrence for the first time in his life was relatively free from financial worries. After the publication of this novel, he decided to get away from the baking heat of Italy and live for a few months in the Swiss Alps, to see whether the mountain air would improve his condition. Although this change of environment benefited him somewhat, his coughing became more frequent, and he suffered increasingly severe haemorrhages. He tried not to let his illness defeat him, writing in a letter: "I feel so strongly as if my illness weren't really me – I feel perfectly well and all right, in myself. Yet there is this beastly torturing chest superimposed on me, and it's as if there was a demon lived there, triumphing, and extraneous to me." Frieda would later remark that she had never heard him complain about his health.

Last Days   With the money from *Lady Chatterley*, Lawrence and Frieda had some choice about where to live, and they selected a pleasant hotel in Bandol, on the French coast near Toulon. Lawrence tried to write newspaper articles and poems, but he could not undertake any further major projects, as his health was now deteriorating rapidly. He began to compose what would be his final work, *Apocalypse*: its purpose was to offer modern man a kind of psychic recovery of his connections with the old world, by providing a fresh view of humanity's "old, pagan vision" and the "pre-Christian heavens". But his physical condition by now was very poor, and he finally agreed to enter the Ad Astra sanatorium in Vence, near Nice. There he grew very despondent, and decided to discharge himself, as he wanted to die on his own terms. He and Frieda rented a villa in Vence, and hired nurses to look after him. On

Sunday 2nd March 1930 his condition worsened considerably; he admitted he needed morphine, and a doctor administered the drug. Lawrence died that evening. Frieda wrote that he was buried "in the little cemetery of Vence which looks over the Mediterranean that he cared so much about". In 1935 his body was exhumed and cremated, and a chapel was erected near his second ranch in the mountains overlooking Taos to house his ashes.

D.H. Lawrence's Works

D.H. Lawrence wrote his first novel, *The White Peacock*, under various working titles, between 1906 and 1910. As mentioned above, the London publisher William Heinemann accepted it for publication, and the book came out in 1911. The novel follows a first-person narrator, Cyril Beardsall, who is continually questioning his identity and his place in the world – even at this stage of Lawrence's career, his writing probes the question of the alienation of modern humanity from its natural roots and instincts. The setting is the countryside around Nottingham (Beardsall, incidentally, was the maiden name of Lawrence's mother). *The White Peacock*

Cyril and his sister Lettie have had a conventional middle-class upbringing: they are cultured and artistic, but they are dissatisfied with their life, and the novel deals with their failure to find genuine love. Cyril courts Emily Saxton, a farmer's daughter, who ends up marrying somebody else, while Lettie, although deeply in love with Emily's brother George, makes a conventional marriage to a narrow-minded man of a much higher social rank. Following this rejection, George marries a pub landlord's daughter, which leaves him unfulfilled, and he becomes an apathetic alcoholic.

There is one further major character, who represents the rejection of modern culture and civilization and embodies the return to nature and the instincts. This is Frank Annable, who had been a student at Cambridge University, before becoming a vicar and marrying a local aristocrat, Lady Crystabel. He has rejected his former life and is now a gamekeeper on a large estate, living in the woods with a second wife and a large family. He is generally disliked by the local men, apparently because, with his animal vitality, he has a great deal of success with their wives. Cyril is attracted by his superb physique and personality, but Annable is found dead at the bottom of a quarry – it is not certain whether he has slipped or been pushed over by a gang of locals. It is interesting to note that, in his very last novel, *Lady Chatterley's Lover*, written around twenty years later, earthiness and return to one's natural instincts are also represented by a gamekeeper who has rejected his middle-class educated background.

George and Lettie therefore are left at the end of the novel feeling that they have not managed to unite their alienated artistic nature with the innate animal instinctive level of their own humanity; neither have they succeeded in bonding at any meaningful level with the members of the human race who are much more attuned with these instincts than they are.

The Trespasser The follow-up to *The White Peacock*, *The Trespasser*, was composed between March 1910 and February 1912. It was originally to be titled *The Saga of Siegmund*, but was finally published in 1912 as *The Trespasser*. Mainly set on the Isle of Wight, with other scenes in north and south London and Cornwall, the novel centres on Siegmund Macnair, an orchestral musician and music teacher, who is married, with five children, to Beatrice. Despite his domestic comforts, he is restless and gets involved in a relationship with one of his pupils, Helena Verden. The bulk of the novel deals with the week they spend together on the Isle of Wight. The relationship does not work on a physical level: he is passionately attracted to her, but she is very withdrawn. Siegmund, in despair at all the conflicts and tensions in his life, hangs himself, and his wife, for the children's sake, deliberately suppresses all memory of him. But something has died within Helena Verden after this tragedy: she has entered a deep period of emotional stasis, and the novel ends with her new friend and possible future lover, Cecil, trying desperately to arouse her from this state.

Sons and Lovers Around the same time *The Trespasser* was written, Lawrence was working on another manuscript, provisionally entitled *Paul Morel*, which was completed in 1912 and published as *Sons and Lovers* in 1913. It incorporates numerous elements of Lawrence's life. The "Bestwood" of the novel is the author's home village of Eastwood, and the Morel family bears many resemblances to his own. The novel charts the protagonist Paul Morel's sexual, emotional and intellectual development from his childhood up to the age of twenty-five. The first part of the novel is devoted to a recreation of the early married life and environment of Paul's parents. Like Lawrence's own family, the father is a miner who drinks, while the mother is intellectual, artistic and well informed; this leads to inevitable arguments. Paul shares his mother's artistic nature and becomes strongly attached to her. Following the early death of his brother from illness, Paul too nearly dies at the age of sixteen and, from then on, the novel concerns Paul's developing emotional and sexual relationships, and his attempt to become independent in all ways from his mother. He has done exceptionally well at school, and wishes to become an artist, but, during the period covered by the novel, works as a clerk at a local factory. At the age of sixteen, he meets his first love, Miriam, who bears many resemblances to Jessie Chambers. They are both passionate about art and ideas, and very much in love, but the sexual side of their relationship is fraught with difficulties. Paul feels he is betraying his mother, while Miriam at first does not want to involve herself in sex outside marriage. Paul constantly tries to force the issue, and Miriam finally acquiesces unwillingly, feeling she is making a great sacrifice for him. This turns out to be a disastrous experience, and Paul ends their relationship. He then enters on a brief and much more fulfilling relationship with an older married woman, but she finally decides to remain faithful to her husband. Near the end of the novel, Paul's mother dies, and he is left on the threshold of his maturity alone, but having become much more aware of his own identity.

The extremely convoluted gestation of Lawrence's next *The Rainbow* novel, *The Rainbow*, should be studied with that of the following work, *Women in Love*, since they are both developments of what was originally planned as one novel. *The Rainbow* was published just two years after the commencement of the first draft, in 1913, but the reworking of the later material as a second volume, *Women in Love*, took until 1920. The preliminary drafts were written between March 1913 and August 1915. The first draft, under the provisional title *The Sisters,* was written between March and June 1913. A complete revision, still with the same provisional title, took place between August 1913 and January 1914. This was then substantially revised again, under the new title *The Wedding Ring*, from February to May 1914, and Lawrence finally took the decision to split the material into two books. The first, now known as *The Rainbow*, was put together between November 1914 and March 1915, and published in September 1915. The book portrays the earlier generations of the Nottinghamshire family whose modern members are treated at length in *Women in Love*. The setting is mainly the industrial counties of Nottinghamshire and its neighbour Derbyshire. Tom Brangwen, a young Midlands farmer, marries a Polish exile, Lydia Lensky, in 1867, when he is twenty-eight and she is thirty-four. Lydia is more cultured and intellectual than Tom, and the novel explores firstly the tensions in their marriage, and the way their relationship gradually evolves into a harmonious loving partnership. The couple live with Lydia's daughter, Anna, by her first marriage to a Polish revolutionary. We are shown Anna's development to maturity, until she finally marries Will Brangwen, the son of Tom's brother Alfred. Their stormy marriage is depicted in detail and, although they ultimately achieve some sort of harmony, this is not to the same degree of happiness as Anna's parents, but represents more of a compromise. One of the major differences is in religion: Anna is a "pagan", in that she worships nature and the instinctive physical life, whereas Will is a Christian mystic, hankering after experiences of the eternal and absolute.

The major part of the novel is taken up with the third generation of this family, and mainly describes the life of Will and Anna's daughter, Ursula Brangwen. She is profoundly conscious of her responsibility to form her own personality, and to gain independence from her early upbringing and family; she questions her father's Christianity, and has various relationships, including a lesbian affair. She trains as a student teacher, later becoming a passionate critic of contemporary industrial society and of the alienation of the natural instincts from everyday life. She becomes engaged to a young soldier, Anton Skrebensky, but she gradually opens her eyes to his conventionality and adherence to social norms. She breaks off their relationship and he, unbeknown to her, marries another woman and is posted on military service to India. Ursula discovers she is pregnant by him, and writes to him asking for marriage after all. However, before receiving an answer, she is involved in a traumatic incident while out walking, becomes dangerously ill and suffers a miscarriage. This leads her to a period of epiphany, self-discovery and rebirth; she is delighted when she learns that Skrebensky is already married, realizing that she must wait for the right man "created by God" to come along. She glimpses a rainbow, and has a vision of a new reality for the whole of society, which will enable it to grow once more from its organic roots, and throw off the shackles of industrialization.

When Lawrence had reworked *The Rainbow* to his satisfaction and sent it off to the publisher, he comprehensively recast the remaining material, between April and June 1916, into a new narrative, and resurrected for it the former title *The Sisters*. Between July 1916 and January 1917 this was once again rewritten drastically, and given the new title *Women in Love* (this first version of the novel has since been published as *The First Women in Love*). Unfortunately, by this time *The Rainbow* had been prosecuted for obscenity and all unsold copies withdrawn and destroyed by a legal ruling. Lawrence submitted the manuscript of his new novel to various publishers, including Duckworth, Constable and Secker, and they all rejected it, commenting that, in the present climate of public opinion, with Lawrence's reputation, it would be unpublishable without drastic revision. Furthermore, several of Lawrence's acquaintances who had seen the manuscript claimed to perceive themselves satirized in its text. Accordingly, Lawrence, presumably fearing not only another prosecution for obscenity, but libel suits into the bargain, rethought the entire project, and radically reworked *Women in Love* over the two years between March 1917 and September 1919. The novel was first published in June 1921, and then further significant changes were made to the second edition, to produce *Women in Love* as it is now generally known, following threats of a lawsuit from the composer Peter Warlock, who thought that the portrait of the composer Halliday in the novel was a scurrilous portrayal of him.

The novel traces the adventures of the Ursula Brangwen of *The Rainbow*, now aged twenty-six, and a teacher at a grammar school. She is the lover of Rupert Birkin, an articulate school inspector who has sufficient private means to be able to retire if he so wishes. Ursula's sister Gudrun is twenty-five, has completed a course at art college and teaches at the same school; she is extremely self-confident and dresses in a bright and bohemian fashion. Gudrun's lover is Gerald Crich, who is around thirty, and the son of a wealthy colliery owner. He is handsome, blond, physically active and in charge of the colliery. However, he lacks a sense of any deep meaning in his life,

Women in Love

367

and his relationship with Gudrun runs into the sands because, rather than striving to achieve a mutual unity of their two personalities, he needs constant reassurances of her affections.

The novel may be said to explore love and sexual relationships in both their creative and destructive aspects. Rupert Birkin contains both of these opposites within himself. He despairs of the modern industrial world and of the human race; however, he refuses to surrender to cynicism and apathy, but persists in his belief in personal fulfilment and integration through interpersonal relationships. These relationships will form the bedrock of a new, organic society, not distorted by over-intellectualism or industrialization. Birkin is, in fact, largely a self-portrait of Lawrence, or Lawrence as he liked to view himself at this period. Like Lawrence, he believes that throughout history the human race has either experienced periods of creative progress or of disintegration. With industrialization and the war, the world is currently, according to him, in a "destructive" cycle. Most of the characters throughout the novel display various degrees of over-intellectualism and alienation from the natural world and from their instincts. Birkin is at the beginning of the novel involved in a relationship with the wealthy aristocrat Hermione Roddice, who is described as "a medium for the culture of ideas" – that is, entirely locked up inside her own head, and cut off from her instincts. Not surprisingly, the relationship collapses. However, the liaison between Gerald and Gudrun is purely sensual, and is ultimately just as unfulfilling. In the end, Ursula and Birkin both resign from their jobs, marry and retire to the Continent – presumably having enough money to do so from Rupert's private income. Their relationship appears to be developing into an integrated and harmonious success. However, Gerald and Gudrun's sensual affair has gone off the rails; she has despairingly taken another lover and, in the Austrian Tyrol, he attempts to strangle her and then flees into the snows in a deliberate suicide attempt.

The Lost Girl   Eight months before *Women in Love* came off the press, D.H. Lawrence completed *The Lost Girl*, a novel he had begun composing as early as December 1912, and which had also undergone several rewrites and title changes. It was eventually published in November 1920.

The novel traces the history of the main protagonist, Alvina Houghton, the "lost girl" of the title, from the age of twenty-three to thirty-two. She is the daughter of well-to-do tradespeople in Woodhouse, a fictional mining town based on Eastwood. Initially, she is "lost" because she seems destined to end up as an old maid, but subsequently she becomes "lost" to those around her because of her rebellion against her conventional upbringing: she plans to move to Australia with her lover, and then, on being talked out of this, moves to north London to train as a maternity nurse – where she gains first-hand experience of the poverty of the capital's slums. On her return to Woodhouse, she finds that no one can afford to hire her services as a nurse on a private basis, and so abandons the idea of earning a living in this manner for the time being. She toys with the idea of marrying various rich men, but decides they are all too cold and inhuman. At the age of thirty, after her father's death, she joins a travelling theatre group, which contains a number of dark passionate foreigners, whom she feels drawn to but ultimately rejects. Leaving the itinerant actors, she takes up her former occupation as a maternity nurse again and becomes engaged to an older wealthy doctor. However, she breaks off this engagement, marries the Italian Ciccio – who was part of her former theatre group – and moves to the mountains of Italy with him. Ciccio is called up for military service, and the novel ends with Alvina, now pregnant, having to bear and bring up a child alone. She is once more lost in an alien environment from which she feels cut off.

Aaron's Rod, a novel which Lawrence had written between October 1917 and November 1921, was published in England in 1922. Aaron Sisson is a mine worker and secretary of the local miners' union in Beldover – again modelled on Eastwood – and also a talented musician, principally on the flute and piccolo. He had originally trained to be a teacher, but he ultimately decided he preferred manual labour. At the age of thirty-three, having inherited a substantial amount of money from his recently deceased mother, he leaves his wife and three children well provided for, and sets off to London in a journey of self-discovery. There he becomes an orchestral musician and frequents intellectual and artistic circles. He is seduced by a scheming female acquaintance, but decides that this is not the type of relationship he left his family for. He falls into depression and succumbs to severe physical illness. The writer Rawdon Lilly, a "freak" and "outsider" by his own description, nurses him back to health, and reinforces Aaron's sense of

Aaron's Rod

369

revulsion at modern marriage, and his fear of being entrapped therein. Aaron goes back to see his wife, who not surprisingly is extremely bitter, so he leaves for Italy at an invitation from Rawdon. There he has a passionate relationship with a noble Italian woman, but Aaron once again distances himself from the relationship, because he wants to withdraw still deeper into himself and avoid being tied down. The novel ends with Rawdon helping Aaron to accept his intuition that the "love urge" has been exhausted by civilization, and that the new creative urge now is that of a power surging from the deepest reaches of the soul, which must be used to renew civilization.

Kangaroo   As mentioned, from June to July 1922, while he was in Australia, Lawrence wrote the bulk of a novel, *Kangaroo*, set around Sydney, which was later published in 1923.

The novel is about Richard Somers and his wife Harriett, who have come to Australia to start a new life after becoming disillusioned with Europe. Their neighbours, Jack and Victoria Callcott, turn out to be members of a clandestine paramilitary organization planning to seize political power by force. Jack offers Somers the chance to become a member, and takes him to see the leader of the movement, Benjamin Cooley, usually referred to as "Kangaroo". Cooley advocates love and brotherhood, but sees this all within a strictly hierarchical model of society controlled by one all-powerful leader. Somers, although in essence sympathetic to his cause, is sceptical and will not commit himself, while Harriett is resentful of her husband's attraction to Kangaroo and the organization. Somers then becomes interested in socialism, but is equally sceptical: Kangaroo's organization is based on love organized through power, whereas the socialists' ideals are based on love for humanity as a generalized and abstract concept, without taking the individual into account. Neither system is what Somers believes he, or humanity in general, needs on a personal level. He is present when the socialists and the right-wingers fight at a rally and numerous men are killed. Kangaroo is wounded, and Somers goes to visit him. Kangaroo asks him once and for all to dedicate himself to the movement, but Somers cannot bring himself to do this. Kangaroo dies, and Somers and his wife start to consider moving to America. Before he leaves, Somers declares that he can only commit himself to nature, to "non-human gods, non-human human being".

Having met the author Mollie Skinner in Australia, Lawrence collaborated on a novel with her, *The Boy and the Bush*, which was published in 1924. Although both names appear on the title page, the precise degree of participation of either author is unclear. It relates the story of Jack Grant, who arrives in Australia from England in 1882 at the age of eighteen, after having been expelled from school and agricultural college, and having been involved in various other dubious doings. The novel depicts how he becomes a successful sheep farmer and gold miner by his early twenties. There is little of the didacticism and pretentiousness of Lawrence's other novels, and it is in essence an uncomplicated adventure story.

The Boy in the Bush

Lawrence turned to Mexico for the setting of his next novel, *The Plumed Serpent*, which he wrote on location in order to immerse himself fully in the country's atmosphere and accustom himself to the mores of the indigenous population. He completed the novel in 1925 and it was published in England the following year. In *The Plumed Serpent* a revolutionary movement in Mexico intends to overthrow Christianity and re-establish worship of the old gods, such as Quetzalcoatl – the "plumed serpent" of the title. The leaders of this movement even assume the names of these old gods. Kate Leslie, an Irish widow of around forty who is visiting Mexico, is at first impressed by the animal pagan vigour of the organization, but then becomes suspicious of its mysticism and barbarity. The novel simultaneously charts the progress of the movement and Kate's fluctuating sympathies towards it. The movement comes to control large swathes of the country, but Kate grows increasingly alienated by its inhumanity. However, she cannot resist the pagan "soul power" of one of the revolutionary leaders who has named himself Quetzalcoatl, and she agrees to participate in a ritual marriage with him. But even after the ceremony she is profoundly dubious, and at the end of the novel we are left wondering whether the movement will be crushed and whether she will become utterly disillusioned and try to withdraw from it.

The Plumed Serpent

Lady Chatterley's Lover was Lawrence's final and most successful major novel. It was written between 1926 and 1928: during this time he completed three separate versions, each of which were subsequently published. The third and final version, the only one to appear in Lawrence's lifetime, was

Lady Chatterley's Lover and The Second Lady Chatterley's Lover

371

privately printed first in Florence in 1928 and then in Paris the following year. In Britain, due to the book's controversial content, it was only published by Secker in a radically expurgated version in February 1932. The first British unexpurgated printing, by Penguin in August 1960, was prosecuted for obscenity; following the collapse of the case, it went on general sale in November of that year, becoming an instant best-seller. The first version of the novel, composed between late 1926 and early 1927, was first published by Dial Press in New York with a preface by Frieda Lawrence. The second version, written immediately after the first one – and reproduced in this volume as *The Second Lady Chatterley's Lover* – was not published in English until 1972, when Heinemann issued it under the title of *John Thomas and Lady Jane*, although an Italian translation was published by Arnoldo Mondadori as early as 1954.

The final version has its setting in Eastwood and other Nottinghamshire towns, as well as Sheffield and Chesterfield – with brief scenes in Venice and London. Its protagonist is Connie Reid, who has had a wealthy, artistic and unconventional upbringing. She and her elder sister Hilda are allowed a great deal of freedom, and both have had sexual affairs by the time they are eighteen. At the beginning of the First World War they settle briefly in London and become part of a coterie of university intellectuals. Hilda marries, and Connie forms an attachment with Clifford Chatterley – a shy and nervous young aristocrat, who had been studying at Cambridge at the outbreak of war, but then joined the army – marrying him in 1917 when he is home on leave. Clifford is seriously wounded in battle, and becomes sexually impotent. Following the deaths of relatives, he becomes heir to the family title and estate. Clifford is not only impotent, but seriously depressed, and takes up writing as a therapy, eventually becoming a successful author. He plays host to gatherings of literati and other intellectuals, and Connie begins to feel more and more empty, frustrated and peripheral. In 1924, when she is twenty-seven, she sees the gamekeeper Mellors (known as Parkin in the second version) washing his naked body in the woods and feels herself flaming back into life. She and Mellors become lovers, and they both rediscover their deep inner selves and connection with nature. Mellors is in fact an educated man who has rejected his middle-class upbringing to revert to a more meaningful working life. Therefore, though he can discourse on intellectual subjects, and can speak with a refined accent, he prefers to talk in broad dialect, and to project a working-class persona. He too, before he met Connie, had become sad and isolated, disillusioned by the war and the destruction of nature by industrialization. He has previously had various loveless affairs with women, including a now estranged wife. However, his liaison with Connie removes all his encrusted bitterness. Connie becomes pregnant, and at the end of the novel they are both waiting for divorces so that they can marry, live on a farm and start a new life together, sheltered from the artificiality they see around them.

The earlier version of the novel contained in this volume, *The Second Lady Chatterley's Lover*, differs from the final version on several plot points, but also, more significantly in its style, outlook and characterization. The novel is less verbose and theorizing, and more tender and bucolic. Significantly, Parkin is not a bitter and jaded former officer like the later Mellors, but a simpler man who was destined to be a miner and chose instead to live away from society and at one with nature.

Mr Noon is an unfinished novel in two parts, which *Mr Noon* Lawrence wrote between 1920 and 1922. Secker posthumously published the first part in 1934, at the end of a collection of Lawrence's short stories, and fifty years later the Cambridge University Press edition appeared, including the very incomplete second part. The novel relates the past life of Gilbert Noon, a science teacher at a school in Nottinghamshire. It is revealed that he came from a working-class background, but proved to be so brilliant at maths, science and music that he gained a scholarship to go to Cambridge University, becoming one of the most outstanding mathematicians of the age. However, due to his somewhat dissipated lifestyle, he did not manage to progress up the academic ladder, and so returned home and became a teacher. He is caught in the act of having sex with Emmie Bostock, a twenty-three-year-old schoolteacher and, upon her apparently becoming pregnant, he is forced to resign his teaching post. In the second part of the novel Gilbert roams around Germany and elopes with a married woman over the Alps into Italy, where he feels himself to be "reborn" – at which point the fragment ends.

During the course of his life, Lawrence issued twelve *Other Works* volumes of poetry and had scores of poems published in journals. He produced three collections of short stories and six novellas, as well as a large number of stories published in magazines which were not collected during his lifetime. He also wrote seven plays, and his prolific non-fiction includes volumes on psychoanalysis and philosophy, travel sketches and hundreds of reviews and articles for the press.

Screen Adaptations

Most of Lawrence's novels – including such lesser-known ones as *The Boy in the Bush* and *Kangaroo* – plus a number of his short stories, have been filmed either for television or cinema. Although the earliest of these date from the late 1940s, they were all extremely expurgated until the late 1960s, when a more liberal social climate began to allow more explicit imagery and language in films and stage plays. By this time, D.H. Lawrence's outlook chimed with that of the new generation, as attested by the 1969 cult classic *Easy Rider*, in which an alcoholic failed lawyer played by Jack Nicholson immediately opens a bottle on his release from prison for drunk and disorderly behaviour with the words: "To ol' D.H. Lawrence". The two protagonists, played by Peter Fonda and Dennis Hopper, on their way across America visit a commune reminiscent of Taos, where Lawrence spent some time, and the film implies that Lawrence was in some way a forerunner of the permissive and sexually liberated Sixties.

Due to its erotic nature, *Lady Chatterley's Lover* has spawned a considerable number of soft-porn adaptations, with even more sequels and spin-offs. In terms of serious mainstream cinema there have been few adaptations however. The first film version dates back to 1955 and is a French production, *L'Amant de Lady Chatterley*, directed by Marc Allégret and starring Danielle Darrieux and Erno Crisa in the lead roles. The next noteworthy adaptation was Ken Russell's 1993 television miniseries *Lady Chatterley*, which featured Joely Richardson as Lady Chatterley and Sean Bean as Mellors. 2006 saw the release of another French cinema dramatization, Pascale Ferran, this time specifically adapting *The Second Lady Chatterley's Lover*, starring Marina Hands as Lady Chatterley and Jean-Louis Coulloc'h as Parkin. This critically acclaimed version won five French César Awards, including the one for Best Film.

Select Bibliography

Standard Edition
The authoritative edition of *The Second Lady Chatterley's Lover* is the Cambridge University Press edition, edited by Dieter Mehl and Christa Jansohn (Cambridge: Cambridge University Press, 1999), which includes extensive annotations.

Biographies:
Aldington, Richard, *Portrait of a Genius, but…: A Biography of D.H. Lawrence* (London: Heinemann, 1950)
Meyers, Jeffrey, *D.H. Lawrence: A Biography* (London: Macmillan, 1990)
Moore, Harry Thornton, *The Priest of Love: A Life of D.H. Lawrence*, 2nd ed. (London: Heinemann, 1974)
Nehls, Edward, ed., *D.H. Lawrence: A Composite Biography* (Madison, WI: University of Wisconsin Press, 1959)
Sagar, Keith, *The Life of D.H. Lawrence: An Illustrated Biography* (London: Eyre Methuen: 1980)
Squires, Michael and Talbot, Lynn K., *Living at the Edge: A Biography of D.H. Lawrence and Frieda von Richthofen* (London: Robert Hale, 2002)
Worthen, John, *D.H. Lawrence: The Early Years 1885–1912* (Cambridge: Cambridge University Press, 1991)
Worthen, John, *D.H. Lawrence: The Life of an Outsider* (London: Allen Lane, 2005)

Additional Background Material:
Boulton, James T., ed., *The Selected Letters of D.H. Lawrence* (Cambridge: Cambridge University Press, 1997)
Miller, Henry, *The World of Lawrence: A Passionate Appreciation* (London: Calder, 1985)
Poplawski, Paul, *D.H. Lawrence: A Reference Companion* (Westport, CT & London: Greenwood Press, 1996)

On the Web:
www.nottingham.ac.uk/mss/online/dhlawrence